ASCENSION

ALSO BY J LJACKOLA

FANTASY ROMANCE

Unbound Prophecy Universe

Unbound Prophecy

Ascension

Descent

Surfacing

Submerged

Riven

Adrift

Unbound Kingdom

Severed Kingdom,

Cursed Kingdom

Prophesied Kingdom

Unbound Kingdom (the trilogy omnibus)

Unbound Prophecy Prequels

Orlaina

Wicked Hues Series

The Forgotten Hues of Skye

The Coveted Hues of Skye

The Shattered Shades of Crimson

The Impossible Shades of Crimson
The Endless Shadows of Pete

Wicked and Fated Universe

Wicked Gods

Trial of the Gods
Tournament of the Gods

Wicked Warlocks

Curse of the Broken Prince
Fate of the Broken Queen

Wicked Shadows

Mark of the Shadow
Touch of the Torch

FAIRYTALE INSPIRED

Wicked and Twisted Tales

Of Candy and Betrayal
Of Petals and Lies
Of Giants and Betrayal

MAFIA ROMANCE

Wicked Cravings

Obsessive Cravings
Forbidden Cravings
Hostile Cravings
Unhinged Cravings

ASCENSION

UNBOUND PROPHECY
BOOK ONE

JL JACKOLA

livshe

Library of Congress Control Number 2018958431

Paperback ISBN 978-1-960784-58-2

Hardback ISBN 978-1-954175-49-5

Electronic ISBN 978-1-960-784-59-9

Fourth Printing Edition 2025

Distributed by Tivshe Publishing

Printed in the United States of America

Cover design by Dark Queen Designs

Map design by C. A. Jackola

Visit www.jljackola.com

AUTHOR'S NOTE

Welcome to the world of the Unbound Prophecy. When I first published Ascension back in 2018, I had no idea it would evolve into six books, a trilogy spin-off, and a prequel. This series started my writing career and the characters in it will always be close to my heart.

As my writing advanced, I looked back at the series and realized it needed some TLC. While I didn't want to stray from the original storyline or intent of the series, I wanted to bring more depth to the characters and their journey. I sat down to revise Ascension in 2024, immersing myself in a world I'd left behind and remembering just how much I love these characters.

If you're new to this series, I hope you grow to love Violissa and Sinow as well as the other characters who call this world home. If you are returning, thank you for sticking with me on this journey and I hope you love the changes.

While revising this series allowed me to look back to where it all began, it also gave me the inspiration to add more stories to this world. And I can't wait to bring them to you!

J. L.

For my family, for always believing in me.

Sac...
Tenebron
Banished Realm

ROVES
CIRILLIA

CHAPTER I

The dew-soaked grass tickled Violissa's feet as she sat with a defeated sigh on the back lawn. Sunlight streamed over the castle, casting long shadows that reached for her like spindly black vines. She was well aware her Council was waiting for her, that the Dark King and his Council were waiting, that the Dark Prince was waiting. Everyone was waiting for her. Yet she was avoiding them all, hiding in one last attempt to shun her destiny.

Power flickered between her fingers, and she reached out to a wildflower, watching as it stretched toward her, the stem lengthening, the bloom growing. The petal met her fingers, its color turning richer, and Violissa's frustration simmered.

Until a familiar voice broke the calm silence.

"Planning to take a bouquet with you to meet the prince today, Violissa?" Daneele said, walking up behind her.

Daneele was the youngest of her Council, although he was still centuries her senior. Ten men made up her Council of Lightbearers, and she loved them all as if they were family. But it was Daneele with whom she was closest.

Keeping her sight on the flowers, she replied, "I'm certain any I took would simply wilt in his presence, but it doesn't matter because I'm not going." She waited for his rebuttal, sensing his tension in the air. "I do not see why you need me there. You've never needed me in the past. It's all formality anyway."

"Honestly, Violissa, do we really need to have this discussion again? We've been over it a hundred times and—"

"And each time I've informed you of my decision," she finished for him, pushing herself from the ground and turning to face him with her arms crossed.

"And so you have, but remember, this is not your decision." He looked at her with a stern brow, but she didn't flinch. "You know you have no choice, so why do you fight it so?"

Of course she had no choice, but she wanted one. Wanted to know she had some kind of free will in her life, that she had some control. Her entire life revolved around the prophecy, and now the first step was here. The Fates had given the sign that she, the child of the Light, and her enemy, the child of the Dark, were to complete their destiny and marry. For the fate of the realms. But what about her fate?

"I am not some pawn you can pull out when it's convenient for the realm. I don't give a damn what some ancient prophecy says about me," she said, her power stirring. "Nothing about marrying a man I've never met, let alone a Darkbearer, could be of benefit to me or this realm. I will not share my bed with the enemy, and neither you nor the Fates will make me change my mind."

Daneele started to argue, but Violissa didn't want to hear it. The sound of her skirts along the ground emphasized her disdain as she stormed off toward the castle.

"Damn it," she heard him grumble as he ran after her. "But you will have met him after today," he said, grabbing her shoulder and turning her toward him. "And you will marry him. The prophecy clearly states it."

"The prophecy can kiss my—"

"Violissa!" Anwell, another of her Council, boomed behind her. If she hadn't sensed his presence first, she would have jumped.

Violissa narrowed her eyes. "Anwell, are you here to bully me as well?"

"Look, we all know your position on the subject, but prophecy aside, you are required to attend the meeting today. To do otherwise could offend the Dark King and cause a war. You assume the throne in an official role in a short while, and it is time you know the protocol that comes with running the kingdom. One does not lead a realm on flowers and meanderings. It's time to grow up and take on your duties. Your people deserve a queen who knows how to govern."

Her lips pursed, and she regarded him with hard eyes. Anwell excelled at the fine art of lecturing, and this time he'd struck a chord. She knew most of her Council thought she fancied too much time outside, walking in the forests or sitting in her gardens, and too little time learning to rule. That wasn't the case. Politics bored her, but she still listened and paid attention when she needed to. She spent as much time as she could with her people, however, preferring them to the boring tasks of running a kingdom. Tasks she let her Council handle.

Anwell's words hurt because she put her people first, always.

"Fine," she said with a sigh, "but I go only in that capacity. I will not be a showpiece to be strutted around in front of that spoiled prince. And do not think for one moment I'll enjoy any of this!"

"We wouldn't think of it," Daneele answered, and she caught the sarcasm that laced his words.

Throwing him a frown, she said, "I'll be down shortly; I need to clean up."

Giving them no chance to answer, she used her power to move herself to her room by shifting there.

Hands balled into tight fists, she stood in front of the window, looking down at the two men as they talked. She knew what they were saying—that she would be the destruction of her people because of her stubbornness. They saw it only from their perspective, not from hers.

The thought that the Fates had decided her path for her, that she had no control over her own destiny, shook her to her core. This was her life, and she should be able to decide who was worthy of her heart. How could the Fates know what she needed? Even if this prince were her true love, she should be the one to decide. Her Council had raised her to be self-thinking and to let her experiences shape her. She couldn't throw all of that away for some dusty old prophecy.

She watched as Daneele and Anwell consulted with the rest of her Council. There were no ill intentions in what they were doing. They were Lightbearers, their nature and their power inherently good. They caused no harm. Lightbearers were immortal men chosen by the Fates, who blessed them in childhood with the power of the Light. They advised the throne and protected the people. The Dark King had a Council of Darkbearers with equal power but gifted with Dark magic. They were the ones to worry about, the ones who would kill and lie, whose people lived under their brutal rule.

Violissa shivered at the thought. She rested her head on the window and closed her eyes. Just thinking of the Darkbearers of Tenebron sent chills down her spine. Their realm was so different from hers, and they lived by a completely different code. While Cirillia lived by the laws of the Light, which were based on love, gentleness and grace, the leaders of Tenebron followed the Dark ways. They ruled through fear, torture, and hatred. And the Fates had bound her to Tenebron's prince, Sinow, in the prophecy that had been the bane of her existence since she first learned of it.

Sighing, she left the window and walked over to the full-length mirror hidden in the corner of the room. A cloth covered it because she rarely used it, never one to be concerned about her appearance. She pulled the cloth down and stared at the woman looking back at her with golden hair that fell in long, loose coils down to her waist and eyes that currently blazed a brilliant emerald. They were qualities that distinguished her from every other person in their world. Her people all had shades of auburn hair with blue eyes; the people of Tenebron had heads of ebony and eyes the color of the soil. There were no others who looked as she did.

Not that she'd ever seen someone from Tenebron. But she knew from her Council and history books. She'd even heard that the Dark King had eyes that were as dark as the color of coal. And to look into the prince's eyes would send you spiraling into a void because they contained no soul. If you looked long enough, you would lose your own soul to that void.

Violissa chuckled. Rumors were all they were. Just as there were many rumors about her. The magical divide that separated Cirillia from Tenebron made it impossible to know if any of those rumors were true. Only the Council had ever come in contact with anyone from that realm, and only in the meeting grove.

Combing her fingers through her curls, she thought about the prince. It wasn't the first time. They had never met—today would be the first time—but her Council had spoken of little but the prince and the prophecy for as long as she could remember. Though she had never divulged it to them, she frequently thought of her impending union. How could she not with all their incessant talk? She'd tried many times to envision herself with one of her own people, but the thought had always been unappealing. It didn't matter that she had no idea what he looked like or who he was. Something about even the thought of the prince called deep down to the core of her soul.

Heat filled her cheeks as she thought of him now. She shook her head to clear it. Any thought of being with a Darkbearer should have been unsettling, but her blood stirred with even the mention of him. It frustrated her because she could not fathom any man from the Dark realm appealing to her.

"I guess I'll find out today," she muttered to herself, sliding her hand down her skirts. "Not that it will make a difference."

She had made her decision long before this day. No matter how curious she was, she would not play by the rules of some ancient prophecy. It had dictated her entire life, and she was tired of it. This was her life, not the Fates'.

Damn that prophecy, she thought. It haunted her dreams, consumed her people and her Council, and irked her beyond words. No one knew the origin of the prophecy or how many eons ago the Fates had written it. But everyone knew it.

The foretelling of the fate of the Cirillians and the Tenebrons rested on Violissa. A prophecy that contained the story of her life and the choices she would make. If one could call predetermined decisions a choice. Even her very existence resulted from the prophecy. She had not been born from a womb, but from magic. The combined magic of the Guardians and the Council on the night Prince Sinow was born, his power marking him as the Dark child within the prophecy. The one whose soul the Fates bound to hers. Immortals grew into their powers; they were not born with them. But Sinow had been, and his birth signaled the calling forth of the chosen Light child, Violissa.

> *With the birth of power shall be*
> *The calling forth of the true light.*
> *The chosen one of light shall unite*
> *With the dark to bring everlasting peace.*

Or so the prophecy read. It should have all been simple, but it was more complex. Violissa was her own spirit and did not want to have that spirit or her freedom reined in by any man, let alone a Darkbearer. The mere thought of it made her stomach turn. They were a hard people who killed without remorse. Had burned, raped and pillaged her people long ago. The border separating their realms resulted from such brutality. It had been the only way to protect her people from the atrocities.

Granted, that had been well before her birth and the treaty between her realm and Tenebron. But if the prince's people were capable of such things, it stood to reason that their most powerful ruler in history could be as well. She couldn't imagine marrying someone like that or, for that matter, bringing him into her realm to rule with her. What completely baffled her was the idea that, according to the prophecy, she would fall instantly in love with him and he with her. It was a ridiculous notion that gave her little faith in the prophecy.

The reflection in the mirror revealed her irritation as she tucked a stray curl behind her ear and opened her mind momentarily to think about the prince. Her heart leaped annoyingly, and she scowled, hating the reaction. It was so instinctual and went against everything she thought about the prophecy because it validated the damned thing. When she let herself think about him, there was a yearning in her soul. Always present, even before she understood what it meant, the sensation existed in the undercurrent of her emotions. She rarely let her guard down about the idea of a union with him, for when she did, she longed for him with an ache so deep that sometimes it seemed unbearable. And that perplexed her the most because she didn't understand how she could feel so strongly about someone she didn't even know.

"Blasted prophecy," she mumbled, shaking her head to clear the thoughts away again. She'd known better than to let thoughts of him in, especially on this day. The intent was to ignore that sensation and prove to the Fates and her Council that she could shape her own destiny. She hoped the Fates were enjoying themselves because she would ensure they wouldn't for long. Not after today.

Picking up her cloak, she hooked the flower-shaped clasp and tugged the hood over her head before shifting to meet her Council.

CHAPTER 2

The meeting grounds were quiet, but the ominous aura of Dark power blanketed the space. Violissa had never been to the meeting grounds, and she was glad her hood concealed her wide eyes. This space was the only spot where both Dark and Light could meet, one that first revealed itself the night of Sinow's conception. It was a sign from the Fates that the first steps of the prophecy were in motion.

Violissa followed her Council. The Dark King and his Council were waiting across from them. The sun, at its full peak, cast its shadow deep behind where they stood, making the Dark King appear even larger and more intimidating than Violissa had imagined. Ebony hair trimmed short bled into a full beard of the same color. His eyes were the closest shade of black and carried a penetrating glare. Swallowing loudly, she reminded herself that even as menacing as he looked, she was just as powerful. Still, she couldn't help but shudder to think of how terrifying his son must be.

"It's an unusual day when any of you arrive late," the king greeted them in a harsh tone that demanded an explanation. "I hope our wait was worth it."

"Where is the prince?" Lann, one of Violissa's Council, questioned, pulling his hood down as he stepped forward. "Apparently, we're not the only ones you wait for, King Drostan."

"Always quick with your observations, aren't you, Lann?" the king quipped. "No, my son has not yet arrived. As for his whereabouts, one can only guess. He will arrive shortly, no doubt. Now, all formalities aside, let me see the girl."

Violissa bit the inside of her cheek, holding back the ire at his insult. Defiantly, she moved from behind her Council. "The girl is here, and she does not like the insinuation you make with that term. Princess will do in the future."

She'd heard enough with that one statement to understand that Daneele had been right in telling her she needed to prove her authority. She was the first woman ruler, and with that came the assumption that she was inferior to her counterparts. Something she would not tolerate.

Now positioned in front of the king, she dropped the hood of her cloak. The Darkbearers took a step back, and the king's mouth fell open before he quickly snapped it shut, his eyes growing a shade darker as if he didn't like that she'd witnessed his moment of shock.

The reaction did not differ from anyone seeing her for the first time. Her looks were too unique to ignore, and with her aura of power and natural beauty, most gaped at her. She wasn't one to acknowledge it, preferring to think she appeared like everyone else, but on this day, the reaction was rewarding.

"If perhaps you could give me the respect my Council and I give you, Your Majesty, then we may proceed with the business of addressing the treaty concerns."

"Feisty, isn't she?" the king replied, regaining his composure and looking past her to Daneele.

"I find it useful in times like this," she answered for Daneele. "Now, I believe there are a few matters at hand that need our attention. Whether or not the prince is present to partake is of no concern to me. Gentlemen, shall we?" She looked at the king's

Council, then confidently strode to her right where a table that encompassed half the glade shimmered into sight. Tall chairs of the same dark oak as the table stood around it, offering enough seats for both Councils and their rulers.

As she walked, Violissa took in more of her surroundings. Trees that towered to the sky encircled the glade, their wide trunks so large they confirmed her suspicion that this grove had stood for centuries, if not longer. She imagined they had borne witness to many meetings, but none as important as today's.

As she walked, the tall grass softly grazed her calves, and a slight breeze played through her hair. Violissa closed her eyes for a moment to savor the peace of the glade. There was irony in such a delicate space being home to meetings between enemy realms. The tension in the air contradicted the calm the grove offered, and she couldn't help but question how it could play such a significant role in the prophecy. If perhaps there was meaning to this grove that only the Fates knew.

It was, after all, an enigma—the only place immortals from both sides could pass. The one pocket free of the powerful magic that made up the boundary dividing Cirillia from Tenebron. The reasons for its existence remained a mystery. Her predecessor, King Viliren and his Council had erected the border, and only one Council remained from his reign, Cyric, who had been so new to his role that he hadn't been privy to the reasons why the space had formed.

The air stirred, and an unexpected tingle made its way through Violissa's body. There was no need to turn. She knew instinctively that the prince had arrived.

This is going to be harder than I imagined, she thought, her chest growing tight.

"Ah, son, so glad you could make it," the king said.

Her head grew light, and she sucked in her core to keep from losing her balance. She was only feet from the table and wished she could rest her hand on it for support.

"Father, my apologies for the delay." The deep baritone swept through her ears, stirring her blood. "She's here, isn't she?"

Pulse racing, Violissa turned around to find that her Council had parted behind her, leaving her facing the Dark Prince. His rich black-brown eyes mesmerized her, and she couldn't look away. Her breath caught in her throat, her heart faltering for several beats. It should have been the mere look of him that caused the reaction, but it wasn't. There was more than the physical attraction that consumed her. This was instinctual, forming deep within her. She struggled to keep from falling, a sudden weakness coming to her knees.

Tall with a massive build, Sinow's fitted black shirt highlighted the muscles beneath. His chiseled jaw would have given him an angular look, but there was a softness that balanced it in the rise of his cheeks and curve of his chin. His coal-black hair held a slight wave to it and sat just above his collar in messy locks, and she momentarily imagined running her hands through its thickness. A few strands fell loose along the left side of his forehead, just brushing the skin. He stood with the stance of a king, of someone who knew the true extent of his power, but without the cockiness one would expect. That power surged from his aura and flickered in the deep hues of his eyes. They were a lush, earthy tone on the cusp of black, the pupil barely discernible. With no reflection of light or herself in them, they almost seemed like they could see straight into her soul, as if she were being pulled by some force into their endless well of darkness.

Violissa didn't know how long they stood staring at each other, but it seemed an eternity to her. The voice in her head was shouting for her to look away, to defy this irrational feeling that had taken over her. Her body, however, seemed to have a mind of its own.

Somewhere she registered the rip of skin in her palms as her nails dug into them, but it didn't sway her. An enchantment hung over her, pulling her body toward him. It accompanied a longing to experience this man, to have his lips on hers, his strength against her body, his touch on her skin. The draw to him was intense and accompanied by a sense that she could never live without him now that she'd seen him.

One step, then another, and he was so close she could almost reach out and touch him. A sharp crack cut the air, breaking her trance and pulling her eyes from his. A whoosh of air rushed into her chest, and she stumbled back a step, her heart racing.

"Tynan, what is the meaning of this?" the king bellowed.

It was only then that her awareness of her surroundings returned. Sinow stood across from her, his eyes hooded as he glared behind her. Following his line of sight, she noted the heat coming from her cheeks. The prince's brother, Tynan, was standing over what remained of the meeting table, a devious gleam to his brown eyes. A shiver slithered down her spine, erasing the pleasant tingles that had been there only moments ago. Where Sinow and his father were terrifying, their power cloaking them in a dark aura, his brother was something different. She couldn't quite put her finger on it, but the word unstable seemed suitable.

"The staring contest was boring, Father. I was having more fun with my magic than watching my brother struggle to kiss the *princess*." There was nothing respectful about the way he had called her princess. Instead, it came out with a sneer that increased the chill in her.

She dropped her eyes from him, staring at the meeting table that was now in pieces. She hadn't realized he'd had that much power; it was a known fact that he didn't. Tynan was an anomaly. He was the second son of a king, an unexpected break in a history where only one son had ever been born, regardless of how many times the king might try. No king had ever produced a second son, yet here he stood, defying the norm and interrupting what some might say was the most important event in their history.

The king looked like he wanted to skin him alive, and she

didn't have to turn back to Sinow to know his reaction. His anger rolled off him in waves that pulsed over her and irritated her magic.

Violissa took a step back, trying to calm the trembling in her body. Every part of her screamed to look at Sinow, to go back to the moment Tynan had severed, but the rational side of her was relieved. Now she stood a chance of avoiding this union...as long as she didn't look into his eyes again. If she did, she knew she'd be lost.

She looked over at the king, whose glare was lethal. If Tynan had been mortal, she had no doubt he would already be dead. A rush of power tinged the air, her own magic fighting against the sting of darkness. The blast of power picked Tynan up and hurled him into the nearest tree, shaking it at its roots and leaving him dazed.

"Take him home," the king ordered, turning to one of his Council, "and see that he stays there. The boy needs a wet nurse at his age," he muttered, ignoring the daggered stare Tynan was giving him as he dragged himself from the ground. "Well then, Princess," he addressed her as if nothing had happened. "I don't believe you've met my son, Sinow."

"I believe we've just introduced ourselves. Isn't that right, Vi?" Sinow replied for her. His voice cascaded over her skin like fingers, and she swallowed back the urge to throw herself into his arms.

"It's Violissa," she corrected, keeping her eyes fixed on the broken table in front of her, "and yes, I believe we have." She stepped further away from him, hating how each lift of her feet felt like her muscles had atrophied. With a slight move of her hand, the air stirred, and the table returned to its former shape.

Keep it together, Violissa. It was easier said than done because she didn't want to discuss business. She wanted to turn back to the prince and acknowledge that the prophecy was right, to confess that thoughts of him all these years left her dizzy and breathless. But she didn't. "I believe you usually discuss the needs of the realms here. And that is what we shall do," she said, glancing quickly at Sinow, careful not to let their eyes lock. "Talk of a union or prophecies will not be any part of today's discussions."

There was a collective groan from her Council and confused mumbling from the Dark Council, but she heard nothing from the prince.

The king started to speak, but Sinow's hand came up to stop him.

"She does have fire, Father. There's no doubt about that."

The inside of her cheek tore with the bite she gave it. They had been talking about her, using their enaigne, the ability to talk within each other's minds. That fact only further strengthened her resolve.

The weight of his stare was heavy, and she dared to meet his eyes once again. She fought with all her power not to fall under the spell and lose control again. Sparks spread through her, awakening her body and strangling her hold on her control.

He continued before she could respond, "But that's a trait I find immensely attractive, along with many others I see before me."

Violissa bit the inside of her cheek harder, tasting the tang of her blood before the wound healed. She needed to keep it together, no matter how his eyes were undressing her and no matter how she wished it was his hands.

Fates, stop it, she chastised herself.

Straightening her spine, she replied, "Since seeing is the only thing you'll be doing with my traits, I hope it's a worthy consolation." She fought her smile when she noticed the tug of his lip as he fought his own. She drew her eyes away, a feat she had doubted she could do, and turned confidently back to the table, walking over to a seat.

"We did have other business to discuss, did we not?" she said, addressing the Councils, resting her hand on the back of the tall chair. "Because I'd hate to think you were wasting my valuable time and that of the prince if we did not."

She heard Sinow chuckle then clear his throat quickly as his father shot him a sharp look.

"This certainly has been worth my time, Vi." She cringed at the nickname, but the smooth tone of his voice soothed the sting. "But I venture to guess you and I are the only thing on today's agenda. Since discussion of our imminent union is presently off the table, I suggest we let our Councils leave us. Perhaps we can find something that appeals more to you to discuss. Unless that is, you have pressing matters back home to which you would rather attend?"

Violissa wanted to stomp her feet and scream, something she was currently doing inside her head. In giving her the out, he'd cornered her. She couldn't deny his request without sparking discontent with his father. From her periphery, she caught Daneele's snicker. He looked away, purposely avoiding her glare and uncomfortably shifting his posture, just like the rest of her Council.

She should have been angry, but this was new for all of them. The Council knew little about the workings between men and women. They took a vow of celibacy for a life dedicated to the monarchy from the moment the Fates blessed them with their power. That calling came when they were children, so they knew nothing about the intricacies of relationships.

Not that she knew anything about relationships other than the familial ones she had with her Council. But she had no plans for this to become anything close to resembling a relationship. In time she would have to, she knew she couldn't deny the Fates forever or the punishment she faced would be severe, but she wasn't ready for a union with the enemy, no matter that even looking at him knocked the breath from her.

She did, however, have to work with the prince on matters of the realm as well as the treaty. They would both be ascending to the throne soon and, as rulers, would have no choice but to work together if she could ever make eye contact with him without kissing him.

She thought about the question he'd posed. He had her cornered. She didn't want to be alone with him for fear that she would lose her resolve, but she couldn't risk offending him or his father. The treaty was unstable as it was, and no matter what she wanted to think, it heavily relied on their eventual nuptials. She had no choice but to stay and talk to him; she'd simply have to avoid looking at him or being close to him.

That should be easy enough, she thought, trying not to roll her eyes.

"I don't know what other matters you had in mind to discuss, Prince Sinow, but I will oblige you." She heard her Council release a breath. Except for Brom, who was always one to worry.

"Princess," he said, concerned. "I must object. I don't think this is a wise idea. Your safety—"

"Safety?" Sinow interrupted, his eyes darkening. "Do you really think I would harm the princess, Brom? Seriously, you must know better."

"Yes, Brom. What are you implying?" King Drostan asked, stepping forward.

Tension struck the air, and Violissa held her breath as her power bucked for release against the Dark magic that spread from both the prince and the king.

"I am sure he meant no harm, Your Majesty," Daneele said as he moved next to Brom. "We simply take the protection of our princess seriously, and leaving her without our guard so close to her ascension, outside of Cirillia, makes us slightly uncomfortable."

"I assure you, Daneele, my intentions are quite honorable. I mean her no harm," Sinow growled, the sound causing her heart to skip. "From what I understand, she's quite capable of protecting herself. She will be your queen in a short while, will she not?"

"I have no doubt she could certainly match your advances, if not best them, Prince Sinow," Daneele replied, his demeanor calm.

Violissa looked to Sinow for a reaction, but if the comment bothered him, he didn't let on.

"I'll be fine," she said, needing the Darkness in the air to fade before she lost control of her power. Light and Dark were opposing powers. Her Council had told her of the natural response her magic would have to his, but this was the first time she'd experienced how powerful it was. If it was this bad just standing with each other, she couldn't imagine what it would be like when they both ascended to their full power. Nor how the Fates could have ever thought putting the two together through their union made sense. "Now if you will excuse us, apparently the prince has urgent matters he needs to discuss with me. You may go."

Violissa, Daneele called to her through enaigne.

I'll be fine, Daneele.

"Go," she commanded when none of them moved.

She may have been their junior by thousands of years, but she was still their ruler, and they knew when not to cross that line. With a bow, they all shifted back to Cirillia.

Violissa turned to face Sinow, only then realizing the potentially devastating mistake she had just made. She'd left herself alone not only with Sinow but with his father and the entire Darkbearer Council.

This could be bad, she thought, wishing she'd heeded Brom's concern. She could take down the Council, and she was sure she could take Sinow, but she hadn't ascended to her full powers, so she doubted she could take all of them as well as the king if they seized the opportunity. *Yes, this could be very bad.*

CHAPTER 3

Rulers didn't come into their full powers until their ascension. It didn't matter if they ruled Dark or Light, their power was substantially weaker until that time. Only when they achieved full power were they able to take the throne. The ruling king would step down, and his son would reign. In Violissa's case, there was no one to step down. The former king had given his life to erect the border between the two realms. Her Council ruled in his stead until Violissa's ascension.

Sinow knew this, as did everyone standing before her, but he wasn't about to go against her, and those with him knew he'd protect her if they attempted anything. She had been his since his birth, and he laid claim on her the moment their eyes met, if not well before. It would be interesting to test her powers, as he'd heard she was already powerful enough to best her entire Council. If she were anywhere near as strong as he, it would be a tough fight, but one that would not take place today.

He let his eyes fall on her again, noting how she avoided his eyes as if she had experienced the same lack of control as he had. Being so out of control had been unsettling. He despised it.

Anything that made him weak was something he needed to over-come, but this...this was different.

The pounding of his heart irritated him, but didn't halt as he studied her. Long, thick golden curls hung loose and draped down her back. Her cloak hid her figure, but he could imagine the soft curves that lay below. Her supple red lips pursed as her green eyes met his. Those eyes mesmerized him. They were so unique, just like everything about her. Green was an eye color no one in their world had. There was talk the Elvin had them, but the Elvin no longer lived; his grandfather had wiped out their population in the last war. The green in Violissa's eyes was in stark contrast to the brown of his people's. There were variations in the hue that shifted with her emotions. It was a subtle change, but he found it fascinating.

Sinow turned to his father. "I'll take it from here, Father. I believe Vi and I need some time to talk." He noted the flinch when he shortened her name, enjoying the reaction. There was no reason for him to shorten her name other than it seemed reserved for him.

Her eyes flicked to his before she averted them to the trees. She was struggling to maintain eye contact, just like he was. But unlike him, she wasn't brave enough to accept it.

"Very well, son. Gentlemen," his father said to the Council, "let us return to Tenebron." He gave a slight nod to Violissa. "Princess, it has been a pleasure."

She gave a respectful nod back to him, then walked away toward the tree line. Sinow watched her, wondering why she was moving so far from them. Running away. That was what she was doing—distancing herself from the intense attraction between them. He planned to push her once his father and the Council left.

She removed her cloak, and the air escaped his lungs. Even without her eyes turned toward him, he could see how her purple gown enhanced the emerald orbs so that they sparkled with an intensity that matched her power. Her golden curls skimmed her bottom, bouncing over the curves of her body, and he clenched his fists, fighting the desire to go to her.

"Son, you know how important this union is. The power you will gain will be unprecedented."

"Yes, Father. Trust me, I understand. It's not as if I haven't heard it since before I could walk," he replied.

"Respect, son. It's a word you apparently missed during your lessons. I may be your father, but I am still king until your time comes to reign. Until then, you will give me the respect I'm due and seek to get this union sanctified." With that, he shifted. The Council gave a bow to Sinow and shifted away as well.

"Let the games begin," he muttered, watching as Violissa sat on the ground, her cloak spread below her, her feet tucked under her.

A startling revelation struck him. This was the woman he would marry, the woman he would spend the rest of his life with, to whom the Fates had bound his heart. The lack of choice had always angered him, but below it was the sense of the connection to her. And if he opened himself to thoughts of her, his body woke, the Darkness in him calming as a sense of rightness filled him.

As he came to stand beside her, he took a moment to study her closer. Any preconceived notions he'd had of what she would look like paled compared to her true appearance. Her tresses had fallen forward, obscuring part of her profile, but he could still see the soft nose and cheekbones, the full lips that called to be kissed. He shook his head, scolding himself for his moment of weakness. Yet another one triggered by her proximity. Weakness was something he didn't tolerate, and he rolled his neck to free himself from it.

Knowing he needed to focus, he glanced past her body to determine what held her interest. At first, it looked like she was picking flowers, an odd thing to do considering the circumstances. Upon further inspection, he realized the flowers were still intact and rose to her outstretched palm. Before her, a plethora of purple flowers had emerged from the long grass. He couldn't stop his gaping as their stems lengthened, and petals filled out. Brow pinching, he glanced around the glade, only then seeing that no other flowers graced the grove, only grass. She had created them with the same ease as he created fire. He had to catch his breath as the reality of her true abilities dawned on him.

"I see you'll be one to surprise me at every turn," he said, moving to stoop across from her. "I must admit, the ability to make plants grow was not on our list of your talents."

He had positioned himself a few feet from her, wary of getting too close for fear that he'd lose control and reach over to draw her into his arms. As desirable as it sounded, he didn't want to risk her wrath.

The smell of lilacs spread from her, and he breathed it in. The smell should have grated on his senses, but it only amplified his attraction to her.

A breeze picked up her curls, where they floated gently before dipping back to her shoulders. He'd seen no one with hair like hers; it was like looking at the morning sunrise. The softness of her skin radiated, and there was a slight pink to her cheeks that added to the allure.

Sinow waited for her to lift her head so he could see once more those emerald eyes she was trying so hard to keep from meeting his. His chest pounded in anticipation, and he had to dig his fingers into the ground to keep from leaning forward to touch her.

"Any other talents I should know about, or will you be saving them for later, maybe our first night together?"

She stiffened, the first movement she'd made since he'd approached her. He watched her closely as she took a deep breath, her chest moving up and down slowly.

"I doubt there are any talents of mine that you'll be seeing in your bedroom, Sinow, or did I not make myself clear?" Her tone was sharp; yes, she had spirit, something that only magnified his attraction to her.

She stood without looking at him, glancing instead toward the sky. There was a twitch in her cheek, and a clap of thunder shattered the silence. She turned and met his gaze briefly, challenging him. Clouds moved over them, but he took no notice, too entranced by her. Her eyes were a rich sage, the color of the forest behind them, and he inhaled sharply as he rose, finding himself stepping into her space.

Time stood still again, just as it had when they'd first met, and for a moment, he almost let himself touch her. But he hated how out of control he was, hated that a prophecy was dictating his moves and forcing this situation, forcing his hand. And no matter how alluring Violissa was, he wanted to show that he held the power here, not the Fates.

Regaining his composure, he stepped back.

Thunder split the air again, and he tore his sight from her to see the storm clouds above them. Clouds that had broken the sunny day in only minutes. He was tempted to stare at her in awe because he knew she had caused the looming storm. But he wanted to ensure he didn't look like some love-struck boy gaping at a beautiful yet powerful woman. He was a Dark prince, not some mortal who held no power.

He let his power course through him, reminding himself of who he was before he retorted, "Impressive. So you can call a storm to show me your irritation. As sexy as I think you'd look rain-soaked, why don't you leave the rain be and use your words to tell me." Lightning struck too close, and he crossed his arms, staring her down, his power masking the need that was surging through him. Her eyes flicked away, then back to him, the tension fading from him for the slight reprieve before it filled him again.

The clouds cleared, and he thinned his lips, not wanting to show his reaction. No one had control over the elements. He couldn't think of anyone but the Elvin who had. There shouldn't have been any connection to them. They'd been extinct for ages. And magic had created Violissa. She had not been born of a woman's womb. She was an anomaly, but perhaps her creation held the explanation.

He shook away the thoughts, seeing that she'd walked over to the table. Turning, he joined her, pushing his discomfort by closing the gap between them.

"Look, I need to make something clear," she said, turning abruptly yet barely meeting his eyes. "I know they've told you there will be a union and that this whole prophecy thing rests on that happening."

She paused and looked him in the eye. The connection between them flared again, burning through him like a wildfire. The quiver of her bottom lip was barely noticeable, but he sensed the brief stutter of her heart. For one, two, three beats before it started again. It was the same reaction she'd had the first time their eyes met. He had his own reactions to deal with: the erratic pounding of his heart, blood rushing through his veins, a tightness in his chest like it would burst. The intense need to grab her by the neck and kiss her was overwhelming. It took all his power to avoid moving.

"It won't be happening," she continued bluntly, obliterating the sensation, "at least not on their terms."

He didn't know whether to laugh at her audacity or to slap her for causing that tightness in his chest to compound. He chose the first option to retain his pride.

"So serious, Vi." He emphasized the nickname he'd given her, knowing it annoyed her. "I thought we'd take some time to get to know one another, talk a little, maybe play a little," he said, giving her a mischievous smirk, "and here you are getting serious on me. Really, a union is the least of my concerns. You can take all the time you want."

He hadn't realized he'd gotten so close to her, and the need to touch her stormed through him when her emerald orbs reached his. Unable to resist, he lifted his hand and picked up a curl that lay on her cheek, letting it drift through his fingers. Her hair was soft as silk, and the longing to twist his fingers into it and drag her against him tore through him. But she flinched at his touch, causing his mood to darken.

"Seriously?" she asked with a rather breathless sound to her voice that tempted him even more. Her sight lingered on him for only another moment before she looked away into the tree line. "I'm surprised. I would have thought waiting would anger you, considering your pedigree."

Pedigree? The insinuation had him squeezing the lock of hair still trapped in his fingers. He noted the catch of her breath and how her chest heaved with it. The cut of her dress exposed the creamy cleavage just enough to tempt him to lower his hand. Dropping the curl and averting his eyes, he replied, "I should take offense at that, but I won't. And I am serious."

He'd had enough of this game. She clearly intended to vex the Fates, something even he wouldn't have considered. It made him curious about Violissa and amenable to waiting like she wanted. He would not, however, give her up, no matter her intentions. The wait for this day had been too long, and he was ready to take what the Fates had promised him. If he had to wait a little longer, then so be it, but he wouldn't give her forever.

Sinow walked over to one of the large mahogany chairs at the meeting table and sat down, propping his feet on the table. He enjoyed the lovely arch of her brow as she considered his lack of respect. Her eyes, however, remained on his feet.

"You see, Vi," he continued, placing his hands behind his head, "you can barely look at me. That tells me you find me as irresistible as I find you. The Fates have a plan, and neither of us can avoid it." He stroked his finger along the tabletop, imagining it was her skin instead, noticing how her sight trailed the movement. "Eventually, you'll give in because that desire you have for me will override your stubborn need for independence."

Her laugh was unexpected, yet the sound was delicate to his ears. "You clearly have no lack of self-confidence. So, what's the catch?" She crossed her arms, her chest pushed further up with the motion. His finger stroked the table harder at the thought of it.

"The catch is that when I tire of waiting, you will have no more say." He stared intently at her and held her gaze when her eyes darted to his. The green in them grew to sage, and he forced himself to continue. He wouldn't allow this damned prophecy to soften him, no matter how he yearned to push aside the Darkness in him and experience her laugh again. "You see, Vi, I've waited an exceptionally long time for you, and I'm willing to wait longer. No matter what you do, you are mine. You've been mine since the moment you took your first breath, and no amount of time will ever change that fact."

He slammed his hand down on the table, sending a loud echo through the silent forest around them, and leaped to his feet. He closed the space between them before she had time to move, standing as close as he could bear without succumbing to the cravings that were pummeling him.

Grabbing a fistful of her hair, he pulled her head back, loving how her lips parted. "So you see, Violissa, I'll wait until you realize you can no longer resist me and come willingly to my bed because I want to enjoy every inch of you," he growled. "And when I'm thrusting inside of you, I want to see those sexy eyes looking up at me while you willingly accept me. I'll enjoy my climax better if no bruises mar that beautiful face." He would never have hurt her, regardless of what she thought, but seeing the flicker of fear in her eyes was satisfying.

Violissa jerked from his hold, those entrancing emerald orbs now so dark they could have been mistaken for black. "Thank you," she snapped.

That hadn't been the response he was expecting. "Thank you?" he asked, not following. "For treating you the way a man should treat a woman?" he snarled.

Her nostrils flared. "No, for affirming my decision not to marry you and for giving me a reason to ignore my Council, the Fates, and my body," she hissed. That she'd mentioned her body confirmed his suspicion that she wanted him as badly as he wanted her. She was just too stubborn to follow that instinct. "To think that the Fates would want me bound to you for eternity. I've never met anyone so rude and self-centered."

"That's because you've never been to my realm," he muttered.

"Goodbye, Prince Sinow. My Council will be in touch, but don't count on seeing me anytime soon." She shifted, leaving him alone in the grove with only the lingering scent of lilacs in her wake.

He raked his fingers through his hair. Back against the wall, he had opted for harsh words he hadn't meant. Her opposition to their union had frustrated him. She hadn't been willing to even give it a chance. The prophecy had led his life, too, so he understood that feeling of weakness. How maddening it was to know he had no free will, that the Fates had already written his life for him. He supposed she was testing the Fates to see if she could outsmart them. She couldn't fight them, though. Prophecy was rare yet powerful, and the one involving the two of them was the most consequential of all.

The Fates had their reasons for pairing him with her, and if she questioned or attempted to change the prophecy, things could go terribly wrong. There would be consequences.

Sighing, he breathed in the lilac that still hung in the air, his chest tightening at the smell. He hated how out of control he seemed around her and hated that she was now controlling the situation. As willing as he was to wait for her, he wasn't a patient man. She would come around, and when she did, she would be his. It was the waiting that frustrated him.

He'd been waiting centuries for this day, and it hadn't ended with her by his side and in his bed like he'd anticipated. Rolling his neck, he fought the Dark power that flared through him, looking for an outlet where there was none. Magic flitted between his fingers, and he gathered it and hurled it at a tree across from him, shattering it to pieces. The noise disturbed the hushed quiet of the woods, but Sinow was gone before the last piece of wood fell to the ground.

CHAPTER 4

Tynan heard the rumble above him as Sinow shifted back to their realm. His lips twitched, his grin spreading. The meeting with Violissa must not have gone well. Sinow had a habit of emphasizing his disdain in his shifts when something pissed him off. And Tynan was certain Violissa and her refusal to move forward with the union had angered his brother just as much as it had his father.

Tynan grimaced as he climbed the remainder of the stairs from the dungeons, holding onto the wall for only a brief second so no one would notice him pause. He knew his father was standing below him, watching for any sign of weakness. The bastard was always waiting for any sign to reinforce his thoughts that Tynan was a mistake of nature put upon him as some punishment doled out by the Fates. Tynan never asked him what mistakes he had made to deserve punishment, nor did he bother to ask why he had to be a mistake. He'd learned long ago not to challenge his father.

When he reached the top of the stairs, he walked down the corridor, far enough to be out of sight before shifting back to his room. Once there, he tore off what remained of his shirt and bit back the howl of pain that threatened to escape. Blood soaked the back of his shirt where his father's magic had hit him, his punishment for creating a disturbance at the meeting today. His father enjoyed flaying the skin from his back in long strokes whenever Tynan made a misstep. He knew Tynan didn't heal as quickly as the other immortals and that it often took hours for bad wounds to heal, where with his brother it was sometimes only a matter of minutes. It was agony for Tynan, but this time it was worth it.

His father hadn't even stopped to consider the timing of his distraction. No one had. They had all just laughed him off as though he were a dumb oaf. Well, he would see who had the last laugh when he destroyed all their years of planning. The crown would be his, and he planned to rip it from his lazy son-of-a-whore brother's head before it even settled.

He smiled through a grimace of pain. It had been worth it to see the expression of surprise on his father's face when he'd disturbed those two foolish lovebirds. The prophecy had always sounded like a pile of lies the Lightbearers had fed to his father to trick him into subservience. To think a Dark King would follow the word of those imbeciles made Tynan see red. It was only after he'd researched the prophecy that he gave it any credence.

Today's interaction had validated it. His brother detested any displays of weakness, and he'd been weak-willed, blindly moving closer to the princess as if nothing existed outside the two of them. The magic of the Fates had been present, and the hairs on Tynan's neck had stood.

But it was over now. He had put the first obstacle in their path, and he intended to do more until the crown was his. Researching the prophecy had led him to uncover something that would change the course of his destiny and destroy his brother. A key to finally taking his rightful place and ridding himself of his older brother. The crown belonged to him, not Sinow, whose whore mother had stolen his father's affection from Tynan's mother, leaving her as leftovers to come crawling back to after the bitch had died.

No, the crown was his. He should have been born first, not Sinow, and now he was planning to make Tenebron his. All that was needed was patience. He'd waited this long, watching and learning, waiting for the day when he'd have his chance. Well, the day was almost upon him, and they were none the wiser about what he was about to bring down around them. He had only a brief time until the ascension, and then it would all be his.

What he'd seen today at the meeting gave him the weakness he had been waiting to discover in Sinow: Violissa. She would be the undoing of them all; she just didn't know it yet.

CHAPTER 5

Doors slammed through the corridor, their motion brought on by the power emanating from Violissa as she stormed by them.

"The nerve," she muttered, on a rampage that had no destination. She didn't want to talk to her Council yet, not after having just left Sinow. Violent shades of black and red flashed in her vision as her temper flared. Servants scattered, knowing to avoid the princess when she was in a mood like this.

Anger was an emotion that few exhibited in Cirillia. The temperament of the people was too gentle. But those in the castle had been witness to it in their princess. And Violissa wasn't shy about holding her temper. She did not, however, loosen her hold on it enough to hurt anyone. Such a thing was not in her nature, and so when her moods swung this way, she did the only thing she knew to do. She escaped into the woods beyond her castle.

She burst through the doors that led outside, irritated with herself that she'd even returned to the castle. Sinow had her so perplexed that she'd left without thinking of where to go and landed there. The confused mix of emotions running through her left her restless.

She was angry at what he'd said, frustrated at how easily he'd rattled her, but most of all, she hated the fact that she wanted to return to him, to lose herself in his eyes, to have his fingers in her hair and on her skin. The thought of his body against hers left her rattled, and she shifted to the woods, closing her eyes to shut out the thoughts. The peace of the wooded world gently pushed out the noise in her head, replacing it with the chirp of the birds, the movement of the insects below her feet and in the trees, and the rustle of the leaves in the breeze. She breathed in the cool, mossy smell of the surroundings, then moved soundlessly forward, draping her hand along the tree trunks.

A sense of calm came over her, erasing the tension in her shoulders. The forest was her favorite place to escape. To some, the forests were a frightening place filled with fairytale creatures and beasts, but to Violissa they had always been a part of her. Her connection to the land and the plants and creatures that inhabited it was like a tether that bound them to her soul. No one understood why she was so tied to nature or how she could influence it so easily. Regardless, her gifts were a blessing. They fed the land, and the land in turn fed her people.

She walked for a long while, trying to clear her head, keeping her emotions and thoughts about the meeting at bay. Avoiding thoughts of the prince. Lush green grass spread before her, covered by a canopy of trees. Through the middle of the small glade ran a stream. The sound of the water splashing along the rocks below added to Violissa's calm. She inhaled deeply, letting the solitude bring her peace. This spot was her favorite and one not even her closest Council knew of. Anytime she needed to think, to settle her mood, or even just escape the weight of her duties and destiny, this was where she hid.

Sitting, she laid back and stared up at the sky, letting the music of the forest lull her to sleep. The afternoon passed by, and when she blinked her eyes open, the stars were sparkling in the darkness.

Stretching, she made her way to the stream and placed her

hand over the water. After a whispered thank you to the land, she cast her magic over the stream. It widened, the water rising to accommodate the change in size until it was deep enough for her to enter. She removed her dress and walked into the cool water, sinking under, then returning to the surface to float upon her back.

Both moons shone high above her, the southern moon a tiny sliver, while the northern moon shone in all its splendor, lighting up the small glade. The reflection caused a shimmer around her body that left her with a slight glow. Anyone seeing her there would have thought a star had fallen and rested in the middle of the water.

She let her mind finally turn back to Sinow, thinking how odd it was that his name came so easily to her, as if she'd known him forever.

Because that's what it feels like, she thought, the realization reinforcing their connection through the prophecy. And he had called her Vi as if he'd known her for just as long. She didn't really mind that he had claimed the nickname she despised from the mouth of anyone else. Even her Council knew better than to shorten her name. But coming from him, it sounded right, as if she had been saving it for him all this time.

Her thoughts turned to his last words, and her mood soured. The tree leaves rustled, and the grass blades lengthened as the water churned. The audacity he had to think he could just take her by force, that he even had the power to do such a thing. It was certainly the kind of thing she'd expect from a Darkbearer, so his words hadn't surprised her as much as offended her. Even so, mixed in his threat had been the suggestion that he would wait for her. That had been unexpected. It had never crossed her mind that he might agree to waiting. Of course, she'd never considered what he might think about the prophecy—if he had the same reservations, the same distaste at the lack of free will.

Sighing, she emerged from the water and made her way back to her dress. No matter what happened, she had no choice but to follow the prophecy. She could postpone the union, but eventually, she would have to go through with it. Her rebellion had its limits, and defying the Fates came with consequences that could be catastrophic. That didn't mean, however, that she had to rush things, that she couldn't take her time playing their game. There were things she wanted to do before she tied herself to the prince.

She wanted to establish her rule as queen once she ascended. When she stepped into her reign as queen, the people would need to grow accustomed to seeing her as more than just their princess. And as much as she frequented the towns and spent time with her people, she worried they would view her differently when she took the throne.

There had not been a ruler on the throne of Cirillia for thousands of years. The Council had been all they had known. So, to Violissa, the change appeared massive, and since she always put her people first, she chose to put the prophecy and this sudden attraction she had toward the Dark Prince aside. Prophecy and the prince could wait; her people could not.

And she needed time to warm her people to the idea of her ruling beside Sinow. As much as the prophecy was talk in the towns, handed down from generation to generation, they were hesitant. The Darkbearers had wronged her people in the past, and history had taught them to fear even their name. Although the border kept them safe from the abuses of those in Tenebron and the Council met with the Darkbearers peacefully now, the fear was still present.

With those thoughts, her resolve strengthened. There would be no union with Sinow until all was in place and the time was right. Besides, as she had told herself earlier that day, being with a Dark Prince was bound to be like living her worst nightmare, no matter how attractive he was. Prophecies and Fates would have to wait until she was ready. The game was in her hands now, and she was not ready to relinquish her control of it.

With the meeting behind her, Violissa returned her focus to her upcoming ascension and to aggravating her Council with her refusal to hear any further talk of prophecy.

The ascension was the most important event in a ruler's life. It was the passing of the reign from one generation to the next, always celebrated on the thousandth birthday of the incoming ruler. Although immortal, there came a time in each king's life when the Fates expected them to relinquish their power and return their spirits to the Fates. It was a voluntary passing of their soul to their next form, but if not done so willingly, the Fates would rip the soul from the king in a horrifically painful form of punishment. She could only think of one Dark King who suffered that fate: Sinow's grandfather.

The Council had prepared Violissa for her ascension, part of which was learning the history of the kings before her, both Light and Dark. All before her had been men, for she was the first female to ever rule. It was a fact that made her even more anxious about stepping into her role as queen.

She tediously studied the ascension ceremony over and over, afraid she would miss something or, worse, forget something. Wringing her hands, she lifted her eyes from the page, seeing that dusk had turned to night. Her eyes were tired, her body craving sleep, so she closed the book in her lap and tossed it into the chair across from her. Rubbing her eyes, she rose and stretched her long limbs before leaving her library and heading to her room.

Only when she closed the door to her room did she realize how exhausted she was. Hastily throwing on her nightdress, she collapsed into her bed, the down pillows around her puffing at the sudden impact. Sleep was fast to claim her, but it did not intend to keep her.

Fog sifted through her mind, corrupting her sleep and pulling her into a dream. Dreams were rare for immortals, so when

Violissa found herself standing in the meeting grounds, she couldn't stop the trembling of her hands. Dreams held the future or a warning, but this didn't seem like a dream.

She stepped forward, glancing around and seeing the meeting grounds take shape. The nightdress she'd slept in still graced her body, which she found odd since she surely could have been wearing something lovelier. It was her dream, after all. Stars twinkled above her, the moons giving the glade a luminescent glow as they shone down upon her.

"A dream," she mumbled. "But why?"

Were the Fates trying to tell her something? This dream seemed so real. She squeezed her hands tightly, the sting of her nails digging into her flesh, yet she didn't wake. The ground beneath her toes was damp, and the warm night breeze caused goose bumps on her arms, which she rubbed away.

The air stirred. A presence entered the dream, one she recognized instantly. Sinow.

"No," she said, afraid to turn, but her body doing it without her consent.

Sinow stood across from her. His black-brown eyes crinkled as his lips lifted in a sexy grin. Her heart stuttered. He was shirtless, wearing only a loose-fitting pair of black pants, his feet bare. Ebony locks were rumpled as if sleep had brought him there as well. He was beautiful in a terrifying way that crept under her skin and settled too comfortably.

His eyes devoured her, lust-filled and hungry, and her breath caught. She suddenly wanted to touch him, to take her hands and trace the definition of each muscle, to experience their strength against her skin. She lifted her gaze back to meet his eyes, seeing the confusion there until a confident gleam replaced it.

"This is just a dream," she said, her voice hushed as he erased the gap between them in a few quick steps.

"Yes, it is," he agreed. "So let's make the most of it."

He was so close, his body towering over hers, his face brushing her skin. A blaze surged through her, waking her body and causing her to lean further into him. His lips ran along her jawline, precariously close to hers, and she closed her eyes, breathing in the scent of brimstone and ash. Hands found her waist, tugging her closer, and she turned her face, her mouth welcoming his as she came alive. His touch and the kiss burned through her, lighting every recess and claiming them as his.

Something nudged at her that a dream shouldn't hold that power, that this seemed too real. It seemed wrong yet so right, and her hands strayed the length of his chest, eliciting a groan from him that erased all her doubts. Thick strands of hair tangled around her fingers as she pulled his face closer, deepening their kiss.

His fingers threaded into her hair, his other hand pushing the loose strap of her gown down before it cupped her breast. Her lips parted as he pushed the other strap down and dug his fingers back into her hair, his kisses growing needier.

"A dream," she breathed through their kisses.

"Yes," he answered, his tongue gently searching for hers.

Had it not been a dream, this would not have happened... although she couldn't truly convince herself of that truth, thinking once she'd kissed him, there would be no going back. The urgent need for Sinow tore through her like an untamable wildfire. Her hands traced the path of his back, pushing at his pants as if this were natural. It wasn't. She knew that, but she couldn't stop because her need was too great.

She'd never kissed a man, let alone touched one, or had one touch her. Yet, she was doing just that. Because this was a dream, nothing more. As his pants dropped to the ground and he picked her up, gently laying her on the grass, she continued to tell herself that.

He kissed her neck, his mouth drifting down to her breasts as his hands encircled her waist. "You're beautiful, Vi," he murmured against her skin, sending butterflies swarming in her stomach.

They swooped and soared, their frantic fluttering escalating when he entered her. A cry built the fuller she became until it scorched the air, silenced when his mouth captured it. She frantically tore at his back as his moves and touches caused an escalating pressure to grow inside her, tingling with a sensation that consumed her until it exploded, tearing through her with an intensity that caused his thrusts to increase.

Hundreds of years of waiting and yearning, of denying her tie to him, of turning away from the flutters that mounted each time she thought of him, freed in a moment of rapture that held them both prisoner. Her body was one with his, her ecstasy shared with him, her pleasure his to take.

And when she could finally stop her heaving chest, she returned the kiss he gave her, smiling against his lips.

"Fates, that was better than I imagined," he said between kisses. "If a dream is this good, the real thing will be worth the wait."

His words should have caused her to pause, to wonder why a dream version of him would say that, but his kisses had dropped to her breasts, his tongue causing her body to wake again. They made love again, this time with no hesitation. Firm touches, bold kisses, and mingling moans made up her dream until rapture struck again, leaving her weakened.

Sinow's hands tangled in her hair, and he raised himself up to look at her. It was so easy to meet his eyes in a dream, and she wished that could transcend into reality. Brown on the cusp of black, his eyes were entrancing, and she thought she could lose herself in them for eternity.

He brushed a lock of hair from her cheek, and she leaned her face into his touch. Sweat lined his brow, and she knew from the way her hair stuck to her face there were droplets on her. His eyes searched hers, and although the craving to have him take her again remained, it was easier to look into his eyes.

"Some dream," he said.

"Mmm, yes, it is," she answered, reaching her fingers up to trace his jaw. He pulled her face to his again and kissed her. She melted, readily giving over to the need that was mounting within her again and aware of the strain on her heart as it sought to reach his.

Violissa woke with a start, sitting up quickly, her eyes darting around. She was back in her room with no indication she'd left. The only signs that anything had happened were the perspiration on her body, the long ringlets of hair stuck to her face, and her naked body. Lifting the covers she'd kicked from her, she found her gown balled up at the bottom of the bed. She collapsed back, bringing her hand to her chest as she remembered Sinow's touches and how real they had seemed. Sleep took her again, this time with no dreams, only a sense of contentment that layered the darkness.

CHAPTER 6

Are you alright, Violissa?" Cayden asked the next morning when she entered the dining room. Breakfast had been laid out over an hour before, so only a few of the Council remained, discussing issues of the realm or whatever it was they discussed when they were all together. Violissa rarely paid attention to it.

"I'm fine, Cayden, why do you ask?" she answered absently, her hand rubbing the spot on her neck where Sinow's touch seemed to linger.

She'd woken disoriented, the dream rushing back to her. The nightdress was still bunched at the bottom of her bed, and she had no explanation of why it was there or why she'd had to clean a strange residue from between her legs before she'd dressed. A part of her knew the answer but refused to acknowledge it because it made no sense. This had been a dream and only a dream.

"You appear to have a flush to your cheeks this morning," Cayden continued, not noticing her distracted thoughts. "I can look you over to make sure you're not coming down with anything."

Violissa placed a hand on her cheek, noting the heat coming

from it. She knew better than to think the flush was anything but a result of her dream, but she wasn't about to share that with Cayden or anyone else in the room, for that matter. All eyes were on her now, awaiting her answer.

"I'll be fine, Cayden. I didn't sleep very well last night. That's all it is." She caught Daneele's eyebrow lift in her periphery but ignored it. Walking over to the bowl of fruit on the sideboard, she chose a few pieces, then sat across from Daneele.

"Well, if it continues," Cayden responded, "let me know."

"Thank you for your concern, Cayden. I'll be fine," she replied, not looking up from her food.

From the corner of her eye, she saw him nod before he left the room.

"Didn't sleep well last night?" Daneele asked. She'd been hoping he'd leave it alone, but that was not Daneele's way. He always had to push her.

"Bad dreams," she stated bluntly. "What's on the agenda today? Not going to torment me with anymore ascension preparation, are you?"

While she didn't mind the reading and the preparations, the Council had been running her through practice after practice of the rituals involved with her ascension. She was growing tired of it and longed to escape, even for a few hours.

Daneele laughed, knowing her too well. "No, I know how much you hate formality."

She smiled. He was right; she had always shunned the formality of her role. She was a free spirit and did not like the confines of the throne. Whenever she could, she would shun the formal aspects and do things her way.

The only time she truly did anything following any type of traditional role was during the gathering of the Masters. Cirillia was a vast kingdom with many towns, and within each one, the Council appointed a Master to govern. While Violissa and her Council could easily travel to each town, it was easier to have someone governing directly in an official capacity to provide direction to the people. Violissa still held the power, and every Master knew this, but in her stead, they were the voice of the crown.

Violissa met with the Masters to discuss concerns in their towns every few moons. It had been the Council's idea that she take on this responsibility centuries earlier. This was the only time she followed the Council's recommendations without question and the only time she involved herself in formal duties.

"However," Daneele said, interrupting her thoughts, "you will be busy for the next few days. The people in the village of Rhann have sent word that there is a sickness spreading through the village. They require healing, and since I thought you'd enjoy getting away from the castle, you'll be coming with us."

That perked her up, and she gave him a wide smile. Being with her people was as refreshing to her spirit as being in nature. "Of course. When do we leave?"

"When the light hits its midday peak."

"I'll be ready," she replied as he rose.

"I have no doubt." He gave her a smile and left the room, which she saw had emptied over the few minutes they had been talking.

The citrus flavor of her fruit made her lips pucker, and she picked up a slice of apple to soothe the tartness. Getting away would be good. She hadn't been able to leave for a while with all the preparations for the ascension. And she loved healing. It was the side of her abilities she shared with her Council.

Healing was only one of the powers her Lightbearers held, but it was the most coveted, since it enabled them to keep their people healthy. Only in rare cases could they not heal a mortal. For those too close to death, they could only provide solace. Their powers were vast but limited in that respect. Once the Fates claimed a soul, there was no amount of magic that could save it.

Healing magic was often a bone of contention with the Darkbearers because it was not a gift the Darkbearers held. They assumed as part of the treaty that their people should be healed as well. It wasn't a terrible suggestion; it was merely an impossible one. There was no crossing the boundary aside from accessing the meeting grounds. With one exception: the meeting of Light and Dark power at the boundary could open a doorway into the other realm. Even with his faith in the prophecy, Sinow's father would never entertain the idea of allowing a Lightbearer in his realm.

That left little ability for her Lightbearers to share their gift. As a compromise, they provided potions and herbs that were known in Cirillia to have healing powers. The Lightbearers shared these, as well as their knowledge of the internal workings of the body, which came as a byproduct of their healing, so the Darkbearers could help their people in times of sickness. Even with all that, Violissa still suspected that some of them thought her Council was purposely not sharing their healing abilities, but it was a long-buried argument she wasn't about to bring back up. She imagined there would be enough contention to be dealt with regarding the prophecy over the upcoming years. No need to add fuel to the fire.

ALTHOUGH SHE STOPPED the illness and healed the villagers on the first day, Violissa spent two more days in the village of Rhann. Being with her people always brought a sense of normalcy to her. She could laugh, sing, dance, learn about day-to-day matters, and be like them...as much as she could. The stark contrast between her and her people remained—the hair, the eyes, the power—but for a short time, it was almost like she belonged.

Daneele and Anwell, the two Council who had accompanied her, had grumbled about her staying longer than necessary, but she stopped them, sending them on their way and knowing she'd hear about it from the others when she returned. The ascension was too close to be dallying about like she was a mortal, she could imagine them saying. Daneele would defend her decision, but she'd still face their disappointment when she returned. Not that she'd pay them any heed. She loved being free from the confines of the castle too much.

On the second night, another dream came. Just like the first, she found herself in the meeting glade, Sinow with her. And like the first time, she lost herself to the ecstasy of what he did to her body. She woke in a sweat, her gown torn in the same place Sinow had torn it from her before he'd taken her. The frayed edges were soft against her fingers when she picked it up from the end of the bed, staring at it in confusion. Had she torn it in the throes of the dream? Her cheeks grew hot thinking of it.

Hastily, she used her magic to repair the gown, thankful the village Master had insisted she stay in his room while he and his wife slept at her parents' home. She cleaned herself up and dressed, again curious as to why there were so many things that had transcended the dream. Biting her lip, she sat on the edge of the bed, searching for a rational explanation, yet finding none.

Violissa spent the morning in the fields beside her people, helping them harvest the fresh berries that she'd grown for them as a treat. Cirillians were hardworking, and she ensured that even though her magic enhanced the land, they knew how to plant and harvest. Wiping her hand on her brow, she looked around at the people. The sun shone down on their auburn hair, giving it depth that never came to her golden locks, and when a young girl turned to question her, the sun sparkled in the blue eyes that matched all the others in her kingdom. All but Violissa's.

They were beautiful, and she marveled at how, even with the same hair and eye traits, each was so different from the other in size, shape, and personality. They were fragile beings, their mortality limiting them to only a few hundred years for most, yet they lived life with kindness and passion. There were times when she would sneak from the castle and disguise herself just to walk through the towns and villages and experience their welcoming generosity. Never had she come across anyone who turned her away or showed her anything but kindness.

That openness was one reason Cirillia had fared so poorly in past wars with Tenebron. The enemy kingdom took advantage of Cirillia, its defenses vulnerable without the Council or, in the past, the king. The Darkbearers wrote it off as weakness, but Violissa saw it as strength. There was no fighting, no turmoil among her people. Life for them was happy and uncomplicated. She saw their lives as worth living. Did the Dark Prince see the same thing when he looked at his people? She didn't know, but as the small child playing in front of her stopped and smiled up at her with those sky-blue eyes, she really didn't think so.

With her dream interrupting her sleep the prior night and knowing her Council was eager for her return, Violissa left the village in the early afternoon. The remains of the day she spent with the local dressmaker, fitting her for her gown. She could easily have created one for herself, but she wanted her people involved in the ascension. Since there had not been one in well over ten thousand years, she knew it was special to them.

The dream returned that night and the night after and each subsequent night. She tried not to dwell on them, throwing herself into the ascension preparations or ignoring the constant hounding of her Council to reconsider her decision on the union with Sinow. As titillating as the dreams were, they tempted her to give up her obstinacy just to experience the real thing. But instead, she made excuses, leading them to believe she was too busy with the ascension to be bothered about it.

Their frustration was evident in the grumbling and the scolding looks, the worry that creased their brows, but she didn't want to think of the union, no matter how her dreams were keeping it in the forefront of her thoughts. She would deal with the union after the ascension. Maybe by then her dreams would stop.

But the dreams wouldn't flee her mind. She couldn't grasp the reason behind their return each night or how real they seemed, but she suspected her subconscious was giving an outlet to the instinctual attraction she'd had to Sinow that first day. He stayed present in her mind just as often as the dreams did, and it did nothing but aggravate her to find herself so utterly out of control about something, especially him.

What really frustrated her was that she was increasingly looking forward to going to bed; it was almost addictive. She would watch for the sun to set, feigning excuses about needing rest for the ascension just to get to bed early. It wasn't far from the truth. The dreams left her exhausted and were cutting in on her rest time.

No one suspected her sleepless nights were anything more than pre-ascension jitters. No one, that was, except Daneele. He read her too easily and questioned her daily about the circles under her eyes, the constant flush to her cheeks, and the bad dreams she blamed. She'd gotten to the point where she tried to avoid him, which had been working quite well, until now.

As she rushed down the hall to scrounge the leftovers from breakfast, she slammed straight into Daneele, who was standing in the doorway to the dining room, arms crossed, waiting for her.

"Oversleep again, Violissa? Honestly, you know any of us can clear your bad dreams up if you'd let us."

"No, Daneele, I'll be fine. Don't worry." She tried to sneak past him, but he blocked her path.

"It is for that reason that I'm worried. Just enlighten me. Share them with me so I can help."

He reached a hand toward her left temple, but she ducked and moved into the dining room. As a child, on the rare occasions when she'd had a bad dream, Daneele would soothe the memory, sometimes even remove it to calm her. It was one of his gifts. All he had to do was place his hand on your temple and the terror of a nightmare would cease. If she hadn't secretly enjoyed the dreams so much, she might have accepted his offer, but for the fear that he would see what she'd dreamed.

"Really, Daneele. I'm sure they'll be much better, if not gone, after the ascension." She grabbed a piece of sweetbread and some grapes, then sat down.

"You really are too stubborn for your own good," he said, following her in. He stopped and stood behind the chair directly in front of her. "But I didn't wait here this long just to lecture you. The prince has requested a meeting with you."

She choked and spat the grape from her mouth, feeling the crimson of her cheeks flare. Trying to recover, she replied, "Really, what could he want with us both so close to ascension? Have you alerted the other Council that we'll be going?"

"No, Violissa. He requested the meeting with you alone. He wants no Council."

"Well then, tell him I'm too busy to—"

"Violissa," he interrupted, "you'll be queen in a short while. You need to act like one. No more games. I told him you'd be there when the sun hits its mid point."

"That's not enough time," she stated, knowing it was a useless battle as her words came out.

"Then I suggest you get ready. You wouldn't want him to see you dressed in your morning clothes, now would you? Oh, and wipe your mouth. You've got sweetbread all over it."

She threw the remaining bread at him, but he shifted before it could hit him. It flopped with a dull thud onto the floor where he'd been standing. She slammed her hand down on the table and screamed in frustration, the sound echoing through the quiet halls of the castle.

CHAPTER 7

Sinow tapped his foot, running his hand through his hair as he waited for Violissa in the meeting grove. He'd delayed requesting to see her, knowing it would bring his craving for her back. Not that it had gone anywhere. It simmered within him like the embers of a fire waiting to be lit. The scent of lilac filled the air, and he savored it, watching as she shifted in. The air fled his lungs as it had that first day, and he tightened his jaw, not wanting it to gape as it was prone to in her presence.

She was ravishing, her golden curls loose again and draping over her shoulder. A thin line of purple flowers wove through one curl and matched the violet of her dress. But it was her emerald eyes, and the exhaustion housed in them, that confirmed his suspicions.

"Hello, Vi," he said, his lip lifting into a sly grin. "I see those dreams have been affecting your sleep." She peeked at him, and the pinkish flush of her cheeks turned the color of a freshly picked rose. "Glad to see I'm not the only one with circles under the eyes. You'd think as exhausted as we were when we finished that we'd have had our fill of beauty sleep."

She held his gaze as her mouth fell open, those perfect lips forming an "oh" as the words he'd spoken sank in. The first dream had come as a pleasant surprise, and he assumed his desire for her had caused him to dream of her. Each dream only further encouraged the need for her because they were so realistic.

The hesitation to meet his eyes was no longer there, further confirming his suspicions because in his dreams, that hesitation had only been there the first time. Once he'd made love to her, it had faded. The air still escaped his lungs when her eyes held his, and he could count the number of seconds her heart stopped, but those reactions had diminished now.

"They were dreams," she mumbled, her brow furrowing as she chewed her bottom lip. She frowned, her lips pursing, the emerald in her irises turning a rich sage as her mood changed. There was a fierce side to her that made her even more attractive, and he imagined it was the side of her that drove the sexual intensity he'd experienced from her. His pulse quickened at the thought of what they'd done the previous night.

"You set it all up, didn't you?" she asked, her tone accusatory. "You knew you couldn't have me in real life, so you invaded my dreams."

If only he had that power. "I don't possess the ability to manipulate dreams. Although it would be a tempting gift to have. Imagine the fun I could have with that," he said slyly, then added, "No, wait, I don't have to imagine. I've experienced it firsthand." He laughed, a wickedly impish laugh, and then ducked as she flung a ball of arcane at him.

He held up his hands in surrender. "I had nothing to do with it. I promise. I don't possess the power to do such a thing. In fact, I thought it was my mind fulfilling the fantasies I was having of you during the day. You certainly do make it hard to concentrate on running a realm."

The arch of her brow was alluring, but she ignored his last comment. "If you didn't know, then why did you suspect it when you saw me just now? Those weren't guesses about my sleepless appearance."

He was finding it difficult to keep talking. The urge to yank her into his arms and kiss her was challenging his strength. She crossed her arms, emphasizing the swell of her breasts, and his sight dropped to them. He had touched and licked those same breasts the prior night, and the thought didn't help his focus.

"Sinow, I asked you a question. How did you know?"

"I didn't. I suspected a few nights ago, but when these appeared," he lifted his shirt to reveal the long scratch marks running down his side, "I knew there was something going on. I asked you to meet so I could have confirmation."

She took a quick breath, biting her bottom lip so hard that a small trickle of blood welled on it. Her tongue came out and cleaned it, the sight only increasing his discomfort.

"I did that?" she asked, her voice hushed. She was clutching her dress, her fingers turning pale with the force.

"I enjoy a little pain now and again, but I'm fairly certain I didn't do this to myself. I don't remember receiving them, so I'd say you had me preoccupied. They didn't heal in the dream, and I stopped them from healing when I woke, so I'd have proof when we met today. You see, even after the scratches, I wasn't totally convinced. It all seemed so real, but the Dream Realm has always been a myth. At least I thought it was, until those deep circles under your eyes, the ones matching mine, validated its existence."

The confusion spread across her features. "But it was all a dream. No one has that power."

"No one here, but what about the Fates? It's possible they don't like the idea of you meddling with their plans or denying me the amazing things you've been doing to me."

Her cheeks grew a delicate shade of crimson. "Stop it, Sinow. That's ridiculous. The Fates don't meddle like that. They draw a lifeline, an outline of what they want, and walk away. They don't mess with your dreams."

He ran his hands through his hair in frustration, pacing as he said, "You and I don't have normal lifelines like our people, Vi. There have been other prophetic dealings with the Fates in the past, but ours is the biggest one of them all. It's not just some random rescue of a village from a rare beast or illness. This prophecy, according to your Council, the Fates wrote at the beginning of our world's creation. It's the only one we have physical proof of in the scrolls your Keeper holds. It's huge, and you...they created you because of it. Without a prophecy, would you even be here?"

A flicker of hurt passed through her eyes before they hardened. He'd hit a nerve, and a very raw one at that. She had no parents, born of magic and not of the womb, and that seemed a sensitive subject for her. Her eyes darkened to a green the depths of the forest behind her as close to black as green could be. The response was an interesting one, and he made a mental note to explore it further if she ever gave up this foolish game of denying their union.

"I refuse to let words rule me," she snapped. "My life has its own course, and I make my own decisions. My decision is that there will be no union between our people and no vows for us. Until I have said otherwise, the Fates will have to wait."

The sky above them rumbled, and he wondered if she'd caused the disturbance with her anger or if it was the Fates expressing their dissatisfaction.

"What is it you're so afraid of?" he asked, daring a step closer to her. "Do you think I wanted this path for my life? Do you think my lack of choice doesn't anger me as well? I suppose if the payoff weren't a lifetime of sex with you, I'd be angry enough to rebel." His power pressed for release, but he kept it at bay. "The thing I don't understand is that you're clearly attracted to me, so what has you so afraid? Because you damn well don't strike me as the timid type."

Her lips pursed, and he noted the flare of her nostrils. "You know nothing about me," she snarled, a sound that only further captivated him. "You think after two meetings and a few dreams you know who I am?" She was trying to put him on the defensive, and he didn't enjoy being put in that position. In fact, he despised it. A growl rumbled in his chest, but before he could say anything, she looked down, smoothing her hands along the front of her dress as if she were shoving away her emotions.

"I know you didn't call me here to rehash the conversation from our first meeting or to torment me about the Dream Realm. It's too close to our ascensions for all that. Why did you request my presence here, Sinow?"

He stared at her, speechless, trying to understand how she'd changed direction so quickly. And with that change, the Darkness in him had calmed. One moment he'd wanted nothing more than to strike her with his magic until she was screaming for mercy, and the next, her demeanor had changed, leaving his mood serene.

"Blasted woman," he muttered. Maybe she possessed some magic that eased his frustration. A kiss would have done the trick, or any form of touching her, but he suspected that was no longer an option now that he'd exposed the dreams for what they really were.

"True, I have brought you here on formal business." Sighing, he let talk of the Dream Realm go. "It would seem my father is conspiring against us."

She opened her mouth to respond, but he didn't give her a chance. "He's decided it would be wise, as our realms will be one... in the future...to have us attend each other's ascensions. Your Council has agreed."

"What?" she gasped, her eyes shifting to a dark emerald. His craving for her flared as her temper ignited. "How dare they—"

"Hold your tongue for a moment, woman, and let me finish. They have agreed, however, to place the final word in our hands, knowing you'd react in this very fashion. Your Council voiced many concerns but thought it best to start our futures with a solid alliance. I've been told it is only for the benefit of the treaty that they've suggested such a thing."

He added the last line so she would not think they were focusing only on the prophecy, which, of course, he knew they were. The treaty had been in place for many hundreds of years, with neither king nor Council stepping foot in the other's realm. The laws of the treaty forbid it, and then there was the pesky issue that no one could cross the boundary without a combination of both Light and Dark magic. He often wondered why that point was even in the treaty, unless it was there as a failsafe. Against what, he didn't know.

That his father had accepted the conditions the Council laid out regarding their ascensions surprised him. This would be unprecedented, but then again, so was the prophecy and the stubborn woman before him.

"Your Council believes, since you will be queen shortly, you should have the ultimate say."

He waited for her reaction and watched as her mind worked it through. Her teeth gnawed at her bottom lip again, a revealing habit he was finding irresistible. Although now that he'd touched her in the Dream Realm, everything about her was irresistible. He should have hated the prophecy as much as she did, hated that it had bound him to his enemy, but he couldn't. Not when Violissa was the reward. There was too much about her that tempted him, and that sensation that seized him whenever he even thought about her told him there was no living without her now that he was this close to having her.

The crystal green of her eyes gave off a prism of color when the sun hit them, beguiling him when she looked up at him. Taking a step back to tame the need to pull her into his arms, he waited for her decision.

"So, what are your thoughts on it?" she finally asked.

He cocked his head, wondering why she'd bothered to ask him when the decision lay in her hands.

"You really want my opinion? That's unexpected." He waited for a response, but only the glitter in her eye registered any. "Honestly," he continued, folding his hands and walking toward the trees.

He'd taken the time to consider his thoughts when his father had come to him about it. Ascensions were private rituals, a sacred passing of the crown and power from father to son. Having someone outside of the Council observe it went against tradition, especially the enemy. And that's what they were, after all. Enemies. His grandfather had led the attack on Cirillia, cornering the last king and forcing his hand. His brutal actions resulted in the loss of the Cirillian capital and its monarchy. The only reason the kingdom existed was the boundary wall that the king and his Council erected before the capital became the void now known as the Lost Realm.

Sinow turned back to her, leaning on a tree and crossing his arms. "I like the idea. It would be a good show of faith from both of us, and...it would get them off our backs. They'd think our amicability was a sign that we were getting closer to the union you dread so much. It would buy you more time, which I venture is the true reason for your avoidance of the union."

Her chin rose, a flash of irritation lighting her features and confirming his thoughts. It wasn't only obstinacy that had her defying the Fates, but fear. He could read it in her eyes, in the tension that lined them before she hid it. Fear of him? Or was it more?

Footfalls that almost seemed like they didn't touch the ground brought her closer to him. She laid her hand against the bark of the tree, standing so close he could see the glimmer of gold in the strands of her hair. It was almost hard for the air to fill his chest when she was this close, and he clenched his hands to fight the lack of control.

"They don't like being used like that unless you ask first," she murmured.

He squinted, trying to determine what she was referring to.

A slight smile tugged at her lips. "The trees."

He stepped from the tree, puzzled by her behavior. She couldn't seriously be talking about the tree. Yet, as her hand caressed the bark, it softened, morphing into something more like moss. She lifted her hand and took his. The contact sent a rush of sparks through him like a current of lightning hitting the ground. She guided his hand to the tree, pressing it into the trunk where his fingers sank into its soft consistency.

His eyes were wide, and he turned them to her, seeking an explanation.

"If you're nice to them and you've just the right touch, they let their defenses down. This one says it's okay to lean now since I've vouched for you."

Sinow wanted to laugh at the absurdity of it, but she was so serious he didn't dare. He continued to stare, astounded by her and the strange nature ability she had. No one had power over nature. Only the Elvin and his grandfather had annihilated them during the war with Cirillia. It confounded him that she would have a power lost ages ago. She had not been born of a woman, so there was no chance of it being in her bloodline. Unless one of her Council had Elvin blood and inherited a dormant nature talent that he'd then passed on when they'd created her. But even that made no sense. Never in history had there been a mixture of the races. He and Violissa were to be the first. He'd need to ask his father's Council to see if they had any insight. There had to be something he was missing.

"So, you spend a lot of time with trees?" he said, giving her a coy smile.

She pulled her hand away, and he missed the touch. For just that moment, she'd let her guard down and he'd enjoyed it, then lost it with his comment. It was too late to take it back, so he continued to tease. "Should I be jealous, worried that you might run off with one behind my back?" He pulled his hand away and leaned against the tree again, crossing his arms and trying to hide his reaction to how comfortable he now was.

"First of all, there's nothing to run off from, and second, there's no competition."

"Finally, a compliment. I knew you had it in you," he replied with an air of confidence.

"I was speaking about the tree," she said. There was a tug at her lips, and he could see she was trying to remain hard but finding it difficult.

Two steps took her away from him but left her standing in front of him. There was no sense of hesitation when her eyes locked on his, but he still sensed the fluctuations of her heartbeat.

"There has never been a Darkbearer on our soil, at least not a welcome one. Our ceremonies and traditions are sacred, especially the ascension."

"And you don't think ours are?" he said, hearing the irritation in his voice.

"There's never been a queen crowned, and my powers...well, they're different, vaster than any king before me." She held out her hand, gesturing to the tree. He understood her reference to her nature abilities, but that still didn't mean his ascension would be any less special. "There are pieces to our rituals that our laws require no one outside of my kingdom to witness. That's why I can't fathom my Council agreeing to this. They must truly be running out of ideas to get us together or running mad."

"Would it be that bad for us to be together? I think the Dream Realm proves it wouldn't be." She bristled, causing a tic in his jaw. Aggravating was a word he was coming to associate too easily with her. He dropped the subject, returning to the ascension. "Listen, we may not hold much sacred in Tenebron, but to my people, the crown and the ascension are. Allowing you to witness it means putting myself in a unique position as well. But I will agree to you and one Council attending as long as you agree to it."

He couldn't believe he was agreeing, but he suspected she had more to lose through this deal than he did, so he had taken the first step.

A darkness came over her eyes again, then cleared as suddenly as it had appeared. It gave him the impression she might be ready to throw a tantrum, and he bit his cheek to keep from laughing.

"All right, the same will stand for you," she huffed. "However, anything either of you sees or hears at the ceremony must not be used to your advantage, and I will swear the same. I cannot believe I'm agreeing to this, but since my Council thinks it wise and you as well, I'll do it. You and I need a good working relationship if the treaty is to continue."

With that, she turned and walked away from him, skirts swooshing as if to emphasize her irritation at the situation. He rose from the tree, feeling as if he should thank it for its hospitality but having too much pride to do such a thing. Imagine if any of the Council were to catch him; he'd never hear the end of it. As he walked away, the tough bark of the tree curved back into place once again.

"So..." he began.

Violissa turned suddenly, a long golden lock of hair caressing her cheek and chin. "Don't think this gets you any closer to my bed, Sinow." He noted a slight blush on her cheeks as his mind wandered to their encounters in the Dream Realm.

"I don't recall there being a bed involved, so that's not a concern." Her blush deepened, and he noted the flicker of lust in her eyes.

"This is business and only business. Don't mistake what happened in the Dream Realm as anything but the influence of the Fates. I am still firm on my thoughts toward a union with you, and nothing will change that."

"You're an aggravating woman, Violissa. And you're playing with fire." He stepped closer to her, towering over her and hearing her sharp inhale when she looked up at him. "I'll wait, because now that I've had a taste of you, I know you'll be worth the wait.

But at some point, my patience will give, and you won't like the side of me that will come out to play. I'm not one to be toyed with."

Her lips parted, and he wanted desperately to kiss her, but he balled his fists to keep from touching her.

"Neither am I." There was a hint of playfulness in her tone. "Goodbye, Sinow."

"Sweet dreams, Vi," he replied with an edge to his voice.

She shifted, leaving only the scent of lilac in her wake.

Power surged through Sinow, his hold on it breaking. His eyes burned, and he knew they were black with anger, anger not even that soothing voice or the lilac could tame. He had more patience than most Darkbearers, but it wasn't something that came naturally. Violissa was pushing him, and it had taken all his effort not to let his Darkness flee from him when she'd turned him down yet again.

As thick black tendrils seeped from his fingertips, urging him to release his angst, the fire within him burned. He fought back the urge to release it, closing his eyes to concentrate on the emotions rioting within him. She needed to come around soon. The closer the ascension came, the more volatile his power was growing. It was changing, becoming darker and more difficult to control. If she made him wait much longer, he couldn't guarantee that when his true powers surfaced, it wouldn't be all-out war.

CHAPTER 8

The air fled Violissa's lungs. She hadn't realized she'd been holding it so tight in her chest when she'd left Sinow. Maintaining control while being that close to him had been painful. She'd wanted nothing more than to give up on her attempts to define her destiny and fall into his arms. His kisses, his touches, and the pleasure they promised tempted her to give in. But she'd fought the temptation. Those things could wait, and he could wait. Once she became queen, once she prepared her people, once she had a sense that there was some free will for her, she would agree to the union. She wasn't ready yet, nor were her people.

She walked over to the windows that overlooked her garden. A violet butterfly flitted among the pansies she'd grown the prior week, carefree and oblivious to the world around it. If only life were that simple, she'd have been able to acknowledge the growing emotions she had for Sinow. Who was she kidding? She'd fallen for him at first glance, and she'd have willingly married him and shared the throne with him if she'd been living a different life.

But things were not simple; she wasn't being given the choice.

He ruled an enemy land. Take away the treaty and that's really what they were, enemies, regardless of how you dressed it up. He ruled over a people who had historically mistreated her own. He was a descendant of the king who'd decimated the population of the gentle Elvin. Annihilation had never been a word spoken from the lips of a Light King, and just the thought drew bile to her throat.

She turned from the window and walked across the room. She supposed he was right. If things were simple, she would never have even been created. Theirs was not a simple life. She was a child of prophecy and, some would say, a child of the Fates. But that didn't mean she had to like it or accept it. There was no choice in how magic had brought her into this world and no choice in being the child of prophecy. But there was a choice in refusing to be a pawn of the Fates. When she married Sinow, it would be on her terms, not theirs.

Violissa ran her hand along the silk sheets that adorned her bed, then collapsed onto them, the lushness of the bedding enveloping her. She stared at the violet canopy draped above her, thinking about Sinow and what she was giving up. A shiver flittered through her when she thought of him, but it was only a physical reaction because all they had was physical. From the instinctual need to the sex they'd had in the Dream Realm, there was nothing there but physical attraction. She didn't know him, nor did he know her, and she suspected what she'd seen of him was not his true self. No one of Dark power could be patient or understanding. All they did was take and destroy.

With a huff, she buried her face in her pillow, hating how exhausted she was from the lack of sleep and from the meeting with Sinow. Keeping up the façade that she wasn't attracted to him, that she wasn't pining for his touch, was draining. She'd taken this path of obstinacy, to be defiant and independent, but now that she'd started down it, she wasn't sure what she'd gotten herself into. Perhaps she should have listened to her Council and played the part of the subservient queen.

"No," she said, "I will play this game on my terms and by my rules."

Sinow seemed to understand, and he had stated he would be patient, but for how long? She'd started down the path, and now there was no turning back. She sat up, threw her shoes off, and rubbed her feet. How she hated wearing these blasted things. Barefoot was her preferred method, but she stuffed her feet into the stiff casings whenever she had any formal function. The first thing she planned to do when she became queen was to do away with any requirement that she, or any female for that matter, wear shoes.

Her Council was likely waiting to hear about the meeting. She could just see them pacing down in the main hall, having sensed her presence the moment she arrived. They'd conferred with the king when she was only days from taking the throne. They could wait. Let them worry about her decision and anticipate her reaction.

And they would worry. The prophecy had been their focus since before magic had created her. The last king had passed his powers to his Council when he'd sacrificed his immortality to save the kingdom. Only Cyric remained from his Council, the king's power passing to the men who now served as her Lightbearers. The history was one she knew little of, but she knew the king had no heirs and to protect the kingdom and the prophecy from Sinow's grandfather, he had relinquished his life.

Although immortal, when eternity became too long, a king and his Council members could relinquish their lives, giving their bodies over to nature and their spirits to the Fates. Typically, a king and his Council would return to the Fates when the next generation ascended. That was not the case for Violissa or the prior king, Viliren.

There were so many firsts with Violissa, and their weight was one she carried unwillingly. The first immortal woman. She would be the first queen, the first to marry outside her race, the first to marry another immortal, and the first to have an arranged marriage. Kings always married mortals. There were no arranged marriages; they married for love. But as romantic as that sounded, she supposed she would be lucky in that aspect.

Mortals had fleeting lives, especially those who married a king. There was tragic acceptance when loving an immortal king. Once a child was upon her, the queen gave up her life for the next generation of power. Sadly, all died in childbirth. To Violissa's knowledge, no Light King had ever remarried. They waited for their soul mate and chose only to marry that one time.

Dark Kings had different practices. Some kings overlooked love and took several wives until they could finally beget a child with one. Some kings, like Sinow's father, would remarry after losing his wife in childbirth, but as that first wife would be the only to bear a child, these marriages often ended miserably, especially if the king's true love had been the first wife.

Each king could only father one child. It was a curse of the immortals. The reason was unknown. Maybe the Fates didn't want too many immortals running around wielding such great power, or maybe they were afraid too many could be a threat to them. She laughed at the notion of a Fate having any fear. Whatever the reason, it was a fact of life that there could only be one child born to each throne.

The only exception had been Sinow's father. His second wife had given birth. The act had killed her, but it had happened. Tynan. From everything she'd heard from her Council, his power was limited, less than any king would have, and significantly less than his brother. But he existed and, from what she'd seen, he was a thorn in the king's side. An anomaly and an annoyance. Or maybe simply a curse on the Darkbearers for all the damage they'd done in the past.

Violissa sighed, wondering if a union of two immortals would change the rules. There were so many unknowns and firsts that ruled her existence. And she didn't want to think about children or marriage with Sinow, no matter how tempting the man was. She rubbed her toes, thinking how blessed the Council was. They didn't face problems of love, unions, or birth. They swore a vow of celibacy when they received their blessing of power from the Fates. Lightbearers were rare, only born when one returned himself to the Fates. All were male. To her knowledge, the last one born had been Daneele, and he was over five thousand years old.

Thinking of her Council reminded Violissa that she needed to talk to them. Glancing at the window, she saw the blush of the sunset on the horizon. There were still too many things to say and do before the ascension. Time was running short. Skimming her hands down the front of her dress, she settled her emotions and walked toward the door.

Her Council was waiting for her in the meeting room. Some were pacing, most were standing, but all were looking at her with anticipation.

"Gentlemen," she said nonchalantly, "I expect you are waiting on me. I must say I don't appreciate you talking with the king without my knowledge... No, it's not quite that, it's really the idea of you making decisions without me that bothers me."

"In our defense, we left the decision in your hands. We merely started the process," Kembal said, stopping his pacing but keeping his hands folded behind his back. His expression mirrored the others in the room. None had sat, and their stress permeated the room.

That they'd waited for her in the meeting room revealed the seriousness of the situation. It was also rare that all ten Lightbearers met at one time unless an urgent or impactful decision had to be made. Mostly they spoke as a collective with enaigne, their ability to talk mentally to each other. This allowed them to continue attending to their many duties within the realm and still be able to discuss matters that needed attention. It was only the impending ascension that had brought them all to her today.

"Thank you, Kembal. I understand that." She waved a hand, and the room was lit by crystal balls of light that appeared in each corner. The room was massive in both width and breadth. Rich tapestries depicting the history of their people draped the stone walls. Plush burgundy carpets covered the stone floor in most places where Violissa's feet walked. An oak table encompassing most of the room stood in the center, engulfed by ten enormous oak chairs, five on each side. A throne-style chair stood at the head of the table, ornamental engravings of flowers running along its borders. It was in this chair that Violissa sat as she waited for the Council to be seated.

She looked out at the ten faces of the men who had raised her. They were her family, the only family she had, which is why she knew they held her best interests at heart.

"I understand that your intentions regarding the invitation to Prince Sinow and myself to each other's ascensions are noble ones. For that matter, all actions surrounding the prophecy that have occurred have been only with the best of intentions. I know you want the best for the kingdom and for me. Understand that I have no doubt of that fact." She took a breath, steadying her nerves. "With that said, it's time for you all to step back and let me lead as I want to. Let me fail if I fail, succeed when I succeed and learn my own lessons. Have faith that the training you have given me over the last thousand years has prepared me for my duties. But understand that I am not the same as any of you. I am going to think and act much differently."

She stopped and leaned back in her chair, trying to read their reactions. From the looks on most of their faces, she'd driven home her point. She would be their queen in a mere day, and for most of them, it would be a relief. Councils were not rulers; they were advisers, protectors of the people. An extension of the throne. They were ready to hand over that duty, which is why she knew they would accept her speech and see it as a precursor to stepping down and letting her reign.

"Now, as for our visitors, I have agreed with your suggestion. The prince and one of his Council will be here to witness my ascension. We will need at least one Council at the border to perform the spell that will give them access. I suspect you've already given them the spell so that they may perform it on their side of the boundary. I expect two of you to greet them when they arrive and accompany them until the ceremony begins. They are then to be under the close eye of at least two guards. I know," she put her hand up as they all began to talk, "no guard could go up against either the prince or one of his Council. It is simply for show. We mustn't have the people concerned about Darkbearers running about unaccompanied in our realm. It will be alarming enough for them to be seen here, let alone without an escort."

"I'll greet them," Daneele offered. "As Keeper, it should be me who performs the spell and greets them."

"Agreed. Cyric, you shall accompany Daneele. As the elder of the Council, you should be part of this historic event."

"Thank you, Violissa," he replied with a nod.

"Then that's settled. Anwell shall accompany me to the prince's ascension. We will leave at nightfall. From my understanding, their event begins an hour following sunset." Anwell nodded as she looked around the table. "One last thing before we move on, although I've agreed to this exchange, it is by no means an acceptance of a union between myself and Sinow. It is merely a development of a working relationship between the two thrones to fortify the treaty. The prince and I will not marry at this time. In the future, we will discuss the prospect of a union upon this throne's readiness."

She waited, knowing the response would be swift. Kembal was the first to rise.

"Begging your pardon, Violissa, but I must protest. It disturbs many of us that you treat the prophecy and Fates with such disrespect. We have spent our lives protecting you and the prophecy. To see you undoing all of our work is disturbing. Have you even thought about the consequences you've brought upon yourself and our people?" His face was red, and she could see her decision had left him visibly shaken. As one of the eldest, she knew he thought he had more at stake for what he saw as her poor decisions.

"Yes, I have, which is why I've only said I won't wed Sinow now. I have not ruled it out and have said it will be an option in the future. He has agreed with my thoughts and will wait."

"Wait? Dark kings don't wait, Violissa. They are not known for their patience. How long do you think he'll be patient? What happens when he tires of waiting? Have you thought about that? Will he fight you? I doubt it. He'll go after our people. With his powers, he'll find a way to bring the border down, and there will be war."

"It won't come to that, and if it does, we'll protect them."

"Ha!" Jar stood up, slamming his hand on the table. "You've obviously never seen war. Fending off the attacks of Sinow and his Council will leave us too drained to protect against his army of mortals, who will enter our lands and slaughter our people. What you're doing, Violissa, is sentencing them all to death."

The others looked from him to Violissa as they watched and waited for her response. She gritted her teeth that no one had spoken in her defense.

"Really, Jar, I believe you're being dramatic. I do, however, respect and appreciate your opinion as well as the others, those of you who have spoken. The union will take place after the ascension. I did not say there would be no union, and I certainly won't let it come to war. I know my limitations." Jar sat back down, rubbing his beard with his hand as he listened to her. He still didn't look happy, nor did the others. She stood, placing both hands on the smooth oak table. The texture of the tree that had given its life to the table revealed the countless years of its existence.

"I need time, time to adjust to my new role, time for the people to see me as their queen, independent of all of you."

"No one says you can't do that," Cyric said, his voice soft. "But we must follow prophecy, Violissa. To deny it is to defy the Fates and risk their wrath."

She could see the concern in the creases on his forehead, the worry in the darkened hue of his cerulean eyes.

"This is not about challenging the Fates or their prophecy. It's about me and my duty to the people. I need to make my place in the history of our people before I can allow someone else to become part of my life, my realm, and my legacy. Do you understand?" She was relieved to see a few heads nodding. "Please know that I do this not to spite you, but for you. If I am remembered as a great queen who did wonderful things for her people, it will reflect on all of you, for I am who you've shaped me to be."

She stopped, pressure building behind her eyes. Daneele stood and addressed the Council in her silence.

"As Council to the throne, our job is to advise, not rule. We no longer decide for this throne, so I say now as I will formally tomorrow," he turned and faced Violissa, "you have my oath to support and protect you as I vowed I would when I first became a Lightbearer. As my queen and the most powerful being in this realm, or this world, for that matter, I am forever in your service. So, I will support your decision to delay union to the Darkbearer throne, as I hope you will support and respect my opinion that it is a mistake." She started to reply, but Daneele held his hand up. "Understanding that I cannot sway you, I only ask that you heed my advice regarding the decision once the ascension is complete."

He sat, giving her a bow of his head, which she returned with a smile. While his words hadn't soothed her completely, they had been an affirmation that he could not change her decision. Her worries lessened, but with them came the realization that tomorrow she would truly be the power of this realm.

"Well then," she said, standing and smoothing her hands down her dress, "we have an ascension to prepare for. Shall we, gentlemen?"

That night, Violissa wove a spell to protect her from any meddling dreams. It was the first night she slept peacefully, the first night that led to the first morning on which she awoke missing Sinow.

CHAPTER 9

When Sinow awoke the next morning, his first thoughts were of Violissa. While it was nice to wake without finding himself drenched in sweat and drained, he had an odd sensation of emptiness in his chest. He shrugged it off and rose from the bed. It was just before dawn, and he wasn't sure why he'd woken so early. Anticipation of the ascension was likely the culprit. Tonight would be the night the Fates blessed him with his full powers, and he took the throne from his father.

Pre-dawn greeted him when he pulled back the window covering. It was too early to be awake, but he was restless. His power pulsed through him in the unsteady current that had started weeks earlier. Magic stirred before an ascension, unpredictable and unsteady. It was a side-effect, his body readying for the addition of power.

Turning from the window, he thought back on his conversation with Violissa. It had taken every ounce of self-control not to have gathered her in his arms against her will, although after the dreams, he suspected she would be more than obliging. And he was certain that if their lips were ever to meet outside of the Dream

Realm, they'd succumb to the prophecy's will. That was the only reason he stood for the nonsense she was subjecting them to, with her refusal to follow the course of the prophecy.

The heat of his power rippled through him, and he rolled his neck, trying to simmer it. The mix of angst and want that came whenever he thought of her left him struggling to maintain his air of indifference. He didn't want her to know she was affecting him, that denying him twisted him into a frenzy of ire and frustration.

She wanted him. The heat of their attraction to one another was clear each time he was close to her. She was just too obstinate to give up on this ridiculous notion that she could avoid her fate. And in letting her do so, he looked weak, something he detested more than the notion that the Fates had decided his path for him.

He pulled a black shirt over his head and pressed the material over his chest, emphasizing the muscles below. Running his hands through his thick black locks, he closed his eyes, the image of Violissa instantly flooding before them. His pulse raced. The flux of power he'd been fighting calmed, just like it did every time he was near her. He could almost smell the lilac that trailed her, see the emerald sparkle in her eyes, the white strands of hair within the gold that shimmered like starlight. But as alluring as she was, there was something deeper that drew him to her. A force he could only credit to the Fates and the prophecy. One that had been driving them toward each other since they were born. No matter how she thought she could deny it, she couldn't. He'd given up trying years ago.

A knock at his door broke his trance, and he shook his head, trying to clear thoughts of Violissa from it.

"Enter," he commanded.

His half-brother entered the room, his beady eyes surveying him.

"Tynan," Sinow addressed him, not caring that his tone was terse.

"I hear you'll be attending the princess's ascension."

Sinow turned away, tucking his shirt in and wishing his brother would leave. "Yes, what concern is it of yours?"

"Well, you gave us no decision regarding who will accompany you."

Sinow gazed upon his brother. At first glance, he bore no resemblance to Sinow. Tynan was a head shorter, much of it because of the slouch he always carried. His looks were not nearly as striking as Sinow's, his face narrower, without the strength of Sinow's. In truth, Sinow found him quite plain to look upon, a reflection of his mother, no doubt. Sinow often wondered what his father had seen in her. He remembered her from his childhood, and upon comparing her to paintings he'd seen of his mother, her beauty did not compare. There was a dullness to her that Tynan had inherited. His brown eyes were flat, lacking the depth of Sinow's. It was haunting to look upon Sinow, his eyes an abyss that could drive a mortal to the brink of insanity or, worse, death. Tynan held none of the Darkness he held, and standing beside him, his elder brother overshadowed Tynan.

Sinow sometimes wondered if it was hard for Tynan to live in his shadow. There were moments when he thought he sensed jealousy or discontent from his brother, a glimmer of something in his eyes that he covered quickly. Whatever it was, it usually disappeared before he gave it much thought.

Mostly Sinow felt sorry for his brother. He was a misfit, an anomaly never meant to exist but somehow defying the odds. No one knew what to do with him. He had no claim to the throne, and with the lack of power he possessed, no one thought of him as a threat.

But because he had some power, he had to remain in the castle, away from the mortals. So, Sinow had taken him under his wing in an advisory role. The title was completely unofficial, but Tynan didn't know it, and it made Tynan feel needed, at least that's how Sinow looked at it. The suggestions Tynan made, Sinow sometimes heeded, and a few had actually been of use. It was something he would never admit to the Council, who considered his brother to be more of a joke than anything.

"I came to find out who you'll be taking to Violissa's ascension as you failed to announce it yesterday," Tynan repeated, breaking the silence as Sinow realized he'd been deep in thought for some time.

He sighed. This would be difficult for Tynan, as he knew how much his brother wanted to go. His curiosity about Violissa and anything to do with the prophecy leaned on the obsessive. But Tynan would have to get over it. A Darkbearer needed to attend, as it was an official visit. Tynan would remain behind.

"I'll be taking Keary since he is our strategic advisor. It will be an opportunity for him to gather information about the Light while being directly on their soil. He'll also be able to witness the amount of power Violissa receives with the ascension. It makes the most sense to take him with me." Sinow was also close to Keary, closer in fact than he was to Tynan, and if anyone was going with him, it would be Keary.

He waited for Tynan to react, his jaw growing tighter as he did.

"Keary is a wise choice," he said, throwing Sinow off with the unexpected response. "One of several you've made lately."

Sinow tilted his head, replying with a cautious, "How so?"

Something was brewing in Tynan's head, and Sinow didn't like the way the air had turned heavier.

"Well, regarding Violissa." He noted the tone of distaste in his brother's voice. "This wait and see idea you've had is brilliant. You don't want to be tied down to a woman, especially her, when you're stepping into your duties as king." Sinow's hands clenched. "There could be nothing worse than sleeping with a Cirillian. This prophecy doesn't seem like a blessing. It's more like a curse the Lightbearers created to enslave our throne to theirs and take control of our people."

Sinow snorted. "You have no idea what you're talking about. You really think the Lightbearers could or would even want to control our people? And as intriguing as it sounds, Violissa does not have the power to enslave me." He stopped as thoughts of their Dream Realm encounters entered his mind. His brother's throat clearing brought him back to reality.

"Honestly, brother, how you can stomach even the thought of touching her is beyond me. The stench of her Light magic would be too overwhelming. Don't get me wrong, she certainly looks tasty."

A growl rumbled through Sinow's chest, and he had Tynan pinned against the wall before he could finish his thought.

"Hold your tongue, brother. You walk a fine line."

Tynan stared defiantly back at Sinow before masking it with a questioning expression. "Did I say something offensive, Sinow?" he managed through the pressure of Sinow's hand against his throat. "I didn't realize you had such strong feelings for the woman."

Sinow released his hand from Tynan's throat. "I don't have strong feelings," he snapped, running his hand through his hair. He didn't know what had come over him, but a protective instinct had surged through him, stirring his aggression. "Just don't be so disrespectful about her in the future. She is to be my queen one day, and your comments are not welcome. Next time, you might not come out so unscathed." He turned his back on Tynan and walked across the room, rubbing his fingers across his temples as he puzzled over the reaction.

"Lesson learned," Tynan muttered, rubbing his neck. "Maybe there's something to that prophecy after all."

"Maybe," Sinow grumbled. He eyed his brother with suspicion, the hackles on his neck rising as a thought came to him. "How did you know I was awake this early, Tynan? Everyone knows I don't rise early in the morn."

Tynan gave him a crooked smile. "I always know when you're about Sinow. It's a brotherly thing."

"Funny, I don't have the same awareness about you," Sinow replied.

"So, I finally found an ability you don't have." His tone was light, but Sinow's mood hadn't changed. "Come now, Sinow, let's not dwell on this." He slapped his hand on Sinow's shoulder, but Sinow shrugged it off. "I simply have different views of the Light Princess and her prophecy from you and Father. You often seek my advice on issues, but on this, you only listen to him and the Council. So, without being asked, I will voice my opinion that delaying this union as you've chosen to do is advantageous. It gives you time to assess this new queen and how she handles her realm and her Council. If the Fates' intention is for you to unite with the enemy, an understanding of who she is and what her weaknesses are will help you rule her and ensure she does not rule you instead." He scratched the stubble on his chin and, not waiting for a response from Sinow, continued, "Someone needs to remain loyal to the realm, brother. Your Council doesn't seem to be concerned, and Father is following their lead. Only I see the prophecy for what it is and worry about what it will do to you and the kingdom."

He shifted away before Sinow could respond, leaving Sinow with only the resounding silence.

Scratching his head, he pondered his brother's words. Tynan's view of the prophecy differed greatly from anyone else's, and he had made valid points. Their father put his faith in the prophecy with no questions asked, which was unlike him. He'd once explained that the day the Light Council contacted him, informing him that Sinow was the other half of the prophecy, he'd had his doubts. There was no blind leap of trust. But the closer to Sinow's birth, the more convinced he was that they were correct. As Sinow's power seeped from his unborn form, the king accepted their word. And he'd been right to do so. Sinow was by far the most powerful immortal Tenebron had ever seen. His power was already twofold that of his father's, and he'd yet to take the crown.

Perhaps Tynan didn't know this. But his thoughts still held validity. Prophecy was nothing more than myth, words written eons ago and credited to be those of the Fates. Words that detailed the intersection of Sinow's life with Violissa's. He understood her frustration with it all, the lack of control and never being able to set your own course in life. But he'd gone along with it all because he had faith in his father's judgment.

His father was an excellent king who differed from many of his predecessors. Unlike Sinow's grandfather, his father followed the true ways of the crown. The ways the Fates had intended. The king and his Darkbearers were there to protect the people and instill order. They were the law: judge, jury, and punisher. Only through the generations had the code of the Dark King and his Council twisted. Dark powers had a tendency to corrupt, and Sinow's father had instilled in him an understanding of how destructive those powers could be. Especially after ascending.

Sinow stretched and ran his hands through his hair. He needed to get away from the castle. Tynan's words had scraped their way into his mind, and he needed to clear his head. Power clawed at him, seeking release, and he rolled his neck, trying to calm it. With the ascension so close, it was battering at him. Strolling to the window, he saw it was still dark, his favorite time to go riding.

He shifted to the stables and prepped his horse. His brother liked to get under his skin about the pleasure Sinow took in riding. He knew it wasn't necessary, but he enjoyed the strength of the horse's strides, the freedom of moving without magic and having the air whip around him. Tynan didn't understand, and Sinow didn't care. He had a stable full of stallions bred to handle him and his power.

He had time for a ride before the hustle of the day began.

The quiet and cool air calmed his thoughts and steadied the erratic pulsing of his magic. The blanket of early morning darkness still enveloped him when he sensed a tug at his mind. Stopping his horse, he looked around to determine what it was. There was nothing around, yet the sensation continued. Closing his eyes, he opened himself to it, trying to determine if it was simply the flux of his power reacting to the upcoming ascension.

Sinow.

His eyes flew open and darted around. Violissa's voice had been as distinct as if she were in front of him, but he remained alone. He rubbed his head, wondering if the pre-ascension was messing with his mind.

Sinow.

This time his name had been clear. The connection to her mind solidified, and his heart raced. There was no way she could speak in enaigne to him. The ability didn't cross boundaries, nor could it cross from Light to Dark. But he couldn't deny it. She was calling to him.

Sinow, follow my voice and find me.

Raking his hand through his hair, he contemplated following her request. He wasn't even certain he could. She was an enemy power, one he shouldn't be able to sense. He could follow his Council, his father, even his brother, sensing their power to shift to their location, but Violissa held no Dark power.

His heart pounded so loudly it was difficult to think. He shouldn't have been able to even hear her, let alone sense her. Yet, when he closed his eyes, he could feel the tie to her and sense where she was in Cirillia. Both were things he shouldn't have the ability to do. But there she was, pulsing like a beacon. Had she always been there? Tied to him, his knowledge of her embedded deep in his consciousness, waiting for them to meet.

"Fates, I can't believe I'm doing this," he muttered before he relaxed and trailed her, breaking the treaty and stepping foot in the enemy kingdom to become the first Dark prince to do so in millennia.

CHAPTER 10

Having laid his seeds of doubt, Tynan shifted back to his wing of the castle. He still had work to do, but every little divide he could put between his brother and Violissa helped. He needed to keep them apart and prevent their union. It was crucial to his plans. Walking into his study, he leaned over his desk. He had left books scattered around the room, stacked haphazardly on the windowpanes and even toppling from the piles on the floor. On the desk sat an older book, the pages open with notes scribbled in the margins. No one bothered coming to his quarters, and even if they had, his study was off the main bedroom. He didn't need nosy Council rummaging through his research, trying to determine what he was up to.

Dawn was still fighting for dominance on the horizon outside his window with what remained of the moon casting shadows across the lawn. Like long, spindly demons reaching for him. Tynan rubbed his eyes, attempting to force away his own demons. He longed to be the one preparing for the ascension, but Sinow was the true heir, the chosen one who would bring ultimate power to Tenebron. Blah, blah, blah. He slammed his hand against the pane of glass, sending shattered shards flying. Blood ran down his fist as the wounds slowly healed themselves. It should have been he whom the Fates had chosen, he who would wear the crown, and it ate at him constantly that it wasn't. Sinow was oblivious to the hatred that burned through Tynan. Oblivious of the plans that would destroy him and of the truth.

It had all started with a letter that had fallen when Tynan had picked up a book belonging to his mother. The book was one of the few things his father had given him, a few random pieces that held the only evidence his mother had existed. Tynan had read the letter so many times he'd lost count. It revealed the truth of what she'd lost, what Sinow's mother had stolen from her and Tynan.

She had been the one to catch the king's eye, to claim his heart first. But it was Sinow's mother who had come along and stolen his affection from her. The whore had flaunted herself so that he couldn't resist, and he'd fallen for it. They had sealed their union by the third rise of the moons, and Sinow had been born first. Only after he'd lost Sinow's mother to childbirth had the king returned to Tynan's mother to beg for her hand. Of course, she accepted, despite how he had previously overlooked her. Tynan had been born only a few years after Sinow, his mother taken the same way Sinow's had.

Tynan had stared at the letter, its words warping and corrupting him until hatred had festered along with a mission. He would take back what was rightfully his: the crown and Tenebron.

He spent years waiting for his chance, looking for every opportunity, but none came. Until he'd buried himself in the ancient libraries in the lower levels of the castle. There, after months of research—reading up on the realm's history, his family's history and lineage, looking for anything that could help him claim the throne—he'd found the key to Sinow's destruction, to bringing down the realm and making it his. He had discovered the location of the Lost Realm. The lost capital of Cirillia and land of the Elvin. Not simply the general location, as everyone knew it was in the Sacred Groves that were split between the two realms. But the exact location and the spell to enter the realm. He'd laughed at how preposterous it was that such a valuable piece of knowledge had been under their noses all this time. He doubted anyone could have figured it out. His grandfather hadn't even after centuries of searching for it. But his grandfather's work had left Tynan the clues to piece it together.

The Lost Realm itself was of no use. It was the treasure buried deep within the realm that would be his salvation. A treasure so sacred that his father and his Darkbearers didn't know it existed. Whatever knowledge his grandfather had held, he'd never shared. But Tynan now had it.

He dragged his finger across the bookshelf, thinking about his discovery that day. Of finding the book hidden deep in a stack of dusty books that no one had touched in millennia. He'd wiped the layers of dust from the book, finding no title on it. Upon glancing at the first few pages, it had appeared the book was merely a history of the last war between the two realms, making it easily overlooked because that knowledge was available in the books on the main floor library. But upon further inspection, he'd found more detail about the lost realm than he had ever learned from his tutors. A scroll hidden in the back of the book gave him even more.

The Elvin had once been protectors of the Fates' word. The scroll of prophecy had been under their protection until they passed it to the Light King Viliren before the war. But Tynan's grandfather suspected they held other relics of the Fates. His war on Cirillia had been a farce. He never cared about finding the prophecy, but he'd made everyone believe he did. Leaving everyone to think he was waging war on Cirillia to steal the prophecy and try to manipulate it when, in fact, he despised any thought of mixing the bloodlines.

He'd been looking for a book that held the power of the Fates. A myth he'd discovered in his research. After the war ended, he obsessed over finding the lost capital, thinking the book was there. He'd been so close, but it was Tynan who pieced the last of the puzzle together. And now, it was imperative to keep his brother and Violissa from their union. If he couldn't, then he'd lose his advantage. Sinow was already powerful. With the ascension, he would transcend that power, but with the union, there was no telling how strong he would be.

Their father claimed that a union with the bitch would make Sinow more powerful than any king before him and as much faith as Tynan had in the research he'd done, he didn't want to tempt the Fates by waiting for that theory to be tested. No, he'd keep them apart until his work was done, then it would be too late for them both, for he would rule both their realms.

The book he held slipped from his hands as he sensed Sinow leave the castle. He'd told Sinow the truth; he did have an uncanny ability to tell where Sinow was. The ability to sense the location of someone with Dark magic was innate, but the seeker had to reach out and search for the person they were trying to find. This was different. It was a strange awareness of his brother. Usually, the connection annoyed him, but lately, he'd found it useful. Finding his brother awake this early had piqued his curiosity, but knowing Sinow had left the castle alarmed him. Tynan cursed and summoned a cape before shifting to where he sensed his brother's presence.

CHAPTER 11

Three women bustled around Violissa, fussing with her hair, her dress, her face. She tried to mask her discomfort with the attention, but her lips pouted all the same. Regret was an emotion she rarely experienced, but it was prevalent on this day. She could have easily made her own dress with her magic like she typically did, and worn her hair loose like she preferred, but she'd wanted to involve the people. So there she was, tolerating the local dressmaker as she made the final touches on her gown and the woman from the nearest town who turned messy hair to styles of wonder. Not that she cared for any of it. There was nothing Violissa hated more than being preened like this.

The grinding sound her teeth made broke the silence, and Nellina, the dressmaker, glanced at her. The young girl with her powdered a dab of color on her cheeks and Violissa inadvertently cringed. She never wore paint on her face, as some women did. The style was only prominent in the a few of the larger towns, and Violissa preferred her natural beauty.

Nellina stepped back, gesturing to the other women to do the same as Violissa stared at herself in the mirror.

They've made me unrecognizable, she thought, blowing a curl up that had fallen over her eye.

And indeed, they had. With curls piled so neatly on the top of her head, she was afraid to move. A few strands remained loose, brushing her cheeks and neck. A dress the color of a field of lilacs fitted her waist and hung loose in fine layers down to skim the ground, hiding the delicate slippers of the same shade underneath. The top of the dress draped just to emphasize the curvature of her breasts and tease with a line that hinted at her cleavage. Capped sleeves covered her shoulders, then flowed toward the middle of her back where they met the silk ties that bound the dress.

But what stunned her the most was the face looking back at her. Gone was the innocence of the girl she had been, and in its place stood the ageless beauty of a queen. Power flickered behind her eyes. That magic and the paint added around them made them stand out even more than she thought possible. They were a blend of green hues, with hints of sage and emerald colliding for dominance. She brought a hand to her cheeks, which now held a permanent pink flush from the powder. Her lips, stained from squeezed berries, made her pout more pronounced.

"I didn't think it possible for you to be any more beautiful, Your Majesty," Nellina said.

There was no changing her mind now. It was done, and she needed to ensure the women knew she appreciated their work. They would no doubt pass the story of preparing their queen for her ascension down to their children and grandchildren. The event was so rare that being part of it was a special honor. "You've done an amazing job. I couldn't have come close to this myself, thank you."

The three women smiled and let out a collective sigh of relief.

"It's truly wonderful," she said, glancing out her window. The ascension was only a few hours away, but morning had already come. "Now, if you don't mind, it would seem I have more preparation ahead of me before the ceremony. Thank you again. You've made the day even more special."

They curtsied again, and upon saying their goodbyes, left Violissa to herself. She turned in front of the mirror again, confounded by how little she looked like herself.

A tremor gripped her hands, and she clenched them into fists, fighting the shake. She'd had a difficult time controlling it while they'd been working on her. Her power had been erratic of late, and over the past few days, it had only grown worse. To add to her concern, her limbs had begun tingling earlier that morning. She was certain the ascension was to blame, but she had no evidence to confirm her suspicion. No one on her Council had witnessed an ascension, and she had no father to tell her what to expect. The unknown left a chill in her bones that didn't settle well with the trembling.

She needed answers, and only one person had them. And that was a problem. Gnawing her lip, she tried to talk herself out of what she was thinking of doing, knowing her Council would be furious if they discovered. As the women had worked on her, her mind had been running through her choices, and she concluded there was only one that had merit. It likely wouldn't even work, but she was determined to try.

Shifting to her library, she warmed the room with a wave of her hand and opened the curtains. Morning light streamed in to reveal a room filled floor to ceiling with books. The soft cream of the walls magnified the light from the windows. A soft green chaise sat in the middle of the room along with several overly large mauve chairs. This was Violissa's favorite room. Its shelves contained all there was to know about her people and her world. She'd read every book in the room trying to understand who she was and the history from which she'd come. The room was a haven to her, just as the glade was. And it was also the safest place to attempt the impossible.

She muttered an enchantment over the room, weaving the

magic to ensure no Council would sense her there and catch her in the act. Then she cleared her mind, closed her eyes, and softly called, *Sinow*.

She waited a few moments, then repeated his name again. Her chest was tight, nerves coursing through her in competition with the trembles. Attempting to use enaigne with anyone outside of her Council was unheard of. No one could speak enaigne outside their race, and only Council and ruler had the ability in each realm. To think she had the power to cross the boundary wall and reach Sinow was arrogant, but she thought it might just work. If the prophecy had indeed intertwined their fates, bound their lives, and made their souls one, then there was a possibility that their powers transcended those before them, and they could speak to each other through enaigne.

But even if it did work, she wasn't sure it would be enough to let him cross the boundary, a boundary that no one had ever held the power to break through. She prayed he did because he was the only one who could explain what was happening to her. The only one who could ease her uncertainty and nerves she didn't want to admit were strangling her. His father would have passed down the knowledge to him. It was assumptive to think he would help her, that he wouldn't laugh and let her suffer. They were enemies, after all. But it was worth the risk, and she suspected after their last meeting that he would.

She cleared her mind again, and this time reached out far beyond where she normally reached, beyond the Council's minds, beyond those of her people, beyond the magical border that separated their realms. Crossing it, the weight of the ancient magic that formed it pressed at her, and as her mind passed through to Tenebron, the air in her lungs grew thick, her breaths shorter. Darkness seeped into her mind, cluttering it with cobwebs and terror, but she pushed it away, keeping her focus on reaching Sinow. A shiver went through her, and she clenched her hands to keep her muscles from quaking. She flitted beyond the sleeping voices of Sinow's people until she sensed his presence.

Sinow.

This time she could feel his mind questioning.

Sinow, she called again.

The silence that spoke back was deafening until she suddenly sensed his full awareness.

Sinow, follow my voice...find me.

She spoke one last time as she slowly withdrew. Back through the dark murmurs into the light, airy tones of her people and finally back to the library.

She opened her eyes and waited. Her heart was racing at the excitement of having reached him and the instinctive reaction her body had in response to being so connected to him. The air stirred, and although the room had not cooled down, a shiver ran down her spine. Sinow had followed her trail and now stood behind her.

"Hello, Vi. Aren't you full of surprises?" His voice sent butterflies tumbling through her stomach. "Have you reconsidered our union so fast? Too excited about the prospect to have your Council reach out so you figured out a way to use enaigne? That's a secret you'll need to share. Being able to seep into your mind whenever I want would be thrilling."

His sexy confidence faltered as she turned to face him. His eyes widened just enough for her to notice. She should have been uncomfortable with his stare, his eyes taking in every inch of her, but she wasn't. Instead, his reaction to her appearance made her feel like the most beautiful woman in the world.

"I thought you were ravishing before, but now you're breathtaking," he said. The words were sincere, and heat rose in her cheeks. But the moment passed by like a rush of wind, his adoring gaze hiding behind shadowed eyes.

She wondered at the change, as if two sides of him existed: the Dark Prince whose power ruled him and the man below. Wanting the man back, she teased, "Flattery will not get you into my bed, Sinow."

"So, I take it there will be no rushed union before our ascensions? You didn't call me here to discuss a change of heart?" He walked around the library, drawing his fingers across the book spines.

"No, I have not."

He turned, folding his arms across his chest. "Then why and how, in the name of the Fates, have you called me here?"

She caught her breath when their eyes met. The reaction was still intense, but after the dreams, looking at him had become easier, even if it still left her weak.

"The how will need to wait for another day, as I really am limited on time. I've placed a spell around the room, so my Council won't detect your presence, but it won't stop them from eventually finding me here. I didn't dare leave the castle this close to the ascension, so calling you here was my only option." She swept a loose curl from her eye, seeing how his fists tightened at the movement. He was fighting the same urges as she was, and she hoped her struggle wasn't as obvious. A battle was ensuing within her body, warring to be close to him, to heed the yearning to invite his touches. She swallowed, the motion like sandpaper scraping over her throat.

"I hope it's important, since discovery of me in your realm, let alone your library, would break that fine thread they call a treaty." His chocolate eyes flicked from hers, and she noted the tension ease in his body before they returned to meet hers.

"Well, as you and I will rule the thrones within hours, I'm really not too concerned," she replied.

"What is it you need, Violissa?"

Her full name fell from his mouth in a harsh tone, and she wondered at the distinction. He preferred to use the nickname he'd given her, but there were moments when he addressed her with her full name, moments when he seemed harder, like his power was more prominent.

Chewing her lip, she doubted her reasons for bringing him to her. It was too late to turn back, however. Taking a deep breath, she said, "I need some answers and...well...you're the only one I know who can give them to me."

He cocked his brow and eyed her suspiciously. "I'm listening."

Violissa folded her hands together and paced slowly around the library. "You see, no one here knows what truly happens during the ascension. What I mean to say is that they know what it looks like and can give me a general description, but they don't know what happens internally to the one ascending. There hasn't been an ascension here in so long that no Council has ever observed one, and it's forbidden for the king to put the details in writing. It's only passed orally to our heirs, and I've no father to tell me." She paused, wringing her hands. "Well, you can see my dilemma. Your father is the only one in our world who knows what it's truly like. I certainly can't go directly to him, but you..."

She trailed off, knowing she was babbling now and not liking how it made her sound. When she looked up at him, she ignored the way her heart seemed to freeze. Its motion stayed caged as he rubbed his chin before running his hand through his hair.

"So, let me get this straight, Violissa. You reject me and any thought of a union with me, in turn rejecting my kingdom and my people."

She bit her lip, seeing how this was turning quickly in the wrong direction.

"And then you have the nerve to call me to you, hoping I'll answer, which, like a fool, I did, and ask that I share information with you that is so sacred it's only handed down from king to son. Words that are only spoken once, what, every ten or fifteen thousand years?" The tremble in her hands grew, and she squeezed them together as he continued to rant. "You really have some nerve. Does your Council put up with this crap as well? Maybe it's a female thing…" He drifted off as his eyes met hers. There was realization there that his words had gone too far.

The hair on her neck bristled, her power flared, and she knew he was about to experience what truly made her stand apart from her Council and her predecessors. Her temper.

"How dare you? You know nothing about me. You think from a few brief encounters that you know who I am and what I'm made of?" She spat the words at him as the tingling increased in her hands, the power bucking for release. She knew her eyes were no longer a crystal reflective emerald, but a deep forest green. Anger was not a Lightbearer trait, and her Council tried to avoid her when she was like this, but it didn't seem to fluster Sinow. He only seemed surprised, his keen eyes evaluating her, a slight tilt to the corner of his lips as if he was keeping a smile at bay.

His reaction calmed her a little.

"I called you here out of blind faith," she continued, "and honestly, I didn't know if you'd help me, but I thought it was worth a try. We are building a working relationship, aren't we?" She bit her bottom lip, fighting the shake that was coursing through her limbs. Looking at him made her tingle more than she already was, and her heart thudded resoundingly through her ears. The damned prophecy made her so out of control and paired with the ascension, she was one step away from crumbling.

Silence hung in the air, and she worried over his response. "Well, Vi…" The nickname was back. "…if I were my father, I'd use this moment of weakness to find out what you were willing to trade for that information." Disappointment flashed through her, and she dropped her eyes, the fight fleeing from her.

She glanced up again, hoping he hadn't noticed. He raked his hand through his hair again, a habit she was beginning to adore, before he looked back at her. The air stuck in her chest, only escaping in small pants as she waited for him to continue. What would he expect in return? She was playing with fire, and she wondered if she would come to regret it.

CHAPTER 12

S age eyes waited expectantly for Sinow to continue. He was still uncertain how Violissa had brought him to Cirillia and into her castle, so that they were now standing in her library like two old friends having a casual conversation. Only there was nothing casual about what she was asking.

He had a decision to make. He could be a complete ass and leave her be. That's what his brother would have advised. Or he could help her. It shouldn't matter to him that she was nervous about the ascension. It wasn't his problem. Yet when he looked at her, he wanted to do nothing more than take her in his arms and reassure her. Being near her made him soft, and he couldn't rectify that with the Dark power in him.

Curse the Fates, he thought.

He studied her. It was true; she had no one. No one to tell her that the spasms that shook her hands were a sign of the oncoming ascension or that the whirring in her head that drowned out normal sounds would recede once she received her power, a power beyond any she'd ever had. Her eyes reflected the chaos in her body. They were a cataclysm of hues. It was as if every shade of green was battling for dominance within them. It was a dance that left him entranced.

He shook his head and focused on their conversation.

"But as it stands, I'm not my father," he continued, seeing the tension flee her body. "Don't get me wrong, I'm no Lightbearer, but my opinions aren't always in agreement with my father's. So, I will offer what I know."

A reflection of relief touched her eyes, and he knew he'd done the right thing, although he didn't know when he'd started giving a damn about doing the right thing. He moved closer to her, reaching his fingers out to touch her quivering hand. She'd been trying to hide the tremors from him, but he'd noticed.

Touching her sent a flood of sparks jolting through him, his body waking along with that incessant need for her.

Ignoring it, he said, "The tingling and spasms you're experiencing throughout your arms and legs will become greater until you think you can't take it anymore. The sound in your head will grow louder until it drowns nearly everything out but the words of the ceremony. Then, upon the ascension, both will culminate in a moment of overwhelming loss of control. At least it will seem that way to you. No one else will know you're troubled one bit, except me, that is." His thumb absently traced the path of her finger. "Once the ascension happens, you'll experience complete silence and calm. The tremors will stop, the noise will cease, and in their place will be a new sense of awareness and power that transcends what you now have."

He brought his hand up and touched her cheek. Her breathing had increased, as had his, and he could hear her heartbeats beneath her gown. She was the most alluring thing he'd ever laid eyes on, her beauty surpassing what it was the first time he saw her. Almost like she grew more beautiful each day.

He was suddenly aware of how close they were standing, of the sound of her strained breaths, of the seductive parting of her lips, of the wayward curl that brushed her cheek. The scent of lilac permeated the air, and he drowned in her presence and the effect it had on him. He leaned down, his mouth hovering so close that their lips were almost touching. His last ounce of control seeped from him as his hand tangled in her hair.

He had wanted to respect her wish and keep his distance, but the ache for her was overwhelming. His lips were so near to hers that her breath warmed his skin, and he inhaled the sweet smell of it. He lifted his eyes from her mouth and lost himself, no longer caring that she wanted to wait. Because this was torture, and he knew what lay beyond that first kiss was ecstasy.

The door to the library slammed open, the resounding sound pulling him from his trance. Sinow dropped his hand from her hair as she stepped back from him. Fury raged through him, his power flaring from the interruption and his moment of weakness. The magical hold that had been binding them was no more, broken when Daneele burst into the room. Sinow fought to contain the ire that was lighting his body like a white-hot heat.

"As excited as I am to see you two together, I hope there is good reason and that no one else knows you are here, Prince Sinow," Daneele said in what was the sternest voice Sinow could imagine a Lightbearer having. "Do you have any idea what this could do to the treaty?"

Violissa bristled, responding before Sinow could react. "I know very well what I'm doing, Daneele. There's no need to question me. I will be queen in a matter of hours, so trust me, the treaty will still stand."

Sinow retreated to the other side of the room, trying to calm his power. The ascension had it so mangled that it was hard to contain, and Daneele's interruption had aggravated it. He glanced at Violissa, seeing that she had grabbed the back of a chair and was looking unsteady. They'd been so close, one slight move away from kissing, one small step to finally having her. But Violissa looked relieved, and that stirred his anger further. She was so stubborn, fighting something neither of them could fight. He wanted to take her by the arms and shake her. It was torment being so near to having her after so many years of waiting. Centuries of being told she was out there, of sensing her, of waiting. Nights of falling asleep thinking of her, wondering what she would look and sound like, of how it would be to touch her. Days of cursing the Fates for binding him to her, for stealing his free will, for dictating his life. And now she was here, and he was still as far from having her as he had always been. Only now it was ten times worse because he knew all the things he'd always imagined, and nothing he'd imagined had come close to what being with her was really like.

He scraped his hands through his hair, a thought breaking through the tirade of noise in his head. Turning to Daneele, he asked, "How did you know I was here? Vi said she placed a spell on the room, and I could feel it. There was no way you'd know I was here unless you were looking for me."

"Your brother alerted me to your disappearance. He said he had found your horse, but you were missing. When he couldn't find you in Tenebron or at the meeting grounds, he reached out to us. His concern was that you had compromised the treaty and somehow broken through the barrier. When he mentioned your powers had been erratic of late, he urged me to check on Violissa." Sinow's teeth ground. To think his brother would even consider he would harm Violissa made his blood boil. "I did a scan of the grounds for Violissa and came upon your presence as well. Trust me, under normal circumstances, we would have been glad to let you two explore your new relationship, but today is not the right day."

Jaw clenched, Sinow realized just what Daneele had said. "Wait, my brother contacted you?"

"Yes, he sent an urgent message for one of us to meet him at the meeting grounds. I will admit, his request had me perplexed, but I didn't give it any thought after learning that you may have breached the boundary, which it appears you have."

Flexing his hands to keep from pummeling Daneele with his

power, Sinow said, "I did not touch the boundary. You have your princess to thank for my presence. But neither my father nor the Council would have let Tynan contact you or even meet you. That makes no sense. He paced the floor in thought, remembering how he'd placed a spell on the horse to keep it from wandering to avoid anyone's curiosity about his whereabouts. How had Tynan even known about the horse?

He stopped, remembering Tynan's words from earlier. *I always know when you're about.* Had Tynan followed him?

"Whatever the situation, Your Majesty, you can take that up with your brother," Daneele said, interrupting his thoughts. "We need to get you back, and Violissa, you need to finish preparations. I don't need or want to know what occurred here before my arrival, just be glad it was me instead of the others. Your first day as queen, and you couldn't wait to stir up trouble." He was standing like a father would, with his arms crossed, toes tapping, and Sinow would have laughed if his mood weren't so off.

Violissa rolled her eyes at Daneele, and this time Sinow couldn't help the tug of his smile. "Fine, give us a moment and I'll be right out."

"One minute or I alert the rest of the Council." Daneele gave Sinow a slight bow and left the room.

They were alone again, and as his eyes met hers, he wished he could return to where they'd been before Daneele had derailed the moment.

"Well, at least he knows how to use doors," Sinow stated, rolling his neck. "Shall we get back to where we were...or no, moment lost?" he teased, enjoying how her smile lit her eyes. "Was that all you needed, Vi? If so, I'll take my leave, as I've got a rogue brother to attend to." And he planned to hunt his brother down the moment he returned to Tenebron.

"Wait. I need to know one more thing. When it's over, are you still..." She paused, chewing on her lip before continuing. "What I mean to say is, does it change you? Are you still..."

"The same person?" he finished for her. There was a flash of vulnerability in her features, and he softened his stance. She was afraid, and he instinctively wanted to shield her from that fear.

She nodded, dropping her eyes.

"Yes. You don't lose yourself to the ascension. You remain the same, just with more power." Although it wasn't the entire truth because Dark power had a tendency to drown a king, twisting him so that he was unrecognizable from the man he'd once been. His grandfather had fallen to its sway. Most fought the change, the power balanced within them, but a few, like his grandfather, lost their minds and no longer followed the code that dictated their magic be used to protect their people. That had never been the case with Light power, so it mattered little that he didn't tell her.

He closed the gap between them. "Is that what all this has been about?" He gestured between the two of them. "That you'll lose your identity? Is that your fear? No longer being you?" He'd clearly made a connection she hadn't meant for him to. He could see it in the flicker of hues swirling in her eyes and the way she sucked her bottom lip further below her teeth. "Because that's your greatest fear, isn't it?" he said, reaching out and tipping her chin up to force her eyes to remain on his. Touching her was risky, but he fought the urge for more, knowing he was seeing more of her than she wanted him to see. "You're afraid of losing yourself to something or someone and no longer having your own identity and control over who you are. That's why you're so against the union."

Her eyes grew wide, the color halting its endless motion and turning a brilliant emerald.

"Perhaps I misjudged you, Vi." He let his fingers brush along her cheek, seeing the glimmer of tears behind her eyes. Tears she was fighting because she didn't want him to think her weak. But he didn't think he could ever believe that of her.

"Perhaps you have, Sinow." Her voice was soft, the sound flittering through him like the wings of a butterfly. "Thank you for being honest with me. You had no incentive to do so, but took the chance, and I won't forget that act of kindness."

He scoffed. "Kindness? That's not a trait of mine, and never let my Council hear you say that."

Her smile grew. "I promise I'll keep it to myself."

He let his finger drift through the curl on her cheek before pushing it back. "Maybe once you've ascended, you'll realize that you will never lose your identity, especially not to me. I'll wait for that day, as I can see it won't be much longer. Good luck today. I can only imagine how glorious you'll be."

Her eyes shimmered, her smile widening.

"You should share those smiles with me more often, Vi. It doesn't quite make up for the lack of intimacy, but it'll do for now."

She blushed, and with a laugh, said, "I'll remember that for next time. Farewell, Sinow, and...thank you again. What you've done for me today means more than you know."

He flashed her a coy smile and shifted, knowing to stay longer would crush any resolve to further satisfy her need to deny him. His attention swiftly changed direction to his brother and the pain he was about to inflict on Tynan for his interference.

CHAPTER 13

Tynan paced the front courtyard, waiting for the pounding of his brother's shift. His stomach turned as nerves rumbled through him. Any time now, Sinow would thunder into the realm, his shift quaking the ground to announce his presence. There was no reason to shift with such force, but when his mood soured, he emphasized his ire through his shift. And Tynan expected Sinow's anger would cause ripples through the ground. Cirillia was the only place he could have gone. Tynan had followed Sinow and seen him shift, but where he could usually follow a shift or still sense his brother in the realm, there was silence. No connection remained to his brother. Cirillia was the only reason that made sense. He only wished he knew how Sinow had passed through the border so easily, a border that was impossible to break through.

Contacting the Light Council had been risky. His father didn't know he had the spell, and if he found out, the punishment would be brutal. But the risk was worth it if it kept Sinow and Violissa apart longer. One kiss and he would lose his leverage. He'd never confirmed it, but he suspected it would be enough and that one kiss would lead to more, binding them together for eternity. Magic from the Fates layered the blasted prophecy, and there was no way to fight it, no matter how Violissa tried. But Tynan was doing his best to undo it or at least delay it.

Time dragged, and his nerves bounded through him like a nervous deer, knowing a predator was coming. Too many variables were out of his control, and he hated it. He could only pray that the fool, Daneele, had discovered Sinow in Cirillia. His violation of the treaty would bring the impending union crumbling down.

The ground beneath him convulsed as Sinow's voice thundered through the quiet morning. Tynan smiled. Things had gone just as he'd imagined and, from the sound of it, even better than he'd hoped. His punishment would be miserable, but the payoff was justified. He looked over his shoulder as Sinow stormed toward him, his body lifting from the ground as the first wave of Sinow's anger pierced through him. He braced himself for the impact, counting the punishment among the others he tracked for the moment he could bring his revenge down on his brother.

CHAPTER 14

Daneele pounced on Violissa as soon as she opened the door. "What were you thinking? Have you lost your mind? If it had been anyone but me walking through that door, they would have sounded the alarms. And the treaty... did you even think of the treaty? A Darkbearer breaking through the boundary violates the treaty." He rubbed his temples as he continued, "You know better. No Darkbearer can step foot in Cirillia until the two of you are married, regardless of who it is."

She rolled her eyes, brushing past him. "You exaggerate, Daneele. Need I remind you I will be queen in a matter of hours?" He caught up with her, his steps emphasizing his disappointment. "If I want to have the prince as a guest, I should be able to make that decision on my own. I would think you would be ecstatic that we were alone and speaking to one another."

Daneele stopped, taking her by the arm and turning her toward him.

"What you don't understand and never seem to want to hear, Violissa, is that there are certain protocols we all must follow. When will you realize this? The treaty clearly states that we do not cross each other's territorial lines until the union. The law protects this kingdom from Sinow if the union doesn't happen, which it clearly is not. Look at how powerful he already is." Daneele gestured to the library behind them. "He passed through the boundary and has not even ascended." He paused, giving her one of his scolding looks. She knew it was pointless to argue and let him continue. "We are bound to the laws, Violissa. If the king had found you on his land, he would have declared war upon violation of the treaty. This is not some kind of game. The people are counting on you. We're counting on you. It's time to step up and fulfill the role of queen."

She wanted to argue that Sinow would be on their soil for her ascension and that didn't seem to be cause for war, but she knew he would reason that it was a mutual decision on both sides, so it didn't count. With a sigh, she said, "Are you done with the lecture, Daneele?"

He threw his hands in the air. "Curse the Fates for making you so stubborn. Yes, I suppose I am. Now, tell me three things: how in the name of the Fates did you bring Sinow here, how did he make it through the border, and does what I interrupted in there mean you've come to your senses?"

She laughed despite herself. "It's amazing how quickly you get derailed. I'm not sure how I brought him here." She began walking down the long corridor again, linking her hands behind her back as she thought about what she'd done to call him. "I surmised that since we were so central to the prophecy, there might be some link between us, so I focused my mind and called to him." She halted her steps and looked at him, bouncing on her feet. "Oh, Daneele, it was amazing. I went beyond you and the Council, past our people, through the barrier and into the Dark realm. I touched the minds of their people until I found Sinow. When I called to him, his mind touched mine. He could sense me, and I him. And he followed that sensation to me. I don't know how he transcended the barrier, but he did, and he was suddenly here."

The pounding of her heart thudded against her chest, beating harder when she spoke of Sinow. Just the thought of his hand weaving in her hair, of how close his lips had been to hers, left her knees weak.

Daneele stared at her, his eyes large. "Do you realize what you've done? The power and control you must have had to do such a thing? This is unprecedented." She watched with amusement as his eyes widened further, his expression of wonderment touching every curve of his face. "Violissa, it is rare for anyone to use enaigne beyond the Council, exceedingly rare. But to use it beyond our realm is unheard of. The amount of power you must have is far greater than we thought. I could say the same for Sinow, which is terrifying. There should be no way he could cross the boundary. We suspected his ascension would give him the ability to, but not prior to his ascension." His hand gripped her arm, his features turning serious. "I don't think any of us are prepared for what the ascension will bring today. We've underestimated the sheer volume of magic you have. The rest of the Council needs to know so we can prepare."

She grabbed his arm as he hurried away. "No, they cannot know. You said that yourself. They don't need to know. I don't want the treaty violated this close to the ascension. Wait until afterward, and we'll discuss it."

"Violissa, really, I think it's safe to say they'll be aware of it by then. They've not been witness to the prince's presence here and need not know. You'll simply leave that scandalous tidbit for later discovery and just reveal that you contacted him. And speaking of scandalous, tell me why I spied you seconds from falling into the prince's arms. Have you changed your mind and given up your hopeless quest to defy the Fates?"

He had pulled free of her grip and scooped his arm around hers, ushering her down the hall toward the front of the castle. He had a talent for changing the subject at just the right moment, and it always worked. "If so, we have little time for a union."

She huffed as she stopped resisting his forward movement and picked up pace alongside him.

"No, I have not changed my mind, and don't even get me started on that subject. But he is...growing on me. There's more to him than I thought there was, and he certainly is something to look at. And boy, can he..." She bit her tongue before she said too much. She didn't want Daneele to know about the dreams they'd shared. Heat grew in her cheeks, and she looked away so he wouldn't notice. "Do you really think it's safe to mention my new enaigne abilities to the remaining Council?" she asked, quickly switching topics.

He gave a loud laugh. "You've learned well from me, child."

THE NEXT FEW hours were like a blur. The Council met with her once more, and during that meeting they discussed her experience with Sinow. Certain details, of course, she and Daneele omitted, and she was glad. The mere fact that she could contact Sinow through enaigne had shocked them enough. They voiced their concerns, just as Daneele had, about underestimating the full power she would receive upon ascending. Anwell proposed they add certain measures to the ceremony to protect the people who were gathering to witness the event. No one knew what effect the ascension would have on Violissa or how far it would spread beyond her. There was very little written about prior ascensions, and Violissa had insisted her people bear witness to the event.

All they knew was that a wave of energy would cascade over Violissa as the ascending gifts joined with her inherent powers. The blast would be enough to throw anyone standing near her far from where they were standing. With the prophecy involved and alluding to how Violissa's powers would far surpass any before her, they were going into this blindly. And it hadn't helped that Violissa had insisted on having her people present. As time grew short, the Council agreed to have the people moved further back from her and to place a magical barrier around them to ensure their protection.

With the meeting adjourned, Cyric ran through the ceremony with Violissa one last time. As the sun reached its midday peak, there was nothing left to delay the inevitable. It was like her body was no longer her own when Anwell informed her Daneele and Cyric had left to meet Sinow and the Darkbearer he was bringing with him. She could hear the crowds outside the castle grounds. They'd been gathering for days, traveling across the realm to witness the event of a lifetime.

Violissa took one last look at her reflection and steadied her breath. The tingling through her limbs had escalated as Sinow had said it would. She could barely keep her hands from jerking uncontrollably. The whirring in her head was deafening, and the only sounds she could distinctly make out at this point were voices close to her. The roar in her ears drowned all else out. It was enough to make her vomit, but since she had been too out of sorts to eat, there was nothing in her to bring up.

Good thing, too. It'd be a shame to ruin such a pretty dress, she thought.

She lifted her head and closed her eyes, sensing Sinow's arrival. Although he was well enough away from where she was in the castle, she still sensed his presence. It was eerie, the connection they seemed to have to one another.

"Best to get on with it," she mumbled. "Wouldn't do to be late and have the whole damned thing take place whilst here by myself."

And so, Violissa shifted outside, ready to face her destiny.

CHAPTER 15

Power flickered between Sinow's fingers, escaping from the violent tempest within his body. Punishing Tynan for his interference had given him some release, but it had also reminded him of how unpredictable his magic was the closer the ascension grew. Now, as he waited for the Lightbearers to signal their presence on the other side of the boundary, he fought not only the surges of power but the steady droning in his head. The sound, like the rushing of the tide as it pounded against the cliffs on the western coast of Tenebron, battered at his sanity.

"Do you feel all right, Sinow?" Keary asked, creases between his thick brows.

Sinow dragged his hand down his face, stopping the pacing he'd been absently doing. Keary was the closest to him on the Council, a friend and more of a brother than Tynan had ever been. He'd come into his power when Sinow had been young, and they'd spent much of their youth together until duty required Sinow to train for the crown.

"Never better," he grumbled, wishing it was the truth. He dropped his hand, curling it into a fist to hide the shake from Keary.

A quiver bent the space before them where the boundary lay, and he glanced over, seeing the telltale sign of magic. If he did nothing, the air before them would continue to look distorted. The boundary wall was not something one could see, but one could feel it. To the mortal eye, the realm continued as an endless forest or field. But if anyone strayed too close, they would become disoriented and end up turned around so that before they realized it, they'd be back at their starting place. Sinow could sense the magic in it, just like his Council and his father could. And now, he could see the magic of the Lightbearers on the other side.

"Ready?" Keary asked, concern still in his eyes.

"Ready as I'll ever be. I'm not certain that being surrounded by Light power is wise at this stage, but..." He hesitated to tell Keary the truth of why he'd agreed to this. But Keary knew him well enough to guess.

"But seeing the princess will make it tolerable?" he teased, bringing his hand up toward the boundary.

Sinow shook his head before raising his hand as well.

"Tell me I'm wrong," said Keary as they both freed their power.

Sinow stayed silent, watching the magic unlock a doorway in the boundary with the help of the Light magic on the other side. This was the first time anyone had attempted it, and the sight was unsettling.

"That's what I thought." Keary laughed just as the doorway opened. He pulled his hood up and stepped through the passage first, Sinow following.

Daneele and Cyric greeted them on the other side. Both were as on edge as Sinow was, their blue eyes guarded. Sinow appreciated that his father had brought him to several meetings with the Lightbearers, prior to the day he met Violissa. It was the only reason he recognized these two from the others on her Council.

"I suspect this ascension will differ greatly from yours, Your Highness," Daneele said to him as the doorway sealed of its own accord behind them. "We will keep the people as far from your presence as possible. Remember, what you see today is sacred to us and to them. We ask that you respect that."

"People?" Sinow asked, confused as to why mortals would be involved in an ascension, or anything their ruler did, for that matter.

Daneele gave him a sly smile, the power in his eyes flickering and turning them brighter. "People. Violissa is a unique ruler, and there is a reason our people adore her."

He pulled his cape up and motioned for them to follow before Sinow could question him. Sinow glanced at Keary, who gave a shrug and pulled his hood further down to conceal his face. Sinow brought his hood up and followed the shift of the two Lightbearers.

The shift trail landed at the edge of a broad meadow. He stared at the sight. A mass of Cirillians filled the field, and his power bucked for release. Bunching his fists, he said, "What is this?"

The only mortals allowed anywhere near the Dark Keep were the servants, and even they knew to keep their distance and their eyes averted. No one dared a glance at Sinow, or any of the Darkbearers. Doing so without permission meant punishment or even death. Sinow tugged his hood further down. A Darkbearer never mingled with mortals unless necessary, and unless doling out a punishment, hoods remained drawn. Were the Light this naïve to disregard his power?

"This is Cirillia, your highness," Cyric answered, his hood still down. It was an action Sinow envied in some respects. There was no permission granted for their people to look at the Lightbearer, no fear that meeting his eyes could induce insanity or death.

Daneele continued, "As I said, Violissa does things differently. Follow us, please."

Are they joking? Keary asked in enaigne.

I wish they were, he grumbled.

Keary grabbed his arm, stopping him. "One wrong move and

you accidentally slaughter half the people here, Sinow," Keary said in a hushed voice, aware of how unstable Sinow's power had grown over the past moon cycle.

It's too late to back out now, he replied in enaigne, noticing how Cyric had stopped and was eyeing them. *Pull yourself together and let's get this over with.*

Sinow straightened his spine, allowing a trickle of his power free to wash over him, fortifying him. A murmur went through the crowd, one laced with fear as the Dark power touched the air.

"Out of respect for Violissa, please refrain from dropping your hood. I'm not sure the reaction our people would have, but based on this, I'd imagine it's a safe bet there might be panic," Daneele said.

Sinow had to fight the laugh Daneele's naïve request caused. He had clearly not remembered, or perhaps he didn't know that Darkbearers and their kings never dropped their hoods in the presence of mortals unless pain was to be inflicted.

"Do anything to our people, and if we don't attack you, Violissa will," Daneele continued.

"Then keep them far enough from me," Sinow replied, feeling his eyes darken. "I don't particularly care for mortals, and my power cares for them even less."

It was a twisting of the truth. He didn't necessarily like being near mortals, but he and his power were there to protect them. The Light didn't understand the code that every king inherently knew because some kings shunned it. Those kings, like his grandfather, were the ones responsible for the current opinion the Light held of Sinow and his father. He didn't particularly care what they thought, and it only helped to solidify the reputation that those with Dark power should be feared.

Silence fell over the crowd, hushed whispers coming as they drew nearer. Cyric and Daneele led them to a spot before a small platform, far enough away from the crowd for Sinow's power to calm. Two men with fiddles stood on the other side of the platform, backing further away as Sinow and Keary approached. Daneele went over to them as Cyric said, "You'll be here during the ceremony. This will ensure you're far from the people and able to witness the ceremony."

"Not far enough," Sinow muttered.

"No, but it's the best we can do. Your presence is hard to conceal, and there is nowhere else we can have you without inflicting more discomfort on you and our people."

The fiddlers began to play, and Sinow snapped his gaze in their direction. Daneele hopped down from the platform.

"Music?" Keary asked. It was a rarity in Tenebron, outlawed in his grandfather's time. Only the Cirillian slaves who had remained in the kingdom after the boundary was in place had sung. When Sinow's father had returned those who remained to the Light Council as part of the treaty, the sound had disappeared. "So, incessant happiness must be an inbred thing," Keary joked. "I thought it was just you Lightbearers."

Cyric glared at him. "The inbreeding stayed on Dark soil. It never made it past the border."

"That's witty, Cyric. I didn't know you had it in you. I figured they had some reason for keeping you around all this time," Keary returned.

Daneele stepped closer, stopping the barbs. "Our people cherish music and..." He glanced at Cyric, who nodded. "... Violissa. We consider her voice to be sacred. It is not something we share or even wanted known, but there is no hiding it now. Only her people have the rare blessing of hearing it, and for her to sing to anyone outside of the kingdom goes against the sacred oath she gave to them. Please understand that what you hear today is her trusting that you will protect that oath and not share this with your Council or your people."

"Violissa sings?" Sinow asked, trying to grasp why that would be any more special than her people singing. Although the thought of singing stirred the ire that the fiddle was already aggravating. "Why would we care if she sang?"

"It's time," Cyric told Daneele before turning back to Sinow. "Stay here and do not move any closer to the crowd."

"That's not a problem," said Keary just as the two shifted away. He scratched his head, his cape following the movement. "What does it matter if she sings? I mean, it's bound to be annoying."

"As annoying as that damned fiddle," Sinow groused.

Keary's laugh broke his tension. He glanced back at the crowd. They had begun celebrating again, their merry voices carrying. Some were singing and dancing along with the music, and Sinow couldn't help but gape at them. It was such a striking contrast to Tenebron and its solemn, dark atmosphere. His power flickered, and he clenched his jaw, fighting the urge to strike out at them. This wasn't his kingdom, but when Violissa finally came to her senses and became his wife, he'd have to tolerate this foolishness.

"Thinking about how annoying it will be to marry a woman who enjoys this," Keary said, gesturing to the crowd.

"That was exactly my thought."

He'd always known Cirillians cherished music, that the Fates had gifted them with a talent for it and voices that weren't shrill and off-key like his people's. It was likely a blessing his people didn't enjoy music. Their voices were terrible, and he could only imagine how dreary their songs would be if they sang. It would be enough to depress even the happiest of Cirillians.

Daneele had brought them near to the front in a small area well removed from the crowd, yet close to the ceremonial area. They'd purposely kept people from positioning themselves anywhere around the space, he assumed as a courtesy to him as well as to the people. Fraternizing with mortals was not something he did. Being in this proximity was discomfort enough.

You know, we could sneak off and wreak havoc in the kingdom before they caught us.

He looked back at Keary. *Don't make me punish you here in front of all these mortals.*

But Keary's comment was accurate and reflected the level of trust Violissa was giving him. Leaving him alone with her people and in her kingdom was risky if he were any other heir to the throne. If he were his grandfather.

The music quieted, the crowd hushed, and a familiar lilac scent filled the air. The crowd parted, splitting in the middle and creating an aisle.

Violissa, he said to Keary, *she's coming with the Council.* Even though he couldn't see her yet, he could sense her presence. It settled on his skin with a familiarity, calming his power.

The white robes of her Council moved up the path, forming two rows. The crowd moved to their knees, but he and Keary remained standing. As Violissa came closer, the annoying thudding in his chest grew. She was behind the two columns of Lightbearers, a lone figure in a white robe layered with embroidered flowers. A bit of green light shone from within the hood. His heart raced, and the pressure in his chest grew as she neared. Not quite the reaction he needed when his body was already a wreck from his approaching ascension. He dug his fingers into his palms so tightly that the skin split around his knuckles. The flare of pain distracted him from the need to run to her and take her away so that he could have her to himself.

He perceived her eyes on him as she passed, and a quick touch of her mind to his. A moment where perhaps she'd wanted to reach out to him, or a reaction caused by what was happening inside of her. Spasms and bursts of pain were likely racking her body by now. He had left that last detail out of their conversation, not wanting to worry her any more than she already had been. She was strong, so no one would notice, but he knew she was suffering. His father had told him it had taken all his energy to get through the ceremony. That he could barely concentrate while he'd fought the urge to rip the skin from his bones to stop the tingling and spasms.

The only blessing was that the climax was approaching for Violissa and would be over in a matter of minutes.

The group ascended the platform; all but two stood to the left in a group. Those two figures, one of which was Violissa, stayed in the center. Kinnel, another of her Council, pulled down his hood to reveal himself. He would be the giver of rites.

The sun above neared its highest point, reflecting light off the white of their robes. Violissa's ascension would come at the sun's peak on the day of her creation, as his would be at the crest of the north moon on the same day. Light powers given from day, Dark from the night.

Silence fell across the crowd, and Kinnel spoke. "Violissa, Princess of Cirillia, leader of the Lightbearers, chosen one of the Fates, you have come before your people to accept the crown and the powers of your birthright."

"I have." Her voice danced like a harmony through the air, drifting over his skin.

"Please kneel."

She kneeled before Kinnel and bowed her head. Kinnel walked to his right, where Daneele now stood, holding a long silver box that, with his heightened sight, Sinow could see had flowers engraved along its length.

The scroll of prophecy, Keary's voice came through his mind. *No one has ever seen it but the Keeper. They say the Fates wrote it in the early days of our world, burning the words into it with starlight and magic.*

Daneele spoke a spell in an ancient tongue of which Sinow was not familiar. The box cracked open. The wind seemed to stir around him as though even it were waiting and watching. Kinnel lifted a thin scroll from the box, and the crowd gasped. He unrolled it and turned back to Violissa.

"And as the sun peaks
On the one thousandth
Day of her birth
Girl shall become woman.
A queen will rise where before none stood.
A force strengthened by ascension
Her gifts exceeding any who came before.
A queen to rule the Light
And unite enemies.
With her, a new era shall rise.
A union between Light and Dark
Land and man.
Peace to balance the world
And free the burdens of souls lost beyond.
A Queen of strength
Of fortitude
Of calm and beauty
And her name shall be Violissa."

The sky rumbled on his last word, and Sinow looked up to see clouds forming above them. The words tumbled through his mind as he tried to make sense of them. There were pieces that spoke to more than just the ascension, references to the prophecy and to more that he could not grasp.

"Do you accept the prophecy and swear an oath to lead your people as it has decreed?"

"I do."

"Do you swear to place your people and your lands foremost above all else?"

"I do."

"Do you vow to rule with discretion, with honesty, with kindness, and to protect your subjects with your life?"

"I do."

Thunder echoed through the sky, and the wind stirred.

"The time has come for you to rise and accept the blessing of the Fates."

Violissa rose, and Kinnel led her to stand before the Council, saying, "Brothers, the last reigning king charged us to protect the prophecy and the realm until the next ruler ascends. The time has come. Will you return the role of rule and all powers passed down to you without hesitation?"

"We will," the voices stated resoundingly.

"Do you swear loyalty and obedience to Violissa and the throne? Swear to follow her with unquestioning faith, offering her guidance and support through her reign?"

"We will. We release the powers given to us back to our queen."

The sky rumbled again, the clouds now completely submersing the sun. A wisp of light flowed from the hands of each Council and collected above their heads, forming a large pool of arcane light that wafted to the clouds above. Those wisps were the powers of the last king, who had given them to his Council the day the Cirillian capital fell and became the Lost Realm. Sinow knew only as much as the Lightbearers had confessed to his father about the day the boundary divided their realms. The king had transferred his power to the Council for them to rule in his stead until Sinow was conceived and Violissa created. He had then given his life to protect the prophecy.

Cyric was the only remaining Council who had lasted, the rest giving their lives over the millennia that had spanned until Sinow's conception. As with anytime a Council returned their long lives to the Fates, their power blossomed in the next mortal chosen by the Fates to receive their blessing of immortality and magic. The king's power coursed through each of them as if the Fates knew it needed a vessel until this day.

Kinnel turned to Violissa, bringing Sinow from his thoughts. He held out his hand and, as she took it, walked her to the center of the platform. He bowed to her and walked back to stand with the other Council, leaving her alone.

Thunder shook the sky, and the earth quaked below Sinow's feet. He watched as Violissa dropped the hood of her cape and untied it. The cape leaped toward the ground, the breeze picking it up, and sending it beyond where his eyes remained locked on her. She was captivating, like a goddess standing before her people for all to witness her most vulnerable moments.

To the mortals, there was nothing they could see that would reflect any weakness. But he could detect it through the shallow breathing, the tight grip of her hands, the slow trickle of sweat down her brow. Pre-ascension side effects were barraging her, and he could smell her fear.

The muscles in her arm spasmed, the slight jerk the only revealing sign. The thunder and wind intensified, then died suddenly just as Violissa paled. Silence enveloped them, and Sinow could hear nothing but her uneven drags of breath and the movement of her chest as it sporadically rose and fell. Anxious tension sat in the air until a trickle of light peaked through the cloud directly above her head.

The light widened until it became a shaft that enveloped her. Gold sparkled over her skin and in her hair until the light turned to a brilliant white, sending tiny beads of light sparkling along her skin like twinkling stars. She tilted her head, an expression of serenity capturing her face, and the white shaft shimmered to a blue the color of her Council's eyes, a vibrant cerulean.

Sinow stared in wonder, closing his mouth when he realized it had fallen open. She was stunning, her power cascading from her in waves of arcane that the mortals could not see. The sight stole his breath, and he had to steady himself. The light danced over her body as she stretched her arms out, her lips curving into a beautiful smile. Its speed increased, the vibrance intensifying until he could barely look at her. Then, in one blinding blast, it charged from her and across the land in all directions, knocking him back a step from the force. The ground below was rocking with the impact, and he had to catch Keary to steady him.

When Sinow looked back up, he was speechless. The light had receded, and there Violissa stood, magnificent as if she were one of the Fates. Her skin shimmered, her hair had turned a shade closer to white, and there was an aura around her that created a warm glow, as though she were an evening star.

Arms lowering, she flexed her fingers, then slowly dropped her head. Her eyes remained closed, her peaceful smile still on her face. She took a deep breath and opened her eyes.

Sinow stepped back as the crowd gasped. Gone were the emerald eyes that had mesmerized him, now replaced by an ephemeral glow, like her eyes no longer held color but reflected only the light within her. They shone so that it was almost hard to look at her. She raised her hands out in front of her and studied them before looking around at the crowd. Hands rising to her face, she brushed them along her cheeks to her eyes like she was searching for something. The more he watched her, the more he realized she was...

Blind.

The word passed through his mind from the flow of her thoughts. One word that explained the confusion she exhibited and the fear that permeated her aura. He wanted to go to her, to pull her into his arms and comfort her, something he never would have considered doing for anyone. But the thought was there, the urgent need to protect her from the madness of the moment. From what the Fates had done to her. Because they hadn't blessed her with ultimate power. They had left her blind.

CHAPTER 16

Emotions barraged Violissa like hail in a storm. Her sight was gone. Power coursed through her, tenfold what it had been, but it seemed unbalanced, swaying too far to the Light power in her, and she could no longer sense her connection to the land. Fear gripped her like a vine, constricting her breathing, and she struggled to move the air in and out of her body. The euphoria of the ascension was a distant memory as was the pain that had wracked her body so that she'd wanted nothing more than to scream and claw at her skin against the tingling that inundated her like bugs crawling over it and the noise that had drowned out even her own words. She should have known a Darkbearer would have relished the pain involved in the ascension, not considering she wouldn't invite the same. But this darkness that covered her vision erased the pain and replaced it with uncertainty and fear.

Her power slipped through her hold on it, twisting within the fear, and a sudden awareness of madness spilled through her mind before she took control of it. It was easy to see how some Dark Kings lost control and even their sanity to the power they received upon ascension.

Calm, Violissa. She steadied her breath, trying to reach out to her Council. The crowd had gasped, so she knew there was some physical side effect to the blindness. Had her Council noticed, and maybe they were trying to reach her through the onslaught of thoughts in her mind? But they likely didn't know the true extent: that she was blind.

She reached out to Daneele in enaigne, but with so much power to control, she overreached, and her mind brushed Sinow's instead. He couldn't help her, and being in his mind would likely escalate the situation. She could barely control herself when she was near him.

Okay, Violissa, now what? she thought after she drew back her enaigne.

She hated how lost she felt, how out of sorts with the blindness and the overpowering amount of Light magic coursing through her. Her power always remained balanced between Light and nature. The two in harmony.

When she was about to give up pondering it and fumble her way to her Council, a gentle pressure built within her, forcing her to expel her breath. Buzzing started in her fingers, then spread to her hands and arms until it enveloped her. It was not the same intensity she'd had before the ascension. This was subtle, almost like a tickle, and there was no pain involved. But even so, it should not have been happening, and she feared something was wrong. She needed to get to her Council and get help, but she couldn't move.

There was another gasp, and she could hear her Council talking in hushed tones. The buzzing heightened, the air froze in her chest, and she lifted her head toward the warmth, her fear abating with the gentle touch of it. Tension fled from her body, and she closed her eyes, welcoming the warmth, letting it run free through her and frolic with her Light power.

A breeze touched her cheek, sweeping loose strands of her hair and freeing it from where it rested on her head. She sensed the land, the swell as it rose to reach her, the scent of the grass and the stir of the trees. A flood of power soared through her, answering the call of the land and balancing the magic in her. She was whole again, and as the magic cascaded through her, she gave herself over to it, knowing this was her destiny.

CHAPTER 17

A second ascension. Sinow couldn't fathom how this was happening, but there was no denying it. Green light flowed from the sky, surrounding Violissa as she tipped her head skyward a second time. Never had there been two ascensions for one ruler. They had theorized that a child born of two realms would have multiple ascensions to accept the powers of each realm, but that theory had always been about a child born from him and Violissa. A child from their union who would inherit his Dark magic and her Light magic. But what was happening to Violissa was undoubtedly a second ascension, and her Council seemed as mystified as he was.

He stared at Violissa, seeing the confusion and concern no longer in the creases of her brow. She looked peaceful, the fear now gone. The ground shook, and the crowd panicked until Cyric stepped forward, hands extended, and sent a calming spell over the crowd. The Light magic aggravated Sinow's power even more. This entire experience had pushed him to his limit, and he wasn't certain he could contain his magic much longer.

Roots burst from the ground, long and thin like vines that ran toward the platform where Violissa stood. They slithered up to her, winding along her dress, some moving around the skirt of her dress almost as if they were weaving. Flowers appeared on the fabric, subtle imprints that decorated the bottom of her gown. The longer, thicker roots continued up her chest, some running down her arms, others continuing into her hair and around her crown. None touched her face, which remained in a state of peaceful bliss, and Sinow wondered if she even noticed the activity.

Finally, the roots stopped their weaving motion and slid away, leaving an imprint of nature's beauty in their place. The light above Violissa faded, the clouds cleared, and the roots returned to the ground as if they had never been there.

Violissa lowered her head. The roots had loosened her hair, and her long golden curls hung free with flowers intertwined within them. Her crown had transformed from a plain diamond circlet. The diamonds it held were now flower shaped, and the silver metal weaved around them as a vine might, the stones holding a light purple hue. Her dress, now with flower imprints covering the bottom, had changed from a light shade of violet to a sheer pale green. And entwined up both her arms were green and violet bracelets that loosely wrapped the upper parts of her arms as a vine would wrap around a post. She was breathtaking, and Sinow had to calm his racing heart.

When she opened her eyes, he drew a ragged breath. Her long black lashes swept around the green eyes, the shade of which had no match. It was as if the sun were shining behind the brightest emerald that existed. The hues shone out of them as a prism of green. But it wasn't only the color that stunned him, but the power behind it.

A drop of sweat rolled over his lip, and he had his hands clenched so tight the muscles in his arms were straining. Everything about Violissa called to his need for her, but his power was rebelling, struggling to escape as much as he was struggling to keep from crashing the stage and kissing her.

Sinow, do you see what I'm seeing? Keary asked in disbelief, intruding into Sinow's mind and breaking through his obsessive thoughts.

Yes, she's not only a Light queen. She's a nature queen as well, Sinow answered.

Do you have any idea what this means? There hasn't been a nature ruler since the time of the Elvin, and there has never been one who also ruled the Light. This is unprecedented.

It certainly is, he said, moving closer to get a better look at her. *I think we need to have a talk with her Council when this day is over. They've left out some details about her Majesty.*

He cut his enaigne as Violissa moved forward. His body went rigid with anticipation as he waited to see what she would do. A breeze stirred his cape, sweeping over Violissa, playing with her hair before it swept back toward him. As it passed over him, it pushed his hood back, and he reached up to stop the movement. The air was warm with an undertone of power. A rustling came from the trees beyond, their leaves jostled in a fury of noise.

Violissa drew a ball of magic into her hands. It reminded him of the light spheres they would create to light the dark. She rolled it between her hands, bluish currents of arcane sparking through it. She smiled at the crowd, a warm, welcoming smile that reached even the dark recesses of his heart. Her eyes flickered to his and, for a moment, all else faded until the world came slamming back when she looked away.

The ball of magic rose, floating in front of her until, with the slight movement of her fingers, it soared over the crowd.

Sinow turned his head, watching the ball grow and pulse until it stopped midway over her people, who reached toward it in a hopeless attempt to touch it.

What in the Fates is going on? Keary asked.

I've no idea. And he didn't. Everything about Violissa's ascension had baffled him. There were no parallels to a Dark ascension. They were so opposite it was hard to imagine how the Fates thought there could be a union between the two. Two distinctly unique powers and two very different rulers. Enemy's. That's all they were, but was it all they would remain?

He glanced back at Violissa, her eyes so bright they were captivating, her smile lighting them even further, the power pulsing around her body in waves no mortal could see. But he saw it, felt it against his skin, summoning his own magic.

The crowd let out a delighted cry, and he turned back to see that the sphere had shattered. Flowers and butterflies drifted down in a sparkling haze of colored light that settled like snowflakes on the people.

He glanced at Keary and elbowed him. Keary's hood had slipped back, and Sinow could see the grin on his face.

Check yourself, he told Keary. *Darkbearers don't smile or gawk at silly shows of magic.*

Keary dropped his head and quickly tugged his hood down. There were times when his friend seemed to forget he was a terrifying Darkbearer, and if Sinow's father had been there, the punishment would have been swift and painful. He was about to tell Keary they should leave, but then remembered they had no way to do so without her Council. He flexed his fingers, wishing he could escape this. The only thing worth staying for was seeing Violissa and being near her. The rest was disturbing his power too greatly to ignore.

As if she sensed this, her eyes returned to him. The wind pushed his hood back again, and her eyes found his. That annoying catch in his breathing returned, his heart thudding so hard it drowned out all other noise. With a coy smile, she brought her finger to her lips.

Stay with me a little longer. Her voice drifted through his mind, calming the Darkness in him and stirring his yearning for her.

She looked away. The crowd grew quiet, and she began to sing.

Sinow's mouth went slack at the sound. Sweet yet powerful, seductive yet with a hint of innocence. Her voice encased him, caressing his skin, moving through his hair, compelling him to crave and love her. He was helpless and weak. And his power rebelled, soaring through him, seeking to eradicate the feeling, but as much as it battered him, it couldn't. The sound of her voice was too enticing.

This was the reason her people considered her voice sacred. This was why she had hesitated to let him bear witness to her ascension. Her voice held power.

The people had gone to their knees. Even her Council were kneeling. He listened to her words sung in ancient Cirillian as they wove a story of struggle and survival. It was the story of the prophecy, one he'd always thought was his to share with her, but he had been wrong. The prophecy was hers, and he was only a part of it. She told of the writing of the prophecy by the Fates, how they delivered it to the Elvin who together with the Light King protected it against the Dark King and his Darkbearers who tried to claim it as their prophecy, a gift from the Fates naming their king's son as the chosen one.

His grandfather. The most violent king in their history. The man who had annihilated the Elvin and forced the hand of the Light King in the darkest days of their history.

Violissa's eyes held tears, which slid over her cheeks, and he wanted to wipe them away. To tell her he wasn't anything like his grandfather, no matter how he worried he would be once his ascension took place. As if in confirmation, his power strained against his control. Focusing on her words again, his magic calmed, and he listened to her tale continue.

The Lightbearers had forced his grandfather back and Viliren, the last Light King, to save his people and protect the prophecy, returned his life to the Fates, giving his powers to his Council and using what innate abilities he had left to seal the seat of the kingdom off, concealing it from the Dark King. The Council met the Darkbearers where the castle had once stood, but upon finding no king and no prophecy, the Dark King had no choice but to give up his quest for the prophecy. As he retreated, the boundary sealed the last connection between Cirillia and Tenebron, severing the kingdoms.

Sinow had heard the story, but the teachings referred to it as a conquest in his realm. His grandfather had spun it to boast of defeating the Light King and destroying the prophecy, which was a threat to his people. Only when Violissa's Council approached Sinow's father, admitting that the prophecy was about Sinow and Violissa, that it was indeed the word of the Fates and not something his grandfather could have destroyed, did the myth of the prophecy return to his realm.

Now he could see there had been even more exaggerations in his grandfather's retelling of the events. He had no reason to doubt Violissa's words. The Light King had tricked his grandfather, and as arrogant as the man had been, he would never have returned home in defeat.

Violissa's song went on. The seat of the kingdom was gone, but with the sacrifice the prophecy was safe, locked away in the Hidden Realm.

Sinow had to think about the name before he realized the Cirillians called the Lost Realm the Hidden Realm. The subtly would go unnoticed if he didn't know the story. His people called it lost, thinking it gone forever. But Violissa's people called it hidden, as if they could find it again. Her next verse confirmed the thought when she told of how the Keeper, Daneele, had received the Fates' sign that the time was near, and the prophecy was in their hands once again. At Sinow's birth, the time of the chosen ones began, and with it, the dawn of a new era was upon them.

She then sang of answering the call of the prophecy and that of her people. Of setting forth to follow the path laid out long ago by the Fates. The resounding sound of voices from the people and her Council joined her. The extraordinary elegance of their voices filled the air, and Sinow was keenly aware of what this said about Violissa and her people. They were hers, trusting her, adoring her, loyal to her without the fear that ruled his people. These people followed because they had faith in her and everything she stood for. It was an overwhelming dichotomy from how his line ruled. Everyone in the field sang with her, knowing every word. Even her Council sang.

If this weren't so irritating to my power, I might enjoy it more, Keary said, interrupting his thoughts.

It was the truth. The sound was setting his magic into a frenzy. And he knew he had to leave. The sun had moved higher in the sky. His own ascension would soon begin.

The song ended, and Violissa's smile lit every part of her face. He couldn't help but think of how enchanted he was with her. Even if he had to deal with her Light power, he was looking forward to the day she would be his queen. Enemy or not, she would be worth it. His magic flared at the thought, and he wondered if the ascension would change his reaction to her. It was an odd thought. Ascensions didn't change a person...but they had changed his grandfather, and that worry haunted him.

We need to leave, he told Keary, his power rebelling further.

As if she'd read his thoughts, Violissa turned her sight to him.

Goodbye, Sinow, she called to him. *Anwell will escort you back.*

He gave her a respectful bow, not wanting to leave but knowing it was time. As he followed Anwell's shift, he wondered again if things would be the same after his ascension. He didn't know what effect the additional Dark powers would have on him. If they would harden his now softened heart. He couldn't deny the emotions that were building in him toward Violissa, the way his heart wanted to burst from his chest when he was near her, the way he desired to go back to the nights when he ravaged her in the Dream Realm. To have such emotions about her when she held Light power caused a battle within him, his power at odds with that of the prophecy.

His ascension was mere hours away, and if the Darkness in him grew stronger, there was a likely chance that it would overpower the call of the prophecy and change their future. As the boundary closed behind them, an unsettling sensation burrowed its way into his chest. One that told him his worries would soon come to fruition, and he might lose Violissa and all the prophecy promised.

CHAPTER 18

The euphoria of the ascension dimmed when Sinow shifted, his departure leaving a vague emptiness in Violissa's chest. She shook herself free from it and smiled at the crowd. Her magic flowed through her veins like the blood that filled them, both Light and nature balanced once again. Her eyes flicked to the place where Sinow had watched, remembering the look of adoration she'd seen when his hood had fallen back partially. He had a dark beauty about him that drew her in and left her wanting to experience more. Thoughts of the Dream Realm fought for entrance, but she shoved them away, knowing she had more pressing matters. The ascension was over, and now it was time to celebrate.

She looked back at her people, holding her hands out, and said, "Welcome to a new era, to a new Cirillia. Let the celebrations begin!"

The crowd let out a cheer that sent her spirit rising, and she gestured for the fiddlers to return to the platform. The celebration would last well into the night, and her Council would make sure their people were well fed and, of course, had plenty to drink. There would be singing and dancing, much of which she would partake in until it was time to leave for Sinow's ascension. A chill sifted through her, and she rubbed her arms as she made her way to her Council. As curious as she was about his ascension, she was hesitant. There were so many unknowns about Tenebron and Sinow. And even with the friendly terms they'd been on as of late and with the prophecy, he was still the enemy, and Tenebron was enemy territory.

"For someone who just surprised us all, you look as if your mind is on other matters," Cyric said when she reached them.

Laughing, she replied, "It is, but it's nothing serious."

"How do you feel?" asked Daneele, his blue eyes evaluating her.

"Like I could eat an entire apple tree by myself." He raised a brow, and she saw the look of concern. "I'm fine," she said, addressing them all. "I'm the same woman I was when I woke this morning."

"I beg to differ, my queen. You are most certainly not the same," Cyric stated, lifting her hands and opening them. "And it would seem there were a few unplanned surprises to your ascension."

Violissa wiggled her fingers, and a purple butterfly emerged from them, flitting around her face in greeting. A trail of multicolored butterflies followed.

"Nature Queen," Daneele said heavily, waving the insects off. "Should have seen that one coming. I don't remember there ever being a dual ascension."

"There never has been one," Kinnel stated as he walked up to them. "You are the first, Violissa. This is a blessing from the Fates."

"It's no blessing, Kinnel. This is her right as queen."

"You've always been entirely too literal, Kembal," he replied. "I consider it a blessing for our people and our lands." He stopped and looked squarely at Violissa. "Are you certain you feel all right, Violissa?"

She smiled and reached a hand out to touch his. "I'm wonderful. I can see and hear, and sense so much, from the smallest blade of grass to the tallest tree. They're all part of the balance within me. If I open my mind, I can hear everyone and everything, from you to the Dark King." She walked toward the trees behind them and waved her hands. "For me, they will bend or they will sway." Looking up at the sky, she said, "The clouds will flow or stop, the rains will come or go. All simply at my word. That power is win me, even greater now than it was. It is an enormous amount of power, and a little frightening to think about. Do you think Sinow's ascension will awaken such power in him?"

Daneele scratched his beard. "I dare say it will, though not to the effect that you have experienced. There is no tie to the land for him as there is for you. But the prophecy does state that his powers will be formidable. He showed greater abilities than any before him, even from the womb. At best, you will have an advantage with your nature powers, but I believe his Dark magic will equal your abilities."

"Violissa," Anwell interrupted before she had time to ponder Daneele's words, "the people have begun celebrating. As you only have a brief time before you leave, I'd suggest you favor them."

"You are right, Anwell, thank you. This conversation can wait. The sunset will be upon us soon, so we must make haste as we will not want to miss the prince's ascension."

The Council spread out into the crowd, creating food and drinks as the merriment continued. Violissa stepped down from the platform and walked to where Sinow had stood. It wasn't possible, but she thought she could still smell him, that scent of ash and brimstone. Closing her eyes, she could almost perceive a lingering touch of his power.

In a short time, she would witness his ascension, something no Light ruler had ever done. Her power flitted through her like a horde of insects clamoring for freedom, and she bit her lip, wondering at the reaction. Light and Dark were not harmonious, nor were nature and Dark. A sense of foreboding passed through her. The sky overhead turned to gray clouds, the wind picking up until she forced her mind to calm. As she mingled with her people, she couldn't shake the sensation or the fear that had sunk into her spine like the roots of a mangled vine strangling the life from a healthy plant.

THE STARS REMAINED hidden beneath thick black clouds, with moonlight trickling down in beams between them. Violissa's nerves sizzled in her, and emerald magic flittered through her fingers from the ominous atmosphere. The sense of foreboding she'd had earlier returned, and she glanced at Anwell to see if he noticed. Before she could ask him, the touch of Dark power tinged the air. Mackay, one of Sinow's Council, stood on the other side of the boundary, invisible save for the aura of his magic. Yet when she blinked, she found that was no longer the case. She could now see through the border's magic into Tenebron.

Mackay waited for them to draw their magic, and she could see him growing agitated that they had not. Deciding not to mention her new ability, she wondered if there was more to it. Sinow had somehow breached the boundary, coming to her that morning and passing right through it. Maybe he wasn't the only one with the gift to defy the magic that separated everyone else. Her Council had long suspected Sinow would have the ability to bring the boundary down once he ascended. The fear that he might do so before that time had been the impetus for the treaty between the two realms. It was clear he could pass through, but maybe they both could and maybe they could both bring down the boundary. Bringing about an end to the separation between the enemy kingdoms and the beginning of their joint reign through the prophecy.

"Are you ready, Violissa?" Anwell asked, but she ignored him, gnawing on her lip and considering testing her power over the boundary.

Thinking of an opening in front of her, she wove a spell to remove a small section of the border. She moved her hand as she muttered the words and watched as the magic took hold. The wall shimmered, the only indication that it existed, then cracks ran through the space, splintering away until an opening appeared. She let out an excited gasp as Anwell stared at her, his mouth agape.

Pulling herself together, she shrugged and said, "It just seemed quicker, and I thought I'd try."

She stepped forward and saw Mackay peer around the opening. His eyes narrowed, his stance defensive and ready to strike if a threat was on the other side.

"Stand down, Mackay. The queen was experimenting with her new powers," Anwell snapped as he stepped through the hole Violissa had created.

"That's impossible," Mackay replied, looking from the hole to Violissa, then back again. "No one has that kind of power."

"The ascension was good to me," she said as she brushed past him. With the flick of her hand, the boundary repaired itself.

The air in Tenebron was thick, the Darkness from its ruler permeating it and the land. A portentous stillness sat within it, and Violissa rubbed her arms below her cape.

"Violissa," Anwell said, his tone scolding, "behave yourself. Mackay, close your mouth. It's unbecoming. Are you the only escort?"

"The prince did not think your presence warranted more, although after that display, I'm tempted to disagree." He drew his hood, continuing, "Follow me."

He shifted, leaving them to follow his trail, something akin to moving through cobwebs, before they appeared at their destination.

Remind me not to follow a Darkbearer shift again, Anwell complained in enaigne. *I need a bath now.*

Hush, she told him.

"You will remain here until the ceremony is over. Do not speak, do not move—"

"Really, Mackay, we are not children," said Anwell with a hint of irritation.

"No, you are worse. You are Lightbearers." He disappeared before they could defend themselves.

Why are we here again?

She shot Anwell a look. *Because you and the rest of the Council thought it wise.*

He huffed, but she dropped it, taking the moment to look around. At first, she thought they were in a dungeon, but on second glance, she realized it was a cavern. The hair on her neck stood, her nerves on edge. Torches lit from the surrounding walls and shed a small amount of light on the group of men gathered in the middle of the space. Violissa recognized the king and assumed from the number that the rest of the group were Council. Sinow was among them as well. Although his hood was up, she could sense his presence.

How quaint, Anwell said, his sarcasm clear. *You don't think they'll try to sacrifice us, do you?*

Like they could. She laughed in reply. *Be calm. I'm sure it's very civilized.*

The king glanced their way and gave them a respectful nod before pulling his hood up. Sinow's eyes burned into her, causing warmth on her skin.

I do believe we're the brightest things here, Anwell said.

I guess I shouldn't take my hood down then, she replied.

No, you had best not. It may cause them to scuttle to the corners like rodents.

Anwell, you're terrible. Have some respect, she said, trying her best not to laugh.

"It's time," she heard Sinow say, his voice sounding slightly weaker than it usually did.

She sought his mind and said to him, *The pain doesn't last very long.*

His sight turned back to her, and she sensed the touch of his mind to hers, then a brief *Vi...*

Longing grew inside of her, but with it was that unsettling sensation that something was about to happen, something that would change everything. The prophecy crossed her thoughts, and a faint worry that she had made a grave mistake slithered its way in. Her chest grew tight, and that fear compounded, but it was too late now. Too late to go back to that day in the meeting grove, too late to question her decision.

The Council formed a large circle around Sinow. The king stood to their side. Torch flames danced in the darkness, creating a macabre display of shadows and movement that caused the hairs on Violissa's arms to prickle. There was nothing about Sinow's ascension that reflected her own, and she fought to regulate her breathing.

The Council, in their robes as black as the night sky, chanted in ancient Tenebron, calling forth the Fates to release Sinow's powers. One of them broke the circle and faced the king, saying, "Do you relinquish title to your throne and to your immortal rule of our people?"

"I do," the king replied.

"So be it. The reign of control is no longer yours. As it is with each ascension, it passes to your heir." A black mist rose from the king and wafted eerily toward the ceiling, evaporating before reaching the peak. He had relinquished the powers granted at his ascension, giving up his claim to the throne so that Sinow could claim it. The Council bowed, and he shifted away.

Violissa scratched her head, trying to figure out why he had left. She had thought he would be part of the ceremony.

He has gone to relinquish his life to the Fates, Anwell said to her in enaigne, sensing her confusion. *There can never be two kings at the same time. He will surrender his life privately, away from Sinow and the people. That is the way of the immortals. Did you not remember, Violissa?*

I had forgotten, and as I've never seen it happen, it seems quite sad now.

Save your pity. He's had a long reign and a full life. He will spend the remainder of his eternity watching the world from above us, or perhaps the Fates will welcome him, choosing him to become a Lesser Fate.

I suppose you're right.

It still seemed sad. Immortality was a gift, but it was one with limits dictated by the Fates. Every ruler and every Council eventually gave themselves back to the Fates, their bodies no longer but their spirits still immortal, never resting. Some became the stars that watched the world and lit the sky, some chose to wander the world as spirits, and a few chosen rulers the Fates offered a place beside them as Lesser Fates. Their power was not nearly that of the Fates, who had created their world, but they spent their eternity doing the bidding of the Fates. Servants to the Fates, Violissa had always thought of them. There was no way to confirm Lesser Fates existed, but the ancient teachings had alluded to them.

The chanting stopped, gaining Violissa's attention. She was not familiar enough to recognize the voices of the Council, so when one spoke, she didn't know which it was.

"Sinow, son of Drostan, next in line to the throne of Tenebron, the ascension is upon us. Do you accept the gifts of your birth and embrace the powers bequeathed to you?"

"I do."

"Will you lead us with thoughtful decisions and calculated risks, putting nothing before the success of this kingdom and the realm?"

"I will."

"Then, it will begin."

Sinow pulled his cape down. As it fell to the floor, flames licked at it. Whence they came, Violissa could not see, but the cape disappeared into their bed. Her pulse was an erratic pounding that would not cease as she surveyed him. He was shirtless and every muscle in his chest was tense with the pain she knew he was experiencing. His eyes were piercing, holding her gaze just briefly before looking up at the ceiling. His chest moved with rapid inhales, and she bit her lip so hard thinking of the violence happening in his body that she broke the skin.

Movement below her feet distracted her from licking the blood away. The ground bellowed, and her nature magic reacted, battling to fix the fear and agony the disturbance conveyed. Sinow threw his arms out just as she had done earlier that day, and the stone ceiling above them crumbled, the pieces falling toward the ground only to become black ash before they landed. The cloudless sky above shone with both moons in their fullest, a reddish glow eclipsing them. Crimson and ebony hues laced with gray poured through the hole and streamed into a cone that enveloped Sinow.

His arms shook, his body one never-ending spasm as he fought for control. The stream continued, power pouring into his body, the hues ebbing and flowing as his powers grew. Violissa's skin itched with the buzzing of her power, the Light in her reacting and struggling against her hold with an instinctive need to strike against the unnatural darkness that had immersed the room. Her own power surged through her in response to Sinow's.

Pitch enveloped the room, all light disappearing, and Violissa peered up to see that the clouds shrouded the moons. She lowered her hood, the glow from her aura providing a low light. The glow had been constant since her ascension, and she hoped it would fade soon since it made her appear as a shining star.

A torch was lit, and Violissa brought her hand to her mouth to stifle her cry. Sinow stood in the center of the circle, his head bowed. He rolled his head from side to side, stretching his neck. The muscles in his arms and chest seemed amplified; his hair darker. His aura was a black fog that seeped from him, long tendrils of ebony smoke stretching beyond it. When he lifted his head, there was no mistaking him as a Dark King. But even his father hadn't emitted the sheer terror that emanated from him.

His eyes were a deeper shade than the darkest black, no pupil even discernible. Where she could lose herself in those eyes before, now they were more likely to invoke terror at the thought of being drawn into them. She shivered as he looked out beyond her into the dark, his hands grasping and ungrasping at nothing. His Council moved to their knees, but Violissa remained frozen.

He turned his vision to her, those lightless orbs an endless void, and a chill went through her. She fought hard to control the power within her that was edging closer to release against his presence. They were now equals with enemy powers, and although he could not best her, instinct was hard to control.

She sensed his mind reaching for hers and opened herself to it hesitantly. She didn't know what to expect. Those eyes bore into her without expression.

Violissa, he said, and she knew immediately that the ascension had changed him. There was no soft voice speaking the nickname he had given her. This was a voice that held authority, addressing her like an enemy, the lack of respect distinct.

She gave a terse reply of, *Sinow*.

You have witnessed what you came for. This is the last we will see of each other for some time. I will call for you when it is necessary. She sensed a hesitation in his words before he continued. *Things are not as they were, nor will they ever be again. Goodbye, Violissa.*

He withdrew before she could respond, his eyes still watching her. Knowing she had no choice, she told Anwell they were leaving and shifted back to the boundary. Sinow had sent no Council with them. He understood as well as she that they both had the power to shatter it.

She looked back into Tenebron as she crossed through, now fully aware that things would never be the same. That whatever the prophecy had held before this day, she had lost it. She only hoped she hadn't doomed them all.

CHAPTER 19

That night Violissa dreamed of Sinow. Just as in the prior dreams, she found herself in the meeting grove. Clouds obscured all but slivers of moonlight, and the night air was thick. She sensed Sinow before she saw him. Power shadowed his eyes as he closed the distance to her. Words wouldn't form; her limbs wouldn't move. She could do nothing when he threaded his fingers through her hair and pulled her to him.

His lips crashed into her parted mouth, and everything faded. There was nothing but the feverish lust that coursed through her and a hunger for him so fierce she thought nothing could satisfy it. Greedy hands, ravenous kisses, and touches that burned through her like a fire she could not tame. Until rapture claimed her, and her climax joined his in a flurry of tangled limbs, husky growls, and desperate cries.

She clung to him as his weight crushed her, his heart pounding so rapidly yet in rhythm with hers. He picked his head up, his eyes flickering from ebony to a rich earthy hue as if warring for control. And she understood then that a battle raged within him, one he might lose. The ebony seeped further in, eviscerating the brown, and he disappeared, leaving her naked and alone in the grove, wishing she could have him back, that she could tell him she had been wrong to fight her destiny. Because her heart admitted what she could not: that she needed him, that no matter how absurd it sounded...she loved him.

Dropping her head back onto the grass, she waited to wake, staring at the clouds and questioning how she could love a man she barely knew. A man she'd spent a sparse amount of time with. Yet it didn't seem that way, not spiritually. He'd always been there, connected to her, her heart bound to his without her consent and without his, but bound, nonetheless.

The wind smoothed over her skin, and she rose, trying to determine why she hadn't woken. Upon her first step, a dressing gown covered her, and with every step that followed, the scenery changed until she was in a garden. The clouds shifted, and moonlight spread across the space. This garden was ancient. It looked as if it had once been connected to the main castle.

Crumbling parts of a dilapidated wall remained, its windows lost long ago. In the center of the garden stood a fountain of crystal-green water that juxtaposed the gloomy atmosphere. Drawn to it, she reached her hand out to the water, but it turned black just as the moon hid behind the clouds again. Glancing back at the broken wall, she saw that streams of moonlight lit the grass, which morphed from lush sage to a brittle ebony.

A loud crack caused her to turn back to the fountain, where the water had stopped flowing and was now a thick, oily consistency. She took another step, and it turned to ash, the fountain crumbling until it was nothing but rubble. The intense thudding of her heart was the only sound, and she swallowed back the flood of fear that was welling inside of her. Looking closer at the rubble, Violissa saw that something was under it.

She kneeled and shoved the fragments of stone away, inhaling so sharply it was like knives tearing through her chest. At the bottom of the rubble lay the scroll of prophecy. She reached out to pick it up, but it crumbled to dust that was blown away by a gust of wind.

"No, no, no," she cried, reaching out in a futile attempt to catch the tiny particles.

Defeated, she rocked back on her knees, burying her face in her hands as meaning took form. She had done this. Her Council had warned her that defying the Fates had consequences, but she had refused to listen, thinking she could make her own path.

"Violissa."

That voice was a whisper on the air. Violissa raised her head and stood, turning with hesitation to find a woman across from her. Power emanated from her. Her silver hair fell in waves over her shoulder, her green eyes shimmering with an otherworldly quality, and Violissa did not have to question who she was. A Fate.

It was uncommon for the Fates to grace the world with their presence. They stayed aloof, letting their world run of its own accord unless prophecy was involved, which was rare. Violissa had heard that in some sightings, they had taken the shape of animals, others as mortals. Either way, they rarely returned to the land. Violissa would have suspected this was a Lesser Fate, but for the sheer power that cascaded from her, touching the surrounding land and air and lighting it a brilliant silver, the color of her hair. There were no female rulers the Fates would have chosen to join their ranks because none had existed save for in the Elvin race. Unless this Fate was taking the form of a woman to make Violissa more comfortable. Either way, this was a true Fate.

Violissa dropped to her knees, her head to the ground in respect. A hand touched her hair, then gently guided her face up. "Rise, my child." The Fate's eyes glimmered emerald that washed over Violissa's skin. She rose as the Fate had instructed, trying to understand why the Fate had appeared.

The power surrounding the Fate dimmed, and Violissa stared

at her. She was delicate, a soft light still surrounding her, with kind eyes and a gentle smile.

"Violissa," the Fate said, her smile dropping, "we laid out your path for you, yet you turned your back on it. Turned your back on us. We cannot force your steps, only offer guidance to direct your path." She smoothed her hand along Violissa's cheek. "Oh, my child, blood of my kin. You have so much of your makers in you. Too much. You are too independent, too stubborn for your own good."

"What do you mean, blood of my kin?" Violissa interrupted as the Fate moved away.

She paid Violissa no mind but waved a hand over the fountain, which took shape once again, the water returning to the brilliant emerald it had been. Within it, she saw an image of Sinow. He was pacing a room, running his hand through his hair in that distinctive way he had about him. She looked up questioningly at the Fate who was watching her.

"We created you both for the perfect pairing. Manipulating it so that when the time came, you could not deny your attraction to each other. Everything we did prepared you for your union. Physically, mentally, emotionally, and sexually, you are each other's equal. No one else can satisfy him but you and you he. You are two halves of the same soul."

She ran a hand through Violissa's hair as a tear ran down her cheek. "But alas, you were too frightened of your own destiny. What have you done, my child? There is no avoiding the complications you have added to your future."

"But the prophecy didn't say there was a timeline. We can still go forward with the union." She heard the doubt in her voice.

"You know that's not true. You realized that today. There is no turning back now, Violissa. The union needed to precede the ascension. Your Council knew this. They understood the consequences but would not go against your wish. Their loyalty runs too deep."

"I don't understand. Why was it so imperative that we unite before the ascension?"

"Think, Violissa, what happens during the ascension? You fully come into your powers. Both you and Sinow are the most powerful immortals blessed by us with gifts beyond those before you."

"But why does that matter?" she asked.

The Fate furrowed her brow. "Because the binding ceremony for your union incorporates a sharing of your blood and hence your Light and Dark powers. Thus, the true union of the realms. The Light power would have been running through Sinow, making his ascension more benign. Your blood has calming qualities that would have balanced the unnatural Dark power we blessed him with."

Violissa went numb, her limbs threatening to give out on her. If normal Dark rulers struggled to contain their power, some like Sinow's grandfather losing the battle to the madness of his gifts, then having tenfold the power would be a burden no immortal should bear.

"Now, there is no balance. He is an unstable threat to your realm, your people, the land, and to you. Before, his desire for you overcame every other urge, even the darkest. You were all he needed and wanted. He's craved you his entire life, even if he didn't realize it. Now, that desire is silenced. It's still there, below the havoc that his power is wreaking on his mind, but dimmed from the intensity of the Darkness. He hungers for that Darkness, for violence, anger, and pain where before he only hungered for you."

"This can't be," Violissa said, her legs finally giving. Sitting on the side of the fountain, she looked down at Sinow. He had moved to a chair and was holding his head in his hands. She reached out and touched the water where his image was, wishing she could take the trouble from his mind.

"He struggles. We blessed him with benevolent traits that challenge his natural inclinations, and the Darkness in him overwhelms him. He's strong. He may stabilize the war within him, but it won't be enough to overcome his Dark needs. You were the essential ingredient."

Violissa peered up from the sight, guilt wracking her. She wanted to wake from this nightmare or return to where she'd been with Sinow, their limbs tangled, bodies as one.

"All is not lost, my child." Hope bloomed only to be shredded with the Fate's next words "But it will be a devastatingly long and agonizing road. The prophecy still stands, however. You have changed its path with your obstinacy, but the outcome remains the same."

She reached into the water, disturbing Sinow's image, and brought her hand back up with the scroll intact. It flowed from her hand, and Violissa watched in horror as the words changed on the fine parchment. The prophecy, her destiny and Sinow's, morphed before her eyes. Death, banishment, pain, and bleakness replacing love, peace, and prosperity.

Tears streamed from Violissa's eyes at the realization of what she'd done. Only when the scroll stopped unraveling did she see the word happiness near the bottom.

"Child of two worlds, you have an arduous road ahead of you. We will be watching."

Violissa looked up to question the Fate but found she had gone. The scroll was now held in her own hands.

Violissa woke with a start, her eyes darting around as she sat up. No garden, no fountain, no scroll. It had been too real to be a dream. All of it, from the meeting grove with Sinow to the Fate. She pulled her covers back and sat on the edge of the bed. Creating a light sphere to break the dark, she rubbed her eyes before lowering them to her nightdress. The same nightdress she'd worn in her dream. One she'd never seen. She pulled at the bottom, bringing the dirty hem up and seeing the ash on it before lifting her foot to find debris from the garden.

Fishing at the bottom of her bed beneath her blankets, her

fingers wrapped around the nightdress she'd gone to sleep in, the same she'd worn in the meeting grove that Sinow had ripped from her. The tear was still there when she held it up, running straight down the chest where his large hands had gripped the material and torn it.

None of it had been a dream, and where she might have returned to sleep with thoughts of Sinow's touch on her mind, that was not the case. The Fate's words played through her mind, reminding her of the repercussions of her decision and the foolishness that she had thought she had some power over her destiny. Her life had never been her own. Not since the moment the ten men on her Council merged their magic to form her with the guidance of the Fates and prophecy. She was a pawn in a greater plan, and no amount of fighting would stop it. It had only altered the course.

With a groan, she lifted herself from the bed, knowing there would be no more sleep this eve. She smoothed her hand down the front of the thin gown and walked to her window. Night still held court, shrouding the land in blackness.

Her mind was a jumble of thoughts and worries. Whatever was coming, she had brought upon herself and her people, and she could not stop it. In a sense, the Fates had offered her the choice: follow the path of the prophecy or step from it. She could not change the destination, but she had switched paths. Unfortunately, she had chosen wrong. She thought of Sinow, and her chest ached at the image of him suffering so. She had caused that as much as she had caused what was to come, and that left a hollow pit in her stomach.

There was no dwelling on her mistake. All she could do now was prepare for what was to come. But she didn't know what that would be. If the threat was Sinow or something else. The skin broke as she gnawed at her lip but healed too soon to be of concern. Sinow may not have been a threat before today, but if he succumbed to his powers, to the pull of the Darkness, he would become one. He had the power to bring down the boundary, and even if her heart still leaped at the thought of him and if she now recognized that it belonged to him, her misstep was the reason. She had made the first move in the prophecy and no matter how wrong she had been, she would face the consequences. She would overcome whatever the Fates had waiting for her, but she couldn't help but worry that her people would suffer the price.

CHAPTER 20

Sinow jerked awake. An unwelcome sense of loss washed over him, and he rubbed his face to clear it away. The scent of lilac still lingered on his skin, confirming that the Dream Realm had once again brought him together with Violissa. He stared into the blackness of his room, trying to calm his mind and quiet the thoughts of her. The longing to return to the Dream Realm and take her again was one he could not deny. If he thought it feasible, he would burst through the boundary and touch her like he had in the dream. Make love to her for real this time, with no manipulation from the Fates, no dream to dull the sensation.

But it wasn't possible. Even the thought caused his power to rebel. No matter how he wanted Violissa, there was no way he could be close to her. The ascension had changed him in ways he had not expected. His attraction to her was now mingled with ire and hatred. The power he had claimed amplified not only her rejection of him as a mate, but everything for which she stood.

Her Light magic opposed his Dark magic, and that Darkness now coursed through every fiber of his being. And it despised any thought of her. If he even tried to think of being with her, his power stirred revulsion. The acceptance of the crown and the power that came with it had obliterated what little he and Violissa had and the possibilities the prophecy had offered. Even brushing her mind when he had told her to leave had sent a convoluted barrage of lust and violence ramming him. It had left him torn between the need to grab and kiss her and the need to torture her until she was screaming in pain. The latter were thoughts he wasn't used to. That had been his grandfather's way. He didn't prolong pain unless the victim warranted that punishment. And Violissa had not.

He sat up and pulled the sheets back. His head was racing, the powers within him conflicting with his will and bucking for release against what had happened in his dream. Dressing, he shifted to the study. A light sphere formed, and he stood for a moment to collect his thoughts. This had once been his father's study, and even though his father had given him the space prior to the ascension, it still seemed strange to call it his.

Fingers dragging over the thick chestnut desk, he thought briefly about his father. They had said their goodbyes earlier that day, and in his father's typical stern fashion, there had been merely a pat on the back and a few solemn words of wisdom. Not that he had expected more. They were Darkbearers, softness and emotion were signs of weakness.

But Sinow had never been as hard as his father, who had blamed the slips of gentleness on Sinow's mother. It was an accusation that made little sense given his mother had died in childbirth, just as every mother of a future king did. Regardless, Sinow had learned to hide it from his father and eventually to hide it from himself. Dark kings were not gentle; they were terrifying and brutal. And so that was the side Sinow had embraced...until Violissa had come into his life.

As if on cue, his magic burned through him, tearing the thought of her from his mind. He balled his fists, waiting for it to pass. When he could function again, he poured himself a drink and walked to the bookshelves that lined the wall, seeking a distraction. Unexpectedly, his power surged again, causing his hand to squeeze the glass so tight it shattered. He brought his hands to his knees and fought for control. Flashes of red and black cut his vision. Dark thoughts clawed at his mind, striking at it as if to shred any last bit of decency in him. He let out a strangled growl and gripped his legs so hard the bones cracked, then healed repeatedly until at last the moment passed. The Darkness calmed, releasing him from its grasp.

His father had warned him that the ascension was only the beginning. That what came after would be the hardest struggle. Every Dark King battled with the power. It was a fight to maintain their control, to harness the onslaught of Darkness the ascension gave them. Losing was not an option because those who lost became the cruelest, bloodthirsty rulers in their history. They'd also been the most insane. With the Darkness came madness, and those who succumbed to the Darkness welcomed that madness. Those kings were rare. His grandfather had been one of them. Many, however, gained control and found a balance within a few moon spans.

Sinow prayed he would win the battle because he never wanted to be like his grandfather. The fate of his kingdom and Violissa's rested on it. Running his hands through his hair, he paced the floor. Memories of his dream surfaced, and he shoved them away. He hated that he wouldn't be able to see her, but he didn't trust himself around her now. If he couldn't even think of her, he didn't trust that he wouldn't hurt her if he saw her again.

She would deserve it. All Cirillians deserve the violence due to them, the Darkness raged.

That was the reason he couldn't be anywhere near her. That voice. Unforgiving, uncaring, and bloodthirsty. It was his heritage; he knew that, but he still didn't like it.

Sitting, he scraped his hand through his hair again, quieting his mind only to have the distinct suspicion he was being watched. Head rising, he looked around the room, but there was no one there. Yet he could sense eyes on him. The sensation of a hand on his cheek, accompanied by the sweet smell of lilac, brushed over him. Violissa. Although she wasn't physically there, some part of her was. Her part of the dream had yet to end. She was still in the Dream Realm and was stretching through it to reach him. There was no way to make that thought rational, yet he knew without a doubt that was what was happening. The scent faded, and the awareness of being watched disappeared.

"Goodbye, Vi," he murmured, hoping the rage would not flare in reaction. Closing his eyes, he breathed in the lingering lilac, knowing it would be the last he would have of her for a very long time.

WITH HEAVY FOOTFALLS, Sinow stalked across the lawn that led to his keep. He'd just returned from riding, taking time to escape the monotony of ruling, and was planning to break his fast. His mood turned swiftly when Odhran, one of his Council, approached him from behind.

"Might I have a word in private with you, Sinow?" he asked, trying to keep up with Sinow's swift steps.

"I don't like being disturbed this early, Odhran. It had better be of importance."

It had been a few moons since the ascension, and he'd finally come to terms with his new powers. He hadn't quite learned to control them but was keeping them in check. Although to most the reality spoke otherwise—their king was bending to his powers.

In attempting to control the Darkness within him, Sinow had created an internal battle that raged constantly. Lately, the depth of that Darkness had been winning, and the man he'd been before his ascension was difficult to find. He had lost the softness in his voice and the pieces of himself that had differentiated him from those before him. The ascension had hardened him. One could not be ruler of Tenebron without a nasty countenance. So, when his words came out demanding and impatient, Odhran gave no reaction. If he had, Sinow would have punished him.

"It is about your brother," he said cautiously.

"And why would my brother be an urgent matter?" Sinow stopped walking and gritted his teeth, irritated that Odhran was delaying his meal.

"After his transgressions regarding the Light Queen, we had hoped there would be repercussions."

"Transgressions? We hoped? So, you are speaking for the Council now, Odhran?" Sinow snapped before walking away.

"I suppose I am, and I'm referring to his contacting her Council about your visit to the queen prior to her ascension."

Odhran was running beside him now, trying to keep up with Sinow's quickening pace. Sinow slowed down and thought for a moment. He'd known the conversation would arise at some point and should have guessed his Council would choose Odhran to broach it. He was the largest and strongest of his Council and so was a wise choice to deal with Sinow's wrath these days. Sinow found humor that his Council sent Odhran to slaughter without hesitation.

"Ah, that. Yes, his actions disappointed me then, but now I realize they were for the best. This kind of power does not come from sharing a bed with a Lightbearer, Odhran. Her blood would have watered mine down, kept my power contained. I see that now, and I don't put it past her Council to have known that would happen. That is why they pushed so hard for a union prior to my ascension. They planned to rein in my powers. To think they almost accomplished it, but they underestimated their queen's stubbornness. I really should thank her for it." He knew his eyes had turned pitch black, as they often did now. "No, what Tynan did was for the best. In fact, I should commend him for his actions." He turned from Odhran and continued toward the keep.

Odhran's sigh was loud and Sinow tensed as he caught up.

Power tinged his veins, seeping from his fingers, but if Odhran took notice, he didn't show it. Instead, he continued talking. "That being so, have you thought any more about the queen and the—"

Sinow grabbed him by the robes, lifting him off the ground. "I will have no more talk of the queen or the damned prophecy. Take that back to the Council." He threw the man across the ground with such force, it rent the land, leaving a divot.

Odhran brought himself up from the ground, brushing himself off. Sinow sensed the anger in him and the flux of his magic until Odhran cautiously dampened it, knowing he couldn't cross Sinow. His features were stern as he stormed over to Sinow, whose magic had formed a haze of black around him. Ire and pride shone in Odhran's eyes. If he faced anyone else, Sinow knew the man would have waged a bloody battle and won, but he would never defy his king.

He glared at Sinow, who didn't blink but waited for Odhran to stand down, which he finally did, saying, "Yes, my lord. I'll see that they understand."

With a bow, he shifted, and Sinow rolled his neck before starting back on his path to food. His mood had turned sour again, the calm his ride had provided washed away like dirt in a rainstorm. As he rounded the corner upon entering the opening hall of the keep, Tynan met him.

"Brother," Tynan spoke in the snide way he had about him, "I hear tell the Council is plotting against me."

Now fully irritated that he had to stop and talk yet again, Sinow paused his step and growled at Tynan. "Why is it so many people are lying in wait for me this morn? It would make me suspicious if I were that type of king. Fortunately for you, I am not. Now, since I have more important things to do than stand around and talk about you all day, was there some urgent matter that led to your delaying my meal more than it already has been?" He waited for his brother's response, ire burning away the last threads of his patience.

Tynan's usual smooth demeanor seemed to unravel slightly at the blight. He recovered quickly, smoothing his expression and giving Sinow an uncomfortable grin. "Yes, brother, in fact, there is. Now that you have settled into your role as king…" Sinow eyed him with suspicion, not sure he wanted to hear the rest. His brother's ideas were not always in line with his. "…it might be a reasonable time to consider expanding the realm."

Sinow stopped him. "You have seriously lost your mind this time, Tynan. Now step aside and stop your prattling."

"No, hear me out, Sinow." He grabbed Sinow's arm as he walked away but withdrew it when Sinow's eyes darkened and blackness spread from his fingertips.

"Beg your pardon, Sinow, but listen. No king has ever expanded our territory. Grandfather attempted but failed. You are the strongest of them. Why not define your reign and be the first?"

"After that debacle, father decided we would never again wage war on another race for their territory. You know that, Tynan. It is a law that's been in place since our grandfather was king. I won't go against that law."

"You are the law now, Sinow. Maybe it's time to change it and take what should be ours."

Sinow wanted to rip his brother's tongue out. His appetite had waned, and what little calm remained, Tynan had shredded. He crossed his arms and studied his brother, who held his gaze. Curios to hear where Tynan was going with this ridiculous notion, he said, "You have my attention, Tynan. Continue."

"The forests to the east of the realm are massive. No one lives there, and the Cirillians do not use them. The Light Council confirmed this during a meeting they held with your Council." Sinow's eyes narrowed, not liking how Tynan was storing random facts from official meetings. "The ground there is fertile in our realm and is likely the same in theirs. Our crops have been poor this season. We could make better use of the land, and with your powers, you could easily take down the boundary."

Sinow had heard enough. He knew exactly what land Tynan was referring to, and he wouldn't touch it even if he thought destroying the boundary made any sense. "Clearly you jest, brother. The Cirillians consider that land sacred, as do our people. Both sides shed blood on that land." Tynan's jaw ticked, and Sinow wanted to punch him. "We protect that land out of respect for all those who lost their lives in that ridiculous war. Violissa's people especially cherish those forests and hold deep beliefs that the spirits of their old king and their fallen kin are there. You cannot possibly expect me to do such a thing." Just saying Violissa's name brought a burning to his chest. The Darkness in him questioned why he was being so protective of her land. "Such a move would not only violate the treaty but also start a war, which I refuse to begin."

"You refuse? Or do you fear the queen's wrath for damaging her sacred lands? You have the power to transcend the boundary and take that land. I thought you were over that wench, yet here you stand basing decisions on the whims of your heart again. The ascension clearly did not change you as I thought, brother."

Tendrils of inky fog fled from Sinow and eclipsed Tynan, throwing him across the room and into the wall, which shook from the force. Tynan fell to the floor, an indentation still in the wall where he'd landed.

"How dare you question me or my powers," Sinow growled. "Brother, you cross the line far too often, and I have been the only one to defend you in the past. Don't force me to stop. It will be a day you regret." He yanked Tynan from the floor and slammed him into the wall, leaving another indent. "There will be no attack on the queen's land and no more talk of claiming territories. And you will touch none of our land that lies along Cirillia's border. Leave the task of ruling to me, brother, and remember your place."

He dropped Tynan and stormed off, not wanting to look at his brother any further. Having lost his appetite, he bypassed the dining room and continued to his study. The door shook on its hinges as he threw it open. This was the only place he could think without interruption. No one dared disturb him here.

Vision now in shades of crimson, he threw a fireball toward the bookshelves, freezing it midair before it lit the books on fire. It floated there, flames flicking in angry hues of orange and red. The need to vent his anger pushed at his control, and he stormed to the window, leaning on the sill and taking deep breaths as he looked out on his land. Winter had come, and the bare tree limbs creaked like old bones in the frigid air.

Once he'd pacified his primal urge for destruction, he thought about the conversation with Tynan. His suggestion had some merit. Sinow was the most powerful of his line. Why not make some advances to a realm that had been static for too long? There should have been nothing in Tynan's words to cause such an extreme reaction in Sinow.

Nothing save for the mention of Violissa. He hadn't thought about her since the ascension, refusing to let thoughts of her into his mind. They did nothing but stir the rage in him. While he'd told Tynan he wanted to avoid war, that was only a partial truth. In reality, the thought of destroying the sacred forests of her people and, in turn, causing her emotional pain was the reason he had turned down the suggestion.

Many of his own people considered what the Cirillians called the Sacred Groves to hold the spirits of fallen warriors from the past war. Some thought it haunted, while others went there to pray to the Fates. Sinow knew the truth as Tynan should have, that the border dividing those woods ran down the same land that had once housed the capital of Cirillia. It was a land of legend to Violissa's people, where the Cirillian king had fought Sinow's grandfather.

His emotions had gone soft with Tynan's words, something he hadn't experienced since prior to the ascension. He wasn't sure what this meant. If he'd had a moment of weakness or if a glimpse of his former self was emerging. And with it, perhaps he could reconcile his powers with his feelings toward Violissa. Ones he had submerged for so many moons to avoid enraging the Darkness within him.

A small glimmer of hope surfaced that this might mean he could see her soon. He missed her. Missed the sparkle of her emerald eyes, the hint of lilac on her skin, the touch of his hands on her body. But all of that had been in the Dream Realm. He had never truly touched her, never had his lips against hers the way he longed. Not in reality, and he wanted that with an intensity that matched the Darkness in him.

The thought of her sent his pulse racing, and anger seethed in his veins with a burning that almost doubled him over. He had let his mind wander too far. Clearing his head, he turned back to the frozen ball of fire that levitated. It had grown in response to his emotions, and flames licked at the spines of the books, singeing them.

Hand stretched, he touched the flames, welcoming the pain. He was so numb now that pain seemed the only reminder that he was alive. He pulled his hand back out and turned the flame to dust, watching as it flittered to the floor.

He stared at it, wondering why Tynan had angered him so. Usually, he blew Tynan off, but this time he'd gotten under Sinow's skin. It wasn't just the conversation or the issue about Violissa's land, but something about the way Tynan talked of her. There had always been some part of Sinow that seethed at the sound of Tynan speaking her name. Anytime he talked about her, it sent Sinow's blood boiling.

Maybe he was overthinking it and this wasn't about Tynan. It was really about Violissa and his buried desire for her. That had to be it, and if it was the case, he needed to find some way to reconcile his need for her with his powers.

He walked over to the chair and sat, propping his feet up on the desk. His mood had been turning but had still been intact until the conversation had turned to Violissa, until he'd spoken her name. Just the sound of her name caused his power to rebel. The ascension had changed every part of him with one exception: Violissa. Thinking of her resurrected some part of his old self. Reminding him of who he had been before the ascension.

Weak, the Darkness whispered.

But he hadn't been weak. Loving her wasn't weakness. His feet fell from the desk with a crash as his power seized control, rioting at the word.

Love, he replied. It seemed an extreme word for a woman he barely knew, but she had been a part of his life from the moment he had taken his first breath. Her name had been one of the first he had spoken while his father taught him about the prophecy.

Skin split over his knuckles as he fought to control the raging fire within him. Closing his eyes, he pictured Violissa, his heart racing in response as the Darkness twisted and turned to destroy the image. Tension lined his body, sweat forming on his brow, but he remained focused on her, remembering the sound of her voice and the sensation of her hands on his skin in the Dream Realm. The war within him raged until the Darkness waned, simmering as if relinquishing its fight. He released the exhale that had been stagnant in his chest.

Violissa, he thought, waiting for a reaction.

There was a flare of painful flames, but they faded to embers. Sagging from the effort, he fell back into his chair with a smile. The battle was not over, but at least he had made some headway. It gave him hope that the Darkness had not completely claimed him. There was still something left, the small piece that belonged to Violissa and the prophecy.

CHAPTER 21

Tynan stormed through the grounds surrounding the castle after Sinow had refused his advice. Anger seared him as he contemplated his brother's words. He knew his place, his rightful place, even if Sinow didn't. Soon he would show him, and never again would Tynan have to tolerate Sinow or his insults.

He took a deep breath and calmed the rage within him. If Sinow wouldn't tear those woods down, he would do it himself. He needed that land, needed the trees gone. The entrance to the Lost Realm was somewhere in that forest. It was the only place in the realm he had found any link to it, and from what he'd calculated, the Cirillians considered those forests sacred because they protected the Lost Realm from anyone trying to gain entry. If he could clear the land in Tenebron, there was hope he wouldn't need the Cirillian side of the forest, that he could find the entrance without Sinow ever knowing what he had done. If not, well, he would deal with Sinow and find some excuse to make his imbecile brother tear the boundary down.

He stared ahead, thinking about how to circumvent Sinow and his Council until a mischievous smile formed. He had the solution, and Sinow would be none the wiser for it. Even if he found out, by then it would be too late. The treasure would be in his hands along with the key to Sinow's destruction, and there was nothing Sinow or his weak Council could do about it. A vicious laugh came from deep in his core, the echo of it lingering long after he had shifted to continue plotting his deception.

***

THE SOUND of the massive tree's fall echoed through the forest and shook the ground below Tynan's feet. He rubbed his hands greedily. This was it. They had felled almost every tree, and Sinow and his Council hadn't suspected a thing. Nothing remained of the grove that had stood since the creation of their world but stumps and a handful of trees on the western edge of the forest. Turning his magic onto the fallen tree, he lifted it and set it on the sturdy wagon with the others. He could have used his magic to destroy the forest quicker than the tedious time it had taken, but Sinow would have sensed such a massive use of his power and come to investigate.

Instead, he had bribed one of the castle servants to find him a crew willing to keep quiet. It hadn't been hard to keep their mouths shut. Mortals were just as terrified of Tynan as they were of Sinow. He had only to give the order as a directive from the king, and they knew not to spread word of their work. There were penalties for spreading rumors, especially if they involved the king.

Initially, he had been worried that the Fates would be cross. Worried they would strike him down before he could achieve his goal. But nothing had happened. Either they didn't care, or they were turning a blind eye to his indiscretions. If it were the latter, he wondered what fault lay at the feet of Violissa and Sinow that the Fates had let him continue his endeavor knowing the result. The Fates didn't like it when someone toyed with their prophecies. History was littered with many a cursed mortal who had gone against them. This time, however, the Fates made no move to stop him.

"Be gone now!" Tynan shouted to the men with a wave of his hand.

They quickly scattered out of the nearly barren grove, leaving their tools behind. They would return to finish with the remaining trees on the morrow. No sense in stopping the progress just because he had found the spot. He didn't want anyone who might come snooping to discover his true intentions, so he would let them expand the clearing toward the west. All that remained of what the dimwit Cirillians called the Sacred Forest lay beyond the boundary that hindered Tynan's path. He smiled. Soon, even the boundary wouldn't make a difference to him.

He waited until the men were gone, listening to ensure there was no one left in the immediate area to bear witness to his actions. Hands held before him, he walked through the clearing, sensing for any sign of magic. His father would have laughed at him, saying Tynan was fooling himself to think he had enough power to find such a thing. His father would have been wrong.

Tynan had learned at an early age to hide his true abilities, to make himself look constantly inferior to Sinow and even the Council. Hunching when he walked to make himself appear smaller than his brother. Letting no suspicions form that he was more than any of them thought him—weak and useless with barely any power. He'd suffered the indignities, letting them assume he was weak, knowing one day he would be the one laughing when they saw the depths of his power. In truth, he was not as powerful as Sinow, especially after the ascension, but he had enough magic and skill to hold his own and more than the foolish Council had.

He continued to move forward, searching for the barrier he knew was within his grasp and brushing past a tingle in the air. It was brief, his hand passing through so that if he had moved any faster, he would never have noticed. But it was there. He stepped back and dipped his fingertips forward, stilling them as the flutter of magic skimmed over his skin.

A wicked laugh fell from his mouth. He had found the one thing his grandfather had spent centuries searching for. He straightened his hand until his palm was now tingling as well, then muttered the incantation he'd pieced together.

> "Realm long ago lost and obscured from sight.
> Reveal your entry and give me light
> To see all you have hidden with my eyes.
> Open your gateway and hear my cry.
> I will pay your price so you cannot deny.
> Realm long ago hidden
> Do my bidding."

The ground below him rumbled, and the sky grew an ominous shade of gray. Energy revolted against his palm, ebbing and surging until ripples formed in the air. They flowed as waves of magic that expanded and brightened as the wind gusted through the empty grove. The ripples ran together, then stretched, forming the outline of an entryway. Like the suggestion of an entrance, a trick to the eye that one would only catch if paying close attention. Tynan pushed his palm forward, his eyes enlarging as his hand disappeared.

Pulse thundering, he moved forward and stepped through the entryway, unaware that where the doorway met the grove, blackness spread as if in reaction to the intrusion he had made into a realm where Darkness was not welcome.

CHAPTER 22

Violissa sat in her garden, looking out at everything but seeing nothing. She was thinking about the changes that had taken place within her over the past few moons and wondering if Sinow was having the same experiences. Time was sparse now, and she relished the moments where she could sit quietly. There had been endless visits to villages and towns too far to witness the ascension, a rash of illnesses that required her aid, and meeting upon meeting. It hardly seemed that so much time had passed.

She had finally snuck away, leaving it all behind to steal a moment of calm. Two butterflies flitted among the flowers in her garden as she sat on the stone bench watching. She leaned down and stretched her finger out to one. It landed, its wings tickling her skin before it flew back to its partner.

Since her ascension, her connection to nature had deepened. Whereas before she had influence over plants and elements, now she impacted all of nature, from the largest animal to the tiniest insect. She didn't quite know what to make of it, but she suspected her Council did. Her suspicion had no proof, but when the matter came up in conversation, they would avoid the subject. She had meant to address the odd behavior but had not had the time. One of these days, she'd corner one of them, maybe Daneele, as he had difficulty keeping things from her.

She rubbed her arms as a chill settled on her skin. Over the past few days, she had been feeling ill. Chills, headaches, and sometimes body aches. Not that she was sick—immortals rarely fell ill—but she had let Cyric look over her anyway. He had found nothing. But something was off, and it was affecting her physically. She simply couldn't tell what it was. Her concern was growing, however, because if it was affecting her this badly, something big was amiss.

Violissa looked out at the butterflies and moved her hands back to her lap. The chill had passed, and she closed her eyes, clearing her head to bask in the last few minutes of peace before she went back to the worries of being queen.

Before long, her mind wandered back to Sinow. She'd thought about him many times since the ascension, and each time, there was an emptiness in her being, an ache in her chest she didn't understand. It seemed ridiculous, especially after their last interaction. But she had come to realize it had always been that way. A hollowness had always been there, going unnoticed until she understood to whom it was associated. There had never been another who had tempted her, another she wanted. Even before she met him, her heart had belonged to him. The Fates had ensured it; she'd simply been too stubborn to see it.

And after her dream with the Fate, she knew Sinow had felt the same. At least before the Darkness had overshadowed it. Violissa gnawed at her lip, wondering if he'd found any peace from that Dark power. Only then would there be hope that they could return to where they had started that day in the meeting grove when she had turned her back on the union. And this time, she would accept her destiny as his queen.

Smiling at the thought, she looked up as a shadow fell upon her.

"Daneele," she said, "tell me I've no more meetings to attend. I really do not think I can bear another."

"You're fine for the moment, Violissa, but I need to talk briefly with you. It won't take long, then I will leave you to return to hiding from us."

She scooted over on the bench and patted the spot next to her.

"You were thinking about him again, weren't you?" he asked, taking a seat.

"About whom?" she asked innocently.

"You know very well whom. You get a faraway look in your eyes whenever the king crosses your mind."

Heat rushed to her cheeks. "Am I that obvious?"

"No, but I know you better than most. Have you changed your thoughts on the prophecy then?"

She had known better than to think Daneele of all people would let talk of the prophecy lie. Looking down at her hands, she contemplated her answer. Only moments before, she had been ready to accept it, but when faced with the question, she didn't want to admit she had been wrong.

"Even if I did, it's too late now. Sinow is a changed man, as I am changed. I fear two with powers as immense as ours would be a dangerous combination. It goes against the laws of nature. Besides, that is not what I've been thinking about."

She smoothed her hands along the fabric of her dress, trying not to meet his eyes.

"The Fates thought it a fitting combination," he said, and she could feel the weight of his stare. When she gave him no answer, he continued. "So, what was it about the king that you were not thinking about?"

She shook her head and laughed. He was always so persistent. "If you must know the truth, I was wondering how he was." She continued to look down at her hands. "He seemed so different when we left the ascension, and I know he was having difficulty adjusting to his new powers." He eyed her with suspicion, but didn't push her to explain how she knew such a thing. "I suppose you could say I'm worried about him. Why have we had no word from his Council? It's concerning not only for his sake but for the safety of our people and the preservation of the treaty."

"You are right to be concerned, but wrong in that we have had no word."

She rose swiftly.

"When and why wasn't I told?" Her pulse raced at the thought of Sinow contacting her Council. Why had he not come or called for her? She sensed the flush of color on her cheeks and wiped at them, hating how flustered she'd become.

Daneele shook his head and frowned at her. "Calm down, Violissa. I'm telling you now. We have not heard directly from Sinow or his Council. This came from our people."

"Go on then," she huffed, fidgeting with her skirt to give her nerves an outlet.

"There is activity on the western border that doesn't bode well. The land within the Sacred Groves is unwell. It is turning black, and the trees are sickly. We believe there is a disturbance beyond the Tenebron border that is causing it."

Her earlier joy gave way to fear that sat heavy in her bones. "In the Sacred Groves?"

He nodded, and she brought her hand to her mouth. He understood how sensitive she was to disturbances of the land. "We think something has happened to the forest in Tenebron. Something we cannot see, but the forest in our realm can sense. The rot is spreading from the boundary, not the other direction."

"But that doesn't make sense. The treaty clearly forbids any new building along the borders. Who would do such a thing? And why?"

"Must you really ask, Violissa? Sinow is the only one with the authority to approve such a thing."

"No, he never would." But there was doubt in her voice she could not hide from him.

"Why not? Is it really so hard to believe? He has changed. You and Anwell both saw it happen. You said so yourself. There is a high probability that he succumbed to the Darkness. Many of them do."

Violissa sat back down and laid her head in her hands, saying, "That would explain why I haven't been well over the past few days. I've been reacting to whatever is happening in the forest. I should have known."

The thought had not crossed her mind, nor had Cyric considered it. Her hands closed and opened as she thought about how the ascension had amplified her tie to the land so greatly that she was sensing it through the boundary.

She looked out past her garden and said calmly, "Show me."

Danelle gave her a simple nod of understanding and shifted to where Cirillia bordered Tenebron in the Sacred Forest.

Violissa inhaled, fortifying herself to what she feared she would find when she arrived, then followed his shift.

Her knees buckled when she arrived, and Daneele steadied her. Through the boundary, she could see the damage. Pain rolled through the devastated grove in waves that drowned her. Daneele's grasp on her was tight; otherwise, she would have fallen. She knew he didn't see the damage beyond the brittle black grass that had bled through the boundary, but he must have realized the extent from her reaction.

Hundreds of thousands of years of life lost with a few strokes of the axe's blade. Agony tore at her, knotting her stomach so that she wanted to throw up.

"Why didn't I realize this was happening? I should have known the land was crying out to me. I feel everything that happens to it."

But she had. The headaches, the weakness. She hadn't been herself for days, and there had been no explanation until now.

"The boundary must have muted your awareness. And they may have placed a spell over the grove to shield you from it. Either way, you could not have known what was happening. That you had any reaction shows how powerful your connection to the land is. It just wasn't enough for you to understand. If anyone is to blame, it's Sinow."

Sinow. He had done this. Had the ascension changed him that much? It was a silly question, considering she knew little about him. A few nights in the Dream Realm and a few meetings did not oblige him to consider her when running his kingdom. She had turned down a union with him. Why would she expect him to protect a grove that meant nothing to him and everything to her and her people?

Calming inhales strengthened her until eventually she could stand on her own. The echo of fractured life still ricocheted through her body, but she ignored it. Wiping away her tears, she replaced the ache with anger. As it rose, her spine straightened. "I think it's time to call a meeting with the king."

"That would be wise. I'll send word and inform you of the result."

She nodded, her eyes still seeing through to the carnage. "I would like to stay a bit longer."

"Then I'll leave you and reach out to the Darkbearers."

He shifted, leaving her alone with only the fragmented screams of the land that circled her like threads in a web. Even though she had dimmed the noise and the pain that accompanied it, its touch slithered on her skin, sinking into her like an unwelcome ghost to haunt her. It begged her to heal the damage, but she didn't think she could reach that depth of magic through the ancient boundary.

The weight of despair caused her to sit, and she folded her legs under her, looking out through the boundary and sensing the spirits of the lost trees. The Sacred Groves housed the memories and spirits of the last war, life lost from greed and the selfish pursuits of a madman. When the magic had formed the boundary that day, it captured the souls of those lost. No one had taught her this, nor had she found it written anywhere in the history of their people. But she knew it to be so. She sensed them, she always had, keeping the grove alive along with the memory of what the realms had lost that day.

Going through the boundary was an option, but Sinow would sense her presence and, given his fragile state the last time she saw him, it was a risk she would not take. She'd speak her mind to him when the time came. For now, she would offer what she could to the land. While she could not heal what damage lay beyond the border, she could ease the corruption it had caused.

Hands firmly planted on the brittle grass, she dug her fingers into the soil below. A song of healing and resurrection came from her lips, soft and in the land's language. The forest was silent. Even the animals and insects paused their scurrying to listen. The towering trees above her shook their leaves and leaned toward her.

From her fingers, a deep aura of green spread, cascading through the grove and beyond into Tenebron. The grass grew strong again, returning to the lush green it had been. And through the boundary, it healed and returned in spaces trampled by careless feet. Violets bloomed around the dead stumps, flowers lifting from the ground and spreading their petals to touch her magic.

The song stopped, and Violissa removed her fingers from the soil. She had done all she could, but it was not enough.

Rising, she placed her hand on the tree next to her. "I will bring your brothers back, I promise," she whispered to it, leaning her head against its bark.

She shifted to plan for her meeting with Sinow, hoping she could fulfill her promise without starting a war with the man with whom she had shared countless nights of pleasure in a dream world. And trying not to think of how her decision to disregard a prophecy that tied him to her had caused this mess.

CHAPTER 23

Open land stood before Tynan. Fields of long grass with trees in the distance. Gone was the grove with the fallen trees. He had crossed into the Lost Realm. Anticipation shivered through him. He had done what no one before him had, and now he was there with nothing to stop him.

The need to head north tugged at him, and he aimed his steps in that direction. He could have shifted, but without knowing his destination, it was a risk he did not want to take. Landing somewhere that put him at a disadvantage would only delay finding the book. There were no inhabitants in the Lost Realm, so there was no worry he would have any opposition to his search. From what he had gathered, the Lightbearers had shepherded the mortals into the countryside and far enough from the capital to avoid being trapped when they invoked the spell. No one knew how the Lightbearers had freed themselves from the realm, but given the secret doorway he had found in the grove, he had his suspicions.

He rubbed his arms under his cape to calm the goose bumps that had risen on his flesh. This place was eerie, even for a Darkbearer. A strange grayish hue sat over the land, as if the sun was shining through the spell, its light muted by the magic.

Walking proved tedious, and the distance to the trees longer than he had calculated. By the time he broke through, dusk was upon him. But his determination had paid off. Just beyond the trees sat the ruins of a castle. Crumbling stone and weeds. The glory of Cirillia was now a pile of rubble. As he stepped through the dilapidated gates, the hair on his neck rose. The sensation of eyes on him was heavy, but that couldn't be. There was no one left in this land.

"Shake it off, Tynan. You're just delirious from walking so long. Besides, there's nothing here that you can't easily destroy," he told himself as he pulled the scroll from his cape, gently unrolling it.

This scroll was the key, and the book was the reward. Years of research, of piecing together knowledge scattered in droppings throughout different writings, painstakingly reading every book on Elvin lore and Cirillian history that time had buried in the deepest recesses of the lower library, had come to this moment.

The Book of the Bound. A book that held the power of the Fates, spells locked away from his ancestors with the power to destroy his brother and make him a king unlike any before him. Absolute power to rid himself of Sinow and his Light whore and to claim both Tenebron and Cirillia as his.

On the back of the scroll, written in ancient Tenebron, were coordinates. Whether a simple guess or precise coordinates, he wasn't certain. But he surmised that at some point, there had been an attempt to find the book. One that had failed badly.

All signs pointed to the possibility that his grandfather's attack on the capital had not merely been about the prophecy. His grandfather's rantings he had found in a small journal, tucked in the far back corner and below so many dusty books no one had found it. Anyone else would have taken the writings in the margins and between lines as the words of a madman, but Tynan was beginning to think his grandfather had not been as mad as people assumed.

He studied the coordinates again, trying to determine where

he was standing. There was no sign on the scroll that told him where the book was, but he knew ancient magic guarded it. He only hoped time and the absence of Lightbearers had diluted it. If he failed in his attempt to break through it, he was sure no one would miss him. But if he succeeded, no one would ever forget him.

Broken fountains and shattered stone peered from the undergrowth, and he surmised he was standing in a garden. According to the map, an indoor garden had stood at the back of the castle. He needed to be at the front. By now, all but a tiny shaft of light from the sun remained. The moons were barely slivers, providing little light. He threw a ball of light up above him to guide his way. As he walked on, a tingling sensation crawled over his skin. Stopping, he sent his power out, detecting the faint pulse of magic and following it to a spot on the ground.

His heart thundered, and his hands shook as he pushed aside dirt and debris. There was wood beneath the undergrowth, and he heard the hollow reply to his knock on it. It seemed reckless to have it unguarded like that, but then he noticed the giant column split to pieces on his left and worn-down bricks that lay beyond the wood. An enclosure had surrounded it at one time, and guards had likely secured the perimeter.

There were no guards to stop him as he stood and blasted the wood with a bolt of power. It splintered, shards scattering to reveal a stairwell that plummeted into darkness. Tynan drew the light he'd created closer and began his descent. He kept his guard up, knowing that even though he could see nothing barring his intentions, the Light King would never have left something this valuable unprotected. The stairs continued until he finally stepped onto firm ground.

He wrinkled his nose at the damp, earthy smell that encompassed the space. Flicking his hand to spread the light out, he looked around, expecting to see the book but finding only an empty cavern. Well, almost empty. To his left and right lay the bones of the previous guards.

He laughed at the absurdity of the dead guards. Even locked away in a realm where no one existed, the Lightbearers had left them to protect the book. Tynan didn't know if they'd been immortal or not, but he couldn't imagine any immortal with the patience to suffer an eternity in this damp hole. It would have been enough to make him surrender his life to the Fates.

The cavern revealed no sign of the book as he walked its length. There was nothing but dirt. He pressed his hands against his temples in frustration.

"Think, Tynan, it's got to be here. They couldn't have moved it."

But what if they had, and maybe that was why no one had bothered to search for this realm after his grandfather? Maybe the notes had been ramblings of a madman after all. Tynan roared in frustration and threw a rage-filled force of magic at the ground, causing fragments of rock and dirt to explode around him.

"Curse it," he muttered as he brushed the dirt from his eyes. To think he'd thought himself so keen as to have outsmarted every-one, and here he was, the fool they all took him for. With a defeated huff, he gave the cavern one last glimpse, then turned to extinguish his light. Just as he lifted his hand, a glimmer from beneath the ground caught his eye. He stepped closer. Something was there just below the unsettled dirt. Waving his hand, he moved the loosened debris aside. A box lined with gold leaves peeked from below a tattered green cloth that slightly covered it.

Tynan almost fell to the ground and cried at the sight before he contained himself. He tore the lid from the container with a flick of his finger. The book was within his grasp. Its worn leather cover revealed its age, no title adorned it, and only its size gave any sign of the priceless amount of information it contained. Without delay, Tynan gestured for the book. It lifted out of the box, hanging in the air before him. Blood pulsed through his veins, his fingers twitching to grab it, but he forced himself to wait, giving time for any spells he may have triggered with its movement. When none came, he breathed a sigh of relief and reached out with both hands, pulling the book toward him.

The moment it was in his hold, the ground shook, and dirt and rocks rained down on him. Those blasted Light had placed a protection spell on it after all, and he had foolishly activated it with his touch. He had mere seconds to flee. Giving it no more thought, he quickly shifted before the spell could grab him and keep him trapped in the cavern for eternity.

Mid-shift, he realized he'd been too late. The band of the destruction spell had snagged the outer part of his right arm. He was stuck between his shift and the spell, which was pulling him back into the cavern. He focused all his energy on holding his shift. The spell had locked on his arm but not the rest of his body, and he strained against the magic to free himself, knowing if he weakened any, the spell would drag him back and entomb him. Sweat dripped from his brow as pain ravaged his arm. He was tiring, and the spell was gaining the advantage. But he was too close to give up, and so, gathering every ounce of energy he had left, he let his power surge forth, leaning into his shift.

Skin splitting, he landed hard on the ground, his other arm taking the brunt of his fall. Clutched in his hands was the book. Keeping it in one hand, he pushed himself to his knees, panting from the exertion. Blood seeped through his fingers when he clasped his arm. The spell had torn his flesh, and blood dripped onto the grass, turning it an ugly shade of black. His wound would heal, and at least the bone was intact. Broken bones were excruciating when they healed.

Removing his robe, he tore a piece and wrapped it around his injury. He would need to conceal it since he healed slower than the others. Making the robe disappear, he conjured a clean one and gingerly put it on, wincing when he moved his arm too quickly. There was no need to bring attention to his wound by leaving the blood-soaked and damaged robe on. Not that he expected anyone to be in his quarters, but he wanted no chances.

He studied the book closer. It didn't look like anything other than an ordinary old book. He'd expected something more ostentatious given its contents, but considering its origins, that would have been unexpected. It didn't matter what it looked like; it was the power it held that mattered. And he was planning to read every word in the book until that power was his.

Rest was what he needed first, but he didn't want to stay in the realm any longer, so he stood, holding the book tight against him and under his cape. Opening the gateway again, he stepped back through to the barren groves in Tenebron and quickly shifted to his room, where he collapsed, never noticing the meadow of violets that had sprung below his feet.

CHAPTER 24

Emotions battered Violissa while she awaited word from the Darkbearers about her request to meet with Sinow. She didn't know how to rectify the confused jumble they presented: anger at Sinow for what he had allowed and a longing to see him and hear his voice regardless of his transgressions. There was no way to balance the two because they were in such opposition. A need for retribution and a need for the man who deserved her ire.

She wandered the castle grounds, seeking solace in the land, but her peace from the morning did not return. Finally, she found herself walking down the long spiral staircase that led to the lower levels of the castle, seeking solace in a voice of reason. Pausing halfway down the stairs, she ran her hands over her hair to catch any strays, lest she look too wild, then continued her long descent to the only place she avoided in her castle.

Cyric was reading what looked to be a dense and extremely boring old book on some history or another when Violissa found him in the Council library. This was not the airy and comfortable library she liked to inhabit but a stuffy and dank one below the castle rooms that contained what her Council referred to as their research books. Cyric peered over the edge of the book as Violissa took the seat across from him.

"Violissa, this is quite a surprise. It is rare to find you down here."

She looked across at him, knowing he could see the worry on her face. Cyric was the closest to a father she'd had. Although he was one of the hardest on her, he was also one of the most understanding. He and Daneele had always been the ones she turned to for a shoulder to cry on or an ear to bend.

"What is it, my child?" he asked in that wise voice that revealed his true age. Cyric was the eldest of the Council and the wisest, yet no one would know it to look upon him. The blessing of immortality left him looking as youthful and strong as the rest of her Council.

She wrung her hands, hiding them behind her so he wouldn't see as he waited patiently for her to speak.

"I'm having trouble," she started. "I am so confused by what is swirling within me so much of the time." The words weren't coming out the way she intended, and she blew a strand of hair from her eyes. Flopping into the chair across from him, she mumbled, "Why does it seem like I'm two spirits living in one body? Like I'm torn in two, and I don't know which half is the right one."

Her words tumbled out. The pressure, the confusion, the longing she'd had since the ascension came pouring from her lips.

"I can't figure out how I have such power over not only our people but the land, the sea, the air. How is that possible? And how do I decide which takes priority? And then there's this new thing with Sinow. Oh, it's so frustrating. One minute I want to kill him, to have the trees plant roots through his limbs and crush his head in. The next minute, I...I...I'm longing to be with him...to... love him. I barely know him, so how can that be, and why is it all so confounding?"

She stopped and took a deep breath, relieved to have so much off her chest. Her teeth gnawed at her bottom lip as she avoided his eyes, fearing his reaction to her confession would show on his face. When he remained quiet for too long, she peeked at him.

Perceptive eyes studied her before he leaned forward, saying, "You are a child of two ascensions. It is no wonder you feel pulled by both sides of your power. You are special, Violissa, unlike any before you. It is your destiny to unite our world, rule both land and people, Light and, eventually, even Dark. Do not fight against your birthright."

He sat back, giving her a broad smile before continuing.

"What is good for the land is good for its people, and what is right for its people in turn should be right for the land. When it is not well, that is where your powers come into play. You will know why the crops dry up, why the flowers wilt or the trees turn bare. What wonders you will do for both our people and the land. Where we haven't known the land as we should have since the time of the Elvin, you now do. With the union to the Dark King, the balance will be complete. You will unite us all, Violissa."

His words should have reassured her, but they did not. The words of the Fate were still too prominent in her mind. The knowledge that doom lingered in the shadows, ready to punish her for not heeding the prophecy as she should have.

"As for the king," Cyric continued, unaware of the conflict in her mind. "I haven't much advice on this piece, as I know little of love and relationships. I do, however, know that prophecy has determined you and the king will unite. Those conflicted emotions you have are understandable. The Darkbearers have done our people wrong many times, and it is in our blood to fear them. Yet, you are different. In you, the Fates have laid the seeds of love. You cannot fight it, no matter how much you may want to. Violissa, part of your destiny to unite our people, comes with your union to the king. Without that, your destiny goes unfulfilled." She cringed, knowing it was unfulfilled because she had made it so. "Now, correct me if I'm wrong, but the Fates usually have their reasons, and giving you this longing, as you call it, to look past Sinow's indiscretions and to love him is part of the plan, my dear. They just never counted on the obstinacy of a young girl."

She wanted to argue that she was a thousand years old and not a girl, but to him she was, so she bit her tongue. His words made sense, although she couldn't help but recall the dream and see the error in those last few statements.

"I wish it were that simple, Cyric, but it is not. And it is too late now. I made my choices, and they were the wrong ones. Now my punishment is to sit by and watch as my people suffer for those decisions."

"Violissa, you can't know that. The Fates are very forgiving. Prophecies can redirect—"

"But that's my point," she interrupted, sitting up in her seat. "The Fates have already redirected its path. I have seen it myself."

His smile faltered, creases forming around his eyes. "What do you mean?"

"The Fates took me to the Dream Realm." She chose not to mention the first part of the dream or anything about her prior time in the realm. "One came to me. She told me the consequences of my decision to delay the union. My actions redirected the prophecy, leaving it unbound from its original path." Telling him lifted a weight from her shoulders she hadn't realized she'd been carrying.

"You see, there will be no union between Sinow and me. Not now, and I don't know how long it will be before one or how much blood will spill before that time. My people's blood and the blood of the land will be on my shoulders." She laid her head in her hands, horrified at even the contemplation of her words.

"Violissa, you do not know if that will happen. All you can do is wait and watch. It's all any of us have done for thousands of years. No one can know the consequences of every choice we make, nor would we want to. If the Fate says we will have war, then so be it. Our people are resilient and, most of all, they adore you. They would not think of blaming you. Don't think of this future as a punishment. What good does that do you or our people? Think of it as a second chance."

"How so?" she asked, wiping the tears from her cheeks and searching his eyes hopefully.

His voice was calm, his countenance no longer reflecting concern.

"You have a second chance with the king, and a better one at that. No more are you under pressure to marry by a certain time. The ascension has passed. Use this time to discover one another, build a genuine friendship with each other so you can accept what is in your heart as can he, without the confusion of the prophecy or what the Fates want. Think of how wonderful it will be if you two have time to fall in love instead of being told to and having the Fates force you into it."

"Do you really think so?" she asked, unsure if she saw this as the blessing he saw it for.

"I do. You never know what the Fates have in store. Perhaps they meant for the prophecy to be written this way. The result is the same, no matter what path you take to get there."

She wanted to return his smile, but his words fell short of lifting her spirits. The path would lead to the same ending, but the journey to get there would be the test. Not wanting to worry him more, she forced a smile.

"Thank you, Cyric. I knew you would be the one to ease my concerns."

"Anytime, Violissa. Now, I believe you have a meeting to plan for. Don't be too hard on the boy. He has a lot on his shoulders right now, and I suspect that some of his doings are not always his own."

Violissa stood, taking a moment to ponder the meaning of his words until she noticed his hand waving her out of the room. Best to leave him to his books and think about his last comment later. She glanced back at him again, shook her head and smiled, then made her way back to the main floor to prepare for her meeting with Sinow.

CHAPTER 25

The floor of his keep trembled when Sinow shifted to the front hall. His cape fluttered behind him, but he had no time to calm its movement. Sinow tore it off, his eyes perusing the signs of the brutal morning he'd had before he turned it to ash. Stepping over the remains, he brushed the blood from his hands, disregarding the servant, who scurried to sweep the ashes up. As with every servant who had the privilege of working in the keep, he kept his eyes down, head bowed for fear of retribution from his king.

The morning consisted of dealings on the outer edge of the realm. The southern fringes of Tenebron attracted the seedier of Sinow's people. They assumed that since these towns were further from his sight, they could get away with more. They never learned that the crown and the Council could detect when things were awry, no matter how far. His father would have sent Council to deal with the trouble, but Sinow preferred to go himself. It helped fortify his image as a king to be feared.

Contrary to the belief of the Cirillians, most of his people were decent folk. When those of less honorable means surfaced, the punishment was swift. Dark kings ruled by fear, and the people feared their king and his Darkbearers. It maintained order, and there were few who dared break the law. Sinow had taken on the task of addressing these situations himself. Where his father had frightened the people, Sinow terrified them. And word was spreading of his quick and agonizing punishments.

His wrath had shown once again this morn. A group of men had settled in one of the southern towns and terrorized its residents. Murder, rape, robbery. All severe crimes that were rare because the Darkbearers did not tolerate them. And the Dark King was swift to act when such crimes occurred. There was no pleading innocence. Darkbearers could read the guilt of a criminal with the touch of their minds. Crimes never went unpunished.

Sinow stretched his neck and rubbed the muscles in his right shoulder. Tension lined his body, even after his release of power. It worried him how he'd gleaned so much pleasure from torturing the men before killing them. He'd taken his time doling out their punishment, making sure the villagers witnessed it. Word of mouth would spread fast, and he wouldn't need to visit other towns in that part of the realm for a while.

He wiped a spot of blood from his arm and headed to his study to contemplate the ease with which he'd tortured the men he'd so easily tracked down. Keary interrupted his thoughts and his path.

"What is it, Keary? I'm not in a civil mood right now, so make it quick."

"We've received word from the Lightbearers. The queen would like to meet with you on a matter of business."

That stopped him. He had thought little about Violissa over the past few moons. To be honest, it was more like he avoided thinking about her. His power remained controlled when she was far from his mind.

The sound of her name nearly knocked the wind from him. "Really? When was this communicated to us?"

Keary gave him a coy smile. He knew Sinow well enough to

read his reaction. Even when Sinow glared at him, the smile remained. "We received the message only recently. The Council recommends that you go. She'd like to meet with you on the morrow."

"Send word that I won't be meeting her." He walked away, wishing to avoid further discussion about it, but Keary followed him. The last thing he wanted was to see Violissa, especially after his momentary lapse with Tynan the last time his brother had mentioned her name. He wasn't sure how he'd react to seeing her. That soft-hearted side of him was not something he had time or patience for anymore, and she brought that side out of him.

"We strongly recommend you meet her, Sinow. The prophecy has not—"

"The prophecy is bullshit created by the Light to weaken us. I'll have no more talk of it. Now, send word that I won't be there."

Keary was more obstinate than the others, likely the reason they'd sent him to deliver the message. Sinow thought of him more like a brother than a friend, which is why he didn't get angry when Keary refused to back down but confronted him instead. He should have known Keary would challenge him; it was inevitable.

"Sinow, I'm going to tell you this as your friend and because no one else has the nerve to say it. I understand that you've changed since the ascension. I realize what it has done to you, but you've lost the person you were before that day. The part that made you so unique compared with kings of the past. It's time to bring it back and stop acting like your grandfather."

Sinow turned his head to Keary with a slowness that emphasized his anger. Power flickered in his aura, clawing at his fingers for release. Keary didn't back down, didn't flinch, knowing to do so would only bring punishment. As it stood, Sinow should have punished him, should have broken a few of his bones, or ripped an organ out and let Keary suffer as it slowly repaired. But it had been a long morning, and as Keary's lip twitched, Sinow couldn't help but laugh, the stress of the morning slipping away.

"Keary, my old friend, you are the only one with the nerve to face his king, especially one as powerful as me, and not piss his pants in fear while doing it." He shook his head as Keary joined in his laughter. "All right, I'll hear you out. Tell me why I must meet with the queen."

Keary took a moment to catch his breath before saying, "Thank the Fates. I was worried for a moment. After last week, when you broke my leg in response to my question, I was uncertain which body part you'd go after this time."

Sinow narrowed his eyes. "I was considering ripping your heart out this time, but I've had enough blood on my hands today."

Keary's eyes widened before he caught himself and replaced the look with relief. "I appreciate that. Don't change your mind when I tell you it is imperative that you meet with her. If you decline, her Council will see it as an insult. To preserve the treaty, the leaders of both realms must meet at the fullness of the northern moon at the very least. She has called you early, but to refuse may provoke war."

"Tell me, Keary, since when has keeping within the bounds of a treaty ever been a priority to our people until now? I understand the importance of this one, but as I see it, there is no reason for me to obey said treaty. The queen and I did not unite, and all seems fine. What does this treaty do for our realm?"

"Have you lost all sense? Or has your brother been bending your ear lately? I hope it's not the latter. The thought of you paying your brother any heed is frightening. So, with the thought that it is the former, let me remind you that we have benefited from the treaty. The Lightbearers aided us on more than one occasion when illness threatened our towns. They provided cures and remedies we lacked. Since the queen's youngest days, our crops have been fruitful every season. They ask nothing of us but to respect the treaty and the prophecy. So as your Council, I insist you meet with Violissa, and, as a concerned friend, I recommend you see her. She has a way of calming your demeanor, which would be a valuable thing for you now. All things considered."

Sinow ran his hand through his hair and tried to keep his calm. Keary was right. He needed to meet with her. As much as he wanted to, he couldn't avoid it. The ire rippled through him at the thought, but deep within him ran a yearning he'd tried to keep buried since the ascension. His pulse quickened at the thought of her.

"You make valid points, Keary, as I knew you would." He sighed. "I surrender. When does she want to meet?"

CHAPTER 26

The day had come. The sun shone high in the sky above them, the warmth taking the chill of Sinow's glare from Violissa's bones. Their distance spoke volumes. There they stood, each with their own pride, their own demons, each too afraid to make a move, so both maintained the distance.

Violissa spoke first. She couldn't take his eyes boring into her, seeing right through her, anymore. He seemed so changed, yet still the same, so familiar. The powers he had gained from the ascension enhanced his broody appearance, which stirred the longing in her. There was a menacing quality to him that should have scared her but left her more addled.

Hands fidgeting, she mustered a simple, "Sinow," but no other words would form, and she cursed how helpless she felt in his presence.

She'd been determined to yell and threaten about what he'd done, and now here she stood speechless, that overwhelming need for him urging her to move closer to him.

"Violissa," he returned, his voice deep and powerful, "you requested my presence. I would assume you have some urgent matter to discuss with me."

He appeared so calm it made her want to run over and smack him. But his hands belied that calm. Bunched in tight fists, they revealed the internal battle that was waging. She considered how difficult it must be for him, that small part of him the Fates had endowed with goodness fighting to survive. A constant struggle to keep that piece of himself intact with the onslaught of Darkness that had invaded him. For any other of his line, she reasoned, it hadn't been as difficult, but he was different, created to love the enemy. And the Darkness in him detested it.

"How are you, Sinow?" she asked without thinking.

He cocked a brow, his jaw clenching.

"Really, how are you? We haven't seen each other since the ascension, and you seem so different."

"I wasn't aware you knew me well enough to quantify a difference, Violissa," he grumbled.

She continued, paying no mind to how he spoke to her. Closing the distance between them, she noted the concern that crossed his eyes.

"You've changed," she said, losing herself in those dark orbs, "but I can sense you're still there. The old you, I mean. Sinow, I'm the only one who knows what you experienced."

"Know?" he snapped. Moving so that he towered over her. "You know what I'm going through? Look at you, Vi." She caught the quick change of her name as he continued, "You don't act any different. Oh, you've definitely changed physically. I'd never considered that you could be any more alluring. Yet you are." He was so close, she could feel the heat coming from him, his power clawing at hers, and it was a challenge to restrain herself from loosening hers. "You can't know the constant torment, the need to see pain and destruction, the desire to cause it. You can't know how hard it is to stand here and not attack you. The need to hurt you right now is overwhelming." He scraped his hands through his hair. "And the damned effects of that prophecy that stirs the need to have you...to touch you. It's impossible to want you and detest you at once, but it's happening."

He walked away from her, rubbing his hands over his face and pacing. The air rushed back into her chest, the world coming back into focus. His words had hurt, but instinct told her to let him continue, that he needed to vent just as she had needed to break down to Cyric.

When he didn't continue, she thought about how to proceed. If she said the wrong thing, it could turn horribly bad, but he was controlling his power, and she knew she could make it easier for him. She silently wove a calming spell and slowly released it, hoping he wouldn't notice.

"You're right. I don't know what it was like for you. My transition was easier. But I know how it feels to detest everything about you, Sinow. To want nothing more than to aim every bit of my power at you and watch you crumble. And I know the madness that emotion creates in my head when pitted against that Fate-driven need..." She stopped, not wanting to give too much away. He was looking at her with his eyebrow arched in surprise. "I guess this means our union is off again?" she joked to break the tension.

He stood frozen momentarily, then gave her a coy grin as his hands relaxed. "I suppose it wouldn't do for the happy couple to destroy one another on their consummation night."

Violissa smiled and added, "Well, we would survive, but I can't say the realms would be unaffected."

He returned her smile, and her heart skipped. "How did you do that?" he asked.

"Do what?" she said, trying to steady her breathing.

He ran a relaxed hand through his hair again. He was more himself now. She could sense the change in his aura, see how the tension had faded from his body.

"How is it I've been fighting this for moons, and in a matter of minutes, you calm the storm within me? It's as if you've turned off the Darkness. I haven't felt this good since before the ascension."

"I don't know. I guess the Fates work in more ways than we know, or maybe that side of you that despises me so much is hiding until I leave."

"That very well may be," he said with a chuckle. "Now, while I have a bit of self-control, correct me if I'm wrong, but I don't think your intention for this meeting was to give me relief from my inner turmoil. What did you really want to discuss today, Vi?" He kept his distance, but she noticed he had moved a little closer to her. She was hoping the next conversation wouldn't throw him back over the edge.

With the wave of her hand, the meeting table appeared, and she walked toward it as a map of the lands spread across it. She glanced up to see that Sinow had walked to the opposite side of the table and was looking questioningly at the map.

"It's the western forests that border your realm," he said. "The ancient forests that are sacred to your people, so I've been told. Why would that concern me?"

She thought for a moment about how to approach the subject, then spoke, "You are correct. My people consider the forests in that part of the realm to be sacred. We call them the Sacred Groves, and the boundary runs through the center. Blood from the last war stains the ground there, and legend claims the groves hide the Hidden Realm, where our king gave his life to protect the prophecy."

"Interesting tidbit, but I don't think you brought me here for a history lesson, Vi. I would get to the point as the ire is building in me quickly."

The twitch of his fingers confirmed his statement, so she decided the best course was to be direct. "Why are you destroying the grove in Tenebron?"

His eyes darkened, and she noticed his aura change, as if his power was seeping from his skin.

"Are you accusing me of something, Violissa?"

His tone was curt, and she bristled. Her power surged in response to the rise of his.

"Someone has cleared the land that borders the boundary in Tenebron, your half of the Sacred Grove. The trees felled, and the ground stripped. These lands are far from any village or town, so why would you need to touch them and why commit such a sacrilege against the land and me?"

A menacing growl rumbled in his throat. "I have done no such thing, Violissa, nor would I. And I take offense at being accused of it. I explicitly stated that those lands were not to be touched."

He slammed his fist onto the table, splitting it in two, the map dissolving in air. His eyes were blacker than the dead of night, and she fought not to take a step back in fright.

"Sinow," she said softly, weaving another spell of calming within her voice as she spoke. "I believe you. But if you didn't, then who did and why?"

Her magic was clamoring for release, sensing his and readying to strike against it. If he didn't control his magic, hers would rebel against her hold on it.

Fists flexing, he snarled, "My brother. Damn him. He wanted to expand the towns closest to the border, but I denied his request. He apparently had trouble obeying my command."

There was something he wasn't telling her. She could hear it in the undertone of his words, but she didn't want to push him.

"I'll rectify the situation. There will be no more destruction of those woods." He moved to turn from her, but she reached over and grabbed his hand. The action was instinctive because she didn't want to leave until she'd restored those woods. She didn't expect the spark when their skin touched or the heat in his skin that sent her blood rushing. Sinow swiveled his sight to her. His features hardened as he looked down at her hand.

"Please, Sinow, I need to see the grove, to..." She didn't know how to explain what needed to be done, the balance within the land that needed to be corrected, and the ache in her heart at the loss. "I must..."

Eyes growing lighter, he stopped her, and for a moment, she almost imagined he could see her pain and straight into her soul. "Yes," he mumbled, "of course you would need to."

It was all he said, all he had to say. With those few words, she knew he understood the depths of her emotion without as much as a word from her. He waved his hand, and the table no longer separated them. He closed the space between them, suddenly closer to her than he had been earlier, and her pulse quickened. Only a small distance remained between them, leaving them one subtle move away from touching.

The power that had flickered on his aura was no longer visible, his eyes the color of damp soil. With a softness that surprised her, he reached his hand out and ran it the length of her jaw. She leaned into his touch, closing her eyes and feeling his mouth brush her ear before he said, "I hope you can keep up."

The magic of his shift skimmed her skin, and she exhaled, trying to remain on her feet with the weakness that had taken hold of her. Opening her eyes, she let her magic seek his shift trail and followed, hoping the calming spell would remain when they reappeared.

CHAPTER 27

No thoughts stopped Sinow from leading Violissa to the groves in Tenebron, but they should have. The emotions she had stirred in him left him out of sorts, and he had acted on impulse. The Darkness in him remained quiet, and a peace he hadn't experienced since before the ascension rested in his bones. For moons, the anger that seemed to spew from him tainted every waking moment. But Violissa had simmered it, providing a temporary balance and return to his former self.

He had been so close to her, his lips brushing the strands of her hair as he whispered to her, and yet his power had not rebelled. The urge to move his mouth a few inches and meet hers had been strong, but that would have taken him over the edge and released the captive Darkness that stalked him, patiently waiting to return.

She had changed since the ascension. Her power encased her, enhancing her beauty, but there was something deeper that the ascension had influenced. A presence she had about her, one that commanded attention from the surrounding world. And he sensed something else, an awareness in her that told him she was ready for what she had denied when they first met. Somewhere in her transformation, he sensed regret in her decision to put him off. He saw it in her eyes, in her actions, and heard it in her words.

But returning to that moment would take time. A union would not come easily, and even the thought sent his power into a frenzy. No matter how he felt about her or how much he wanted her, the cost was too high, his power too unstable. Even the brief touch of her hand to his had sent fire scorching his veins.

If not for the sadness in her eyes, the need to correct whatever was wrong in the forest that poured from her, he would have left. A desire to protect her from that pain, to ease the sadness, reared up in him and forced his ire down. The tears in her eyes had burned straight through him, twisting like a knife. Which was why he was standing in Tenebron, staring at the devastation and waiting for her to join him.

The wind stirred the grass, moving its blades along the stumps of the lost trees as if mourning their absence. He had half expected to find the grove intact, not quite believing what she had told him. He was scanning the carnage when she shifted in, her agony flooding in waves from her before it morphed into anger. His eyes jumped from her to where her sight landed.

"No!" Her scream rent the silence, stopping the fall of the axe. It disintegrated to shards of wood and metal as magic in shades of greenish blue encased the mortal, capturing his cry of terror. The magic stopped, and the man fell to the ground.

"Fates, I didn't mean to do that," Violissa said, her voice shaking.

Darkness beckoned for release, and Sinow heeded its call. He stepped forward as the mortal picked his head up, his expression morphing to sheer terror when he saw Sinow.

"Your highness..." He brought his hands to his face, trying to hide from his king, but it was too late.

Sinow sensed another mortal, and a long tendril of ebony darted from him, surrounding the mortal and pinning him to the ground. Rage scorched his veins like an inferno set free.

Sinow, Violissa's voice was like a gentle breeze, soothing the flames. It still stunned him that they could use enaigne with each other when never before had it crossed between Light and Dark wielders.

He walked to the mortal before him, jerking him from the ground with his power and digging through his mind with his power. The man struggled against the invasion and the pain it brought, a silent scream trying to find its sound. Sinow searched through the cobwebs of memories until he found what he needed. He dropped the mortal, who crumpled into a ball, holding his head and sobbing.

Sinow, Violissa said again. *This is not my way.*

He glanced back at her, seeing the concern in her eyes. *But it is mine, and this is my kingdom.*

I won't watch you kill them.

He studied her, wondering how the Fates had expected them to be one when they were so different. *Their crime does not warrant death because it was not of their doing. Someone tricked them into believing the crown ordered the work.*

Her eyes grew wide before they glanced at the man, who was still writhing on the ground. *So, he will live?*

Yes, but with consequences.

He turned from her, addressing the second mortal who remained with his head to the ground, not daring to look at his king.

"Take him," he said to the other mortal. "And let him be a reminder of what happens if you dare look at your king without permission."

"Yes, my liege," the second man said, keeping his head lowered, his posture bowed while he gathered his companion.

It was too late for the first man. He would go mad within days for making the mistake of looking Sinow directly in the eyes without permission. In fairness, Sinow had no cape to warn the man of his identity. All of Tenebron knew their king and his

Darkbearers wore black capes, shielding the innocents from their power. But this would be a warning to others that their king made no exceptions. Only with a spell of permission could a mortal withstand looking a Dark King in the eyes. The power was too intense. This mortal was lucky he hadn't died from the sight...or perhaps that would have been a blessing.

"Do not return. Tell the others who inflicted this damage that I did not sanction this. Any who return to bring harm to this land will experience my wrath."

His magic strained to cause more pain, to dole out more punishment, but their crimes had not been their own, and he could not justify it. Doing so went against the code of the Darkbearers and their king. Harm only those who deserve the punishment. Protect all others. It was a code he struggled to maintain under the constant sway of his power.

"Thank you, my liege." He scurried away, dragging his friend behind him and leaving Sinow alone with Violissa.

Rolling his neck, he looked at her. Pursed lips and serious eyes informed him of her thoughts.

"I am a Dark king, Violissa." He didn't know why he had the impulse to explain. "My people fear me for good reason, and no one meets my eyes without my permission."

"What will happen to him?" she asked.

"Madness will take him. If he's lucky, the Darkness will infect his mind so badly he will die within days. If he's not, then he will live in a constant state of terror and visions, incoherent ramblings and agonizing voices. To look a Dark king in the eyes is to see death itself. No one comes out unscathed unless they have my permission."

"And when do they have that?" Her curiosity surprised him, especially with how weak he'd always considered the Lightbearers.

"Never."

The crease in her brow deepened, and she sucked her bottom lip in, giving him a curt nod. He studied her, seeing a side he had not expected from her, a strength to understand what went against her code. Her eyes dropped to his hands. He balled them into fists to hide the slight shake. Reining in his power had been difficult. A balance existed within him, one that teetered dangerously close to the lure of his power, and each time he used it, the need to decimate and ignore his code challenged that balance. This had been no exception, especially with the irritating sting of Violissa's magic against his skin.

A loose curl skimmed over Violissa's cheek, and he had the sudden urge to touch it. Moving closer to her, he reached his fingers out just as her eyes darted back to his. The lock was soft, the golden hue holding variations of yellow and white that captivated him. He twisted it around his finger, drawn to her again and wanting to close the remaining distance between them. But the demon within reared its head, seething at his proximity to her, at the Light power that sat on her aura and collided against his like a sworn enemy brandishing a sword.

"What do you need to do here?" he asked, seeing understanding cross her eyes.

"I need to heal the land." The sadness returned as if she had forgotten about it, and it was rushing back to remind her of what surrounded them. She grabbed his arm, stumbling slightly, like remembering had opened a wound.

"Vi?" he asked, his internal battle calming at seeing her this way.

He held onto her to steady her, hating how she suddenly seemed so fragile.

"Is it the land?" he asked, wiping a tear from her cheek.

She looked up, her lip trembling, her eyes a brilliant emerald that would have enchanted him if he weren't so concerned. He saw the truth then. The damage to the land was doing this to her, and in her anger at the mortals, she had masked the effects. But now, she could no longer hide it. Her power tied her so close to the land that she suffered as it suffered. The Dark side of him celebrated at finding her weakness. It screamed to ravage the land and see her crumble further. But he would never do that to her, and so he shoved the thoughts away, fortifying them behind the need to make her better.

He thought of her ascension, of the way the land had come alive with her song.

"Sing," he said, understanding her in ways he shouldn't have been able to, but did.

"But—"

He stopped her words with a finger to her lips, his eyes following its trail as it dragged over them. Desire gripped him, threatening to take his moment of rare selflessness and destroy it.

"No buts," he said, fighting the need to replace his finger with his mouth. "Sing and heal the land. I'll shield the area, so no one will know. I'll be the only one to hear."

She gave him a smile, the sparkle returning to her eyes. "Thank you," she said, and he noted the sincerity of her gratitude.

His finger lingered on her chin before it slid over her neck. "Do it now before my bad side returns." He snatched his hand back, fearing what he would do if he let it move further and the repercussions his power would wreak if he did. It was stalking, searching for a way to break free from the binds he had trapped it in. He was still in awe of how close he was to her, but it was taking all his will to keep his power restrained.

Forcing himself to step back from her, he formed a shield around the forest, ensuring no one would hear her sing. He could still sense the two mortals who had not run far enough yet and so he threw out a spell to block the sound from them. Her voice was sacred to her people, and he would risk no one outside of her realm hearing it.

The air touched his skin, a gentle breeze that seemed to wrap around Violissa, stirring the long locks of her hair. She took a few steps further into the stripped grove, and a stillness settled over it.

It was almost like every creature knew something special was about to happen and was waiting with anticipation.

Violissa closed her eyes and sang.

The sound drifted through him, touching the deepest recesses of his darkened soul and reminding him of what she meant to him, of the binding that tied them to one another. It soothed his conflicted mind, asserted a claim on him, and deepened the emotions he held for her. The words were not quite words but more like an ancient language of the land, far older than either of their tongues. They reminded him of the sounds of the forest, and he realized she was speaking to the trees, singing to their spirits, and calling them back home. Her song was hauntingly beautiful.

Breaking the trance he was under, Sinow walked around to see her face and watch her. Her sight focused far beyond his vision, and her features held serenity. She bent down and placed her hands on the stump closest to her, and a green aura eclipsed it before spreading across the barren grove until it had reached every stump. Her voice lifted to a crescendo, the emerald magic rising as she stood and filling the surrounding space. Arms spread, Violissa held a high note, the ground shaking slightly in response.

Sinow looked around, his eyes wide as the trunks lengthened, following the movement of her arms as they reached to the sky. He watched them rise, stepping back in surprise to see wisps of light diving into the climbing trees. Almost like souls returning home. He rubbed his eyes, thinking it an impossibility, but then everything he was witnessing was impossible. Immortals could destroy, they could build, they could create, but none had power over nature. None could bring back life, but that's what Violissa had done. Maybe not a mortal life but the life of the land, the plants that were living things.

Her song had ended, but Sinow stood riveted, staring at her and, for the first time, seeing the true depths of her power. The Darkness rebelled, seeing it as a threat, and he balled his fists to hold it in.

"Souls?" he mumbled. "Those were souls?"

Emerald irises fell upon him.

"The spirits of those lost in battle that day protect this forest. The trees hold their essence, and we hold their memories."

The rustle of trees spread through the forest as if in confirmation. A breeze whipped past him, carrying a line of flower blossoms that danced in its current. They flowed past her outstretched fingertips and settled in her hair. Violissa smiled and said, "The balance has been restored. Thank you, Sinow."

Her smile lit her eyes and left him spellbound once more. Parting lips and a pink hue that climbed her cheeks encouraged him to disregard the rebelling magic inside him, and he took a step closer before something caught his attention, ripping his opportunity from his grasp.

"My Council. They're coming," he said, hearing the disappointment in his tone. Their voices were battering him with questions. "They noticed the magical disturbance. It's best that I be here alone to explain it."

"Yes, you're right," she replied, her smile dropping. "Goodbye, Sinow, and thank you again."

"Vi," he said, right before she shifted.

"Yes, Sinow?"

"What you did for me today, calming the Darkness...thank you. You've no idea how I needed that."

"I think it's safe to say we know each other better than we thought, Sinow. Until we meet again, goodbye."

"Goodbye, Vi."

Keary and Faolan shifted in as Violissa vanished. Sinow could still smell the lilac in the air.

"Sinow?" Faolan asked as he looked around, searching for something.

"What's going on here? There are remnants of Light magic all over this place and," Keary squatted, rubbing his hand over the grass, "is that nature magic?" He glanced at Sinow, giving him a smirk. "Need we ask, Sinow?"

"No, you need not. Everything is under control."

Keary shook his head. "And what were you and the Light Queen doing?"

"The Light Queen was here on our lands? Why were we not informed, Sinow?" Faolan asked, ignoring Keary's teasing tone.

Sinow snapped, "I do not need your permission for any decisions I make, Faolan."

"He knows that, Sinow," Keary replied, knowing it took little to send Sinow over the edge these days. "It's best to warn us as a precaution. Otherwise, it sets overzealous ones like Faolon into a fit with worry." Faolon scowled at him, and Sinow had no doubt that if his king had not been present, a scuffle would have ensued. Keary enjoyed stirring trouble a little too often. "As I see no damage, I think it's safe to presume you and the queen were not fighting. But since you're fully clothed, I'm guessing you weren't having fun either," he said with a sly grin. This time it was Sinow's turn to scowl. "So why did we detect the massive surge of Light magic here?"

"Because I gave Violissa my consent for her to clean up the mess that was here. Someone authorized the clearing of these lands under my name."

Keary's grin faltered as Faolan scanned the forest. "There is nothing wrong with the forest, Sinow."

"Not anymore, Violissa repaired it. But when we arrived, the trees were gone. Only stumps remained. And these," he kneeled and plucked a flower from the thick grass, "were here where I suspect only mud and trampled land had been."

"Violissa?" Keary asked.

"Yes, I'm positive. Flowers aren't a norm for our lands. I think she somehow sent her magic through the barrier. She certainly didn't cross into our realm before I brought her here. I don't care how she did it, nor am I concerned about it. What concerns me is that someone destroyed this grove—"

Faolan stopped him. "But there is nothing wrong with the grove."

Sinow gritted his teeth as Keary shook his head. Faolan had tested his king one too many times and interrupting him had been the final blow. Faolan was on his knees, fighting to hide his pain within seconds. Sinow's magic encased his lungs, gripping them tight as Faolan kept his eyes locked on Sinow. One sign of weakness, one small cry or reflection of agony, and Sinow would compound his punishment. To show weakness went against everything they were as Darkbearers. "Never question me again," Sinow growled, the power tipping the balance and calm Violissa had weaved in him.

"Yes, my liege," Faolan rasped.

Sinow released his hold on him and watched for any sign of relief, but Faolan didn't move until Sinow began talking again. "Violissa brought the trees back. If I hadn't seen it with my own eyes, I would have doubted her ability to do so."

"Nature queen," observed Keary as Faolan stood.

Leave us, Sinow commanded Faolan, who bowed before disappearing.

Keary did not react, likely assuming Sinow had sent Faolan away.

"Yes, she is." The thought of her calmed Sinow, and he flexed his hands against the tide of Darkness. He looked away, thinking of Violissa and how beautiful she'd been standing in the green haze of her magic.

"Any thoughts about who circumvented you and allowed the clearing of the land?" Keary asked. Sinow glanced back at him. Keary was sharp, and Sinow could see his thoughts clearly in the lift of his brow.

"I have my suspicions, but I'll handle it myself."

Keary grabbed his arm. "Something needs to be done about him, Sinow. You have a soft spot for him, and he's taking advantage of it. Don't let him blindside you."

Sinow dropped his eyes to where Keary's hand sat on it. "Be glad I've better control than I had before, Keary, or you'd be across the forest right now tending to your bruises. Don't test that control."

"Just watch your back, Sinow, that's all I'm saying."

SINOW STORMED into his brother's room. The topless woman on top of Tynan jumped up and tried to scream, but Sinow muted her with the flick of his hand, keeping his eyes from her to avoid accidentally killing her. To her benefit, she kept her sight down and dropped to her knees, head touching the floor in deference. Even if she didn't know he was king, she had been smart enough to know better than to risk it.

His brother sat up, buttoning his pants. One of Tynan's vices was women. He was always biding his time with one, bringing them in from various towns, taking his fantasies and then his frustrations out on them. There were reasons the Council took a vow of celibacy and a reason kings were selective about their bedroom habits. One slip of power in the throes of ecstasy, and the mortal was dead. And Tynan had left a trail of death to satisfy his appetite. The women knew what they risked, but the temptation of bedding a Dark prince and touching that power often proved too much. Of course, turning one down was just as much of a risk.

Tynan's vice was not one Sinow shared. He had no taste for it. Only one woman tempted him. There had only been one who ever had, and any thought of anyone but Violissa turned his stomach even as far back as he could remember. No one else would satisfy his need for her, and the violent reaction at the thought of even considering another woman was enough to keep him faithful to her. The prophecy ensured he and Violissa would fulfill its intent, even if she had rebelled against it.

His brother more than made up for his lack of sexual experience.

"Sinow, what a surprise," Tynan said with a sneer.

The woman's fear permeated the air.

"Get out," he told her, staring his brother down.

She ran past Sinow and out the door, holding her dress in one hand and her breasts in the other. Thankfully, her departure would go unnoticed, as Tynan's quarters lay on the outer edge of the castle.

"Why do you disturb me so, Sinow? It's difficult to function for the rest of the day when interrupted like that. I'll have to find myself another wench now."

"That's far from your primary concern, Tynan," Sinow answered. Fire blazed within him, licking at his fingertips to be freed. "I thought I told you there would be no expansion of the realm on Cirillian territory."

"You did. Why do you ask?" Tynan calmly rose from the bed and pulled a shirt on, but Sinow detected the subtle pitch of his voice. "Brother, you look upset. Have I offended you? Did you want the whore for yourself?"

Sinow glowered at him, the muscles in his arms twitching as the Darkness crested. "I don't need your women, Tynan."

"That's right. I forgot you have that little *problem*." The snicker that accompanied the word caused a growl to rumble in Sinow's chest.

"Why did you order the mortals to cut down the ancient groves on the eastern border? And why were they under the impression that the order came from me?"

Tynan's eyes darted to his. "They what? I explicitly told them the venture had been called off. It's true I made an initial request, but when you expressed your objection to the idea, I called it off."

His answer lacked conviction, and so Sinow pressed him. "You planned all of it before the discussion with me? You even hired men to do the work?" Sinow's hold on his control loosened, and a haze of black filled the room. "You are in no position to begin ventures on my behalf, Tynan."

"Now don't get all upset. I know how busy you are. I simply thought I'd do some pre-planning for you, save you the trouble," he said with a wave of his hand. "Clearing those woods would have allowed camp setup for our troops."

Fury scraped through Sinow in a violent rage that spurred the Darkness and escaped his grasp. Ebony tendrils spilled from him, slamming into Tynan and sending him flailing across the room into the wall behind him. Stone fell in broken pieces that crumbled to the floor as Tynan pulled himself free.

"Thank you for restraining yourself, Sinow," he said, popping his arm back into its socket. Sinow took pleasure in the flicker of pain in Tynan's eyes and the clenched teeth that Tynan had intended to hide that pain.

"You are in no position to make decisions for me or speak on my behalf," Sinow snarled, trying not to throw his brother out the window. "What you did was out of line and could have had dire consequences for the treaty and the land."

Tynan dusted the rubble from his clothes. "You sound as if you have fixed whatever damage was done. I take it you stopped them in time." He tilted his head as if waiting for Sinow to disagree.

His confidence faltered when Sinow said, "I've taken care of it with the help of the queen." He instinctively chose not to say her name. Something about Tynan's reaction to Violissa always rubbed him wrong.

"Violissa?" he hissed, and Sinow's alarms went up as they did anytime Tynan talked about her. "She was here on our land?"

"On my land," Sinow corrected. "And that's not your concern." He walked over to his brother and lifted him by the collar. A subtle choking sound escaped Tynan's throat. "I am the only reason no one has banished you from these lands. The Council has no fondness or need of you. I have no need for someone who does not know his place. Stay out of realm business, Tynan, or you will no longer be welcome anywhere but the Banished Realm." He dropped him and walked toward the door. Hand on the door handle, he glanced back at Tynan. "Keep your whoring contained. Have some respect for the dignity of my crown. Otherwise, I will have no choice but to burn away any need you have for women." A burst of flame filled his hand, where it lingered until he turned it to smoke.

He slammed the door behind him, hearing Tynan mutter, "At least mine gets used. Someone in this family needs to act like a real man."

Sinow balled his fists tightly and suppressed the urge to crash back through the door and beat the life out of Tynan, as he had done when they were children. His brother was always keen on identifying Sinow's weak spots, what few he could find, and would remind Sinow of them constantly. Sinow usually let it roll off his shoulders, assuming it was his brother's way of compensating for not being king. Today, however, he didn't have a sense of humor about it.

There were times he questioned why he put up with Tynan, as he knew his Council frequently did. Loyalty was the only reason he had. It had been there since they were young. They'd been close before their father decided it was time for Sinow to learn the duties of his future role. Only then did they grow apart. Slowly at first, but as they aged, the distance became too formidable to surpass. After the ascension, it worsened. Tynan's behavior was more secretive. He uttered comments under his breath, eavesdropped on conversations, and now this.

If Sinow had been more mistrustful, he would have suspected Tynan's intentions, but he wasn't and, to the Council's frustration, he never did. If he'd heard the words of the rewritten prophecy, he might have put the pieces together, might have had some idea of the snake that lay among them, but he didn't, nor would he until it was too late.

CHAPTER 28

The sun filtered through the large window in long streaks that banished the shadows to the corners of the library. Violissa stared at the book, the words out of focus as her mind slipped again to Sinow. Several days had passed since their meeting, and no matter how she tried, she couldn't keep her mind from returning to him and the events of that day. It was as if two different people lived within his one body, both vying for rule. He had begun the morning possessed by that Darkness within him and then suddenly he was back to the man she'd first met so many moons ago. She knew the calming spell she had quietly woven held some explanation, but she suspected the man she first met, who had repeatedly brought her to ecstasy in the Dream Realm, fought for dominance when she was near. It almost seemed as if that part of him rose to protect her from whatever the Dark side of him might try to say or do to her.

The thought of him protecting her brought a smile to her lips. She could defend herself, yet she still thought it a sweet gesture. With a sigh, she set the book aside and gazed out the window. Two sides to one man. And if she was being honest, both sides attracted her. The side that reveled in the Dark power, the broody, dangerous side, stirred something deep within her she didn't recognize, something almost feral. And the other side of him made her heart race in an entirely different way. It leaped and soared at the smooth sound of his voice, the flickers of brown in his eyes, the soft touch of his hands on her skin.

A quiver passed through her as she considered what he would eventually be like when he accepted his Dark powers and his split identity finally merged back to one. She wasn't so certain she would have the strength to resist him once that happened. She was having such a difficult time as it was.

Cyric's voice disrupted her thoughts, and she jumped, the book crashing to the floor.

Violissa, we need you down in the lower wings. There's something you need to see, he called in enaigne.

She picked the book up from where it had landed. "A lot of good you did clearing my mind," she mumbled as she stood and placed it on the seat where she'd rested only moments before.

I'm on my way, she replied to Cyric.

Arms stretching, she shook out the stiffness from sitting so long, wondering what could be so important that Cyric would call her away from her private time and to the lower wings at that. The only things down there, aside from the Council's library, were dampness and spiders; both things she could do without on this beautiful sunny morning. Glancing out the window one last time, she let out another sigh and shifted where she sensed Cyric.

Where she landed was nowhere she'd been before. The light sphere that hung above Cyric did little to remove the dank, dreary feel of the space.

"Cyric, what is it and why the urgency?" She looked beyond him and noticed Brom in the background. He bowed slightly, and she smiled in return, silently wondering why both had brought her here. A sense of foreboding crawled over her skin, solidifying when Daneele appeared from behind Brom. She blinked, leaning to determine where he had come from. Only a stone wall stood behind Brom, yet Daneele emerged as if from somewhere past the wall.

"We need to show you something," Cyric answered. "Daneele, if you will." He gestured to Daneele, who turned to the wall. Mumbling a spell, he waved his hand over it, and Violissa's jaw dropped. The wall dissipated, and a hallway now stood in its place.

She moved next to Daneele and studied the space where the wall had been. "How did I not sense the magic in that façade?"

"It's old magic. An Elvin spell only I know as your Keeper," Daneele responded as he continued forward. Keepers held the secrets of the past and protected the prophecy. There was only one for each generation of rulers. Daneele was Violissa's. He was the youngest of the Council, his calling coming when the last king's Keeper handed his knowledge down and returned his soul to the Fates. "You are entering a section of the castle locked away from the time of the last Light king. The only time anyone other than me has been here was the day of your creation."

Drawn to the end of the hall, Violissa walked past him, not stopping until she was standing before a doorway carved into the stone. Although to the mortal eye, it only appeared to be a dead end, the door, carved delicately into the stone, emitted a rich and ancient power whose source could only have been Elvin. She brought her hand up to it, and a line of beautifully scripted words appeared over the top of the doorway. Etched upon the door, a pattern of flowers rose to greet her hand.

Along the seam of the door lay a thick black film that seemed to stretch around the outer edges of the doorway to escape whatever lay beyond. As she watched, it appeared to move slightly. She took a step back in reaction.

"This is similar to what I saw at the Sacred Grove," she stated, looking back at the men. "What is it doing in my castle?"

"That's what we need to find out, Violissa, and the reason we called you. We don't know what it is or why it's here, but the fact that it's escaping from that doorway is a troubling sign," Daneele replied, the concern in his eyes revealing the true seriousness of the situation.

"The three of us have been down here debating who we should inform of this, other than yourself, of course, and we can't come to an agreement." Violissa scrunched her eyes at Cyric as he continued. "Some of us are of the thought that we need to inform the Dark King, since this will surely impact his realm as well as ours."

"What?" she asked, her voice rising a pitch. "Why would he need to be informed? There's no reason I can't simply send this stuff back where it came from, like I did in the grove."

"Violissa, I don't think you understand what this means." Daneele stepped up to the doorway and rested his hand almost reverently on the door before them.

This was no ordinary door. The engravings told her that much. But the way he had approached it had her thinking it was something sacred.

"You said you used it on the day of my creation? This can't be..." A thought took shape in her head, one that sounded too impossible to be true. "This is a doorway to the Hidden Realm?"

Daneele gave her a somber look and nodded.

"It was under us all this time? Why didn't I know?"

"Because you did not need to know yet," Cyric replied. "The Fates said the doorway would open again only at the fruition of the prophecy."

"We can discuss this in depth at a later time, Violissa," Daneele said, cutting Cyric short. The quick interjection made her question what else her Council was hiding from her. "What matters now is that something is happening beyond that door, and if this is indeed the same substance we saw at the realm borders, the problem may be worse than I fear."

It worried her to see the deep concern that lined his eyes. He took his role as Keeper seriously and was protective of any knowledge of the Hidden Realm and the prophecy.

"Daneele," Violissa began, "that part of the border where I

found the damage in the Sacred Groves, does that area touch the Hidden Realm?"

His shoulders slumped, and for a moment, he seemed defeated. "Yes, in fact, it sits at the exact place where the capital once sat. This is why I encourage you to alert the Darkbearers, Violissa. When the last Light King cast the spell, the capital and the land surrounding it became lodged in a collapsed piece of our world. The magic he and his Lightbearers used caused our world to fold in around it as if it were in an eternal void. If it were to reappear, it would now sit within both our realms, splitting the boundary in half. If this substance," he gestured to the black part of the doorway for emphasis, "is indeed leaking from the Hidden Realm, then it stands to reason that it appears in both our realms. Since we don't know what it is or what it can do, we need to warn them."

Chewing her bottom lip, Violissa paced the corridor. She didn't have an issue with sharing this with Sinow, but she had a concern about how to share it. There had never been a Darkbearer on their soil apart from her ascension, and there certainly had never been one in their home other than that day. Having him down here with the Hidden Realm, the birthplace of their people and that of the Elvin, well, that was something unprecedented. If she invited Sinow in, she would give him a glimpse of something so sacred that her Council had not even shared it with her until now.

She pulled at one of her curls and looked back at the three Council before her. "Send a message to Sinow's Council that I request his presence at the height of the day and that it is of utmost importance he meets me."

"I would recommend he bring Kanine," Cyric said. "As the king's eldest Council and one who was present during that fated day, he may add insight." Violissa wanted to object, but she knew that Cyric, the only Council left from that period, would know best. He and Kanine were the eldest of any living Council, and if anyone could figure out what was happening here, they would be the ones.

She nodded. "Brom, please send the message." She looked up at the blackness around the doorway one last time. "I'm going back up to think about this. I'll be in my chambers if you need me. Please call me when they arrive."

They nodded to her as she turned to leave. Daneele walked ahead of her and released the magical force that shielded the corridor from the rest of the castle. She knew fully that she had the power to walk through without him, but she kept it to herself.

"Daneele," she said as she stepped past him, "do you have any idea what it is or what it means?"

"No, for once I am at a loss. I have never seen or heard of such a thing, Violissa. I only hope that we can figure out a way to stop it. Something is going on beyond that door to cause it."

Violissa gave him a weary smile, then shifted. She needed time to take in all she had been told and to think about what all of it meant. Then there was the fact that a doorway to the Hidden Realm sat below her castle, where it had been all this time. The information kept from her. But why? She couldn't find a reason that made sense. It was common knowledge that the Sacred Grove had once been home to the capital, so why keep this from her?

Worries tumbled through her mind, and she knew returning to her book would give her no more reprieve than it had before her Council had called her. Returning to her quarters, she peered out her window, thinking of the spreading blackness that was creeping beyond the doorway. Something gnawed at her, telling her there was a connection to what she had found in the Sacred Grove. No matter how she turned it over in her mind, she couldn't fit the two together, nor could she determine the answer. Whatever it was, she needed to stop it and what she had done in the Grove had not been enough. But how could she stop something she didn't understand?

Rubbing her hands, she noticed the oily residue remained on

her fingers. The lower levels had left a grittiness on her skin, and the need to wash away the sensation of the black substance convinced her that a hot bath was necessary. Walking to the tub room that adjoined her sleeping quarters, she used her magic to fill the tub, warming the water with it.

As she removed her clothes, her mind drifted back to Sinow, anticipation building that she would see him this day. The warm water only further heated her body and the flush that settled in her cheeks. Brushing her fingers over one, she thought of how he'd been so close the last time they had met, how his fingers had lingered in her hair and his breath had been warm on her ear when he had leaned in to her. Sinking under the water, she chastised herself for letting her mind wander, hoping the next few hours would pass quickly. Otherwise, she wasn't certain if the situation in the lower castle wing and the prospect of seeing Sinow again wouldn't drive her to madness.

CHAPTER 29

Sinow handed the reins of his horse to the stable boy, who took them and quickly backed away from him. He gave the boy a hard stare, noting how he squirmed under the weight of it. The boy, like the others who served Sinow, had the spell of permission granted to him, yet he still kept his eyes on the ground.

Sinow leaned in closer to him and said, "You are wise to fear me, young man. Remember that as you get older. I am not someone you ever want to cross."

"Yes, my liege," the boy stuttered, then ran off toward the stables with the horse.

Sinow chuckled, knowing there was no reason to scare the kid, but the earlier in life he understood that fear, the more of an obedient citizen he would become when he aged.

Sinow brushed the dirt from his pants as he walked toward the castle. He had gone riding upon waking to clear his head but had spent the entire time thinking about Violissa. The calming spell she had woven had worn off quickly, so thinking about her was a struggle. He had clamped that unpredictable power down deep within him, but it had seethed, waiting for the right opportunity to overtake him. That opportunity came when Kanine shifted before him.

"My liege, I have urgent news." Sinow looked at his eldest Council. Dealing with the unhinged Darkness he was fighting to control had put Sinow on edge, and the last thing he wanted was urgent news.

"Can it wait until later today, Kanine? I've just returned from a ride and would prefer some peace before I'm hassled with matters of the realm."

"No, Sinow, it cannot wait. We've received a message from the Lightbearer Council. The queen has requested your presence at her castle at the day's high point. For some inexplicable reason, she has requested that I come as well."

Sinow scratched his chin, thinking the request an odd one. "Just the two of us and no other Council? And at her castle, on Cirillian ground rather than the meeting grove?"

"Yes, my liege. Strange as it sounds, that's what we were told."

Sinow stopped. The Dark power within him twisted and howled for escape as a thought came to him. "So Violissa thinks she can summon me now? As if I'm one of her Council? I don't like being summoned anywhere, do I, Kanine?"

Kanine eyed him questioningly but held his tongue.

"I don't want the queen to have the pleasure of thinking she can summon me at her command." He emphasized each word with a flex of his hand, black shadows slipping from them. "Are you in the middle of anything, Kanine?"

"No, nothing in particular."

"Then we are going to pay the queen a visit. Only we're going to do it on my terms and not hers. If the matter is that urgent, then it mustn't wait."

Kanine opened his mouth to argue, but clamped it shut when Sinow let a tendril of power seep around his neck.

"Let us see what the queen wants." He closed his eyes and reached his power out to sense Violissa. It seemed such a natural thing, the connection they had like a beacon that tied them. But a war raged within him when he touched her essence. Her aura emanated so strongly she could have been standing across from him rather than a realm away.

Sinow reached over and grabbed Kanine's arm, knowing Kanine couldn't travel into Cirillia as he could. He allowed himself to follow Violissa's power and shifted toward her. The Darkness rebelled at the prospect of being in her realm, but the anger it held at having been summoned by her kept him focused.

He shifted in with a fury, the floor beneath him buckling in protest. His eyes landed on Violissa just as she screamed. The ire fled with his ability to speak. She was standing in a water-filled tub, holding a long towel in front of most of her body. His arrival must have startled her, so the towel had nearly dropped because it only covered part of her, leaving the curve of her hips and thighs exposed. His eyes traveled the length of those curves, the smooth skin of her stomach, the flesh of her breasts that bulged from where she held the towel tight. There was a pounding sound that wouldn't stop until he realized it was his chest.

Kanine cleared his throat, waking Sinow from his trance. Sinow could only function enough to smack the man across his chest and say with a growl, "Kanine, turn now."

Kanine turned around, muttering, "Yes, my liege."

Sinow swallowed, trying to control the urge to rip the towel from her and devour every inch of her. Magical alarms were scorching his skin, his presence setting them off, but his focus remained on Violissa.

"Sinow, what is the meaning of this?" Her eyes forced his attention, and he saw the spark of power in their green. She made no attempt to cover more of herself, and the thought of her being so naked and so near made it difficult to form words. "Sinow?"

Brom shifted into the room, dragging his attention from her. "Violissa, is everything all—"

He stopped mid-word, his expression shifting from concern to horror upon seeing his queen in such a vulnerable state. Sinow chuckled as Brom averted his eyes quickly, and a pink hue colored his entire face.

"Yes, apparently the king misinterpreted my message," Violissa answered. Sinow noted a bit of playfulness in her tone. "I clearly said the day's peak, but he took it to mean immediately. Please take Kanine to Cyric so they can talk. The king and I have some things to discuss."

"Yes, my queen. Would you first like me to remove said king so that you may be more...decent for your discussion?" Brom continued to look at the floor while he addressed her. Violissa's eyes, however, never left Sinow's.

"No, that won't be necessary. I can take care of that myself, and I think it's just punishment for his assumption. Thank you, Brom."

Brom turned and looked with relief at Kanine, who still stood with his back to Violissa. "Kanine, shall we?"

"With pleasure, if you don't mind, my liege?"

"Go," Sinow said, holding Violissa's stare. Brom shifted, and Kanine followed, leaving them alone.

"I imagine you have good reason to come crashing into my tub room, Sinow? Judging from your entry, I don't think seeing me in such a state was your intention, so why is it you've assumed that this is appropriate?"

Her quip angered him. "The assumption was on your part, Violissa," he said, saying her full name even though the Darkness didn't have him in its grasp. "I do not take well to being summoned, especially by you." The power swelled slightly in him, and he knew his eyes had darkened another shade.

"Ha, this is about your pride? You don't get summoned?" She stepped from the tub, and his vision fell to her long legs and the inviting shape of her calves. He jerked his eyes away as she continued. "Sinow, you really think this is only about you? That I was making some power play? I asked you here to share urgent matters that will affect both of our realms, and you complain about how I asked you?" She threw up her hand, and as the towel shifted, the skin of her right breast slid free, more of her hip becoming visible with it. He took a step back and grabbed the chair behind him. Desire raged through him, only to be challenged by the fire within. He growled in reaction and glared at her.

With a smirk, she said, "Seriously, Sinow? You deserve to be flustered right now, and I'm thoroughly enjoying your reaction."

"Vi... Please put some clothes on and we'll talk. I may have made a mistake rushing here." He hated giving her the upper hand and admitting he'd been wrong, but he had to remove himself from the situation before he destroyed the entire room.

"Why hold back, Sinow? Maybe it's time to give into it. Maybe this is our opportunity." The green in her eyes turned to a lush hue, and he watched as she released the towel. It dropped soundlessly, but his eyes stayed riveted to her body. Every detail he remembered from the Dream Realm was there for him to see. And he took each one in, memorizing them again, just like he had each night in his dreams.

He closed the distance between them and threaded his fingers into her hair, pulling her head back and smashing his mouth into hers. His body came alive, the thrill of touching her again outweighing the Darkness that surged with the heat that scalded him. She gripped his shirt as his hands slid over her curves, touching her supple skin and relishing her deep inhale.

Her mouth was sweet and needy. Her skin possibly the softest thing he'd ever touched. She tore at his shirt, her breasts pressing to his chest, and he couldn't stop the momentum. There was no way to stop it as he backed her into the wall, lifting her leg and sliding his hand until she was groaning deliciously. Her hands were at the buttons of his pants while his ventured further, discovering her need for him was just as desperate and the sensation of it coursed through him. He dragged his lips down her throat, licking at the sweetness of her breasts, ready to claim her.

"Sinow."

He dragged his teeth over her nipple, prepared to devour her.

"Sinow?" he heard again, and this time, he stopped. The voice no longer held the passion it had, and he lifted his head to find her across the room, the towel still covering what his mind had subconsciously uncovered, what his mouth had dreamed of tasting. Ragged breaths scraped his throat. The chair behind him was so tight in his grip, the wood disintegrated as he released it. Violissa's cheeks were flushed, as if she'd caught every minute of his fantasy.

Dropping his eyes, he tried to calm himself, to understand what had come over him. His power flared at the weakness, scorching him and hardening him, but when he looked back up, he couldn't help but notice the hunger that sat in her eyes.

The crimson on her cheeks darkened. "Is that what you want?" she asked, her voice so soft it was like the touch of a feather to his skin. "We could, you know. There's nothing stopping us. Now would be the perfect chance to put it all aside and finally give in to those emotions, Sinow. To finally fulfill our destiny."

There was a hint of a plea in her voice, her way of admitting she was finally ready. Of telling him she wanted him to do what he had envisioned, wanted him to touch her as he had in the Dream Realm, to take her as his wife and his mate for eternity.

As much as he longed for those things, this time he was the one to turn away from them. He could no longer have her. If he took advantage of her offer and did the things he had fantasized, his Dark powers would tear through him. The storm raging inside him would overcome the hold he had on it, and he didn't think he could ever regain control again. There were too many consequences to that happening, and he wouldn't risk it.

"Put some clothes on, Violissa," he said, running a hand through his hair. It killed him to turn her down, but he was one step from losing his battle to the Darkness. Her expression changed, hurt passing through her eyes before they turned the color of the forest in the dead of night.

"Fine, if that's how you want it, then that's the way it will remain, and you can deal with your frustrations," she snapped, glaring at him.

She dropped her towel, throwing him completely off guard again. Reaching behind him for the chair, his fingers slipped through the air now that there was nothing left to grab. His chest constricted, need consuming him as his eyes perused what he so desperately wanted. But the moment passed as quickly as his racing pulse, and her magic draped a lilac gown over her curves. He exhaled, his muscles shaking from the tension within him.

Violissa shook her head, and the wet tangles that hung over her shoulders and down her back dried. Lush golden curls now cascaded down her body, stopping at her hips. She gracefully gathered her curls and piled them all atop her head, a few shorter wisps freeing themselves in the process and bouncing gently along her cheeks. Again, his heart rate quickened, the air in his lungs freezing as emotion stole his breath. She was the most alluring thing he'd ever seen, and every part of him ached for her.

She looked up at him, her eyes softening. "One day you'll tire of watching me do that."

His fingers relaxed, releasing the tight grip they had within the fists hidden behind his back. "I don't think I ever will, Vi." Her calming spell swept through him like a soft breeze, pushing back the Darkness until he returned to himself once again. He wasn't certain how she did that so easily. It almost seemed like an ability she reserved just for him.

She had opened the door and begun walking down the hallway it fed into when she glanced back at him and asked, "Are you joining me or do you plan to stand there gaping the rest of the day?"

Her tone was playful, and it skimmed through his ears like the wind on a summer day.

He tried to scowl, but his power was too at peace and her eyes were dancing too seductively. "Joining you," he replied. "Although I don't think I have a choice."

"Oh, you do. But I'd rather not leave you alone in my tub room with those fantasies of yours."

She threw him a coy grin before walking further. The Darkness in him shoved against the calm, but he pushed it back, shaking his head and following her. He kept enough distance to avoid disturbing his calm. If this seemed unusual to her, she made no mention of it, and he suspected she understood his reasons for it.

"Are we really walking there? Not shifting?" he asked as they walked the long corridor, the side of which was lined with floor to ceiling windows. The light cascaded in past their thick amber drapes, which looked as if they always remained open to the world outside. Sinow thought of the halls within his own home, dark and somber, with barely any windows. The distinction was startling.

"I don't like to shift unless necessary. I prefer to stretch my legs and view my surroundings," she admitted matter-of-factly.

They came to a long, winding staircase lined with a scarlet rug that sank with his steps. At the bottom of the staircase, Violissa turned left and continued down a wide hall. Sinow didn't have time to look around as he tried to keep up with her. She was walking more hastily now, like she didn't want to give him that luxury, and that made him deliberately slow his pace. Portraits lined the hall. Towering men with broad shoulders and auburn hair. Blue eyes that shone with power stared back at him.

"Vi, are these the Kings of Cirillia?" he asked, halting his steps and studying them. The Council had taught him about the more important Light Kings, the ones who had influenced his people's history, like Viliren, the king who ruled before Violissa. But never had he seen paintings of them. He had expected they would not bear any resemblance to her since she was the first in her line, but he thought he might see her green eyes or golden hair on at least one of them. Instead, they all had the auburn hair and piercing blue eyes he saw on her Council, the distinctive traits of all Cirillians.

"So, you truly are unique," he murmured.

Her sigh echoed in the hall's silence. "In every way," she replied before continuing her journey. He wondered at the sadness in her voice, but she distracted him, saying, "We need to keep moving. They are waiting for us."

The temptation to say they could have shifted and saved time crossed his mind, but he thought better of it. As they came to the end of the hall, it widened until it suddenly ended at a dark wooden doorway. Violissa opened the door and walked beyond into the darkness, waving her arm up to create a light sphere to light their way.

They followed the light down an old corridor. The ground crunched beneath Sinow's feet, and the air smelled of must. He wondered where it led, his curiosity driving him, but when they reached a dead end, his power clawed at his patience, leaving it tattered and one thread from unraveling. If this was some kind of game, Violissa would lose. He needed answers soon or there would be no stopping the Darkness from slaughtering his control and everything within reach.

CHAPTER 30

Violissa listened to Sinow's shallow breathing behind her, noticing his frustration increase. He was standing closer to her now that the corridor had narrowed, and her own breathing quickened in response. Her mind wandered briefly to the incident in her tub room, heat climbing in her cheeks. She wasn't sure how he'd unknowingly projected it to her, but it had stirred her blood, regardless. He wanted her, and she wanted him to act on it, just as he had in his mind. But he had shut her and his desires down. The act confirmed that her defiance of the prophecy had indeed cost her.

"I hate to state the obvious, but this is a dead end, Violissa." Sinow's voice cut through her thoughts like a sword through flesh, and she jerked her sight to him. The ebony of his power drifted around him like shadows feeding from the blackened corners of the corridor. "Is there a point to all this?"

She couldn't help but notice the venom in his tone, and she let another calming spell slip from her, hoping he wouldn't notice. The battle within him was one he fought constantly, and she carried the guilt, knowing her decision to delay their union was the cause. If she could turn back to that day, her decision would now differ, but even she did not have power over time.

"Yes, there is," she replied. "Be patient."

"I'm not a patient man," he grumbled.

He scratched his head and stretched his shoulders. The battle was tipping, and Violissa's time was running short.

Daneele, she called. *Let us through.*

She was certain she could have broken through the spell that hid this passage from sight, but her respect for tradition and Daneele's role as Keeper kept her from doing so.

The wall before her shimmered.

"Violissa," Sinow growled. That sound slinked over her skin and sent her pulse racing. But he had used her full name, and that added an unwelcome chill.

The wall disappeared to reveal the corridor, and Sinow swiveled his head to her.

"What is this?"

Pursing her lips, she said, "It's a corridor, Sinow. Now keep up."

He grabbed her arm as she was about to walk through, and Violissa noticed Daneele tense.

Go, Daneele, let me handle him.

Are you certain?

Sinow slammed her against the wall, stealing her breath, as Daneele's power surfaced along with her own.

Go.

He left them, but Violissa didn't let her sight leave Sinow's nearly pitch orbs.

"Where are you taking me?" he snarled.

"You need to trust me, Sinow. We can't very well be lovers if you don't trust me."

A shimmer of brown flashed in the ebony of his eyes, and he tipped his head, seeing too far into her soul with his steely gaze.

Her power flickered on the edge of release, and it sizzled in the air where it met his.

"We're not lovers, Vi." The nickname was back, but she remained alert, knowing one word or move could stir the Darkness. It clawed at her Light, the sensation disturbing.

"No…we're something else, aren't we?" And she didn't know what they were now. They could have been lovers, married and enjoying each other the way they had in the Dream Realm, like they both now craved, ruling side by side. But they weren't.

"What are we then?" he asked, his tone softer.

The grip on her arms loosened, and his hand drifted up her arm. His fingers skated over her neck, and he stepped closer. She let her head fall back as he towered over her, and she struggled to find the words to answer him. Maybe the Fate had been wrong. Maybe they just needed a moment like this, and they could return to the prophecy's path.

"Fated," she murmured, barely able to form the word.

Her lips parted, and he dropped his eyes to them, his thumb brushing her bottom lip. The heat coming from him was enough to scald her, the sparks of their power warring around them enough to bring the corridor down on them. Somewhere she registered stone cracking, rubble falling, but she could do no more than stare at Sinow. The change in him both fascinated and devastated her. Brown eyes succumbed to sable, the softness in his jawline overtaken by tightness, the caress to her lip becoming painful.

The air sizzled. The sharp stings of their warring magic pecked at her skin as he said, "You're wrong, Violissa. We are nothing more than enemies. That's all we ever were, and it's all we'll ever be."

Penetrating orbs of endless black returned to hers, and she inhaled so that it was as sharp as nails scraping her lungs.

"Why have you brought me here?" he said, stepping away from her.

She didn't know what to say and stared at him, still comprehending the sudden change. She wanted to go back to the moment before, when he had been so near that she could have pulled his face to hers and kissed him.

"There's something you need to see," she said, pulling herself together.

Power settling now that they were no longer as close, she glanced at the destruction of their moment. Stone had split, and there was now a crack in the wall behind where Sinow stood. In other sections, the stone had turned to rubble, which lay scattered at their feet. He was correct. They were enemies, but it was their magic that made them that way. The Fates had made them lovers, and now the two sides fought for dominance in a battle neither could win.

"Then show me before I bring this tunnel down on us."

With a sigh, she walked past him and through the doorway that shimmered with ancient magic. She followed the path, sensing him behind her, the silence a reminder of what could have been.

As they rounded the bend, she came upon Daneele. "Violissa, King Sinow," he said in greeting, creases lining his forehead as he looked between the two. "Cyric and Kanine are waiting for us at the doorway. Would it be wise to ask why the walls of a corridor that has stood for millennia now carry damage?"

"No, it would not," Sinow snarled. "What doorway?"

"You'll see momentarily." Daneele led them further.

"I don't appreciate this game and would like someone to tell me..." He trailed off as they came around the bend and to the doorway to the Hidden Realm. Shoving past her, Sinow went to the door and put his hand up to the engravings, tracing the writing with his fingertips.

"I know some of these words," he said, confusion in his tone. "This is ancient Cirillian mixed with, what? What is that?"

"That, Your Highness, is Elvin," Cyric responded.

Sinow snapped his attention to them. "No one speaks Elvin. No one since my grandfather's time. Not since..." He stopped, and Violissa could see him working it out.

Her skin still burned from his touch, and no matter that his mood had turned, her body was still reeling from the effects of it. His brow creased, and she couldn't help but think how beautiful he was, standing there like a Dark Fate. "Where does this door lead to, Violissa?" His eyes grew a deeper shade of ebony, and she could see he already he knew the answer he sought. Stepping toward her, his jaw clenched as tight as his fists, he said, "Where, Violissa?"

"I only just discovered this myself, Sinow," she said.

"I'll ask once more before I bring this corridor down around us. Where, Violissa?"

"To the Hidden Realm."

A tic of his jaw and a flare of anger that streaked across his face like lightning. Violissa weaved another calming spell, and his eyes narrowed when she released it. She saw the Darkness rebel, but the spell worked, and the earthy tone returned to his eyes. He looked as though he wanted to say something about it, but turned from her, studying the doorway. Her exhale clawed at her throat.

Hand resting on the doorway, he said, "All this time, and the doorway has been underneath your castle?"

"Yes," Daneele answered. "But we cannot enter the realm. The doorway has only opened for us once."

Sinow lowered his hand and turned to Daneele. No anger remained, only curiosity, and Violissa relaxed a little more.

"When?" he asked Daneele.

"The night of your birth."

Sinow's sight landed on Violissa as his brows furrowed. He scraped his hand through his hair, and she couldn't help but think it was a move she adored every time he did it.

"They created you in the Hidden Realm," he stated. "Why? What reason would require it?"

She didn't have an answer, but Daneele spoke for her.

"For reasons we cannot share," he stated flatly. Violissa watched Sinow bristle at the answer. "We don't control entrance to the realm, Your Highness. The magic from the spell that hid the realm from us created the doorway. It is a portal that grants entrance only when the Fates allow it. The night of your birth was one of those times."

"So why have you brought me here? It's clear no one intended this to be shared with me, so why bring me here at all?"

Violissa stepped closer to him, her power flaring in reaction.

"Because there is something wrong on the other side of that door, and we fear it could threaten both our realms." She gestured to the blackness at the corner of the door. Concern lined his features when he turned his attention to the corruption. He reached for it but drew his hand back quickly. His aura changed, ebony shadows spilling from him.

Violissa, this isn't a good sign, Cyric warned as Daneele's enaigne joined his to state the same concern.

Sinow's hands tightened, and anger morphed his features. She had expected him to react, but not in this way, and she took a step back, thinking of how he had threatened to bring down the corridor on them. The potential of that threat had never seemed so possible until now. And if he lost himself to the Darkness, the risk extended not just to her castle and those in it, but to her entire realm.

CHAPTER 31

Darkness threatened to drown Sinow, and every time he tried to gain control over it, that control evaded his attempts. Being this close to Violissa stirred it, but the calming spells he sensed drifting over his skin had helped until now. There had been a moment when they were alone where he had almost forgotten his struggle. Where all that existed was Violissa and the temptation to kiss her. He had been so close, his body one move from having her against it, but the Darkness had destroyed the possibility, tearing it to shreds he could no longer make whole.

Now, his power was rebelling again. The black consistency bordering the doorway had been like a charge that sent it roaring through him. He hadn't had time to even contemplate the idea that this was an entrance to the Lost Realm. The reaction had been too intense. It was almost innate, as if it were calling out to the Darkness within him. Whatever it was, there was no good reason for it to be anywhere near Violissa's castle, let alone a magical entrance to the lost capital of Cirillia. He wanted to reach up again and touch it, but instinct screamed for him to hold back.

Something about it drew his power out, like it wanted him to touch it, to let his magic merge with it.

He flexed his fingers, taking another step from the substance, and tried harnessing his power, but as always, it felt too good when the Darkness flowed through him.

"Why is this of any matter to me or my Council? It seems to me this is your problem, Violissa." He gritted his teeth at the brittle acidity of his voice.

"It matters more than you realize, Sinow," Kanine said, surprising him. He turned to face Kanine, who was the last person Sinow had expected to hear from. "If this is happening here, then it will happen in our realm as well."

"Our realm doesn't border the Lost Realm, Kanine. You know that." The anger swept through him again.

"He's right, Sinow," Cyric said, stepping forward. "Although I didn't realize you knew so much, Kanine."

"I know more than you can imagine, Cyric."

Cyric eyed him with curiosity, but Sinow didn't have the patience to stand and listen to their banter.

"Someone help me understand, because I fail to see how this impacts me," Sinow demanded.

From the corner of his eye, he caught Violissa shooting him an irritated look, then noticed the surrounding space had grown brighter, the more out of control he'd become. Light magic poured from Violissa in response to his powers. The same had happened when he had pinned her to the wall earlier. The memory spawned a need to have her that way again, and he ground his teeth to stay the emotion.

"Anything that impacts the Hidden Realm, or Lost Realm, as your people call it," Cyric explained, "impacts both Tenebron and Cirillia because of how the spell over the realm worked."

Sinow ran a hand through his hair in frustration. What in the Fates was the man talking about? Violissa stepped to the door, suddenly too close to him again. His chest tightened, her lilac essence filling it as his sight followed her hand. Her fingers traced the intricate engravings on the door. He had seen samples of Elvin writing in his studies, but the Elvin had never been allies with Tenebron, so their language remained a mystery to him and his Council.

"Is the boundary part of the Hidden Realm?" Violissa asked.

"In a way it is," Cyric answered. "After we hid the capital, we called forward the same magic that hid it and stretched it upward until it was a full boundary dividing our realms." That was a fact Sinow had never heard. "I believe that is why the two of you can travel so easily through the border."

"How so?" Violissa asked, but there was never an answer. Sinow had positioned his hand across from hers as he listened to Cyric, fascinated by the patterns on the door. A sharp stab made him draw his hand back quickly, Violissa doing the same as she let out a quick yelp. Two handprints, one black, the other cerulean blue, were now on the door. The colors bled into the engravings and began moving on opposite sides of the doorway, tracing the details.

"Our magic," Violissa mumbled as Sinow followed the movement of the colors.

No one spoke, and he imagined they were all watching the two flows of magic meet in the center of the door and crash into one another, merging in a beautiful shade of purple that cascaded over the door. A deep rumbling shook the corridor, and the doorway crumbled. Sinow stared at the essence of magic, a light purple mist that slowly evaporated.

"I thought you said this door never opened without the Fates," Sinow said.

"It looks like the Fates have decided that time has come once again," answered Daneele.

Violissa peered up at Sinow with eyes that sparkled with curiosity. "We shouldn't keep the Fates waiting."

The opening before them gave no sign of what lay beyond, but that didn't trouble Sinow. Nothing frightened a Dark King. He took the first step forward only to have a hand grip his arm and tug him back. His snarl broke the silence, and shades of red slashed his vision as he whipped his head toward the offender. Cyric was quick to remove his hand.

"The realm is sacred," Cyric explained, though the explanation did nothing to simmer Sinow's anger. "No Darkbearer has set foot on that soil since your grandfather's attack forced us to hide it. The Guardians will not look kindly to having your steps break their rest before Violissa's can."

"What Guardians?" he asked, his aggression still present and ready to pounce and crumble what remained of his patience.

"The Guardians of the Hidden Realm," Daneele said, as if this was common knowledge. Sinow searched his memory, but he had never heard of Guardians.

"I'll go first," Violissa said before he could question further. "It seems only right, since this is the place of my creation."

The dark world enveloped her before it brightened with her presence, almost like it had been waiting for her to wake it. He pushed Cyric aside and followed Violissa, aggravated that she had taken the lead. Light power barreled at him from every direction, and he shrugged the sensation away. His magic battered his hold on it, screeching to break free. He was in enemy territory, far worse than Violissa's castle. This was ancient land, and he noted the pulse of power that differed from the Light power in Cirillia.

A large room sat before him, one that led him to believe it may have been an indoor garden at one time. The walls had crumbled, but their essence remained like a ghost rising to surround the empty windows. Above him, the shell of a glass ceiling stood, the glass no more, shattered perhaps when the realm disappeared, then disintegrated into the sand that crunched below his feet.

Withered trees and plants, dead longer than he had lived, yet somehow even in death they seemed somewhat preserved, spread through the room. And in the center stood the foundation of a stone fountain, cracked and deteriorated. He could almost envision what it had looked like at one time, imagining it carved with detail and spewing shimmering green water that cascaded along every side. He blinked, and the vision was gone, replaced once again with the dilapidated, rotted scene.

"Why do I sense Darkness in my kingdom?" a voice boomed from nowhere yet everywhere. "Be gone. You have no place in my realm!"

Sinow grimaced, not caring for the insulting greeting.

"Not just Dark but Light," came a woman's voice, as gentle as a breeze in the warm season.

Turning his vision to where the voice had emerged, Sinow saw the shape of a woman shimmer in the air. She faded in and out, no color to her, only a mist-like consistency giving her definition.

"She is here...she has returned." The woman floated to where Violissa stood, bringing her hand to Violissa's cheek. "The Light child has come home," she said, as the figure of a man took shape next to her with the same misty appearance. Snapping her head toward Sinow, the woman disappeared, only to form again before him. Her sudden movement surprised him, but he didn't step back or reflect any emotion. He glared into her colorless eyes. "But she did not come alone. So much power. Never before...yet so untamed."

She reached toward Sinow, and he swatted his hand to keep her away.

"Why am I here?" he demanded, not wanting to deal with the shade and her unnerving statements.

"Because the Fates have deemed it so," the man said. The woman continued to hover before Sinow as her companion continued, "You are here because they so desire it. There is something they need you to see here. Otherwise, the doorway would not have allowed you entrance."

"The blackness," Cyric said, stepping forward.

"Cyric."

"My liege, Viliren," he returned as he bowed before the shade.

Sinow's eyes went wide as Violissa gasped.

"The last reigning king of Cirillia," Violissa said.

There could be no denying it, no matter how impossible it was. The king, who had returned his form to the Fates to protect the prophecy and the capital, now hovered before them. Sinow glanced at the female who had backed from him and floated next to the king. He didn't know who she was or why she was here with the king, but she must have been someone important.

Guardians. That's what Cyric had called them. The king and the female were Guardians of the Lost Realm, which led Sinow to believe this woman had been someone important to Cirillia and to the king. The queen, perhaps? He had never read of the king marrying, but the history was not complete, so it was possible. But queens were always mortal, so she couldn't be. Sinow scratched his head, trying to figure it out.

"Rise, Cyric. You bow to only one king now, and that is no longer me." His hand gestured toward Sinow.

The shade rushed forward, her hand resting on the king's arm with too familiar a touch. "No, he cannot bow to the Dark child yet. Remember? They have delayed what should have been, denied their hearts, ignored the prophecy's path."

Sinow had heard enough, and his power was resurfacing, clamoring within him against the vast amount of Light magic in the space. "Enough," he said. "Tell me something of importance. Why is it the Fates have brought us here?"

"There are things you need to hear," the woman said, reappearing before him. "But only the two of you. The Fates do not allow visitors to this realm anymore, even you, Keeper."

"We're here to protect," Daneele exclaimed, but Viliren interrupted.

"Protect? Whom? The most powerful Light queen and Dark king our world has ever seen? It's you who need protecting. Either of them could return your souls to the Fates, and you think they need protecting."

Sinow opened his mouth to question why he would say such a thing. Not even a king could kill another immortal and send their soul back to the Fates. But the king stopped him, saying, "Ah, but you have not gained that power yet, have you?" His faded eyes were penetrating, seeing into the deepest recesses of Sinow's soul. If he'd been the type of man who knew fear, Sinow would have buckled under the accusations weighted within that stare. The old king turned to Violissa. "The Fates protect us all if he ever does."

Sinow steadied himself, his mind turning the words over and struggling to find answers to the questions that were like a cacophony he couldn't quiet.

To Daneele, Cyric, and Kanene, the king said, "You are not welcome in this realm now. Only the chosen ones can seek entry. Now be gone." With the wave of his hand, the three disappeared from the room and the door reformed with a thunderous boom.

The Darkness reared its venomous fangs, and Sinow rubbed his forehead to silence it. He was about to protest, but the female's voice silenced him.

Have patience, Dark One.

"You can use enaigne?" he asked aloud.

"Sinow?" Violissa said, the look of concern in her eyes calming his ire. The urge to take her hand and support her through this gnawed at him, a warmth lancing his heart before the Darkness halted it.

There it is, the shade said to him. *Why do you deny it?*

"I don't know what you're talking about, but get out of my head and get to the point so I can get out of this forsaken place."

She took form too close to him and placed a hand on his chest before he could react. Pressure sat where her ephemeral hand was, and the sensation of warmth spread from her fingertips.

"Such Darkness. So much power," she said aloud. "More power than even your grandfather before you." Her voice filled his head again as she silently continued her flow of thoughts only to him. *So different from him, yet so alike. It's your heart that differs. It is what tames the Darkness.* She glanced at Violissa. *Two hearts, one soul. Listen to your emotions and accept your love for her.* Anger rose within him, and he could see that she sensed it, her hand momentarily pulling back. *Do not fight it, Dark child. You must learn to embrace your powers before they destroy you and everyone you love.* Her eyes fell to Violissa again on her last words, and he couldn't stop the slithering of unease that washed through him, like a predator seeking refuge.

"Why have you brought us here?" Violissa interrupted, and Sinow gave a sigh of relief as the shade moved from him. "What is it we need to know?"

"You need to know about the corruption," the old king said. "Someone has entered our realm and stolen from it. Someone uninvited."

"Someone with Dark power," the woman finished, wringing her fingers with worry.

His power flared at the accusation. "Tread carefully, shade," he growled, "for I do not take well to false accusations."

Violissa shot him a look just as a calming spell settled over him. Even though it simmered his rage, he narrowed his eyes, ready to complain about how she had assumed she could blast him with the damned spell once again. But she twisted to the female shade, her brow puckered and said, "A calming spell? How can you weave a calming spell if you have no power?"

So, the spell had not come from Violissa. That revelation made him consider once again who this woman had been.

"No powers?" the woman asked. Sinow studied her, knowing now she could not have been the queen. Mortals had no magic. So who had she been? "My dear child, you of all people should know that you carry your magic in your core, and not even death can strip that from you. Weaving is innate, and no matter what your state, it can still be done." The woman floated delicately up to

Violissa and laid her hand over her chest. "It is here that your true power lies. It is important that you never forget that."

Violissa tilted her head, and Sinow could see her trying to work out who this woman was, just as he was. Weaving was a word that came to mind any time Violissa's calming spell settled over his skin, and it was the word the shade had used, too. But weaving was not a word associated with the magic of the immortals. Only the Elvin had used the term because only they could truly weave a spell. Immortals wielded their magic differently. He remembered Tynan babbling about it when they were in lessons as children. His brother's fascination with the Elvin had bordered on irritating, and Sinow had been relieved when his father had separated their lessons.

His curiosity piqued, Sinow was about to ask her to elaborate when the king continued. Sinow couldn't help but think he'd done so deliberately.

"Dark blood has tainted our land, corrupting it, and that corruption is spreading into your realms."

Sinow bristled again at the accusation. "I can assure you no one from my realm has been here."

"Are you so sure, Dark One? Only someone with skills in magic could have done so."

"If my Council was looking for a way into this realm, let alone found one, I assure you I would know. Besides, you said yourself the Fates decide who enters and when."

"Rightfully so, for this entrance." The old king gestured to the now sealed doorway. "The magic that encased this land was powerful, but we all knew there would be weak spots. Tiny pockets exist which, if given just the right persuasion, might grant one access."

Sinow drew in his breath. He racked his brain. No one on his Council would go behind his back, and even if they did, he couldn't fathom why anyone would want to come to such a Fateforsaken place. "Who would do such a thing? Why bother? There's nothing here."

"Your Council is not the only one with power, Sinow," Violissa stated.

He laughed. "Are you referring to Tynan? Really, Violissa? He couldn't summon enough magic to scratch his arse, let alone find his way to the Lost Realm." As he spoke the words, doubt crept in. But Tynan didn't have the power to do something like this. Even if he did, there was no reason to venture here, nothing that held any value. Light power saturated the air and the land, and not even Tynan would want to deal with that invasion of his senses. As it stood, Sinow was barely sane from the sensation. It didn't add up, and he was about to say so when something occurred to him.

"Wait, you said someone stole from the realm. What was stolen?" The king's features flickered, but Sinow caught the distinct look of concern within them. Power burned for release, and Sinow clenched his fists. "What are you hiding?"

He looked at the female shade, whose emotions were clearer, shifting from worry to sadness. But the king spoke, drawing his attention back. "It is of no concern to you now, Dark child. The only thing that matters is that it be returned."

"How can I return something when I don't know what it is?" he snapped. "I don't play games, and that's what this seems like. You want us to deal with this mess, this black corruption that started here in a realm you were supposed to be guarding, yet you won't tell us what you hid here before you cut this realm off from the rest of the world? Either tell me what you have lost or I'm leaving."

As a bear lifts onto its haunches, ready to strike, the shade king stretched his form, towering over them. "Do not presume to order me around, boy."

"Do not presume that I will stay here any longer, old man," he raged back, the Darkness rising within him.

"Sinow—" Violissa started.

"No, Violissa. This blackness and this realm have nothing to do with me or Tenebron. I am leaving." He turned and stormed to the doorway, hoping the Fates would reopen it before he reached it.

"Fool!" The shade's voice boomed. "This has as much to do with your realm as it does with Cirillia." A force pushed against Sinow as though the king's very voice was power.

Sinow whipped around, black tendrils spilling from his fingertips as the power tore through him. Anger scorched his veins as the Darkness took over, coursing through him like unhinged flames. He was not about to let a mere shade attempt to overpower him.

His hand raised to show the old king his true power when Violissa yelled, "Enough!" and a blasted calming spell hit him from two directions, suffocating him and smothering the Darkness.

He roared, arching his back as his power fought the violation. He bent over, his body at the mercy of the internal battle, gripping his hands on his knees. Clambering for freedom, the controlling part of him encompassed the fire, dousing the flames and burying the vicious side of him. A ragged inhale scraped down his throat, and he straightened his body. Hating the display of weakness, he averted his gaze from Violissa. She had used another calming spell, she and the female shade.

He glared at the king, who had crossed his arms and was giving him a smug look. Violissa placed a hand on Sinow's, and he jerked back, not realizing she was so close to him. He met her eyes, finding concern and understanding but no pity, like he had feared he would.

"Vi," he said, the need to give her an explanation strong.

Shh, she called to him, her emerald orbs sparkling in the room's shadows. The calm sank deeper, and he wanted to lean into her touch, to bring his hands to her face and draw her lips to his. To have this dance between them end and finally have her. The Darkness stirred, and as if she sensed it, she gave him a soft smile. *Let's hear what they have to say.*

He nodded, his sight falling to the shape of her mouth that he longed to trace. For a moment, they remained there, her hand on his skin, their eyes locked, the chambers of his chest hammering. But the moment passed, and she dropped her hand, a sadness dimming her eyes.

"Please continue," she directed her words toward the king and a hollow sensation passed through Sinow at the loss of her attention and her touch.

"Dark blood has corrupted this land, and the blackness spreads. It will continue to seep through the magic that borders this realm and into both your realms."

"My realm does not border the Lost Realm," Sinow stated, his frustration mounting again. He'd thought he had made it clear this was not his issue, but here they were again discussing the same thing.

"Do you know how we hid the capital, Dark child?" the female shade asked quietly.

We. She had said we, and that piqued Sinow's curiosity further.

"The spell hid it from sight," Violissa answered for him. "Sinow is correct; only Cirillia surrounds the Hidden Realm. The boundary created is the defining line between my land and Sinow's."

"Not so, Light child," the shade continued. "The land surrounding the capital was vast and included the Elvin realm and Cirillian land that we considered sacred. I believe you now refer to it as the Sacred Groves." And more questions mounted in Sinow's mind. He had thought the groves to be considered sacred only because of the war. "All of which was encompassed within the spell. The border erected by the Council came from the same magic we used to hide the realm. It was extremely powerful, and they expanded the boundary along the dividing line of Tenebron and what remained of Cirillia."

"Then we are correct," Sinow began before the king cut him off.

"No, you are not. You think a shield of magic surrounds this realm and keeps it from sight, don't you? If that were the case, how could you see through to each other's realm?"

Sinow glanced at Violissa, who was now chewing her bottom lip as she tried to figure out what the shades were trying to tell them. He was growing tired of this game. "Enough riddles, get to the point," he said, awaiting the shade's response.

But it was Violissa who answered. "It couldn't be a dome as we've always thought." Her eyes widened as if the answer had come to her. He was too busy battling the irritation that threatened to break the hold the calming spell had on him.

"The spell didn't cover the realm. It collapsed it," she stated, pursing her lips as she pondered her realization. Her words tumbled through his head as he tried to imagine the power required to fold land into itself but leave everything intact, as if it were in its own unique space. "All this time," Violissa continued, "we thought the spell hid the realm from view when, in reality, it moved the realm into a pocket of space."

"Yes. The spell folded the surrounding land into itself and moved it into its own world, so to speak," the king explained. "That is why you should both be concerned about the blight that is slowly leaking from this realm."

Sinow spoke up this time. "You said your Council created the border between our lands from the lingering spell that hid this realm. When you hid the realm, it re-created Cirillia, moving the lands that bordered the capital so that they now bordered Tenebron."

The female shade nodded, the king speaking, "As the blackness bleeds from our land, so it spreads through that boundary and into both your realms. The magic of the spell surrounding this land is acting as a barrier, but that barrier is breaking down."

Now it all became clear. This was no longer only a problem for Violissa. It was much bigger. "So, if the blackness is seeping from here, it will seep into both our realms. I see why we might be concerned. Will it overtake everything?"

The king shook his head. "No, it is simply a gateway."

"A gateway? To what?" Violissa asked, her voice rising a pitch.

"To Darkness."

"That's not a bad thing," Sinow said. "I welcome more Darkness."

The female cocked her head, and the sensation that she was seeing far into him passed through him. "Do you, Dark child? Do you really? Has more Darkness been good for you?"

Violissa stopped his reply. "What will that do?"

"The Fates created our world with the balance of Light and Dark. What was taken from this land has shifted the balance, but the corruption it unleashed will distort that balance further. If not stopped, it will eventually mean the end of our world. Dark cannot be without Light, and Light cannot be without Dark, the two sides are intertwined. The two of you are the embodiment of that idea. If you do not stop the corruption, you will lose everything."

"Then how do we stop it?" Sinow's head was hurting, and he had little power left in him to contain his frustration.

"You cannot stop it."

"What? Then why bring us here? Why all this talk if there is no answer?"

"Because you need to know."

Sinow lost his patience. The thought that he'd wasted all this time and energy just to find there was no answer drove him over the edge. "No, I don't. I couldn't care less if more Dark power enters this world, especially after being stuck in this Light pit with all of you for so long. This has been a waste of my time, and I'm leaving now." As he turned to walk away, the doorway shimmered before him. Even the Fates recognized there was no changing his mind this time.

"Sinow—"

"I'm done, Violissa. I would drop it now, or I'll let this whole place experience the power I've been holding back." He didn't bother to pause his strides or look at her as he spoke. But something stopped him.

It will happen, Dark child. The female's voice invaded his mind. *There will finally be a time when you both know the true gift the Fates have given you.* Images burned through his head as she spoke. He saw Violissa smiling up at him before kissing him. Saw her laughing, the sunlight shimmering in her golden hair, her eyes brilliant jewels that took his breath away. Saw her looking down at something in her arms before looking up at him with emotion that stopped his heart. In her arms, the tiny hands of a babe reached up to him, power pulsing from them. The image shifted once more, and Violissa was sitting beside him, her hand upon his as they watched a young black-haired boy run, giggling through a field. Power streamed from his hands as he ran, creating a rainbow effect. He turned toward them and waved, his emerald eyes gleaming with joy.

The images faded, and the air he'd been holding fled his lungs. Mind a jagged mess of thoughts and emotion, body a flood of Darkness that threatened to submerge him, he did the only thing he knew to do. He composed himself, glared back at the shade, and stormed from the room. His insides were in torment, part of him excited by the prospect, and part of him writhing in anger at the invasion of the images in his mind and what they signaled.

Hands clenched in tight fists, he didn't dare look at Violissa, too worried he would lose the brittle piece of control he still had. And too worried that the consequences of losing that control would be more devastating than the realization that the visions he had seen were of a future that no longer existed.

CHAPTER 32

A war was raging in Sinow, and it hurt Violissa to see him in such turmoil. There was nothing she could do to help him. Anything she tried would only worsen the situation. He paused briefly just before the doorway, and she wondered what was going through his mind to make him do so. The quick glare he shot at the female shade was enough to inform her that the shade had said something to cause his hesitation. Something Sinow had not liked, or at least his Dark side had not.

She turned back to the shade king and bowed. "I believe our time is up. Thank you for allowing us entry into your realm and for sharing your concerns."

He gave her a gracious bow in return. *Violissa,* the king spoke in her head. *The blackness that seeps from this realm is more than it seems. Do not let your guard down for even an instant. Only through your combined powers can you hope to fight it.*

Why didn't you say this while Sinow was here?

I don't trust him yet. The Darkness runs deeper in him than in any who ruled before him, even his grandfather, and he has not learned to balance his powers.

"But the Fates trust him," she said aloud.

"Do they? There is a reason the Fates wanted the union before his ascension. You know that. There is so much conflict within him he doesn't even trust himself," the female said, her form flickering in and out. "Why do you think he keeps his distance from you? He knows the prophecy and understands full well that being with you will bring him inner peace. He doesn't trust the Darkness running through him enough to allow himself to do such a thing."

"Enough," said the king, quieting her. "Remember, Violissa, only with both your powers can you hope to fight this blight on our lands."

"Both powers," Violissa repeated. "How..." She stopped, glancing back at the doorway through which Sinow had walked, the answer coming to her. She and Sinow would need to join forces to combat this. "Of course. Thank you both. Thank you for all that you've done."

Gathering her skirts, she rushed after Sinow. The faint call of her name followed her, but the doorway sealed too quickly behind her to heed it. She re-entered the hallway just in time to catch Sinow stepping beyond the corridor, their three Council behind him.

"Sinow, please wait!" she called.

He stopped, lowering his head as he did. "I thought I made it clear I was finished here, Violissa," he responded, his back to her.

"We are, but I need to ask one last thing before you go." He turned, his eyes black as a moonless night. "Daneele, Cyric, please escort Kanine out." Daneele looked like he wanted to object but stopped and bowed, clearly seeing there would be no arguing the point with her. Cyric followed with Kanine.

Sinow crossed his arms once they passed. "You do not speak for me, Violissa, and I did not release Kanine."

She huffed, having no energy left to argue about the petty comment.

"Call him back and then send him away if you must, but I need to speak with you alone."

His jaw went rigid, the muscles in his arms twitching. "This had better be important, Vi. My temperament is currently unstable, and I'm having an exceedingly difficult time keeping my powers at bay. Make it quick." He ran his hand through his hair, and she caught the momentary closing of his eyes as he tried to deal with the internal battle. If he lost control of his powers, the consequences would be dire to any mortal on the grounds above them.

Maintaining her distance to cause him no further torment, she started, "We need to work together."

His laugh was vicious. "This again. I thought I made it clear there would be no more talk of this. Now let me out of here, Violissa."

"Hear me out, Sinow. The ascension was hard on both of us… well, mainly hard on you," she corrected as he raised his eyebrow. "We still have the prophecy hanging over our heads, and at some point, we need to deal with it. It's not a question of if; it's a question of when, and I think we both realize that."

"Do we?"

"Yes, we do. There will come a time when we must fulfill it, but we need to first give *us* a chance." The right words kept eluding her, and she wanted to kick herself for sounding incoherent.

"You had your chance the day we met, and I distinctly remember you turning me down." There was an acidic edge to his voice that stung her, but she was tired of assuaging his Dark side.

Hands on her hips, she snapped, "And I distinctly remember you telling me you would be patient and wait for me."

His lips pressed together, his facial features became so tight she thought he might break a bone. Silence filled the space, and she waited for him to erupt. But the tension faded, his features softening.

"What are you asking, Vi?" She noted the change in his tone and the return of her nickname.

"That we should meet regularly. Ever since the ascension, we've avoided each other and have had our Councils hold the treaty meetings. We should take over those meetings and conduct them without our Councils."

"And what would that accomplish aside from completely torturing us both?" he asked, giving her a coy grin. Her heart raced, warmth filling her cheeks at the insinuation of his words.

She smiled. "It would bring us closer to each other. Maybe acclimate our powers so we could stand to be near one another." Her chest held a heaviness in it, the air passing through her lungs in tiny inhales.

"What did the old king say to you back there, Vi?" Startled at the change in subject, her head went back. "You were in there longer than a normal goodbye would take. Did he say something to spur this new idea of yours?"

"What did the female say to you?" she asked, not liking how he was suddenly grilling her.

Eyes narrowing, he said, "I asked you a question to receive an answer, not another question."

She wanted to argue, to tell him if he needed answers, so did she, but she let it go. Whatever it was, he wouldn't share it, and that made her wonder again what the shade had said. Maybe he would tell her one day. When they were through being enemies who craved being lovers, when the Darkness no longer ruled him.

With a sigh, she told him the truth, knowing he would read a lie and walk away from the possibility of a future together.

"He told me it would take both our powers to defeat the corruption. It seemed like a good excuse to see you more often." She winced at the desperation in her voice and saw from his expression that she'd given away too much. She groaned inwardly, not knowing where to go from there and waiting for him to cut her with his words.

But he did something unexpected. He smiled. It was beautiful and frightening at once, and she had to force herself to breathe.

"At the rise of the next full northern moon, I'll be at the meeting ground. Now let me out before I change my mind, and I bring this tunnel down on us." He held her gaze longer this time, causing the heat to rise in her cheeks before he turned and walked toward the barrier that separated them from the others.

She waved her hand, and the barrier disappeared. Walking through, he grabbed Kanine by the shoulder and shifted.

A dull ache filled her chest, a strange sense of loss accompanying it. So much had happened, and she knew it would take time to process it all. Eyes turning toward the doorway to the Hidden Realm, she surveyed the black substance that still lingered around the edges. It hadn't moved in the time they had been in the Hidden Realm, but she wondered how long it would be before it spread and infected more than just this part of their world.

"Violissa?" Daneele had leaned through the opening that still stood where she'd let Sinow leave. "How did you let him out?"

"With the wave of my hand. Why?"

He squinted at her, and she could see him thinking it through. "I thought only Keepers had the power to do that. Did you know you could do that on the way in?"

"I did. I didn't want to hurt your feelings." She smiled innocently and walked past him. "I think I'll take a walk now. I need some time to think."

With that, she shifted to the lawn of her castle and wandered, her mind milling over all she had seen and learned and her heart pattering swiftly at the thought of seeing Sinow at the rise of the northern moon.

CHAPTER 33

The rich lilac skirt Violissa wore spread around her as she sat in the middle of the meeting grove. Face tipped toward the sky, body resting back on her hands, the full sun above shimmered on her skin, giving her the appearance of one of the Fates. Golden tendrils of hair swayed in the breeze, the brightness of the sun reflecting within them, creating a look of stardust upon them. She was breathtaking, and Sinow didn't dare disturb the moment, so he silently watched her, taking in each beautiful inch of her.

She tilted her head back down and gazed across at him. He noted the skip in the beat of her heart as her breath caught for just that brief instant, as it did each time their eyes met. She smiled at him, the sun sparkling in her emerald eyes.

"Are you purposely trying to sneak up on me, Sinow? You should know by now that I can sense you shifting in."

"Ah, I'd forgotten that slight point, Vi. I was simply taking a moment to enjoy the scenery." The calm he experienced each time they met swept through him. It would last almost until their next meeting and had helped him keep the full extent of his inner turmoil at bay. He still wasn't sure how she managed it, but regardless, he didn't question it.

The urge to move closer to her, to be by her side rather than so far removed from her, tore through him. He quickly pulled himself together as a brief surge of power ran down his arms and into his hands, threatening to destroy the calm she'd given him. Time away from her, as well as being too close to her, were the only things that disrupted whatever spell she placed on him.

The years following their ascensions had advanced rapidly, but to Sinow, it seemed as if only a few moons had passed. He and Violissa met formally four times a year when both moons were at their peak in harmony, discussing matters of the realms and talking of their lives. His time with Violissa was short, but he looked forward to it with an eagerness unlike any other.

Although their relationship had grown, neither moved to make more of it, nor to even ask for more time together. He knew they both wanted to, but neither knew how. It seemed a curse to have so much power yet to be so powerless. The Darkness sat coiled and ready to strike whenever he drew too near her, and even her powers seemed unstable now, as if they sensed the need to defend her. So, distances remained in place, neither testing if they could surmount the destructive need for their powers to obliterate each other.

The result was a constant frustrated state and sexual tension that pierced the air. The habitual distance became second nature to them, no matter how Sinow hated it.

"Sinow?" The enchanting sound of Violissa's voice broke his thoughts and brought him back.

"Forgive me, Vi. My mind wandered."

She gave him a sly smile, and his pulse raced. "Hopefully, nothing that would make me blush," she teased, her eyes shimmering with playfulness. "Sit and relax. The day is fully here, and the sun is shining its blessings upon us." She patted the ground, even though he couldn't possibly sit next to her like he wanted.

"That's not something that would invite a Darkbearer to sit, especially not their king. What is it with you and your nature gifts? I'll never quite understand the connection." He sat at a suitable distance from her. Each time they met, he tried to be closer to her, but so far had only removed about a foot of what seemed like miles. In reality, only about ten feet stood between them, but to Sinow, it was an enormous gulf that symbolized the hurdles they had to pass before they could even consider thoughts of a union.

"Have you any news from your realm?" Violissa asked.

He was tired of discussing realm business when he met with her. It was the time that followed, when she shared her secrets and her smiles, when he learned of her childhood and the small things that endeared her to him further, that he wanted this day.

"Right to business, Vi? Will you never allow yourself to simply leave business aside and spend the entire time discussing other things?"

"Such as?"

Raking his hand through his hair, he rose, pacing to ease his frustration with the situation. She was trying to turn the conversation back to his lead, but he wanted her to confess that the emotions stirring in him were ones that plagued her as well. To say that she wanted to test the distance, to fight their powers, to regain the proximity they'd had before the ascension.

"You know damn well the things to which I refer."

"We've been through it before, Sinow. We can't even bear to get close to one another, so how can we dare to discuss anything further until we accomplish that feat?" She stood, glancing over her back as she brushed her skirts off. He took in the curves of her profile, the softness of her chin, the delicate cheeks upon which now sat a light blush. The blush deepened as she met his eyes once more. "What would you have me say? That I welcome you to my bed when I know the risks that would bring?"

He stepped toward her, stopping when the scorch of his power rose once more. It was still a mystery to him how he could overcome the internal response at certain times, like when she had healed the ancient groves. Yet that ability continued to elude him most times, even with the calm that washed through him with her presence. He thought perhaps it had been an impulse or an emotional reaction that had given him the ability, but no matter how he tried, he could not replicate it.

A curse came from him as she gave him a knowing look that told him he had just proven her point.

Needing to take back control of the conversation, he said, "So, you would welcome me into your bed now, Vi? How quickly your feelings have changed."

Her lips parted, a quiet exhale fleeing them.

"They have, haven't they?" He dared to take another small step closer.

She turned from him and walked away, lengthening the distance between them.

"Vi, don't walk away from the truth. You can't run every time the subject of our union hits too close to home. You are no longer the innocent queen in waiting who could get away with playing games with me and your Council." He'd gotten to her. She turned and stalked back toward him. The closer she came, the more his power spiked through him like daggers shredding his insides, and the more her eyes showed the struggle within her to control her own powers. She stopped about a foot in front of him, the closest they'd been able to get since that day in her castle.

The strain of keeping her power contained was showing, her teeth clenched, her hands, glowing a brilliant greenish blue hue, balled into fists. Arcane snapped from her in sparks of blue and white, tingling against his skin and stirring his power to rebel against his hold on it. If either released their control, the result could inflict serious damage. Flames ran through his fingertips at the thought of the fight, and he sensed his aura darken, a haze of black beginning to shroud him.

"You are brave, Sinow, to challenge me with such words." Her voice, although holding strength, quivered as she continued, "I am not running away. I don't know what to do now. Can I deny that we've grown closer? No, can you? Can you stand there and tell me thoughts of the union have not crossed your mind again?"

He smiled against the angst of his magic, saying through gritted teeth, "No, I cannot. Nor can I deny that thoughts of you in my bed have ever left my mind."

He relished the blush that returned as she chewed her bottom lip. She tipped her head down and drew a deep breath before meeting his eyes again. The sight softened him, his power settling some.

"Sinow," she murmured. "It cannot yet be. Don't you remember telling me the same thing that day in my tub room? Or do you forget what you gave up that day, telling me the same thing I am telling you now? You were right. The forces within us are too strong, and yours are too unpredictable. Someday it will happen, but not until this..." She brought her hand before her and opened it. The arcane within rose in her palm, and he could see it seeking an escape from the shield she had created around it. "Not until this has dissipated can we be together, and I just don't see how to overcome it at this point."

He moved to grab her hand, but the power upon which he'd had such a tight rein seized its opportunity and burst forward as Violissa lost control of hers in the same instant. The two met with a thunderous roar and sent him flying backwards. Trees crashed, ground severed, and Sinow came to a stop far from Violissa, who sat in a pile of debris. He rubbed his head and stood, brushing himself off.

"See?" Violissa yelled from across the grove. She was pushing herself up from the ground where she'd landed, wiping the dirt and bark from her skirts. "Even if we were to admit our feelings, nothing could come of it."

She looked up suddenly, as if realizing, just as he had, the meaning in her words. He wondered if she felt for him as deeply as he did for her. The emotions he held for her had changed over time, so that lust was no longer the motivator. There was more there, something in his chest that sat like a weight he could not escape. A part of him recognized it had always been there. But no matter how he wanted to admit or act on it, the Darkness kept him from it.

He brought his hands to his head in frustration, knowing she was right. They still needed time. The rage tearing through him was evidence enough of that. A calming spell cascaded over his skin, and he closed his eyes, relishing its touch and releasing a long sigh.

"I believe we've had enough for the day, Sinow," Violissa mumbled, repairing a rip on the side of her dress.

He rolled the tension from his neck and moved toward her, leaving a safe distance between them. Her eyes gleamed, and he wondered if the brightness of the sun had caused their glossiness or if it was something more.

"Once, long ago, we stood in this very spot, Vi, and I told you I'd wait for you. Even though the tides have turned, and both of us need to work things out, I'm still waiting. I do believe I will always be waiting." It was a moment of tenderness admitted in the stillness of his inner chaos.

A smile, sad yet lovely, touched her features. "No, not always, Sinow." She looked off toward the sky for a moment, her chest rising with a deep inhale. "One day it will all come together, and our patience will pay off. The Fates have their reasons for delaying things, and I have faith they'll reward us soon."

He lost himself in her eyes and the lilac in the air before he composed himself and spoke the two words he dreaded every time they met. "Goodbye, Vi."

CHAPTER 34

Violissa focused her thoughts on Sinow again, trying to quell the power that had surged when she last conjured an image of him in her mind. The emotions that flowed like an undercurrent below her magic caused conflicting sensations. Dampening the rise of magic, she concentrated on the emotions instead: the swell in her heart, the rushing of blood, the rightness that sat in her belly. As those sensations grew, her power dimmed until it was just a buzz below the rest.

With a relieved sigh, she sat back, knowing these exercises, although taxing, were necessary. She hoped that by doing this, she would eventually conquer the instinctive rebellion of her power whenever she was with Sinow.

Standing, she stretched, realizing she had been sitting for too long, letting time slip by with her focus. Awareness of something out of place tugged at her, and she froze, arms still stretched above her head. Tilting her head slightly, she tried to determine what it was. The tugging reached her core, a violent stab that made her double over just as the room shook.

The land. That's what she was sensing, a disturbance in the land. She shifted to the back lawn and dropped her hands to the ground to detect the issue. The ground rippled, the land bellowing in response, and she jerked her hands back.

As she sought to determine the source of the disturbance, an angry roar split the air. It hadn't come from nearby, so she sent her magic out to find it. Knowing Brom was in the outer courtyard, she called to him.

Brom, did you hear that?

Yes, I was just coming for you.

I'm going to find out what it is. Alert the Council that I may need them.

Yes, my queen.

Honing her powers to the sound, she shifted, landing on the western side of her realm, not too far from the boundary. Her feet sank into the same dark substance she'd seen on the border near the Sacred Groves and on the walls below her castle. After the warning from the Guardians, she and her Council monitored the black substance, but the spread had been so slow their concern had diminished. She kneeled, letting her fingers slide through it. Not only was it oily and thick, but it emitted an aura of Dark magic.

A cry stuck in her throat as she spotted the source of the deafening sound in her periphery. There had never existed a creature as hideous as what she spied bearing down on the village. It was massive, casting a shadow over her even from the distance. Another roar rent the air, and she stood, craning her neck to figure out what it had in its hand.

"Fates," she cried, realizing its grasp was around a mortal who was thrashing violently. Her hand flew to her mouth to stifle the bile that rose in her throat.

Daneele broke her traumatized stare as he moved beside her. She hadn't realized her Council had arrived.

"I told you to wait for my call," she mumbled, unable to take her eyes from the sight.

"We disobeyed. You can lecture us later because I'm certain you're going to need our help," Brom said from behind her.

Daneele looked at her with wide eyes and asked, "What is that thing?"

"I don't know, but we need to get it away from that village."

Ripping her attention from the vision of horror before them, she glanced around for a solution. They were close to the western border where her realm met Tenebron, so they had little area to work with before the boundary cornered them. It didn't matter; they had to distract the beast and draw its attention from the village and the mortals.

"We need to get it away from the people. I'm going to distract it and try to move it back some. Once I do, Brom and Daneele get the people to safety," she commanded. "The rest of you wait for my signal to attack."

Shifting, she landed in front of the beast. It stood at least twenty feet tall and was broader than the house it had just destroyed. Skin, blackish-green, covered its body, and a foul odor that caused Violissa's nose to crinkle came from it. Two enormous black eyes stared down at her. She tried not to look away, but the sight of it horrified her. When it opened its mouth and roared at her, spewing flecks of blood and an oily consistency, her stomach turned violently. Its teeth were each the size of her body, and it had no nose, only a flat section with gills that flapped with each breath it took.

It was something from a nightmare, and she would have backed away if the mortal in its hands hadn't still been struggling for freedom and a town of mortals hadn't been running scared behind her.

The beast reached for her, and she summoned the roots below it to climb and tangle around its legs, throwing it off balance. It teetered, dropping the mortal, and Violissa let out a relieved sigh when magic encased the man and brought him safely to the ground. The beast tore free of the vines before she could bring it down, and Violissa threw her power at it, forcing it to step back. She continued doing this, shifting in front of it, blasting it, then repeating until its body slammed into the boundary. It shimmered, sending a vibration through the air that rattled her bones.

Before she could cast the next spell, the beast's paw careened into her and sent her flying. She shifted mid-air, calling for her Council to attack as she landed back in front of the beast. The Council's magic barraged the creature, and it roared, waving its arms around. She braced for another impact, but instead of hitting her again, Violissa watched in horror as five smaller versions of the creatures burst forth from its arms. They scurried toward her Council, who continued to throw their magic out. She didn't have time to comprehend what had happened as the beast turned on her. They could no longer help. Their attention was now on the smaller creatures, leaving Violissa alone with the monstrosity that had given birth to them.

CHAPTER 35

Sinow's head was pounding. The calming spell Violissa had placed on him during their last meeting had worn off faster than usual, and the Darkness had surged back in response to being kept at bay for so long. Release was necessary before it threatened to overwhelm him, but he had yet to think of a satisfying way to release it. He was contemplating heading to the dungeons to torture the prisoners when the air rippled. A massive thud echoed through the keep, following the reverberation. He turned his head toward the eastern boundary, sensing the disturbance had come from that direction. Calling out to the Council nearest the keep, he commanded them to report to the area of impact and shifted.

Keary was the first to arrive. "Can you see anything through the boundary shield, Sinow?"

Since the ascension, he'd been able to see through it right into Violissa's realm. The magic of the border caused a slight misting of things on the other side of it, but he could still make out Violissa through it. His heart raced, and the power within bucked again until he realized she was fighting something the likes of which he had never seen. The thing towered over her as she fended it off.

Around her, Council fought creatures who were smaller yet just as disturbing and lethal. She was holding her own, but even with all her powers, she still appeared taxed.

His rage flared as the creature grabbed her, throwing her straight toward the boundary. Her body flew right through it, and she landed just feet from where Sinow stood. She looked up, her eyes growing large upon seeing him, and the skip of her heartbeat didn't go unnoticed by him.

"Sinow?"

There was no time for her to say more, nor was there time for him to respond. The creature tore through the boundary, and flashes of warped magic from the invasion stroked the air. Its massive, black and slimy hand grabbed her leg and dragged her back through. The boundary healed itself immediately. The sequence of events happened so quickly he knew she hadn't had time to shift away from the beast.

Sinow shifted to follow her, not bothering to even look back at Keary. The noise of the battle assaulted his ears. He shifted closer to the creature, catching Violissa's attention. She looked curiously at him and opened her mouth to yell something when the creature's hand slammed into her and sent her careening across a field of downed trees.

"Violissa!" he yelled out of instinct. Nothing could harm her, but still the rage exploded, currents of power eviscerating the control he'd had on it. Drawing on that anger and power, he poured it into the beast, which roared and swayed at the impact. Sinow took the moment of weakness and went in for a second round, shifting to its other side. Ebony tendrils of magic swirled around him, and he sent another blast of it at the beast. But the creature didn't respond this time.

"Sinow! Stop!" Violissa yelled as he blasted the thing repeatedly with a mix of fire and Dark magic that swirled in a red and black haze around it.

Sinow! she screamed in his head. *Stop, it's feeding off your Dark magic!*

Sinow paused and stepped back to look at the creature. His chest seized. She was right. It had grown and was getting bigger.

No, this can't be, he thought as he backed further from it.

Violissa ran to his side, and this time, his power didn't rebel. The sight of the creature straightening and now towering at twice its size had him too transfixed.

"You can't fight it," she said, "but you can restrain it for me. I want to try something."

He tore his eyes from it and glanced at her.

"Whatever I can do to help," he replied, thinking he needed to rectify the damage he'd just caused.

He shifted to the creature's backside and sent his powers out to grab hold of it. Long, thick black tendrils of magic encased its head and arms, wrapping around its torso. Sinow pulled back his power to tighten the binding. He struggled as the use of his magic to such a degree allowed the Darkness within him to creep further out. That part of him looked around at the chaos and destruction the creature had caused and relished it. He instinctively wanted to release the thing and watch it wreak havoc. Here he was in Cirillia with a creature even Violissa couldn't seem to defeat. Why was he helping?

Because it's attacking my fated, his mind answered, a sudden possessive protectiveness crawling from below the Darkness.

He focused his attention on Violissa, ignoring the rebelling Darkness, and watched her blast the beast with a massive bolt of Light magic. Blue streams of arcane flared from her hands, and the beast howled in anger. They engulfed the thing as a mist of green spread through them. That green mist was what Sinow had seen in the Sacred Groves the day she had healed the trees. Nature magic.

The beast howled, showing signs of weakness, and Sinow reined the bindings in tighter as it fought to break free. Weakening, the beast let out a screech that shattered his ears before it exploded, sending black clumps the consistency of tar-like blood flying everywhere.

Sinow relaxed slightly, called his power back, and looked over at Violissa. Even covered in splatters of the creature's guts, she still looked beautiful. He shook himself free of the muck that covered him as her Council shifted to where he and Violissa stood across from each other. The smaller beasts they had been battling had suffered the same fate when Violissa had killed the larger one.

"What in the Fates was that thing?" he asked her.

She shook her head, apparently just as baffled as he was.

"It was a Torathar," Cyric answered, and all eyes turned to him. "We have not seen one in our world since the beginning days of our people. I've only ever read about them."

"Where did it come from?" Violissa asked, still mindlessly wiping the black muck from her arms.

"King Sinow," said Cyric, "I think you'd better summon your elder Council for this. Kanine would likely be the best choice as your eldest."

Sinow bristled at the idea of Cyric giving him orders, but the concern etched on the man's face stopped him from reprimanding him. He had never seen such a deeply worried look on a Lightbearer.

Eyes closing, he called to Kanine. Then, because Cyric's assumption that he could command him still irked him, he called to Keary as well.

When he had summoned them both, he told Cyric, "I took the liberty of adding Keary to your...*request*. You will need to let them through, since they cannot cross on their own. You'll find them directly across from us, awaiting your arrival."

Violissa frowned, and he gave her a smirk as he shook beast gunk from his boot. Daneele glanced between them before shifting. Sinow looked toward the boundary, detecting Keary and Kanine standing on the other side, waiting. He knew they'd be able to sense Daneele's Light magic only when he drew close enough to it. Once they perceived the magic, they would use their own to open a space in the boundary, just as they had done for the ascension.

Silence hung over them while they waited, and Sinow glanced at Violissa. Lip tucked below her top teeth, her eyes focused behind him as if her thoughts were elsewhere. Likely trying to determine what this was all about, just as he was. Images of her magic destroying the creature kept running through his head. His magic had only strengthened the thing, yet hers had decimated it. Ire slithered through him at the thought of his weakness. Considered fiercer and stronger, he should have downed the beast within seconds. Yet it was Violissa who had done what he could not.

He thought back to when she'd destroyed it, lingering on the image of her at that moment, her golden hair flowing in the wind, her face lined with determination, and her eyes a brilliant shade of green. They had radiated and shimmered. The magic that flowed from her hands had been unusual, not the shades of magic a Lightbearer would exhibit, but a mix of both the bluish hues of her arcane Light powers and the vibrant greenish glow of her nature gifts. His skin had prickled at the sensation, the unfamiliarity.

Before he could ponder it any further, Daneele returned with Kanine and Keary.

Worried that the ire stirring within him would escape if he came too close to Violissa, Sinow kept his distance. As if she noticed his battle, she stayed back. Her gaze lifted to his, and his pulse increased as heat built in his chest. Weakness his power recognized and revolted against. Fisting his hands, he turned from her, directing his sight to Cyric.

"They're here. No more delays. Tell us about those creatures," he demanded.

Keary moved next to him, confusion etched in the lines on his brow. He remained quiet, likely knowing from Sinow's tone this was not the time nor the place for him to question his king.

"The Torathar," Cyric began.

"What did you say?" Kanine blurted.

Sinow gave the man a threatening look, and Kanine lowered his eyes. "Let him continue, Kanine. You'll get your answers, but I want mine first."

"As I was saying," Cyric continued, "the Torathar were an abomination created by the Fates long before any other race walked these lands. I know only what legend says of them. Kanine may know more."

Kanine looked at Sinow before answering, and Sinow nodded in approval. "Probably not. The last time I even heard stories about them was as a young child. Those stories are long forgotten by most."

Sinow brought his fingers to his forehead, squeezing the skin to alleviate his mounting frustration. Before he could strangle Kanine for his lack of input, Cyric spoke again.

"Then your stories are likely the same as ours. I will share what we know from them."

"Keep it short," Sinow snapped. "I'm losing patience."

Violissa's lips thinned, her eyes on him when he glanced up. They were a rich sage. Tiny lines creased their corners, and he could see his comment had aggravated her.

"As you know, the Elvin were the first race, followed by the Tenebrons, then the Cirillians. Before the Fates created the Elvin, however, they made the Torathar. It was their first attempt at a higher creature, and it went horribly wrong. The Fates formed the Torathar from the very ground we stand upon, molding the mud and clay from it, before adding their magic. At first, the things were only mounds of senseless muck, and the magic did nothing more than give them shape. They had no sense of intelligence and simply wandered the world, much as a leaf caught by the wind might. So, the Fates decided they had made a mistake and left them be. They turned their attention to creating smaller creatures to hone their skills. Animals of all types that still grace our lands.

"Not all the Fates wanted to give up on the Torathar. They decided they would work at adding more life into the forms and began experimenting with them without the knowledge of the other Fates. But as they poured more magic into the shapes, they realized too late they had made a mistake. Those Fates had powers bound to the Darkness, giving it unheeded to creatures with no mind to comprehend and no morals to gauge its destructive force. Although the beasts held no magic, their bodies were weapons forged from the magic of the Dark Fates. They were massive and unrelenting, destroying everything the Fates had built, pulling down trees, tearing up the land, killing the animals. Worse, they seemed to multiply on their own.

"The other Fates were furious. To balance the mistake, they made a second attempt at higher life and created the Elvin. There was hope that the nature abilities would counteract the destructive need of the Torathar since they too had been born of nature. The Fates were wrong. The Elvin were too weak and the Torathar easily defeated them, sending them hiding into the forests of what is now the Hidden Realm."

Cyric took a breath, pausing his words, and Sinow wondered how much of this story was myth and how much held merit. Bedtime stories, watered down over millennia, often morphed from their origins.

"The Fates then created the Darkbearers," Cyric continued, "hoping, as their powers were bound to the same Darkness that drove the creatures, that they could control them. Again, the Fates were wrong. Instead of restraining their powers, the Dark magic of the Darkbearers only strengthened the creatures. The Fates realized they'd made yet another mistake. They had tilted the balance of power to the Darkness. The world they created suddenly fell into chaos, and so in one more attempt to fix things, they created the Lightbearers, hoping they, along with the Elvin, would balance the Darkness and work with the Darkbearers to defeat the Torathar."

Patience running thin, Sinow dragged his hand through his hair, trying to determine why this history lesson was so important. He had only asked what the creatures were, but Cyric had never been one for brief replies. Sinow had learned this the first time he'd met the man, and with each subsequent meeting, Cyric reconfirmed the opinion.

"As you know, this didn't go as planned. The Darkbearers and Lightbearers were enemies from the beginning, and so the Torathar continued to wreak havoc on the land. The Lightbearers and the Elvin, however, became allies, and it was by chance the leaders of the two races were together when a Torathar attacked. They fought side by side, their powers intertwining as they fought. That blend of power was the force the Fates had been looking for. The combination brought the beast down and was the beginning of the end of the Torathar. Until today."

Brows scrunched, Sinow jerked his head up. "Wait, Elvin and Light magic defeated them when nothing else could?"

An uncomfortable silence followed a sharp inhale from Violissa's Council, and Sinow noticed a few glances between them. Cyric's hands were flexing nervously.

"That's what I heard," Violissa added, her eyes narrowed, a frown marring her features.

She cast her gaze at Sinow, the emerald brilliant in the midday sun. Awareness slammed into him, pieces falling into place, and he shifted his sight abruptly to Cyric.

"You've been hiding something from her, haven't you? Hiding it from everyone. There's a reason only she could defeat that creature, isn't there?"

"Now, Sinow," Daneele interrupted with concern in his voice.

"No, you lied to her all these years. Lied to us," he said, ignoring Daneele's protest.

Turning back to Violissa, he saw it now. All the unique aspects of her made sense—the golden hair, the green eyes, the nature abilities. Characteristics no longer seen in their world because the race that held them no longer existed. "Why can Violissa defeat the creatures when no one else can?" he demanded, still holding her gaze and watching realization settle in her. Her eyes grew bigger, her teeth gnawing on her bottom lip.

"Someone needs to answer me now," he growled. But the answer came from someone unexpected.

"You know why, my liege. Why force them to say it when you know the answer?" Kanine said.

Sinow turned around and glared at the man, but before he could speak, Cyric said, "You knew? How?"

Kanine didn't dare drop his eyes from Sinow. He knew the consequences, and with Sinow's anger now tenfold, his power one word from erupting, it had been a wise move. Sinow would have unleashed his wrath on Kanine if he had. "No, I suspected."

"What are you saying?" Violissa asked, her voice fragile as if she might break with the next answer. Sinow glared at Kanine before glancing at her. She looked so unsure and almost broken, and he detested the sight of her that way. As much as his Dark side disliked her, he still held the heart the Fates had bound to her, and it tugged at the pain reflected in her eyes. "Someone, please tell me the truth." Her voice trembled, and it nearly destroyed him.

Power flared through him at the intrusive weakness, and he clamped his fists tight to harness it. Her Council were shifting their feet, their sight everywhere but on their queen. He almost laughed and wished he had. It would have soothed the Darkness. They almost looked like children she'd caught doing something wrong.

It was Cyric who finally answered her. "It was not our place to tell you. The Fates, they swore all of us to secrecy. They told Aradisa you were not to know the truth until the time was right."

"I would say now is that time," growled Sinow. "What in the Fates is going on? And who is Aradisa?"

Cyric glanced at him with a look of frustration, as if to tell Sinow he wasn't helping, then let out a heavy sigh and turned back toward Violissa.

"Her mother."

Violissa's gasp was so loud it stopped his mouth from falling open. "But I don't have a mother," she said. But the certainty in her words was missing.

"The history is not as it seems," Cyric said, his cerulean eyes shadowed with emotion. "King Viliren wed an Elvin princess, Aradisa. We warned them, her father warned them, but they didn't listen, and perhaps it was the Fates' doing. There was no stopping the love between them. It infuriated your grandfather, Sinow." He could only imagine. His grandfather had hated the Elvin so much he had decimated their race. A union between the Light King and an Elvin princess would have sent him over the edge of madness. "Aradisa conceived many years later, but too soon for the prophecy. A Fate came to her, telling her it was too early, that the Dark child would not come for another generation. The two had to be born the same day."

Violissa brought her hand to her mouth, and Sinow could only guess she knew what was coming. They both did. The history, even if it did not include these details, remained.

"With the threat of Sinow's grandfather, who was growing agitated by the day, and the grave time difference, the Fate told her there was no choice but to hide you away until Sinow's birth. His grandfather was already stirring trouble. He discovered she was with child, and he had this unhinged determination to steal the scroll of prophecy from us. Spouting that his son was the Dark child and there was no way he would let him touch a..." Cyric hesitated, but Sinow knew what he had started to say.

"Mongrel," Sinow finished for him. The sadness in Violissa's eyes tore at him, and he hated himself for saying the word. "My grandfather hated the Elvin. He had many choice words in his writings for the race, and that would have been his word. Not mine." Because Violissa was anything but that. She was a glorious specimen of what the two lines could create. Beautiful in every aspect. But he couldn't tell her that. Not here, not now...maybe never if he failed to grasp control of his Darkness when he was near her.

"So all this time, I've had a mother? A father? I've been the true heir of the Light line and..." Tears pushed behind her eyes, making them glossy, the green a misty sage. "...the Elvin line? All this time you've let me believe I was so different. That I wasn't born into this world like everyone else. That I was flawed because of it. And you, you all," she looked around at her Council, "knew the truth and kept it from me?"

"We didn't have a choice, Violissa." Daneele spoke this time, his face lined with guilt.

"You had a choice," Sinow shouted. "You chose not to tell her and to lie to me and my father."

He didn't know if he was angrier at the hurt Violissa was experiencing or about being misled all this time. He turned and glared at Kanine. The Darkness rebelled, reading the treachery in Kanine's actions. A burst of magic fled from him and hit Kanine square in the chest, encasing him and sending him to his knees.

"And you...you're a traitor to me, my father, and my grandfather. How could you not tell us? How could you mislead all those you claim loyalty to? There is no excuse." He moved his hand, and Kanine straightened, pulled from where he had landed as Sinow's magic gripped him. The skin around his neck blackened, his breathing silenced, but he didn't dare show his pain or Sinow would worsen the punishment. Every Darkbearer knew that to show weakness, especially in front of his king, was cause for brutal, unrelenting torture.

"Sinow. Stop this now!" Violissa screamed. "You are on my land, and this is not the way we use magic here."

He turned, his dark eyes burrowing into her. The man he had been moments ago was gone, drowned far below the fury that swept through his veins. He fought it, aware that he needed more answers, needed to understand why no one knew this part of the past, how it had disappeared. Summoning his strength, he dropped Kanine. He could tell ebony had glazed his eyes so they no longer held the brown Violissa was used to seeing. A light blue aura sat around her as she held her own power at bay. He could sense it clawing at her for release against the Darkness that permeated the air.

"There must be an explanation. Right, Kanine?" she asked Kanine directly.

Defiance flickered in Kanine's eyes, and Sinow took a step closer, his power sparking through the air, waiting for Kanine to invite more punishment. But he stayed in the crouched position he'd landed in, one hand bracing himself against the ground.

"You don't understand, Sinow. I couldn't tell your grandfather."

"Then make me understand," Sinow snarled.

"You have no idea what your grandfather was like."

"I know exactly what he was like." Like me, he wanted to stay but silenced it, not wanting to voice the admission. If it was one thing he never wanted to be, it was his grandfather. A man lost to the Darkness, his code ignored, his duties to his people left behind in the Darkness that warped him. His grandfather had been a monster, and a moment didn't pass when Sinow thought perhaps he was one spark of power away from crossing that line and becoming the man he hated.

"No, you don't," Kanine said, standing, the defiance back. "He was a madman. Do you have any idea what he would have done if he had made it to the capital that day? If I had told him what I remembered and all others forgot. If he remembered his reasoning for breaking through the Cirillian border that day? He wanted the prophecy to be his. Wanted to warp it and make it fit his agenda. Wanted your father to be the child in it so he could manipulate him and the words of the Fates. And Aradisa was in his way."

He pointed to Violissa, fire in his eyes, and Sinow fought to contain the power that wanted to slam the man back to the ground and break every bone in his body for his defiant words. "If he had made it that day, he would have killed Aradisa. Would have marched right in and ripped the child from her womb. He would have crushed the life out of her before he even finished killing her mother. I kept silent to protect her. To protect the prophecy. There were some of us who believed it would come, believed there had to be a better king. Believed you would be born and complete the prophecy. I don't know why I remembered, and all the others forgot, but I kept the secret, knowing the truth the moment the capital disappeared. Knowing the Fates had protected her, and she would return when the rightful king was born. If I had told your grandfather...you wouldn't be standing here next to her because he would have turned over every inch of these lands to find a way back to the Lost Realm. And trust me, he searched until his last breath. That was just to find the prophecy. If he had known the truth of what that realm hid, he would have found it." Kanine dropped to his knees, bowing his head. "I knew it was a risk. Staying silent all these years, but it wasn't my secret to share, and I would risk your wrath again to know that your destiny is intact."

Cyric stepped forward before Sinow could react. "He speaks the truth. Your grandfather was obsessed with the prophecy. He never understood why there needed to be two sides to the power. He only wanted one child to rule all of us: his child. He would have killed Violissa and her mother, and none of us, not even Viliren, could have stopped him."

Sinow ran his hand through his hair. His anger had abated some with the thought of losing Violissa to his grandfather's madness.

"Your grandfather was a formidable man," Kanine said, looking up at him. "That same Darkness you struggle against, he failed to overcome. It infected every part of his mind, and he could never have reasoned a union with a Lightbearer, especially not one that was half-Elvin. Viliren's choice of an Elvin as his queen disgusted him. He saw her pregnancy as a blight on the purity of the races. It was our undoing and his own."

Silence blanketed them. Never could Sinow have fathomed all that had come to light. Violissa was half-Elvin, half-Cirillian. She was the daughter of the last Light king, not a child made from magic as he'd always been told.

"The woman in the Hidden Realm is my mother, isn't she?" Violissa's voice split the silence, stopping his thoughts. "I was standing in the same room as both of them, and no one told me? I don't understand why you could tell me none of this prior to now. Sinow's grandfather has long been dead. Why did no one think to speak of this?"

Cyric let out a long sigh. "The Fate made it clear when she warned your mother you were not to know until the Fates deemed it the right time. Your parents gave their lives to protect you, to protect the prophecy. Aradisa gave you up, removed you from her womb and sealed you into a protective sphere so you could have the life the Fates had prophesied. So you could lead our world into a better life alongside Sinow. The Fates removed all evidence of her existence. Kanine and I are the only ones who still remember her. I carried that secret with me until the day you were born, and I shared it with the Council. Who were we to go against the Fates?"

Sinow's head was pounding, and he needed time to think through everything he had learned. His power was so agitated it was knocking against his skin, looking for an escape.

Turning to Kanine, he said, "I understand why you made your choice, but I will still deal with you when we return."

Kanine bowed his head to the ground. "Yes, my liege."

There were no words he could say to Violissa to express his thoughts. Too much had been said, and he needed time to process it, just as he imagined she did. He didn't know if he could look at her the same anymore. Her powers were greater than he had been told, greater than he had imagined. She held two lines of power within her, and although nature magic was weaker than Dark and Light magic, added to Light magic, it gave her an advantage.

His power bucked at the thought, stinging his insides like a hive of hornets. Doubt and thoughts of weakness plagued him, feelings that only increased the discomfort in him. He needed to leave before he exploded, but he knew if he did, Violissa would take his departure as a slight against her. But he had no way of expressing what was running through his mind, and his current state would only make it worse. The power escaped from his bunched hands, threatening to strike, and he knew he had to get away before it erupted.

Hating himself and the war within him, wanting desperately to stay and comfort her, to take her aside and have her soothing voice tell him her concerns, her doubts, her emotions, he did the only thing he could. He gave Violissa one last glance and shifted away.

CHAPTER 36

With the remaining pieces of her heart now fractured, Violissa stared at the space where Sinow stood no more. He had left, and she couldn't help but think it was because of her. This day, which had begun so well, had become an emotional nightmare. First, the Torathar, then the admission that her Council had deceived her, that her parents had been so close, and she hadn't known, that she even had parents after thinking she was an anomaly, and now this.

The weight of eyes on her had her looking up to meet Keary's gaze. Sinow had left without even taking his two Council with him. If she needed any further proof of his discontent with the situation and the revelations about her, there it was. As if the Cirillian part of her hadn't been enough to place distance between them, now she was half-Elvin, everything a Dark king detested. And the Fates had forced him to love her.

Love? No, that was not the word for what they had, no matter how her heart reacted to the word. Love didn't leave like he had. Love didn't bend to Darkness. No, what he felt for her was not love.

"I'm no different from who I was before," she told Keary, his chestnut eyes unwavering.

"No, but you're now more powerful than he thought, and that's a threat to all of us," he replied, his dark eyes only a shade lighter than Sinow's.

"The prophecy states they are equal in power. This changes nothing," Cyric said in her defense. "He witnessed her two ascensions. You were there, Keary. You saw it, too."

Kanine remained quiet, but Keary continued to question on Sinow's behalf. "But, Cyric, Elvin? You expect Sinow, us, to be content with this information? No one but you and Kanine has even seen an Elvin kind, let alone witnessed their powers. We needed to know this. He needed to know it."

Daneele stepped up. "It was not our place to tell any of you, even our own queen. Would you have had us disobey the Fates?"

Keary glared at him, then looked at Violissa.

"This changes nothing, Keary," she murmured.

"It changes everything to the Dark blood that runs through him, and that is what you should fear, Violissa. He was already over the edge from fighting. If he can't regain control, I can't promise there won't be repercussions for everyone involved in hiding the truth from him." He looked directly at Kanine when he spoke those last words.

Kanine sighed and simply asked, "Can someone get us through the barrier so we can return home and deal with this?"

Violissa watched as Daneele left with Kanine and Keary. Arms crossed, she waited for his return, unsure of what to say to her Council. They had lied to her, left her in the dark about her history. Confusion and anger swirled in her, but hurt enveloped it. Hurt from what they had done and from Sinow's reaction. She still didn't know how to read it, even after what Keary had told her. He might have only been angry at the situation, but then it might have been more. Her heritage could be the culprit, leaving him repulsed by her. The thought caused a sharp sting of pain in her chest.

Daneele returned, and the silence remained until it was too uncomfortable, and he broke it, saying, "Violissa, you must understand—"

"No, Daneele. I don't have to understand anything," she replied, cringing at the harshness in her voice but not willing to soften it. "The destruction from that creature needs to be cleaned up. There are villagers who will need healing. See to them, all of you, and clean up this mess."

There were no other words. She wasn't ready to deal with them. Never had she acted like a commanding queen, but she needed them to know they had wounded her by hiding the truth from her. Letting her believe she'd been different, not born the same as all of them. Believe she had no parents. She gave them one last look and left them, shifting but not sure where to go. She had no one else, no one to cry to, and the only man she cared about was a realm away dealing with his own sudden repulsion to her. Her Council were her only friends, her only family, but in that moment, she felt very alone.

Landing in her shift, she stared at the door to the Hidden Realm. All this time, it had been under her, and all this time, her parents had been there. It seemed like such an odd thing...parents. Hours ago, she'd had none. Her Council had always told her that their magic and that of the Guardians had created her. That she had not been born of flesh and blood. But the only truth in that had been the magic and Guardians involved. Magic to free her from whatever spell her mother had placed her in the day the capital was lost and the Guardians who protected the Hidden Realm and the secrets of her birth—her parents.

Anguish washed over her at the thought of all she had lost, all they had lost, and she fell to her knees. All of it lost for the sake of a prophecy, and all to appease the will of the Fates.

She put her hand to the door, hoping it would open but

knowing in her heart it wouldn't. Leaning her head against the door, she said quietly, "Mother, Father, if you can hear me, I know now who you really are. Help me. I don't know where to go from here. I don't know who I am anymore or what I'm supposed to do." A tear slid down her cheek and splashed on the stone floor. "He hates me, and it's my fault. I did this. It's all falling apart, and I can't fix it. I've made so many wrong choices and cursed us all."

A sob escaped, more tears falling, and she turned her body, resting it against the door as she hugged her knees to her chest. She kept her head touching the doorway, wishing it would open, and her mother would embrace her, or her father would wrap her in his arms and take the pain away. Disembodied remnants were all that remained of them, and even if the doorway opened, she would find no comfort there.

Eyes closing, she thought of them as they must have been when they were whole, picturing the portrait of her father in the castle hall and imagining they were on the other side. The thought gave her little comfort, but even a little was enough to ease the ache.

CHAPTER 37

Sinow stormed through the castle, heading for the lower levels. Rage clawed through him, but it wasn't enough to keep his mind from how he had left Violissa. Keary had told him about her reaction when he had returned, and Sinow hated that he had hurt her. There had been no choice. The Darkness had him in its grasp, and if he had stayed, he would have lost control. Anger had already dug its talons into him when he had been useless at defeating the beast. When Violissa had done what he could not. He had been weak, and the Darkness in him loathed it.

He knew his powers were equal to hers, but seeing the blend of her powers and seeing her use them had stirred the aggression in him. When the truth of her lineage and the lies her Council had told to deceive her had come to light, added with the fact that Kanine had deceived him, it had sent him over the edge.

Regardless of what she thought, her heritage wasn't what had bothered him. It made sense and only further increased his desire for her. The idea of the unknown, the mystique of the Elvin, a race they knew so little about, intrigued him. That Elvin blood ran through her made her more irresistible.

Sinow reached the lower dungeons and paused. He hadn't been past this point in the castle since he was a child and had to think about which direction he needed to go. He briefly reached out with his powers to find the room he was looking for and sensed it, along with another presence. Tynan. The hackles on his neck raised, and he gripped his fists. Whatever his brother was up to, it didn't matter. Sinow would kick him out when he got there. He couldn't deal with Tynan's prying questions.

Continuing down the hall, he rounded a corner and came upon another set of stairs. Why his forefathers had hidden this room so far down, he didn't understand, but figured anyone who needed it would have taken the smart route and shifted. He had avoided shifting, knowing in his current state, the force of his landing would likely have brought the entire keep down on him. Besides, he had needed the walk to clear his head, even if it hadn't worked.

As he approached the bottom of the stairs, he finally came upon the room for which he'd been searching. He could see light coming from beyond the closed door. Tynan was still there.

Teeth grinding, Sinow pushed open the door and stormed in, causing Tynan, who sat hunched over a table covered with books, to jump slightly.

"Sinow, this is the last place I'd ever expect to see you. In fact, have you ever set foot in this library, or any, for that matter?"

Sinow ignored the jab and looked around the room. Stacks ran the length of the walls, stuffed full of books layered in dust. Tattered and frayed, the bindings reflected their age. The castle had a main library on the upper levels, but this one was older and rarely used now. It housed the special books that kept the history of their people, as well as what they knew of the Cirillians. Most importantly for Sinow, it held everything his people knew of the Elvin.

His curiosity about the race had driven him to the lower depths of his home. The lessons from his childhood had covered only the basics of Elvin history. Not enough to answer the questions he now had. He wanted to understand their magic, but even more, he wanted to find out about Violissa's mother. The Fates had to have missed something when they erased knowledge of her existence. Someone couldn't simply disappear from history that easily, even with the Fates involved. And someone that important to the Fates must have left her mark somewhere.

The images she had placed in his mind in the Lost Realm slinked through his consciousness, and he rubbed his temple to erase them. Even when he hadn't known who she was, she had gotten to him, and even in her current state, he surmised she held some sort of power. He needed answers, but what he didn't need was Tynan underfoot asking him questions.

"Leave, Tynan," he ordered as he continued walking through the room, past him. He didn't bother looking back at his brother and, thankfully, Tynan didn't care to argue. He heard him gathering the books he'd been using before he left without a word.

When Sinow could no longer feel Tynan's presence, he began looking among the rows of books. He didn't know if there was a method to how they were lined up on the shelves, nor did he have the patience to figure it out. The spell to locate the books on the Elvin was in the air within seconds, and Sinow waited patiently for it to find its mark. After a short time, the lower corner of a shelf to his far right rattled.

A touch to the books that were moving broke the spell, and Sinow kneeled to look at them. There were several, most layered with dust and cobwebs, but a few had fingerprints like someone had used them recently. Several empty spaces told him someone had taken a few of the books as well. It had to have been Tynan; no one else had been down here in ages. Sinow made a mental note to question Tynan later, but he had other things on his mind and put the question aside.

He pulled the books from their shelf with a flick of his hand and dropped them on the table where Tynan had been. They spread out as they fell, filling the table. He ran his hand through his hair and sighed. This was going to be a long night, and sifting through books sounded like torture to him. Unlike his brother, libraries were the last places he wanted to be, and books were the last thing he wanted to spend his time with.

As the pages flipped in the first book, his irritation settled, and he slipped into a calm that he doubted would last. Hours later, he had gone through most of the books. Looking at the remaining few, he wondered if this had been a fruitless quest. Cyric had said the Fates had erased all memory of Aradisa besides his own and Kanine's. An odd thing to do, in Sinow's opinion. Leaving one Council in each realm to hold a memory that the Fates had deemed concerning enough to strip from the world's knowledge. Why keep two memories intact? And why the only surviving Council from that time?

Head in his hands, he contemplated giving up and returning to the main floor for a strong drink. One book remained, and he grabbed it, his frustration causing it to slip from his fingers. He caught it before it crashed to the floor, the pages flipping quickly until they slowed toward the end like something was keeping them from the same steady motion. Bringing it back to the table, he smoothed out the pages, noting the difference. Turning more pages, he found a page with depth, as if someone had folded it multiple times to fit into the book. He turned the book sideways and unfolded the page. Sucking in a breath, he stared at the family tree before him.

The writing looked too foreign, too meticulous to be from an ancestor or even a former Council. No, this was Elvin. He could tell from the flare of the letters, the gold that glittered in the ink. Someone had stolen this and hidden it. The script was similar to what he had seen on the doorway to the Lost Realm.

Sinow spread the page out further, trying to determine whose family it was. He could have kicked himself for not paying closer attention to his lessons as a boy. Elvin history had been brief, and he hadn't given it much credence since they were all dead. Trying to recall the letters he had learned of the ancient Elvin tongue, the one used from the early days of the Elvin before they had learned the common tongue, he deciphered the word 'royal' at the top of the page.

The chair screeched as he sat back with the discovery. This page held the royal line of the Elvin house. Cyric had mentioned that the Cirillian king, Viliren, had married an Elvin princess. Scanning the names, his frustration growing the further down the page he came, Sinow found nothing until he reached the last branch of the tree. He brought the page closer, seeing dashes below the name of the last Elvin king, Veneran. Two dashes led from his name and that of his queen. The first dash led to Faraname, who married Rinalian. His name sat below the king's name, but where the dash for his second child ended, no name appeared. More intriguing was a lone dash midway between, showing room for another name through a union. Sinow rubbed his finger along the blank spaces and noted the indents where the two names were missing.

"Found you," he mumbled, hoping the Fates wouldn't realize their mistake. They'd erased the names but not the evidence of their existence. He clenched his hand, then released his fist over the page. A cloud of black poured from his palm and splashed over the page. He picked the page up and blew the blackness from it. Where the spaces had once been blank, his magic revealed two fresh additions to the family tree.

"Aradisa and Viliren," he muttered, sitting back again in his chair, the confirmation of what he'd found just hitting him. Violissa wasn't only heir to Cirillia, but heir to the Elvin throne, exactly like Cyric had said. That was why she'd had two ascensions. But the Elvin had been weak. Sure, they had control over nature, but flowers and trees proved useless against the Dark powers of Tenebron. The royal line must have been different, but how so?

Sinow slammed the book shut.

Kanine! he bellowed in enaigne, knowing Kanine would drop everything and appear before him. His Council knew when their king summoned them in such a tone, it was best not to make him wait.

Violent flames coursed through his body as his powers pulsed. The Darkness still possessed him, and the thought of Kanine's deception and what he had just learned brought it pounding back like an incessant maelstrom. Kanine appeared seconds later, each second only adding to the chaos in Sinow.

"Yes, my liege," he said, bowing. Sinow tossed the book to Kanine. "Every book on Elvin history in this room and this lone one has the only evidence of Violissa's mother."

"As we told you, Sinow, the Fates erased all knowledge."

"All knowledge but yours and Cyric's. Why do you suppose that is, Kanine? What makes the two of you so special?"

"I don't know."

Sinow didn't pause to reflect on the question or Kanine's answer. They weren't his priority now.

"Tell me about Aradisa," he demanded.

Kanine stuttered. "There isn't much to tell. She was the daughter of the Elvin King. Her brother inherited the throne since he was born first. Cirillia and the Elvin were always close, so it made sense when Viliren married Aradisa. Your grandfather hated it, however. There was a rumor he had once fancied Aradisa, but if it was true, he would never have admitted it. He was against even the thought of mixing the bloodlines. As far as I know, Viliren was the first to do so."

Sinow stood and slammed his hand down on the table. "I don't need a history lesson. I want to know what her abilities were. Were they greater than the average Elvin? If so, how?"

"Ah, I see. Well yes, they were greater than the other Elvin. She was royal, and as with any royal line, the Fates blessed her with special powers."

Sinow impatiently interrupted, "So what could she do? Were their royals any threat to the Light or Dark?"

"Well, there were differences. Where the normal Elvin could

grow flowers or even a tree here and there, one from the royal bloodline could call a storm or fell a forest." He paused a moment, then looked keenly at Sinow. "Is that your worry, my liege? That Violissa's Elvin gifts might be a threat to you?"

Sinow growled but kept his mouth shut so Kanine would continue. "Elvin powers, even their royal line, were weak. They were never strong enough to fight a Darkbearer, let alone a Dark King. The nature powers Violissa possesses from her mother's side are strong, but only because her Light magic enhances them." The pacing Sinow had started paused as he considered Kanine's words. "This simply brings her to an even level with you, my liege. It certainly does not make her stronger. No one can surpass the power you possess, nor has there ever been a ruler as formidable as you."

Sinow didn't know whether Kanine was trying to make up for his past indiscretion or if he was simply being honest.

Taking strides closer to Kanine, he said, "Thank you for your honesty, Kanine." Kanine bowed and turned to leave, thinking incorrectly that Sinow was dismissing him. "I'm not finished," Sinow snarled, and Kanine turned back to him, a moment of fear passing through his eyes. One he should not have shown his king.

The Darkness pummeled Sinow, slashing his vision with crimson and black. Kanine's pulse thundered, causing Sinow to grin. Even with all their powers, his Council knew to fear him. His rage and strength could make even an immortal suffer, especially when he was as out of control as he currently was.

Sinow moved his hand, and Kanine struggled not to collapse in pain. Palm closing with excruciating slowness, Kanine's bones snapped one by one until Sinow's fist was clenched completely and Kanine fell to the floor. He was healing, but Sinow's magic was countering every setting bone and crushing it again. Healing bones was painful enough, but to have them broken and refused repeatedly was torture. To Kanine's benefit, he didn't let his king see his agony. If he had, Sinow would have ripped every organ out of the man.

Sinow leaned down next to Kanine's ear, hearing the tight panting and uneven heartbeats. "If I ever find out you've hidden something from me or neglected to tell me something again, I will send you to the Fates myself." He released his hand, and Kanine's body flopped forward, his broken hands unable to stop its motion. Sinow planted a foot on his back, crushing him further into the floor. He stepped forward, hearing the snaps and pops of Kanine's spine as he walked over him. "Do you understand, Kanine?"

Kanine struggled to answer but managed a low, "Yes, my liege." Sinow could see the healing of the vertebrae as he glanced once more at him. He'd be up and moving again within minutes, but Sinow had made his point. "Oh, and clean up my mess before you head up."

Shifting, he left Kanine to deal with his misery and the mess.

CHAPTER 38

Quiet sat over the town, which the Torathar had so recently ravaged. Two mortals had fallen victim to the creature's violence, and Violissa had taken part in the mourning ceremony, lighting the pyres that returned their bodies to the land.

Walking the path that led from the village and making her way beyond into the open land where she had fought the Torathar before guiding it toward the boundary, she thought about her Council. She had made peace with them, forgiving them for the secrets they had kept from her. They had done it out of fealty to their former king, her father, as well as the Fates. Only she had the nerve to disobey the Fates, and she knew from experience what punishment that could bring.

Instead of holding onto her anger, she had shed it and embraced the idea that she wasn't as different as she'd always assumed. Although she knew her appearance and her power made her stand apart from every woman in her lands or even in their world for that matter, knowing she had been born to parents who had loved her enough to give their lives to protect her made her differences seem small. Discovering the truth had finally brought her closer to those she ruled.

She shifted further, stopping close to the boundary and overlooking the place where she and Sinow had fought the Torathar and life had changed for her. A breeze played in her hair, picking up a few golden curls and scattering them across her face. Brushing them away, she took a deep breath, her brow puckering. There was still something there, something slight in the air, which she couldn't quite name.

She walked forward, all thoughts of what had happened here banished temporarily from her mind as she tried to determine what it was. Bare feet stepping through the tall grass, she noticed the surface change with each footfall. Her toes sank enough for her to stop. Scrunching her lips, she closed her eyes and sent her senses out through the ground into the roots and sediment that lay below. Something was deep below her, and she sensed movement but couldn't determine what was causing it. Chewing her bottom lip, she dug deeper with her magic, reaching for definition, but whatever it was, it wasn't something tangible. There was only a sensation. Dark, hungry, angry.

She jerked back, her magic fading as her eyes burst open.

"No, it cannot be," she mumbled.

Cyric, I need you here now. There is something happening, she called out in enaigne.

Cyric shifted to her within seconds. "Violissa? What is it?" he said, his vision darting around the open field.

"Do you sense anything? Anything Dark?"

His blue eyes questioned her before he closed them and sent his magic out to find an answer for her.

When he opened them, he shook his head. "No, nothing. But you sense something, don't you?"

She did, but had no way of verbalizing what she sensed. Instinct told her it was something she should fear, but how did she explain that when there was nothing to see?

Kneeling, she placed her hand on the ground, saying, "Yes, below us. Far below, something stirs and moves toward the boundary. Like it's being called by something."

A look of concern passed over his features. "The Torathar feed off Dark power, Violissa." She swiveled her gaze to his, the admission striking fear in her heart. Her hand shook when she brought it from the ground. "If their return broke through in our realm, it would only make sense that their essence is trying to reach that Darkness to strengthen themselves and re-emerge like the one yesterday." She looked back to where she sensed the boundary, only now seeing the connection between where the beast had been when she'd discovered it and the proximity to the boundary. Cyric continued, "Sinow's powers are volatile, and they are without precedent. He is the strongest of his line."

"The Torathar are feeding from it," she said, swallowing back the terror that thought caused in her. The creature had been enormous, and even with both her powers in use, it had been difficult to destroy. She couldn't imagine battling more than one. And after seeing what Sinow's power had done to that one, picturing more emerging in Tenebron, where the source of that Dark power sat, was terrifying.

"I am inclined to agree with what you sense below us. They must have been dormant, and something woke them. Now they're trying to find their way to the Dark power and take form like the one yesterday."

"Fates, if that happens..."

"We're in for a fight we'll have a difficult time winning. You are only one, and they will be many. In their current form, locked below the surface, they are harmless, black ooze like that surrounding the Hidden Realm entrance."

"That's what that was?"

"I suspected so after seeing the creature. It has the same consistency as the Torathar."

She dropped to her knees, leaning her head toward the ground to see if she could detect whatever it was stirring below, to confirm that it was indeed the Torathar. "That's the infection my father was speaking of." Calling the former king her father seemed such an unusual thing that she almost laughed about it, but the seriousness of the situation stopped her. "Cyric," she said, picking her head up and meeting his eyes. "If they reach Tenebron, they will find form again, won't they?"

"Most certainly."

"Then I need to stop them."

"Violissa—"

She ignored him, sending her magic back into the ground. Movement met her magic, laced with emotions: desire, anger, envy. Their need for form and movement slunk through her thoughts. When she touched the blackness that ran deep below them, a jumble of thoughts and emotions, chaotic and frantic, slammed her as if they were one massive collective mind. And within the havoc, one primal urge that screamed for more. It was something more than just the Dark power, something far more dangerous and unhinged. A power with which she wasn't familiar and couldn't name. Something older and beyond her knowledge.

Shoving her power deeper, she tried to grasp what it was, but something latched onto her magic, ensnaring it and dragging it further down. She tried to rein her powers back, but to no avail. A sensation of total darkness engulfed her mind, fighting into her consciousness. Control dangled just beyond her reach, the escape she needed so close yet too far to grasp as tentacles of black ooze invaded her mind and her senses. She fought, knowing from the outside, Cyric could not see her battle. She wasn't even sure if his magic would detect any trouble. The invasion continued, the blackness seeping through her like a strangling vine from which she could not free herself.

There was nothing she could physically fight, and her mind raced as it warded off the violation. In desperation, she reached into her body for her power, leaving the safety of her mind and grabbing onto her nature gifts, demanding her body release them. Her gifts smashed into the ground, pushing the blackness back.

A chorus of voices screamed in frustration, but before it had time to attack again, she freed her mind, called her power back, and withdrew into the protection of her body. Staggering back, she heard Cyric's questions but drew her Light magic, pouring an explosion of arcane into the ground as her fingers sank into the mud. Commanding it to weave through the Elvin magic that was still cascading from her, she watched as the two powers moved quickly across the land, surrounding the border, and burrowing as one through layers of dirt and rock below. The ooze shifted lower, the ground bucking before her power engulfed it.

The breath caged in her lungs escaped, and her muscles relaxed. Nothing remained below; the land was quiet once more. She had expected to feel the essence flee, but she felt nothing. It was gone, the land silent, the chaos no more. Destroyed by her magic, just as the Torathar had been.

Violissa looked over at Cyric, who was staring at her with wide eyes. Magic still spread from her hands, and she quickly stopped it, pulling her fingers from the mud.

"Did you sense any of that, Cyric?"

"Any of what, Violissa? I was speaking to you, but when I looked to see why you didn't respond, you seemed almost asleep. Your eyes had glossed over, and as much as I tried, I couldn't wake you. What happened?"

After giving Cyric a summary of what she'd experienced, she waited for his response.

Pacing, he scratched his head before saying, "Your nature gifts have always been a mystery to us. Even when the Elvin walked the land, their magic was so different it was hard to understand." He stopped and turned to her. "I witnessed nothing of what you experienced, but I would wager that is because Light magic is not sensitive to what you sensed below the surface. If it is indeed essence of Torathar, it makes sense that your magic would respond to it, given their consistency is land-based. But what you described—leaving your body and moving into the land—is not a power we share with you."

It was the same sensation she had when she had reached out to Sinow with enaigne, crossing the boundary and finding him.

"Sinow and I do," she stated with a shrug.

"Gifts from the Fates," Cyric muttered. "Violissa, can you still sense it? Do you have any notion that the black matter is still near us?" He waited momentarily for her to respond, then added, "Don't send yourself out beyond your body again, though. We can't take the chance that whatever it was that tried to ensnare you isn't completely gone."

She laughed. "Don't worry. I never want to experience that again." She drew in a breath and closed her eyes, listening with her magic but not daring to move beyond the boundary of her body. There was nothing she could detect nearby or in any part of Cirillia. Tenebron was what now worried her. If there was black ooze underground preparing to take the form of the Torathar, she wasn't sure if Sinow would sense it if he were waging an internal war with his power. There would already be enough Darkness surrounding him. A little more would easily go unnoticed.

"I'll be right back," she said to Cyric before shifting closer to the boundary. She could see beyond it into Tenebron, but didn't venture through it. There was enough connection to the land to do what she needed from this point, and she didn't care to upset Sinow any further by crossing into his realm.

Eyes closed, she listened, making certain there was no hint of the voices she'd heard earlier. She detected nothing, but that didn't mean Tenebron was clear. Kneeling, she placed her hands to the ground and drew upon both of her powers, weaving them together before casting them along the land and through the border into

Tenebron. A wave of green and blue magic cascaded across the land and spread as far through Tenebron as she could reach. No one would notice it except for Sinow and his Council. She just hoped he'd understand what she was doing as she waited for the repercussions if he didn't.

CHAPTER 39

Sinow held his head in his hands to assuage the pressure that now never seemed to abate. The Darkness had been surging through him since he'd left Violissa that day in the clearing. Part of him wanted to reach out to her, to see her again and have her weave one of her calming spells through him. The other part of him reared in objection at such a weakness.

He questioned whether there would ever be a time when he wouldn't need a spell to be in her presence. If this was how they would spend the rest of eternity if they ever wed. The anger swelled, and he tried to calm himself. He was being irrational. After all, this couldn't be how the Fates expected them to live.

He needed to speak to her, to have her talk some sense back into him. Still needed to talk to her about all that had occurred the last time he had seen her. He had left abruptly but had known he needed to. Keary had talked to him about what had happened afterwards, and Sinow's hope that he had not offended her seemed unlikely. He briefly contemplated opening his mind and removing the barrier he'd placed within it to keep his mind from hers. Maybe that's what he needed. A few minutes to speak with her, even if only through enaigne.

He stopped as the Darkness rose once again. It was so hard to keep that side of him at bay. He concentrated on reining it in and had just grabbed hold of it again when he sensed the power race across his land, the combination of nature and Light woven together just as it had that day in Cirillia. Then, just as suddenly as it had been there, it was gone as a wave might pound the surf, then disappear with only a line of froth as evidence it ever existed.

"Violissa," he mumbled. He thought briefly of confronting her about it before an onslaught of Council voices barreled through his head.

Quiet! he yelled in enaigne. *There is nothing to be done. The spell is gone, and there is no evidence there was any ill intent to it.*

On the contrary, he understood exactly what she had done. The spell was the same he had experienced that day with the Torathar. She was cleansing the land to avoid any future occurrences. He should have been angry—in fact, part of him yearned to confront her—but he had just caged that part of himself and instead he let her go. There was no need to confront her about something he understood. No sense in stirring the monster in him that threatened to escape whenever he was around her. He would broach the subject at their next meeting.

Staring out the window, he rubbed his jaw. The scheduled meeting with Violissa would not be for another two moon cycles. Long enough for him to gain control or... He pushed the thought aside, determined that he would win this battle, that the Darkness would ease and he would find balance just as his father had. That he would not follow in his grandfather's footsteps. If he did, he would lose everything. Lose any chance of leaving a legacy like his father had, of being a respected king, of finally having Violissa.

His chest swelled at the thought of losing her completely, an unexpected wave of emotion sweeping through him until the Darkness rose and pounced on it, snuffing out any sign of weakness. And love was weakness. Loving his enemy was weakness.

Head dropping against the glass, he wondered if that was

indeed the emotion he had for her. The Fates expected it of him, his place in the prophecy guaranteeing his heart belonged to her. But love was a foreign emotion, one not expressed by a Dark King or his son. A word not heard in the Dark Keep.

Every king had an undeniable draw to the woman who would bear the heir to the throne, the next Dark King. It was unavoidable, and there was no turning from it. The Fates chose their mates as much as they chose Violissa as his. The only difference was that those unions did not guarantee love. Sometimes love developed, and from what he knew, it had for his father. But most times, the union only guaranteed an heir. The woman was nothing more than a vessel, a tool for the Fates to bring the next king into the world.

If he had been a soft man, he would have found sadness in such a situation, questioned the cruelty of the Fates for sacrificing each king's wife and the mother of his child. But Sinow was not a soft man, and his Dark power made him more objective, seeing the necessity of the progression and not the sacrifice. Besides, it was an honor for the woman, knowing the Fates had chosen her, that the king was drawn to her, that she would be queen if only for a short time, that she would bear the next Dark King. Every woman in the kingdom prayed to the Fates that the king would choose her, even though only one every ten thousand years or more had her prayer answered.

A stirring outside his study distracted him, and he turned his attention to the door, rushing to it before swinging it open. The hall was empty, shadows spilling in from the lightless corridor. But someone had been there, and although Sinow didn't have the same awareness of his brother as Tynan had of his presence, Tynan's scent lingered in the air. Dust, dank, charred rot. That's what his brother's scent had been of late, something twisted with more than the Darkness that flowed in his blood.

What had he been up to? Trust had been something Sinow had always given Tynan. Blind faith, protection from the harsh words of his father and the Council, brotherly affection. Those were things he offered Tynan, with no expectation of anything but the same in return.

Yet as the years passed, they became less balanced, Tynan withdrawing from him and the world. Sinow continued his loyalty to his brother, regardless, and only recently had he grown suspicious that Tynan had used that loyalty to his advantage, taken it for more than he should have. There was no proof, only a nagging suspicion that Sinow continued to brush aside in hopes that he was wrong. But the sneering remarks of late, the vile way he spoke Violissa's name, the sneaking around, had tested the solid bond Sinow had kept in place.

Rubbing his forehead, he closed the door, frowning as he tried to determine what Tynan was up to now. If he didn't stop, the Council would approach Sinow and force his hand, something he did not want because turning against his brother was not an option. Tynan had no one on his side, no one who believed in him, no one who cared about him other than Sinow. It would take an act of serious betrayal for Sinow to ever think of turning on him, and he didn't want to think of the consequences if that day ever came.

THE DAYS PASSED QUICKLY, and with each one, Sinow lost himself further to the Darkness. His power simmered just below his skin, ready to strike at the slightest provocation. Deep in the recesses of his mind, his former self rested, waiting to break free of the binds the Darkness had on him, but he slipped further, no matter how he tried to cling to the remnants of Violissa's calming spell.

"What are you doing out here, Sinow?" Keary said, coming to stand next to him.

"I came out here to escape my nagging Council, and you think it wise to interrupt my solitude?" He had meant the words to tease, but each came out like jagged shards of glass scraping across skin.

"I see you're in a good mood, as usual."

Power snapping at his bones, Sinow snarled, "What do you want, Keary?"

Keary's sigh was palpable, and it simmered Sinow's ire. No matter how the Darkness took him, Keary remained a loyal friend, often the only one brave enough to approach Sinow when his moods were like this.

"You're due to meet Violissa at the full day's rise."

Violissa. Even the sound of her name roused the stillness of his heart, causing it to rebel against the madness that had Sinow in its grasp.

"And I suppose you're going to tell me I have no choice but to meet her."

The snort Keary emitted caused Sinow to turn his head and eye his friend. "I'm not going to tell you that, or I risk losing a vital organ."

"Maybe a limb this time?" Sinow suggested, his brow arched. "You healed too quickly the last time I turned your liver to ash."

Keary paled, the only indication of the agony he'd experienced the last time he pissed Sinow off. "Maybe," he said. "A finger might be easier."

Sinow stared back over the ravine, annoyed that Keary had intruded upon his only place of escape. With his enhanced vision, he could see Violissa's castle far off in Cirillia. He could almost smell the lilac in the air.

"I'm thinking both legs if you don't leave me alone," he grumbled.

"At the risk of your wrath, Sinow, you need to meet her. The treaty—"

"Is bullshit. We all know it. The treaty was in place until Violissa and I met. It was a way to ensure we saw the prophecy through, which we didn't."

"The treaty is in place because it benefits us. It does nothing for Cirillia, but it helps our people."

Head dropping, Sinow let out a sigh before running his hand through his hair. Keary was right. No matter how Sinow wanted to avoid seeing Violissa, he had to for his people. And seeing her wouldn't be horrible. He always returned more at peace when he was with her.

"Fine. Now leave me alone until I must leave. I don't need you breathing down my neck anymore."

"You're a cantankerous bastard," Keary joked, testing Sinow's patience. He always pushed, toeing the line between friendship and disrespect, and he was the only one who got away with it.

"I'm about to add an arm to my list unless I change my mind and just sever your head. Reattaching that should make you reconsider calling me names in the future."

Only the echo of Keary's laugh remained, his shift taking him away before his comments forced Sinow to act. If any other Council had been present, Keary would be lying in agony at his feet now. If he collapsed any further over the edge of Darkness, it wouldn't matter if there was anyone present. Sinow would torture Keary properly regardless.

The ravine was silent, with the sun above casting long shadows far below. Sinow had been coming here since he was a child, stumbling upon it while hiding from the Council and his studies. Ever since, it had been his oasis, an escape from the pressures of inheriting the crown, from his father, from learning to rule, from his impending ascension, and now from the Darkness that consumed him every waking minute. The latter was inescapable, but at least here, away from everyone, the chaos quieted.

There was another advantage to the location. It offered him a chance to see into Cirillia. He'd spent countless hours wondering what the girl on the other side of the world looked like, wondering what it would be like to finally meet her, to fall in love with her like the prophecy foretold. Not that he would have ever admitted such a thing to anyone. And as far as he knew, no one else could see beyond the ravine. Boundary magic blocked their sight.

He cocked his head, only now realizing he'd always had the ability to see through the boundary in this spot as if it held some sort of magic that differed for him. No other part of the boundary had been penetrable before his ascension, but this always had. A deliberate connection, perhaps? One the Fates provided to strengthen his bond to Violissa?

Shrugging out the tension the thoughts had raised in his shoulders, he glanced back at the sun's position. It was midday, the sun's peak near. Time to meet Violissa. As if in answer, his power roared through him, searching for an escape and when denied one, coiling, ready to strike at the enemy it knew awaited him in the meeting grove. The one who owned the only part of Sinow the Darkness hadn't fully penetrated: his heart.

CHAPTER 40

Sunlight streamed across the grove, warming Violissa's skin, but even it could not stay the nerves that had her wringing her hands. She'd been dreading this day, avoiding thinking about her last encounter with Sinow, wishing the days would slow at the same time as she wished they would quicken. It confounded her that she wanted to hate him for how he had left her the day they'd discovered the truth about her, yet a longing still existed to see him. To still the confusion, she blamed his abrupt exit on his mood and the Darkness that owned him.

Two moon cycles had passed, but the incident was still fresh in her memory, the wound still raw even with the blame placed elsewhere. She paced the open field where the Councils usually met and over to the patch of grass where she and Sinow had spent their last few meetings. Her heart skipped a beat at the thought of him, but it returned to its steady rhythm when reminded of the reality at hand, and she let out a long exhale. He was so unpredictable. One moment he was everything she wanted, leaving her lost in his presence, and the next he was another man, drowned in terrifying power that left him cruel and her hurt. If only he could find the balance.

A stillness sat over the meeting grove until the air stirred and the heaviness of Sinow's shift settled over her skin. His presence was easy for her to sense, his aura drowning in the ebony of his power. Calming the fluttering of her heart and the involuntary rush of her magic at the cloak of Darkness, she turned to him.

Her heart sank as she studied him. Eyes blacker than the darkest abyss glared back at her. Streaks of black power curled in long tendrils of haze from his body. His ebony locks were messy, as if he had repeatedly run his hands through them.

She swallowed back the ache in her chest at the sight of him and drew on her power, ready to weave a calming spell to soothe the madness that lurked on the edge of his aura.

"Don't hit me with one of your blasted calming spells, Violissa," he commanded before she could finish. His hand raised to shield himself from it if she even tried. "This is not the time, and it will only aggravate me."

She didn't bother to argue. He was not himself, and no matter what she said, it wouldn't matter. There would be no cordial talks, no friendly banter or flirting words to straddle the distance their powers required. This was business only.

Sinow swiped his hand in the air, and the meeting table appeared. He leaned over it as a map of the western part of Tenebron rose to cover its surface.

"We have an outbreak here in our western lands," he said, pointing to the area. "Any medicines your Council can provide will be helpful. We used the reserves we had on hand long ago."

Violissa took a deep breath and prepared herself. She was not about to stand there, pretending nothing had happened the last time they'd seen each other. He may very well want to keep this short so he could avoid being with her, but she refused. A moment passed before she gathered her thoughts and responded.

"You didn't really come here to discuss what healing magic we can send your people, Sinow." His jaw ticked, the only sign of his irritation. "Our Councils could have discussed that. We need to talk about what happened with the Torathar. If anything, we need to discuss the threat to our people. The black scourge that is threatening our lands, not to mention the creature it brought about."

"Your lands, Violissa." His eyes darkened, and she noticed a flicker of red appear around the haze of his power. That was new and worrisome. "There is nothing threatening my lands, and so there is nothing to talk about."

"Damn it, Sinow." She refused to stand for his dark mood or his avoidance any longer. "Is it really such a problem to you that I am part Elvin?"

"Half Elvin," he snapped. "Honestly, Violissa, I don't really care that your mother was Elvin. If anything, it makes you even more alluring." He let his guard down for only an instant as he spoke the words, and his eyes softened before they dropped to the ground. The moment passed quickly, his sight returning to her. "I care that I was deceived," he growled. "And I don't like being lied to."

Pitch black, his eyes bore into her, sending a chill crawling over her skin and sinking into her spine. This was why people feared Dark Kings.

"I never lied to you, Sinow, and from what I heard that day, there were reasons we weren't told the truth of my origins." She bit her lip and watched him for a reaction. When she saw none, she continued, assuming that was his sign that she could continue. "I have just as much right to be angry. No, I take that back. I have more right to be angry. Sure, my Council and Kanine deceived you, never telling you the whole truth, but they fabricated my entire existence." Anger nosed its way into her blood, loud and hostile, and for the first time, she recognized the Elvin in her. The side that fed her intense emotional shifts that were unheard of among the Cirillians. "All this time I believed I was different, that I was alone. So much about both of us separates us from being normal, but for me, there is much more. My hair, my eyes, my nature powers, my emotions. I was alone with all of that, believing I was not born of parents, of flesh and blood."

She paced as her thoughts mangled her focus, spilling out like she would explode if the words didn't find a way out. "Do you know what it's like thinking you were not born but created? That no one in this world was like you or could understand you? And all this talk of prophecy and the Fates made me feel as if...as if..." The words wouldn't take form even though they were battering for escape, to finally admit what had nagged at her since she was young.

"As if the Fates put you here for only one purpose?" he said.

Swiveling to face him, she snapped her mouth shut to hide her surprise. She hadn't expected him to understand, yet that one line spoke volumes. Her eyes searched his, recognizing the lighter shade of brown, the softness they now held. Breath catching, she ignored the tightness in her chest, the strange skip of her pulse that seemed to act on instinct each time she looked at him.

"Yes," she whispered with a nod. Eyes dropping to focus on the fabric that sat bunched in her hand, she continued, "I always wanted to be more than that. More than something the Fates made to fulfill a goal, more than something that had no lineage, no past, only a future as the queen destined to marry the Dark King." She peeked up at him. "And now, even that doesn't seem like it will ever happen."

He stepped closer, and she saw the struggle, noted how the hues of brown danced in his eyes as they fought for dominance before he reversed the step. There was something in his expression, a longing that went unanswered because his power wouldn't allow it. He gripped the corner of the table, and she could hear the wood straining against his hold. Summoning a calming spell to ease the battle, she saw the understanding in his eyes as he shook his head and raised his hand to stop her.

She called her power back and quieted it, knowing he wanted to do this on his own. Her chest ached for him. No matter how frustrating her situation was, his was impossibly more difficult. He closed his eyes, and she watched his breathing calm, waiting for him to look back at her. When he finally did, his eyes were a rich brown.

"I'm not angry with you, Vi. This entire situation is overwhelming. We're both pawns in the Fates' hands. It's not all bad though," he said. The longer he held her gaze, the warmer she grew and the harder her pulse pounded. "I think we can both agree that the Fates did their job well." A coy grin grew, sending her breathing into an unsteady pattern. "Would it be that bad to be my queen?"

Words escaped her. She wanted to tell him it wouldn't, that she craved his touch again, to experience it outside of the Dream Realm. That if putting up with his changing moods meant she could have his mouth on hers every day, then she would happily accept that fate.

His grin curved deliciously, humor touching his eyes, and heat rose in her cheeks.

"No, I don't think you'd have any trouble with that," he answered for her. "I can think of a few benefits of taking you as my queen."

She swallowed, the sound too loud in her ears.

"One day?" she asked, unable to condense any of her thoughts into words.

Hands clenching in and out, grin faltering as the earthy hue of his irises morphed a closer shade to black, he said, "One day."

Dropping his eyes, he scraped his hands through his hair and took a seat at the table, resting his head in his hands. "Where do we go from here, Vi? This is torment."

He lifted his head, and Violissa sucked in a breath. He looked like a tortured soul, and she wanted to go to him, to take his face in her hands and kiss away the pain, to hold him until the Darkness abated and he could be free. But that was a fantasy that would never see fruition, at least not anytime soon. She knew this was a consequence of her decision to turn her back on the Fates. To deny the prophecy so stubbornly without thinking of what would happen.

"I don't know," she answered honestly. Defeat sank into her shoulders, weighing her down.

Sinow's fist came down on the table and she jumped. Rising, he placed distance between them, and she wondered if he was doing it to ebb the rise of Darkness she could see flickering around him again. A calming spell would ease his suffering, but she didn't dare weave one, knowing he had stopped her twice.

She rubbed her forehead with her palm, noting her own power increase in response. It was a struggle to keep it at bay every time his surged. An instinctual urge to fight him and rid the area of his power overcame her, no matter how attracted she was to him.

"What do you want me to say, Sinow? Neither of us knows the answer. I don't know what to do except to be patient and hope this phase in our powers, your powers, finally passes."

"I'm tired of being patient!" he roared, and she saw the flinch of regret before he shielded it behind his anger. "I crave you, Violissa, and knowing I can't act on it is maddening. How can this be part of the Fates' plan? Does their prophecy really mean to have us live like this?"

Heart thudding so violently it pained her, Violissa tried to hide her shock at his admission. He craved her, and she wondered if his emotions ran as deep as hers, or if it was just her body he wanted. She couldn't ask and, on some level, she recognized it ran deeper. The Fates had ensured that.

"Sinow," she said, stepping toward him. He shook his head, moving away from her, his mouth so tight she could tell he was grinding his teeth as he fought his power. "This isn't the work of the Fates. It's my doing." Admitting it was risky. He could take it the wrong way and leave her again as he had before. He could blame her for the agony he was suffering and never speak to her again. The thought left her gutted, and she fought her reaction to it. Sinow started to speak, but she continued, needing to tell him the truth of what the Fate had shared with her. "If I hadn't been so stubborn, the union would have taken place before the ascension, and you would not be suffering so. We would both have what we long for without our powers warring."

He wrinkled his brow, saying, "What are you talking about?"

"That was their plan. Only I deviated from it, and now you're suffering for it. If I had followed the rules of the prophecy, our union would have merged our powers. My Light power would have eased your ascension, but now—"

His harsh laugh stopped her, his features sharpening, twisted by his power. Once again, she had made the wrong decision. And once again, she would pay. Driven by the Darkness that now consumed him, he stalked closer, towering over her as he sneered. "You really think I need your powers for anything? That your weak Light magic would influence me or my power?" It took every bit of strength not to put space between them and even more to contain her magic as it whipped through her, seeking to smother the Dark magic that hung around her like a sinister shadow. "I need nothing from you, Violissa. And your words only confirm that Tynan was right, after all."

"Tynan?" she asked, confused by his words. "What does Tynan have to do with any of this?"

Excitement flittered in his eyes, and she could read the expectation there as the air grew thicker. He wanted to see her fear, to have her cower before him. But it wasn't fear she experienced. It was sadness, and he must have seen it there because a flicker of brown emerged from the depths of ebony in his eyes before it sank back below. His moment of conflict seemed only to agitate him further, and his lip curled into what she could only describe as a snarl.

"Tynan always said your Lightbearers manipulated the prophecy to weaken us. In fact, he's always thought it was a lie fed to us to entrap me and weaken my powers."

Her blood froze, followed by her body as he leaned down,

dragging his cheek along hers. His mouth was so near her ear that the warmth of his breath draped over her skin. The moment should have left her frightened, and that was exactly his goal, but that part of her the Fates had bound to him, the part that loved him, even under the influence of the Darkness, lurched at the heat that encompassed her.

She leaned into him without realizing it, almost turning her face so that her mouth would meet his. Envisioning the force with which he would destroy her if he took her this way, if the Darkness was in control, warring with her power in a battle of flesh and will. She almost tested his reaction until a growl rumbled through his chest as he said, "Now that sounds exactly like what you just told me, Violissa."

The accusation stung, defeating all her urges, and she shoved him away, letting her power seep out to beat back the shadows.

"You take my words out of context, Sinow. It is your brother whose intentions you should question, not mine. Your father believed in the prophecy, and deep down, you do as well. If you don't, then why are you here?" She glared at him, knowing her eyes had lost their brilliance and likely matched the color of the forest behind them. Hands on her hips, she waited for his answer. The fight she'd seen in him earlier was gone, the Sinow she knew lost below the gnarled claws of his power.

"That is an excellent question, Violissa. Why am I here? In fact, why are either of us here? It's clear we can't stand being near each other. If what you say is true and we needed to wed before the ascension, then why bother?"

Those endless orbs of terror watched her with anticipation, waiting for her to break. And it worked. Her guard slipped, disappointment stabbing her chest along with a fear that this was it, the moment she would lose her chance to make things right again. But that's what he wanted, to hurt her with his words, and she was too proud. Gathering her strength and letting her magic shield her, she readied herself to respond, but he gave her no chance. Instead, he went in for the kill.

"So why don't we just walk away, Violissa? There are plenty of attractive women in Tenebron who would die, no pun intended there, to be my queen and bear their king a son. Why should I waste any more time on you?"

The words tore at her, shredding her to the core, and she struggled not to bend over from the agony they caused. That's what he was looking for. That vicious side of him, and she hated it. If only he could learn to balance his powers. This wasn't the man who had talked to her for hours in this same grove. It wasn't the man who, only moments before, had confessed that his craving for her was torture. But this was part of him, and no matter that he couldn't straddle the line between drowning in his Darkness and burying it, she would not let him win, nor would she let him know how badly he had hurt her.

She bristled at his words and drew her power further, seeing the Light pour from her as the Dark swirled around him.

"Then don't," she blurted before she could take the words back. "Maybe you're right. All of this has been for naught. It's too early in our reigns to take a mate, anyway." She waved her hand as if dismissing the idea, but his response was unexpected.

"Never too early, Violissa. In fact, a mate right now might help me release some of the angst you seem to have built up in me."

"Now?" she asked, her eyes going wide before she caught herself.

He couldn't. He wouldn't. The very thought was sickening. The prophecy said he was hers. It said nothing about another woman having him. But it wasn't as if they were young. They had lived for a thousand years. Enough time for him to have had lovers, enough for him to still indulge now that she had turned him down. The idea left her stricken because she had never once entertained the idea of being with anyone else; even the thought made her nauseous. It always had.

"Why not?" he said, his eyes narrowing, his expression unreadable. Fury seemed to pulse from him in waves that bounced against her power as if searching for a weakness. "Maybe I'll take a few before I'm ready to deal with you, or maybe I won't deal with you at all."

"Fine," she snapped, venom protecting her from the agony that was currently eviscerating her. "If that's good for you, then it's good for me." She tipped her chin up, forcing a confident smile. "I don't know why we even bothered with the prophecy or each other. It's clear we're still the enemies we started as. In fact, I think I'll start the search today so I can finally be done with you." She didn't know where the words had come from, but they were out now, spoken and irretrievable. A look of surprise crossed his eyes, but she didn't care to hear anymore from him. "Goodbye, Sinow. I'll have my Council contact yours from now on. I wouldn't want you to be burdened with me more than you already have been."

Shifting, she landed in her room, collapsing to her knees as they buckled under her. What had she done? But she hadn't done it. He had. Accusing her of lying to him, of manipulating him so she could weaken him. It was a ridiculous notion and one she should have shut down immediately, but he'd distracted her being so close, his mouth over her ear, his power encompassing her body. And that moment of vulnerability had led to heated words that neither of them could take back.

Even though she recognized that his Dark side had influenced his words and that somewhere inside the man she knew and cared about was fighting to be heard, it hurt nonetheless. The concern now was whether he would follow through with his threat. She wouldn't. There was no way she could even consider another man. Stomach turning at the thought, she dismissed it, hoping he would gain control.

Lifting herself from the floor, she smoothed her skirts, knowing there was nothing to do but wait and see. For now, there were bigger issues to deal with. The Torathar and the reason for their emergence.

After pulling herself together and containing her emotions, she shifted just outside of the meeting room. Her Council had been busy while she was gone. Books and maps lay spread across the table, hands flipping through pages as voices carried with different suggestions and theories.

Lip sinking under the weight of her front teeth, she tasted the bitterness of her blood as she distracted herself from thoughts of Sinow. There was no room to worry about him. Too much needed to be done, and if he remained on her mind, the day would be even longer. The belief that his threats had been a bluff reassured her as she walked into the room, greeted by ten pairs of eyes eagerly awaiting her return.

CHAPTER 41

What had he done? A heavy sense of foreboding rippled down Sinow's spine as he jerked his sight from where Violissa had been. There was nothing in his words that had held truth. They'd been malicious, spoken to evoke a reaction, but not the one she had given. He didn't want another woman. There was no possibility to even consider it, which he never had. He ran his hand through his hair. Maybe she was just calling his bluff. Or maybe he had pushed her too far. Fates, if that was the case, he might lose her.

The part of him that cared about her clawed from deep below, trying its best to surface and reclaim control. It wanted to go after her and take the whole conversation back. But that part wasn't in control, and the Darkness slammed it back to the depths where it held him hostage.

She couldn't do what she'd threatened, though. Just like he couldn't. The prophecy ruled them both too tightly. Even if he tried to get near another female, the reaction would be severe. He knew the consequences he faced with just the thought of another woman. He'd made that mistake before. Long before he'd met Violissa, when she'd simply been a bedtime story. Tynan had tried to get him interested in one of the serving maids. The thought of her had made Sinow violently ill for days. The reaction was one he had avoided since then, his brother often evoking it whenever he had the chance.

No, Vioissa would never take another man. Her response had to be the same as his. The Fates' way of ensuring they stayed loyal to each other and the prophecy long before they met.

Angry splashes of crimson and ebony blinded him at the thought of how weak the prophecy made him. Weak for a woman who had pushed him away and threatened to take another. He grabbed his head in frustration. This was his fault. His power was out of control and pushing to hurt her. Calm was necessary, but he had repeatedly refused Violissa's attempts at a calming spell. He would need to assuage the Darkness himself.

Head lifting, he looked to the place where Violissa had sat during their last visit, the sun glittering in her emerald eyes and streaking the golden strands of her hair with silver. Desire rippled with a ferocity through every vein in his body, giving the weak part of him the moment it needed. He surfaced, tearing through the Darkness and taking over. Vision clear, mind calm, he exhaled. It was good to be back in control, but the reality of what his lack of clarity had cost him pummeled him.

Turning his eyes to the sky in agony, he cried, "Why?" As if the Fates would answer, he waited before saying, "Why can't I gain control? What am I missing?"

Maybe Violissa was right. He was terrified of becoming his grandfather, and nothing terrified him. He was the Dark King, the most terrifying man in their world. And there was no denying he was already becoming his grandfather. Tipping to the Darkness far too easily now, becoming another person. At times, it almost seemed there were two different people fighting for dominance within him.

The Fates gave him no response, and he dropped his head in defeat. He had no choice but to head home. The right thing to do would be to go after Violissa and admit he'd said the wrong things, but although every part of him screamed he needed to do this, he was too proud. And so, he left the grove, unaware that his pride would soon cost him everything.

***

THE DINING ROOM was empty when he returned from the grove. He expected no one to be present, mid-day had passed, but he was famished. The tug of war inside him used all his energy and always left him feeling as if he hadn't eaten for days. Luckily, lunch had recently been served, and some scraps remained on the table. Taking his seat, he grabbed a thick leg of meat and bit into it, savoring the taste and realizing he hadn't eaten all day. Movement broke his blank stare, and he looked up to see Tynan taking the seat across from him. Tynan leaned back in the chair and propped his feet on the table.

"Really, Tynan, I'm trying to eat in peace."

"Trouble with Violissa again, brother?"

Sinow's skin prickled as it did every time Tynan said her name. "Why do you ask, Tynan?"

"Well, I overheard—"

Fist dropping to the table, sending food and plates scattering, Sinow snarled, "Were you spying on me?" The Darkness reared its fangs, and this time, he welcomed it.

Tynan's lips thinned, and Sinow detected the slight tension in his posture. "As your advisor, it is my place to know what goes on in this realm."

"It is your place to respect my privacy," he growled, standing and leaning over the table. "It is not your place to spy on your king. You've gone too far this time, Tynan."

Tynan rose, his eyes hard as he stared Sinow down. He never stood up to Sinow, never showed any backbone, and Sinow couldn't help but wonder at his sudden ferocity.

"And you haven't gone far enough, Sinow. What you did today was the first step, but if you don't follow your words up with action, if you return to her side, then you'll doom yourself and the kingdom. The kingdom needs a terrifying king, not one whipped into subservience by some idiotic prophecy and an enemy queen who would chain your potential."

Anger flared through Sinow like an inferno devouring the land. His eyes scorched with Darkness, and he knew they had turned black. Fear crossed Tynan's face before he hid it below a firm downward turn of his features, leaning toward Sinow as if to challenge him. With an inhale that scraped his lungs, Sinow straightened to his full height. In his current state, he could have cared less about what Tynan had said regarding the prophecy. It was the knowledge that his brother had dared spy on him and the way he was now speaking to Sinow. His voice raised in defiance and with the confidence of someone with power. Commanding and challenging his brother, his king.

A growl rumbled from Sinow's chest, and he drew his power, sending Tynan across the room and pinning him to the wall. Rubble fell, and the hall shook as Sinow shifted to appear in front of him. He grabbed Tynan by the collar, his continued glare further angering Sinow.

"You will watch your tongue, Tynan. No matter that you are my brother, I am still your king. Your role is to advise, not to command."

He released his brother, who fell to the ground where he remained on his knees. Tynan held his stare, and Sinow detected something within it that taunted his power before Tynan lowered his head. "Your pardon, Sinow. My passion for your reign to be the greatest in our people's history has once again bested me. I will speak more wisely next time."

"And," Sinow continued, ignoring Tynan's groveling, which soured his stomach, "if I ever find that you've spied on me again, I will banish you for all eternity, brother or not."

"Yes, my liege."

Sinow walked away, but the power had hold of him, and something Tynan had said piqued his interest.

"Tell me why you think my conversation with Violissa went well."

The sound of Tynan rising had Sinow swiveling back to his brother. "Did I tell you to rise?"

Tynan dropped back to his knees. Flexing his hands, Sinow gestured for Tynan to rise. The disdain that curled on Tynan's lips before they curved to a grin caused Sinow to tilt his head and study his brother. Tynan ran his hands down his shirt, smoothing down the material and taking his time to respond. The gesture informed Sinow that Tynan was carefully measuring his words before speaking. It was a calculated move and a smart one given Sinow's current state.

Patience thinning, Sinow was about to release his power again when Tynan said, "You don't need her." He walked to the table, picked up a piece of fruit and held it in his hand as if he were weighing its worth. "Her Council told Father that a union with her would make you more powerful. You're already the most powerful king we've ever had. What difference would wedding her make? Why bother harnessing your inner nature just to bed her?" Tynan glanced over his shoulder at Sinow, who had crossed his arms, listening intently.

"Go on."

"Why not walk away like you said today? Take a break. Wed one of our own and have her bear the next king."

The thought was the same he had voiced without merit to Violissa, only to see her reaction. She'd had a momentary lapse, the hurt passing over her features before she called his bluff and made her own ridiculous statement about taking another. Neither of them had a choice. Even if the prophecy weren't in place and Violissa were not his, finding his future queen would never be as easy as Tynan had made it.

Heirs never came so early in an immortal's life, nor did a queen. Sure, he could take mortals for pleasure, likely killing them, as few could withstand the power of a Dark king in the throes of his climax. But he didn't have any desire to, and then there was the prophecy.

He tried to envision bedding another woman, touching and kissing someone other than Violissa. The hasty reaction was the same as it had always been. His stomach lurched, his head pounding as emotion strangled him and warred with his power. But that didn't stop the violent physical reaction he now realized Tynan had wanted. Sinow fought against the rising tide within, not wanting to suffer the embarrassment of having Tynan witness this moment of weakness. Try as he might, the bile rose in his throat, and he turned away from Tynan, heaving the contents of his stomach onto the stone floor.

Tynan chuckled while Sinow spat and wiped his mouth on the back of his hand.

"Even with all that power, you're still a pawn of the Fates."

Sinow threw his hand out and sent his brother careening through the room again, this time crashing into the doors. "There will be no more talk of another union," he roared, his two sides in agreement for once. "Nor will there be an heir yet," he followed, trying to remove the vile images from his head. "It's too early. You know how it works. That won't come for thousands of years. And it most certainly will not come from anyone but Violissa."

He sat, eyeing the food on the table he had once hungered for and hearing his stomach tumble.

Tynan brought himself to his feet, rubbing debris from his hair. "Fine, no heir, and apparently no other woman. I'm not sure why the two of you even had that talk earlier, if this is where you were going to end up."

Sinow ignored him, his mind working something out. An heir would come when he and Violissa finally wed. It was inevitable. "Imagine," he drawled, power whirling within him.

He thought of the heir their union would bring. He was the most powerful Dark King in history, and she the most powerful Light Queen, with Elvin blood gracing her. The child would have power beyond any he could fathom. Unlike his grandfather, that thought did not threaten him, but instead enticed him. A strange sense of calm, a balance of sorts, rested over him. Rolling his neck, he stood and smiled at Tynan. He had found a reason for his inner Darkness to consider Violissa, and he didn't want to risk losing that sensation. A place of contentment within the turmoil and an acceptance of the prophecy.

"No, there will be no other union. Violissa will be mine, just as the prophecy states."

Tynan looked confused, and Sinow wondered briefly at the irritation he saw in his brother's features, but his thoughts had him too distracted to think further about it or mention it.

"Imagine the power our son will possess," he continued. "There have never been two rulers as powerful, and never with the potential for the two to mate. A union will bring power like no other to our realm, Tynan, and that is worth any sacrifice I need to make."

Tynan looked as though he wanted to object before his shoulders slumped. Sinow pounded his hand down on the table, seeing Tynan jump and relishing the reflex after Tynan's earlier enjoyment of him emptying his stomach. "Never spy on me again and never dare to think you can tell me what I need to do when it comes to Violissa. Not unless the thought of life in the Banished Realm sounds appealing."

He shifted, leaving Tynan as the power to which he had reluctantly given himself over coursed through his veins at his revelation.

CHAPTER 42

Rain pounded against the windows and rattled the panes as Tynan slammed the book closed. He rubbed his temples and leaned his elbows on the desk. What had seemed a simple task had become more troublesome than expected. The book contained spells written in an ancient tongue he didn't recognize. Deciphering them was excruciating. Using various books sourced from the lower libraries, he had broken a handful, but with them came the discovery that there was more to the book. The spells were only the first step. To release the power held within the book, more than just mastering the spells was required, and he had yet to determine what that was.

Peering out at the rain, he sat back in his chair. He was losing ground with Sinow and Violissa. Keeping them separated was growing difficult, and he had run out of ways to interfere without looking obvious. Each day he failed brought them closer to their union, and he feared there would be no chance for his plan to succeed once that happened. Sinow would be too powerful and, with Violissa by his side, undefeatable.

After spying on their last meeting, he'd had hope. He'd caught only a fraction of their conversation. The cloaking spell he'd taken from the book had been more difficult to master than he'd thought. By the time he made it to the meeting grove, Violissa was sulking about something, and Sinow was at the table holding his head like some weak mortal. He'd barely contained the laughter the sight caused. And he'd almost given up until the tone changed and Violissa said something that triggered Sinow's power. Something curious about their union that was exactly what Tynan needed. A pissed-off Sinow was hard to control, but with the Darkness out of balance like it had been, he was unhinged. And that's exactly how he'd been when he left the grove.

Tynan had returned expecting to fuel the fire, but his conversation with Sinow had gone sour quickly. The bastard had convinced himself that he still wanted the bitch.

Tynan rose, his sight falling to the storm outside. Wind howled, and streaks of lightning colored the sky. He needed something more, something to ensure the two did not wed. Fortunately, regardless of Sinow's insistence that he would continue forward, his powers opposed Violissa's enough that the two could barely stand to be near one another. There was irony in the idea that they wanted each other but couldn't stand each other. Almost like the Fates had a sense of humor. Whatever it was, it bought him more time, but not enough. At some point, they would overcome it, and his plans would disintegrate.

The wind rattled his window, catching his attention. He needed a failsafe, something to ensure there was no turning back for them. To rattle their foundation like the wind was doing to his windows. Turning back to the book, he flipped through the pages.

The wind was the key. There had been a spell he'd deciphered earlier about the wind. Pages shuffled by as he searched for it, his frustration mounting until the page opened. He fell into his chair, reading through the spell. Power to manipulate the wind to do his bidding. His lip curved, snaking into a wicked grin.

Sinow was due to hold a full Council meeting soon, and the Council would want a decision on Violissa. Their people were getting restless for a union. Idiotic mortals who knew nothing about the ways of the immortals. Kings never took wives this early in their reigns. The less mortals knew about their ruler, the better, and in this case, it would benefit Tynan.

The meeting was the perfect way to stir up doubt among the Council and throw in some suggestions of his own to make the others think. If a trusted servant were to be present in that meeting and overhear something that Tynan could further manipulate with his power, well, then a little fun could be had. A wind spell to overhear the rumors that would spread, then carry those words to Violissa. With her strange abilities over nature, understanding the message tangled in a gust of wind would be easy for her.

Propping his feet on the desk, he placed his hands behind his head, ideas spinning. It was time to take his game to a new level. If this didn't work, then he would have no choice but to come out against Sinow before all his pieces were in play. He was hoping it wouldn't come to that yet. Not without understanding the power the book held. For now, he would trust in the wind to do his dirty deeds and twist Violissa's emotions. If she were truly the nature queen they said she was, then she would see the wind as a friend. A friend cloaking the unseen enemy below. And setting the stage for her undoing and Sinow's.

CHAPTER 43

Sinow sat before his Council, who met regularly with him to discuss issues in the realm. Those meetings were one of the few instances when they were all together. It had been over a moon cycle since he'd last seen Violissa, and he wished he had let her use one of her calming spells. He struggled daily to maintain clarity, to keep the Darkness from overtaking him. The moment with Tynan when he had returned from seeing her had given him balance, but it had been short-lived. The internal battle returned and wore him down endlessly.

Slumped in the corner, Tynan caught Sinow's attention. His eyes were focused on the ground, darting back and forth like he was searching for something. The movement stopped when the servant handed him a drink. Muscles tense, Sinow ignored him, intending to give him an earful when this was over. He didn't like servants in their meetings, but his father had allowed it. The meetings sometimes ran long, and rather than interrupt discussions by using magic to make food or drink, the most trusted servants remained in the room for any needs that arose.

Sinow had dissuaded the practice, thinking it too lax, but it seemed his brother hadn't given his request heed. He would address it when this was over. He didn't have the patience to deal with Tynan now, and his power was so charged he'd likely kill the servant inadvertently.

Flexing his fists, he looked back at his Council. "Let's get this started," he said. "Are there any urgent issues to bring forward today?"

A few of them exchanged looks, and Mackay cleared his throat before addressing Sinow. He suspected what was coming and tensed in his seat.

"My liege, we have a concern that needs to be addressed," Mackay said hesitantly. His Council knew how volatile Sinow's power was these days, and they avoided stirring it. Mackay's hesitation led Sinow to believe the others had chosen him to do the stirring.

"Go ahead," Sinow said, leaning forward in his chair. An orb of light flickered somewhere behind him, lending an even more frightening edge to his appearance.

Mackay cleared his throat again and continued, "As you know, it's been years since your ascension, and there is talk among the people, questions frankly about when you will..." He stopped as Sinow shifted back in his seat and crossed his arms. He already knew where this was going and didn't like it. Mackay continued, "They want to know when you'll take a queen."

Tynan broke the sudden tension, spitting his drink all over the table in response.

Not bothering to look from Mackay, Sinow snapped, "Pull yourself together, Tynan, or leave." Rolling his neck to ease the tension that had mounted, Sinow watched as Mackay fought to hold his glare. "So tell me, Mackay, since when do I care what my people think? I fail to see how this constitutes a matter of urgency." Hands stretching to the table and gripping the edge, he looked at the other Council. "Are people really concerned with this, or are you using them as a scapegoat for your own agenda? My father didn't take a wife until well into his reign. I see no reason not to do the same."

"What of the Light Queen, Sinow? Do you not think it's time to act on that union?" Keary asked, standing up to address him. Sinow swiveled his head to him, scrunching his eyes. Keary knew his answer, and he'd discussed his reasons with him earlier in private. It irritated Sinow that he'd taken this moment to bring it back up.

"You know very well the situation with the queen, Keary. It will happen of its own accord."

"Why will it not happen now, Sinow?" his brother asked.

Eyes penetrating, he stared at Tynan. His power sparked in jagged strikes against his skin, and he considered unleashing it at his brother. Sinow was about to threaten to remove him if he didn't keep his thoughts to himself when another Council followed Tynan's question.

"He brings up a good point, Sinow. Why can it not happen now?"

Sinow's jaw tightened so that the taut tendons strained to snap. This conversation was not what he'd intended to discuss today. He didn't feel he needed to explain himself to his Council. He was king. "Because it is too soon."

"Is that really it?" Tynan asked, his eyes too excited.

"Since the answer your king provided was not enough," Sinow said, raking a hand through his hair. "No, it's more than that. Our powers oppose one another too much now that the ascension has occurred. We cannot even be close to each other yet. A union at this time would be disastrous for both the realms."

Voices filled the room, each vying to be heard, each rallying for further explanation and answers. Sinow pounded his fist on the table, silencing them. "Enough! Let us end this conversation—"

"It begs the question, Sinow," Faolan interrupted. "Why bother with the Light Queen at all now? Obviously, a union is unnecessary, as their Council had previously insisted it was." The voices murmured again. "You are the most powerful king the realm has ever had. Why not forget this prophecy garbage and look to one of our own?"

Many of the voices asserted their agreement. Sinow watched Keary shake his head as he met his gaze.

Stay calm, he said to Sinow in enaigne.

But it was difficult to maintain control. Heat was rising in his chest, his magic stabbing at him and escaping from between his fingers. They knew better, knew how things worked, that even if Violissa wasn't a factor, he would need to wait until a sign from the Fates to find a queen. But that didn't mean he couldn't dally in the flesh of mortals until the right one appeared, and that's what they were suggesting. The thought was nauseating, but he would never admit it. A storm of emotions had his Council in its grasp, their frustration heightened that the prophecy thing had never seen fruition.

Tynan shattered Sinow's patience, rising from his seat and exclaiming, "That's a fantastic idea. That's exactly what you should do, brother. Marry one of our women. They may not be as stunning as Violissa," once again the sound of her name coming from his mouth grated on Sinow, "but I'd bet your crown they're more exciting in bed."

Rage ripped through Sinow, and he erupted. Standing, he brought his fist down against the table, shattering it. A fire blazed within him, and ebony shades of black swirled around him. He had no doubt his eyes were the color of a moonless night.

"There will be no more talk of unions," he bellowed. "I will have no one but Violissa, and that will be on my terms and not yours. If I hear anyone suggest I bed a mortal or, worse, wed one, I will leave you in a perpetual state of torment for the next century. Now leave me, all of you." Flames licked from his fingers and scorched the broken piece of the table that remained in his hand. The room had grown silent, and guilt sat on their faces. It was almost like they had woken from a spell and realized their suggestions had been foolish and dangerous. Each stood and bowed before shifting, leaving only Keary and Tynan.

"That includes you, Tynan." He released his magic and wrapped it around Tynan's body, slamming him into the floor where a sharp chunk of table sat. It pierced through Tynan, who grimaced as Sinow raised Tynan's body back up. He didn't break his eye contact with Sinow or show his pain. If he had, Sinow would have made the punishment twofold.

Sinow walked over to him, standing above him. "I no longer want you in my presence. And if you dare do something like that again..." He ripped the chunk of wood from Tynan's chest, enjoying the blood that gushed from the wound before his body began to heal. "I will spear your body on the tallest point of this keep and ensure you remain like that until you're in so much pain, you return yourself to the Fates and rid me of dealing with you."

Tynan pushed himself from the floor, holding his hand over the wound. He glowered at Sinow before he disappeared.

The tension fled Sinow's muscles, and he looked over at Keary, who shook his head.

"You let him get away with too much, Sinow, and you always have. I will tell you again, he is a weakness you need to address, and soon."

"I will," Sinow replied, looking at the chunk of table in his hand. Keary ran a hand above the smashed remains of the table, making it whole again.

"It's been some time since the ascension, Sinow. Maybe it's time to approach Violissa about the union again. It's clear you will give yourself no other option."

Sinow sat back down and ran a hand through his hair. "You know what happened last time. I know I don't want another option. She's the only one, but the last time we met, there were words exchanged. The kinds of words that are difficult to take back."

"Many things can be taken back, Sinow, especially words. I've known you since we were kids, and I can tell what you feel about her is deep. Actually, I'd venture a guess that's an understatement. That right there should be worth risking the humbling task of apologizing for what you said."

"You're probably right." Sinow leaned forward, his elbows on his knees. "But I don't know if that's enough, Keary. The instinctual hatred buried in our powers erupts when we even attempt to get close. It's getting better, but still not like it was before the ascension. I don't know that we'll ever surmount it."

"Why is that, I wonder? Maybe that was the reason the Light Council wanted the union before the ascension?"

"Apparently," Sinow said, rubbing his hands over his face and leaning back again. "Violissa mentioned something about it when we last met." He clawed his hands through his hair, thinking of how he'd reacted. Taking offense at her words instead of really listening to them. "And I overreacted like a fool when she did."

Keary laughed. "It wouldn't be the first time, and I'm sure it won't be the last. Look, Sinow, I know you tried pushing through the reaction before, but you need to keep trying. What's the worst that could happen? So, you blast each other with power and end up with some injuries. You're both immortal. You can't kill each other, and you can heal. If I were you, I'd try it again. Don't pay the Council any heed. They're just trying to do the right thing for you and the realm. Unfortunately, what they brought up wasn't the right thing."

Standing and giving Sinow a slap on the shoulder, he said, "As long as we've known each other, Sinow, I've never seen you want anything as bad as you want Violissa. You've always been obstinate about maintaining your celibacy, as if you were one of the Council. And while we had our struggles with it, you've made it look embarrassingly easy. I guess what I'm saying is, the Fates have joined the two of you together since before you were born. Don't let more excuses keep you apart."

Sinow peered up at him, wondering when Keary had become the sage.

"Well, I'm off," Keary continued. "I have the honor of soothing egos my hot-tempered king bruised once again." He gave Sinow a playful smirk. "Good day, my liege."

Sinow sat quietly after Keary left, thinking back on their conversation. Maybe Keary was right. Excuses ruled his relationship with Violissa. Her excuses had pushed them apart initially, and now his excuses were keeping them apart. He had enough control now; it was time to take that control and use it. Time to make her his. Their next meeting wasn't for two more moons, so he would use the time to his advantage. Work on containing his power and its reaction to hers so that by the time he saw her next, he'd walk right up to her, take her in his arms, and kiss her like he'd wanted since he first laid eyes on her. Then he'd bed her again as he had in the Dream Realm, but this time it would be no dream. His hands would touch, his mouth would taste, and the pleasure would be undeniable. A smile grew at the thought.

The air flickered in the corner of the room, and his smile faltered. Squinting at the slight distortion, he tried to determine what it was, a nagging at his mind that he needed to worry about it. But a crash outside the room tore his eyes from the spot, and when he looked back, the air was still and his vision clear.

Shrugging, he left to find out what had caused the disturbance, unaware that with his instinct ignored, the prophecy strayed further from its original path.

CHAPTER 44

Violissa rose from the water of the small pond. The sun glittered off the surface of her skin, creating a haloed effect about her. She'd taken the morning to escape and clear her mind, but as always, her thoughts had strayed to Sinow. The longing for him was growing. It increased after each meeting and even after the words spoken at the last meeting, it hadn't simmered. She knew he hadn't been himself and that the words they'd volleyed had merely been idle threats. At least she hoped they had been. It was so hard to guess what he would do if completely under the influence of his powers. The possibilities of what might have happened since that day were not ones she wanted to entertain, but still they crept in. And with them came an envy she didn't like.

"Don't be stupid, Violissa, you know he hasn't done anything," she told herself, shrugging off the negativity.

If his connection to her was as strong as hers was to him, then he had merely thrown words out to hurt her. There would be no mortal in his bed, no other woman to touch him like she wanted. Even the thought stirred her envy so that the water turned hot.

Shaking the images away, she turned to more positive

thoughts. A future with Sinow. It was time to relent and admit the Fates had been right, to give up her independent ways and let the Fates take the lead. She had established herself as queen, become comfortable with her duties, and embraced her new powers. And she now realized she was in love with Sinow. No matter which way she looked at it, love was the only word to describe it. Giddiness came over her when she thought of him. Her heart raced in anticipation of each meeting. A part of her even wished she'd accepted it all before the ascension, but not even she had the power to turn back time.

She chuckled as she thought of how worried she'd been after her dream with the Fate. Maybe it had all been a dream and not a warning. Years had passed, and no disasters had occurred. If anything, she and Sinow had only grown closer, even if they couldn't be near one another. She was confident that one of them would test the safety boundary they'd set up between each other again. Sometimes they crossed it, but those times were rare, and touching each other was never the goal in those moments. It was strange how when his power had him in its grasp or he focused on something other than the need for her, he could be so close she could reach up and kiss him.

Leaving the water, she walked to her dress and drew it over her damp skin. A breeze blew through her hair, causing a chill to tingle down her back. The breeze wrapped itself around her as voices touched her ears.

Violissa. It was an eerie tone reminiscent of a chorus of voices.

She looked around as the breeze tugged at her dress like it was trying to get her attention. Communication with the trees and plants and even with the land was something she had done often, but never had she heard the wind speak. Excitement flittered through her, causing her skin to pebble.

Violissa, it said again, drifting away as it rebuilt its strength. *We have heard talk of a union.*

She perked up at the word, and the wind whipped across her skin.

"Sinow?" she asked, feeling even better about her decision to move forward with their relationship.

Yes, it replied, a flutter rippling in her chest at the confirmation. *For Sinow, but your name was not in the air.*

Her smile faltered. "What are you saying?" But her heart had dropped, and every warning in her mind was telling her she didn't want to know the answer.

It is being spoken that a union will be to one of Tenebron.

"No..." Memories of their last meeting flashed back to her. "I don't understand. Who else would there be?" The words came out in a string of pained syllables, her emotions clamoring for freedom. Her chest ached with throbs like feet stomping repeatedly on it.

There is merely talk that it will happen. We have not heard a name.

"From whom did you hear this? It cannot be true." She was grasping at the thought that it may have been a rumor, but knew the wind would not have bothered her about just a rumor. Why she trusted the wind for its word was a question that never crossed her mind.

From servants at his castle and people in the towns. The word has spread quickly. We hear all and have not heard otherwise.

The air froze in her lungs, her legs shaking with the effort to remain standing. "He's taking another," she mumbled, not wanting to believe the words. Tears rolled down her cheeks, and she rubbed them away, trying to calm her emotions, but the wrenching of her heart wouldn't stop. The breeze caressed her face, drying the moisture on her cheeks before drawing away.

If Sinow's words weren't so fresh in her mind. If she hadn't threatened to find another to replace him before he could replace her, then she might have doubted the words the wind had spoken. But the words were too fresh, the pain too raw, and so she dropped to her knees. He had told her he would no longer wait, and she had disregarded his words, thinking it an empty threat. But she should have known. Dark Kings didn't play games. And they weren't patient. She had pushed him too far, and he had given up on her.

Another tear left a trail down her cheek, and she brought her hand up to wipe it away. He was taking another. He would touch another, kiss another, bring another woman to climax, and do all the things she wanted him to do to her. Those things she had believed he would reserve for her, just as she had reserved them for him. But he hadn't, and the agony the thought brought cut so deep that the tears spilled until the ground below her was wet with them. Anguish welled in her chest, and she doubled over before collapsing on the grass and holding her legs tight to her.

The emotions that pounded at her were unknown to her, bringing an ache that left her riven. She never stopped to doubt the words the wind had spoken to her. Never wondered how this could be, simply assumed it must be truth based on that last conversation. Her mind forced it to make sense.

Their lack of intimacy had frustrated Sinow, the distance they maintained, one he no longer wanted to fight, and so he had given up. He was a man, a Dark King, no less. He had needs she had not met, and so he had turned to another, just as he had said he would. She had made the first step in denying him and the prophecy. Now it was his turn.

Her mind rationalized his motives and the consequences, the impending union to a woman who was not her. And so she lay there, her tears unstoppable, as the land wove a blanket to cover her and the trees bent to shelter her. Providing the only comfort they could to their queen.

Night fell, but the pain did not abate. When she could cry no more, Violissa pulled herself from the ground, whispered thanks to the land, and shifted to the castle. She appeared in the Council's study, knowing at least Daneele would be there. Hoping he could explain the pain she was experiencing and her inability to breathe.

She imagined she looked a fright. Her hair had dried while

she'd lain there and had matted in clumps around her neck. Knots had formed around her face. Her tears had left her eyes swollen and itchy, and when she'd last rubbed her cheeks, the dirt on her hands had likely left streaks. Her dress barely covered her, buttons she could not reach lay open, and she hadn't the energy to summon her magic to close them.

Daneele saw her first and leaped from his chair to catch her as she collapsed in his arms. The others gathered around, concern etched on their faces.

"Violissa, what is it? What's happened?" Daneele asked, brushing the hair from her face. She tried to speak, but a sob escaped her throat, and she buried her face in his chest.

"There's nothing physically wrong with her," Cyric said, kneeling next to them. "I scanned her."

"Then what is wrong with her?"

The voices overwhelmed her, making it hard to distinguish one man from the other, and with the sobs gutting her, she gave up trying. The air continued to stir as more Council joined them. Finally, the room quieted, and she forced down the remaining cries that fought to escape and lifted her head. Tears still streamed from her eyes, no matter how she tried to halt them.

"Violissa, talk to us, please," Daneele pleaded softly.

She looked up at the concerned faces. All she could manage was, "The pain...it hurts, and I can't heal it." She caught a sob before it burst forth and wiped her face on the back of her arm as a child might.

"What pain, my queen? I find nothing wrong," Kembal stated. He had leaned forward to scan her for something that would explain her condition.

"Tell us what happened, Violissa," Daneele pressed.

She looked down at her hands and played with the binding of her dress. She felt such a mess, so foolish for acting out of control. With a sniffle, she said softly, "Sinow is planning...a union."

"Well, that's wonderful news," Kembal declared. He was always a little slow at figuring things out.

"I don't think she means to her, Kembal," Cyric blurted, the elder man giving the younger Kembal a disgusted look.

"No, he's…it's to one from his realm." Another sob clawed free.

"How can this be?" Daneele responded, leaning back on his feet. "He can't. He can only unite with you."

"Why?" Cyric asked. "There's nothing that says he must."

"The Fates have spoken. It can only be Violissa," Jar stated.

"I didn't listen to them," Violissa said. "So, why should he? It's just prophecy. He has no requirement to abide by it."

"But I thought things were going well?" Daneele asked her, pushing her hair back from her eyes.

"I thought so too, but we bickered the last time we met, and so I guess I was wrong."

"Wait. Where did you hear this, Violissa?" Cyric asked, taking her hand.

"From the wind." She waited for the questions she knew would follow.

They all talked at once until Cyric held up a hand to silence them. "The wind told you?"

"Yes, it's never spoken to me before, but it sought me out. Well, really, a breeze found me and told me it had heard people talking."

"Where did it hear the talking?" Daneele inquired.

"From the castle servants and the villagers."

"This makes no sense. Someone send a message to the Darkbearers and summon Sinow to a meeting. Now," Cyric demanded.

"No," she said, looking around wildly. "No, I can't face him."

Cyric grabbed her shoulders. "Get hold of yourself, Violissa. This is too important for you to act like a child. The truth needs to be confirmed by Sinow. Not the wind. Until then, we cannot believe there is any truth in this." She cringed at his tone. Never had he or any of her Council scolded her. She wanted to crawl away and drown in her misery. "Someone send a message demanding that the king send representation if he cannot come himself," he continued, turning to the Council. "We must know the truth."

Two Council left to prepare the summons, and Violissa's hands shook at the thought of facing Sinow and hearing him confirm the wind's story.

Cyric turned back to her, his voice softer. His cerulean eyes so kind she almost started crying again. "Now, my dear, the pain you're experiencing, I believe, is what they refer to as a broken heart. There is nothing we can do to soothe it. You need to rest until a response comes. Then you will meet the king and find your answer. It will be fine. I'm sure there is a reasonable explanation." He wiped a tear from her cheek. "Daneele, please take her to her room. I'll let you know when we hear something, Violissa." He kissed her forehead, and Daneele scooped her up, then shifted from the room.

———

AFTER A LENGTHY BATTLE TO convince Daneele she would be all right, he left her room. Alone, Violissa washed her face, fixed her hair, and changed her clothing. Those tasks took her mind from her woes only temporarily. Lying on her bed, staring out the window, she tempered her urge to cry. Storm clouds had gathered, and rain fell, a stark reflection of her mood. Normally she could control it and keep the weather from revealing her emotions, but she didn't have the strength today.

A knock on her door sent anxious nerves bouncing through her.

"Enter."

Daneele entered, peeking over to read her mood. "We've heard back," he said, concern lining his features. "They will meet you at the rise of the north moon, but not for three days."

Violissa sat up. "What? But that's so long." Her voice grew shriller with each word. "How can they expect me to wait that long? Do they not realize this is an urgent matter?"

He looked at her with those striking blue eyes that seemed to read her every thought and sat down on the bed next to her. Pushing back a strand of hair that had fallen forward, he tucked it behind her ear. "Violissa, you need to relax and calm yourself. I know you're upset, but working yourself up like this won't help the situation. They made it very clear they could not meet us until then. They gave no reason, and we have no choice but to wait."

A groan came from her as she dropped her head on his shoulder. Daneele had always been the big brother to her. Guiding and comforting her, clearing away her nightmares or fixing her scrapes when she fell. She was comfortable sharing her thoughts and feelings with him, just as she was with Cyric. It was Daneele, with his incisive eyes and knowing looks, to whom she was closest.

She picked her head up and looked at him, taking in the shoulder-length auburn hair and the full beard that had so often tickled her when she was a tiny child. He was a good man, as were all her Council. It saddened her that he would never find love as she had. Never experience the joy of it. The laws of celibacy bound the Council. They were Fate driven and no Council ever challenged the Fates. From what they had admitted, the desires of the flesh faded with time, their power overtaking it until it was nothing more than an occasional thought. Still, it seemed a harsh penalty for their gifts.

But then she thought of the pain that now coursed through her chest and the irrational emotions that were battering her and thought perhaps he was lucky. He would never experience a broken heart, and all that came with it. Perhaps it was she the Fates had cursed, and he the one they had blessed.

"Violissa?" Daneele asked, worry dimming his eyes. "Are you

still with me or have you completely lost all connection with reality? I hope we don't have to confine you for madness like they do the Dark Kings when they lose their minds."

"Funny, Daneele," she said, swatting his arm. "No, I'm still here. I was just thinking about how lucky you are not to have to experience what I am."

"It depends on how you look at it," he replied, patting her leg and standing. "You see it only from this moment in time, but what if none of this had happened? You would still have the joy of love." She crinkled her nose at the term that had yet to be spoken aloud, and he chuckled. "Remember, there are different sides to all stories, Violissa. Perhaps this one has a side you have not considered."

She smoothed her skirts and gave him a half-smile. "You're right. I have no choice but to wait the three days before I can resolve the issue. Maybe the wind was incorrect, and I'm overreacting. I'll have to be patient." But she didn't believe her words, her gut telling her she had reason for concern.

"That's my queen," he said, walking over and kissing the top of her head. "Will you have one of us come with you when the time arrives?"

"No, thank you, Daneele. I need to do this on my own."

"Have you tried to contact him at all? That would seem the easiest approach to all of this."

"Through enaigne?" He nodded. "Yes, over and over, but he's blocked me. We agreed it would be best to block each other. His new powers are so volatile we didn't know if enaigne would set him off. I can't reach him now."

"Well, be patient. Find something to occupy yourself with over the next few days and try to keep your mind from worrying on it. Everything will be all right. The Fates would never change a prophecy as important as yours and Sinow's so drastically." Her chest went rigid as she pictured the prophecy in her dream and how it had changed before her eyes. Doubt crossed her mind, but she quickly hid it from Daneele. No one realized the extent of the damage she had already caused, and there was no need to worry him more.

She shook away the doubt and smiled at him as he continued, "You know we are here for you. We may not know exactly how to make things better, as we have had so little experience with female emotions, but we will try our best."

Giving him a quick peck on the cheek and a squeeze of his hand, she said, "I know you will. Thank you, Daneele."

His feet fell soundlessly on the brightly patterned rug covering her stone floors, and Violissa watched the greens and purples disappear under each footstep, only to return as his foot lifted. It made her think of the ebbs and flows of life and how quickly things she once considered constant could disappear from grasp. The door clicked behind Daneele, and she turned back to the window to watch and wait for the long three days to pass her by.

THE RISE of the north moon bathed the meeting grove in silver and shadows. Below it, the south moon climbed to reach its partner in the dance they performed each evening. Always reaching for each other but never touching, like two star-crossed lovers. In a few days' time, they would both be at their fullest and highest positions in the sky, the only time they came close to meeting.

Wringing her hands, Violissa waited for Sinow. Her nerves were high, and every noise made her jump. She had prepared herself, ready to hear him shatter her heart further. She hoped he would be the one to come and that he wouldn't send someone from his Council. That he would tell her the doubts and worries had been for naught. That he only wanted her. Thinking rationally and keeping her emotions under control was hard, but she convinced herself there was a reasonable explanation. She and Sinow would laugh at how absurd she'd been to take the word of a breeze and blow the situation out of proportion. And then, they would overcome this disastrous battle of their powers and finally unite.

A disturbance in the surrounding air alerted her to someone shifting in behind her. But unlike the usual flutter of her heart, the hair prickled on her neck. It wasn't Sinow; she didn't sense his aura. She turned, biting back her disappointment.

"Tynan? I called for Sinow or his Council. What are you doing here?" she asked.

"Well, I hate to disappoint you, Violissa, but I was the only one available." The sound of her name from his mouth sent a chill down her spine.

"Where are they, and how dare they send you in their place? Treaty rules forbid it." She didn't like the way he stared at her. It made her feel violated, like he was taking her clothes off bit by bit and touching her. Rubbing her arms, she waited for his answer.

"I am Sinow's ambassador now. He doesn't have time to deal with you, nor does his Council. They're too busy preparing. I'm sorry to disappoint you, but I'm all you get."

"Preparing?" she repeated, hating how his eyes gleamed like he was enjoying her reaction. The bile built in her throat at the understanding of what those preparations might comprise. "What could they be preparing for that would require them all to be present?"

"Sorry, but I am not at liberty to discuss the Council's activities." He rubbed his hands together and stared back at her, his eyes beady. He reminded her of a wolf about to attack its prey.

"No matter," she said, keeping her voice steady. There was no way she would let him see how his presence was disarming her. "I requested this meeting to find the answer to something that has recently been brought to my attention."

"It would be my pleasure, Violissa. Ask away." Something about the calm in his voice sounded as though he knew what she would be asking. As if he had expected it.

"I need to know if Sinow is planning to wed one of your people."

A smirk formed as he feigned thinking. "Hmm, that is an interesting question. I really can't answer it, though." The smirk widened, and she wanted to smack it from his face.

"What do you mean you can't answer it? It's a simple yes or no answer. It really isn't that difficult."

"I understand that, but I am forbidden to discuss the business of the realm."

Frustration mounting, Violissa huffed, "But if he's not planning to wed, then...oh...then there would be nothing to discuss and so you'd have an answer. I see." She heard the disappointment in her voice. The hurt she experienced was too strong to hide.

"Tell me this," she said, needing more. Needing a definitive answer, even if it broke her. "Has there been discussion of a union with someone other than me?" she continued.

"Now, Violissa, you know I can't answer that."

"Please, Tynan, I deserve to know that much." She hated that she sounded like she was begging him.

"Well, I guess I can reveal that much. Yes, there has." His grin thinned, turning his appearance maniacal, and she suddenly wanted to be extremely far from his presence.

"So, it's true," she said as she rubbed her forehead with her palm. Tynan didn't reply. He simply stood there watching her with that smirk, his eyes boring into her.

"May I ask how you knew, Violissa?"

She stifled a sob at his words, not wanting him to see how he had destroyed her. "The wind told me."

"Really? How fascinating." His reply was condescending, and she shot her head up to see that he had moved closer to her. The skin on her arms prickled, chills nesting in her core and reaching through her limbs. He was too close, and she wanted to run.

"Leave me now, Tynan," she demanded.

He reached over and ran his hand along her neckline, saying,

"You know I'm second in line for the throne, Violissa, and I guarantee I'm much better in bed."

Reflex unchecked, she slapped him across the face so hard it drew blood from the force. Snarling, he touched his bleeding lip. Hatred flared in his eyes, which were almost as black as Sinow's. "You'll regret that, you Cirillian bitch. Don't think my brother and his Council won't find out about this. I'm sure when he does, he'll be happy to have any whore spread her legs for him rather than you."

He spat the blood from his mouth at her and shifted, leaving her too stunned to move. His words had held such venom, and the threat within them was one she couldn't ignore. He had pushed her, touched her without her permission, insinuated that she would be better with him than Sinow, and left the image of Sinow with another woman burned into her mind. And she had snapped, losing her temper and hitting him even before those nasty words had fallen from his mouth.

Burying her face in her hands, she tried to hold back the emotional storm brewing within her. Everything was falling apart, and now she'd gone and done that. He'd deserved it, but it was all Sinow's Council needed to declare a breach in the treaty and start a war.

She crumpled to her knees and curled into a ball on the ground. Every emotion she'd held back over the last few days battered her at once. Tears flooded her face when she thought of how Sinow was choosing another over her. But the more she cried, the angrier she became at how easily he'd given up on her and turned to another. She was angry at the lies he had fed her over the times they had met, telling her he would wait for her. Telling her such things when he hadn't meant them. The anger deepened with every thought. It raged through her like an uncontained fire, threatening to destroy all other emotions until she satisfied it.

Images swept through her mind—Sinow touching another woman, that woman touching him, loving him, his mouth on hers, his hands bringing her to ecstasy and doing the things he had done to Violissa in the Dream Realm. And with every image, jealousy and a need for revenge twisted her pain until it no longer existed. No one hurt her like this. No one chose another woman over her. The intensity of her emotions should have given her pause, but it didn't. Instead, it swallowed her, taking over all rational thought as her Light side succumbed to the call of her Elvin side.

She stood, a deep green entering her irises, as the glade went silent. Agony had been her companion for days, and now she would inflict the same agony on Sinow. He would know what he had done to her and feel it twofold. She wouldn't be the pitiful end of this situation; she was the Light Queen and heir to the Elvin throne. That Elvin blood flared within her, feeding her emotions and stirring them as her Light powers never could.

Eyes turned to the sky, she roared, "If this is what you want, Fates, then I won't be the one left weakened and abused. Two can play at this game, and I will come out victorious!"

Lightning slashed the sky, thunder destroying the silence until the sky turned vicious and gray. The grove shook as she shifted, leaving only the echo of her anger in her wake.

CHAPTER 45

The floor quaked below her feet when Violissa shifted to the castle's front hall. She stormed through the halls, summoning her Council in enaigne.

"Well, Violissa?" Cyric asked, meeting her as she rounded the corner into the meeting room.

"From the looks of it, I'd guess the news wasn't good?" Daneele asked as he and the others backed away, fully aware that her mood was precarious.

"No, it wasn't, and I may have started a war with the Darkbearers."

A cacophony of voices flooded the room, but Cyric held his hand up to silence them.

"We're due some explanation, Violissa. What has happened?"

"It's true. Sinow is wedding one of his own," she said, suppressing the urge to cry.

"Did he tell you that?" asked Cyric.

"No, his brother did."

The chatter erupted again.

"Tynan?" Daneele questioned. "Since when does he speak for Sinow, and why was there no Council there?"

She flopped into her seat, too defeated to stand anymore. Their questions were only bringing the discomfort in her chest back. "Apparently, they were all too busy with preparations to be bothered with me. Tynan was the only one available. Shows you the level of importance I now have," she said, scratching her neck where Tynan had touched her.

Cyric looked at her questioningly. "That doesn't sound right, Violissa. Are you sure?"

"Yes, he confirmed all of it. So, if that's the way it's going to be, I won't sit back and play along." She sat up, a solution to her situation forming. "Find me a husband," she blurted before she could think through her decision. "I want a union of my own. Two can play this game, and I won't be playing the fool. Start the preparations."

"Are you mad?" Daneele said, leaning his hands on the table. "You can't unite with anyone else, Violissa."

She met his eyes, knowing hers were hard and likely a rich shade of green. "Sinow is," she said, crossing her arms and daring him to argue.

Shouting commenced, voices all eager to stop the madness their queen was displaying.

"Enough!" The walls shook from the power of her voice, and they went silent.

Emotions such as hers confounded her Council, and she was in a state beyond any they had seen her in. If she had to describe the scorching in her veins, she would liken it more to a Darkbearer than to a Lightbearer. And she imagined they had known all along that her vacillating emotions came from her Elvin roots.

They backed up a step from the meeting table as she continued. "This is not your decision to make. Now be gone and start preparing." She rose, ready to leave them, when she halted her steps and said, "No, on second thought, don't find me a husband. I'll find my own." They stared at her in confused silence. She clapped her hands and shooed them away. "Go now. There is work to be done. He'll regret his decision when he experiences the same pain he cursed upon me. It's the only way."

Vengeance would be hers, and he would regret ever turning from her. Fury whipped through her, heating her skin and darkening her eyes. She left the room, no longer interested in talk of the Dark King and his treachery.

Silence hung over the library as Violissa sat staring out the window. She had been there since her outburst two days prior, locking herself away from the others. It was the only quiet place she had in the castle, and she needed time to think. Though her temper had calmed some, her mind had not changed. Anger, embarrassment, shame. The emotions still clouded her judgment and her pride.

Gray clouds sat low in the sky, the weather having held its gloomy state since it had turned. She rested her head against the window, thinking about what she intended. Out of control was a place she'd never been, and the emotions that accompanied it were unfamiliar to her. She'd never been jealous or wrathful. Darkness drove those emotions, and she was a Light Queen.

A deep sigh fled her, and she muttered, "Am I doing the right thing?"

Her voice cracked, the tears welling up again. She didn't like being so weak, didn't like the helplessness that washed over her when she cried. She did, however, like the way those darker emotions made her feel in control again.

The idea of wedding another man made her want to vomit. She didn't know how Sinow could stomach it, but perhaps the Fates had only cursed her to suffer. Sinow was the only one for her, but now she couldn't have him. And she'd gone and declared that she would wed a Cirillian.

She dropped her head to her knees, cursing herself, the situation, Sinow. If she weren't proud, she would hunt him down, throw herself at his feet, and beg him not to do this. But she was a queen, and rulers did not act in that fashion. He had already damaged her pride, already tossed her aside as if she were nothing. With the thought, her anger crept back in, sinking under her skin and disturbing her calm.

No, she would not debase herself. There was no changing the path now. It wouldn't be Sinow on the other side of her bed, wouldn't be him kissing and touching her. She tried to think of someone else in her bed, but her stomach turned. Chewing her lip, she debated how she would deal with such a thing when Sinow was the only one to whom she had ever been attracted. That instinct to vomit when she even considered someone else frustrated her. Before she had thought it a protective response from the Fates so the prophecy would remain intact. Now, with the prophecy about to fracture completely, she didn't know what to think. It was clear Sinow didn't have such a response.

Balling her fists, she rose and paced the floor, chiding herself for being such a fool. All this time, she had thought they were both powerless in their attraction to one another. Maybe she'd been wrong. Maybe he'd never had that sensation. Perhaps it had all been a deception, and he had played her for a fool. Foolish was how she felt now.

She thought about it for a long time, trying to think of a way around her dilemma. A way to wed someone without having to share a bed with him. What man would settle for that? Unless she united with someone who knew she didn't need or want that intimacy, chose someone who respected her need for chastity, who understood the union was only for show.

That was the answer. She would have her revenge, but on her terms. Excitement welled in her until she thought about how she would be in a loveless union with no intimacy and Sinow would be reaping the rewards of his union and indulging in the flesh of another until he'd had his fill and maybe then would turn to her.

White-hot jealousy slashed her vision. She would not be his second choice, the one he turned to after he satisfied his needs with other women.

The images in her mind helped convince her that her plan was necessary. She would marry someone who would honor her need for no intimacy and someone who could outlast Sinow's appetite. No mortal would live that long, and since he was likely to take many with as long as immortals lived, she would settle for one. The thought never crossed her mind about an heir or how Dark Kings chose their queens. It was something she had never learned, and so the knowledge was not there to give her pause before she reached out to Daneele.

Daneele, I need to see you.

She paced the room, waiting for his arrival, chewing on her bottom lip as she did. Never once did it cross her mind to take more time to think things through. There was no awareness of the haste with which she was deciding, her emotions driving her every move.

Daneele arrived within seconds.

"I hope you've changed your mind about all this, Violissa," he said, walking to where she stood, anxiously waiting. "If Sinow unites with another, then we will be patient until he's gotten over it. Mortals have brief lives." She wanted to roll her eyes but refrained. "The Fates have said the two of you will be together. Perchance you have to endure knowing he's with this other woman for her lifetime as punishment for not following the prophecy."

"How supportive, Daneele, thank you," she replied, sarcasm coating her words. She wouldn't put up with another woman in what should have been her bed. If the Fates were this cruel, she didn't care if the prophecy never came to fruition. "Now sit, please."

"Oh, this can't be good if I have to sit."

"Just sit and listen." She gestured to the mauve chair that sat in the middle of the room, a sage couch across from it. Holding her hands together to keep them from shaking, she sat on the couch as he settled in the chair. "I have not changed my mind, nor will I. If he intends to unite with another, then so shall I."

Daneele stood up, saying, "I can't listen to this."

But she stopped him, grabbing his hand to pull him down. "I need you to hear what I have to say. I've thought this through and—"

"You've not thought this through, Violissa. You're acting out of emotion, and you're not being rational. I've been told this is how females act, but I've never witnessed it until now. This is insane."

This time she did roll her eyes at how presumptive he was to assume women acted irrationally. As if his brief exposure to women gave any credence to his comment.

"Regardless of what you think, Daneele, it's going to happen this way. I won't be made a fool of...oh, never mind. Just listen. I need to choose someone, but I don't want any physical contact with that person. It's the one part I can't bring myself to go against. I need someone who will understand that and respect my wish. Someone who will not want to take what should have been Sinow's. Although why, I cannot tell you. Especially since he won't be doing the same. It makes me sick to imagine it." She paused and massaged her temples with her fingers.

"Violissa, what are you rambling on about?"

"Daneele, you promised me once that you would do anything for me. And at my ascension, you vowed to follow me. I need you to trust me now. Will you do that for me?"

"I don't believe I have a choice. What is it you're asking of me, Violissa?"

"You will be the one to unite with me, Daneele."

He stood quickly and backed away from her. "What? Have you lost your mind? Of all the idiotic ideas." His eyes had gone so large the white portion washed out the blue.

"No, Daneele, please hear me out. Please," she begged him, "just listen."

He ran a hand over his beard. "This is madness, Violissa."

"Please, Daneele," she begged, tears pushing at her eyes.

Sighing, he sat back down, resting his head in his hands before he peered back up at her. "I'll listen, but that in no way means I'll agree."

She nodded, picking at the skin on her fingers before saying, "I can't unite with just anyone as he's doing. He may be able to push all thoughts of me away, but I can't do the same. So, I must unite with someone who will let me maintain my chastity, will let me continue as I am, with no pressure. A mortal male will expect intimacy, regardless of whether I am his queen." She rubbed her arms, chasing away the churning in her stomach. "One of you would be ideal because of your oath to remain chaste for the crown. You will do whatever it takes to protect me, and this is what I am asking of you. Daneele, you are my closest friend. Like a brother to me."

"Even more reason for this to be very distant from your list of options, Violissa."

"But that's what makes you perfect. You will ask nothing of me. You will only see that I am safe. If it must be any of you, I choose you. Please, Daneele, do this for me."

Her eyes misted, and she bit her lip to stop them.

"That's what makes me perfect? Do you hear yourself? What you're suggesting is madness, Violissa. A Council cannot unite with you, cannot..." He stopped as the tears returned to her eyes. Sitting back in the chair, he studied her, his eyes heavy, the blue in them almost navy. "All any of us have ever wanted was for you to be happy, Violissa. Seeing you like this leaves us helpless. When you were small and you hurt yourself, I could heal the wound and that would stop the tears. But I don't know how to heal this wound." He put his head down in his hands and asked in a defeated voice, "Will this make the pain go away?"

"No," she answered honestly, "but it will help with the other emotions: the shame, the embarrassment."

He peered back up at her, and she saw the resolve flee from his shoulders. "If the Council approves, then I will agree to it. Understand the seriousness of what you've asked, Violissa. Once finalized, there is no going back. No changing your mind once the Council announces it. No place on the Council for me going forward." She winced as he said it, knowing all he would give up for her.

"I understand," she mumbled.

"Call the Council before I change my mind."

She hated the anguish his voice carried, but there was no turning back from this. Closing her eyes, she summoned her Council. Even those working in the villages heeded her call, knowing the situation was tenuous. When she was done, she reached her thoughts out to Sinow once more, trying one last time to reach him. As with all the other times, there was nothing but silence. She swept her mind back quickly past his people, hearing the excited talk of a coming union spoken in their heads. That had been another way she'd checked for the truth after meeting with Tynan. What she'd heard had hurt her almost as much as Sinow had.

The arrival of her Council broke her thoughts. They came quickly, knowing the importance of her summons.

Taking one last look at Daneele, whose eyes pleaded with her to reconsider, she stood, saying, "I have decided that I will not unite with one of our people."

Relief swept through the room, halting when she continued. "I will instead unite with Daneele." The gasp was deafening. Shouts, confusion, outrage. Violissa raised her hand to silence the chaos.

"Please hear me out. I do not wish to give up my entire self to a union. I still wish to remain untouched. There is only one who tempts me to give that up and, as he apparently does not feel the same, there will be no one. Only some of you understand that enough to respect my request. As Daneele is the youngest of you and he and I have always been close, it makes sense to choose him. Of course, I ask your blessing for this decision." The noise started again, but she continued. "Know this, though. What Sinow has done has hurt me as no one ever has. I cannot undo what he has done. His actions have already embedded that agony into my being. But the satisfaction of seeing his reaction, of seeing him realize he didn't make a fool of me, will help ease that pain."

They talked among themselves for a long time, with Violissa anxiously chewing her lip and twisting her hands. Daneele continued to sit, holding his head in his hands, his elbows propped on his knees. A hush fell upon the room, and Cyric stepped forward.

"Is this really what you want, Violissa?" he asked, looking aged and weary.

She nodded, unable to give voice to the lie. It was the furthest thing from what she wanted. Sinow was what she wanted, and she had lost him.

"Do you understand that by the laws of the land, your choice, once announced, cannot be undone?"

She nodded again.

"Do you understand the consequences of your decision on yourself, Daneele, and the future of our people?"

"I do," she murmured. He looked back at the Council, who all nodded to him.

"Then, with a heavy heart, we concede. We will not deny you what you ask, but let it be noted that we do not agree with it. This is a sad day, Violissa, but if this will help dry your tears, then we will agree to it with reservations. Are you certain Sinow is marrying another? Do you have any more proof than Tynan's word?"

There was no proof she could share, but on one attempt to reach Sinow through enaigne, she had let her senses skim the minds of his people. The wind had been correct. Talk was spreading through the towns. Excitement for a new queen, condemnation that their king had originally thought to wed Violissa, slander at any mention of her. The minds she had skimmed had left her wounded, and she'd stopped herself from hearing more.

"Word has spread through the towns," she said, blinking back the tears at the reminder of the harsh thoughts. "I have heard the thoughts of his people, and they confirm what the wind and Tynan told me. Sinow is marrying another." Her voice splintered, a tear spilling free.

Their faces fell before Cyric, holding his head high, said, "Then we support your decision and will silence any reservations. But let me be clear once more that we do not approve of this and what it means for the future of this realm." She dropped her eyes, hating the disappointment on his face. She glanced back up to see him shake his head sadly before he said, "Let the arrangements begin and word spread."

They bowed and shifted, leaving her alone with Daneele.

"Are you certain, Violissa?" he asked once more.

"In truth?" She turned to him, her strength faltering. "No, but he has given me no choice."

He pulled his hand down his face. "Then at least give it time before the ceremony."

"Time for what? Once we announce it, there is no going back."

"Then I'll say once more, Violissa, don't do this."

But she had to. The idea of Sinow marrying another and having to sit by and watch without acting angered her. She shook her head, her fingers digging into her skin. "The union will move forward. I will not stop the announcements." She paced, her hand under her chin as she thought. "But we will need time. Preparations will need to be made, celebrations planned." Although she knew she would not be celebrating, her people would. "Let the others know we will hold the ceremony at the height of both moons. That should piss Sinow off." It would mean the union would not occur until after their scheduled meeting and likely not before his union, but since his union defied treaty rules, she wouldn't bother going to the meeting. There would no longer be a need. The treaty stood on the idea that she and Sinow would wed and, with that now lost, she had an excuse not to see him again. Doing so would be too painful.

"Great. Pissing off a Dark King sounds like as perfect of a plan as marrying someone who is not part of the Fates' prophecy," Daneele grumbled. She shot him a look, and he added, "I'll let the others know."

He left her, and as she plopped herself back in the window seat, she tilted her head at the stir of the land. Like a tremor beneath her. As quickly as it had come, it was gone, and she returned her sight to the window. If she had followed her instinct and searched for the source, she may have noticed the quake ripple outside of the doorway to the Hidden Realm. For deep inside, the words of the prophecy were changing once more, altering the path and leaving it completely unbound.

CHAPTER 46

A breeze swept through the meeting grounds, ruffling Sinow's hair as he waited. Violissa was late. She'd never been late. In fact, she was usually there before Sinow arrived. He was patient with her, unusually patient, but this was ridiculous. Reaching out in enaigne, he tried to talk to her, but once again there was only silence. He'd tried multiple times, but she had blocked herself off from him, which was unexpected. They had agreed that he would block himself off since his powers were so unpredictable, but she was to remain open for when he was ready to contact her.

Disappointment nagged at him, and he ran his hand through his hair. This day was one to which he had looked forward. Every day he had worked on his control, thinking increasingly about Violissa until he could picture her in his mind without losing that control. Today would have been the ultimate test. His excitement had plagued him all morning, and when he arrived, he had planned to go right to her and pull her into his arms with no delay. But she hadn't been there.

The breeze gusted across the grove with more fury, whipping around Sinow where it remained. Scratching his head, he walked from his spot, only to have it blow over his back. Oddly enough, it seemed the wind was determined to aggravate him. The rest of the grove was still, not a blade of grass moving. The sting of the breeze on his skin stopped him. There was something more within it. A subtle vibration that sounded almost like words.

Waving his hand to break the air's movement, he cursed as it continued to drag and push at him like it needed his attention.

He froze at the thought. That couldn't be it, but Violissa wasn't there, something that gave him pause, and the wind would not stop battering him.

"You're trying to tell me something, aren't you?" he asked.

The air whipped at him again, and this time, the trees joined in its frantic movement.

"Is it Violissa?" he asked, feeling idiotic that he was talking to nothing and thankful no one was there to witness it.

"Something is wrong, isn't it?" he asked.

The trees shook violently as if to give a resounding yes.

"Damn it," he cursed, needing no more affirmation.

He shifted back to Tenebron and reached out to sense Keary, finding him in the dungeon. Screams echoed through the space as Sinow made his way over to him. The source of the noise was a traitorous servant who had made the mistake of spreading rumors about Sinow, a crime punishable by death. Eyes missing, limbs twisted, the prisoner hung from chains that had peeled his skin down to the bone. Sinow had never had a taste for torture, regardless of the Darkness that reveled in it. He would have simply killed the man outright, but Keary enjoyed doling out lengthy torture.

Sinow had always believed a swifter death was better for both him and his victim, a difference that caused him to stand apart from his predecessors and his Council. Only when the Darkness had him completely in its grasp did he take the same enjoyment from it. In this case, he had left the punishment up to Keary and the Council, all suggesting that torture was the best example to deter any future actions against the crown.

Words taken from the last meeting with his Council had been the servant's undoing. This was exactly the reason Sinow had demanded no servants be present during meetings. While there had never been a servant bold enough to go against the king, precedent was always possible, and this man had done just that. The rumors had spread like wildfire, distorting the discussion he had held with his Council until the people believed he'd been preparing to unite with one of them and had turned his back on Violissa.

The prophecy was common knowledge to his people, stemming from the days before his grandfather. Sinow's father had found no reason to dissuade the talk that Sinow was part of it. But that didn't mean they liked the idea of their king wedding the Light Queen. The Light were still their enemy. Taking her as his queen would be a challenge, uniting the kingdoms even more so.

The rumors that had spread, however, gave him insight as to just how resentful his people were about the union. Jealousy that his queen would not be of Tenebron and a deep hatred of Cirillia and its Lightbearers fueled the misinformation.

An agonizing scream from the servant brought Sinow back to why he'd sought Keary out.

"Sinow, what a pleasant surprise." Keary said, stopping the man's scream with a flick of his finger. A note of sarcasm tinged Keary's greeting. "You don't come down here often."

"There's no need to. That's what I have you for. Look, have you or the others heard from the Lightbearers recently?"

"No, we're not in regular communication, Sinow," Keary replied with a chuckle. "Why? Did something happen?"

He wiped blood from his hands and moved closer to Sinow, concern changing his demeanor.

"Violissa didn't show for the meeting today, and I'm worried." He didn't say what had sparked his worry for fear of evoking more laughter from his friend. The thought of anyone knowing he'd been talking to trees was humiliating.

"I wouldn't be, though that is a bit out of character for her. I'm sure everything's fine. Maybe she just forgot."

"I don't think so. Isn't it a requirement of the treaty? You know what sticklers they are for following that treaty to the word."

"True." He rubbed his chin. "You want to start a war over a missed meeting?" He arched his brow, giving Sinow a smirk, which Sinow returned with a glare. "Sinow, she's fine. It's not like she's sick or wounded. She's a healer, remember? Not to mention the immortal thing. Although there are illnesses that even the healers prefer to let run their course. Perhaps she is sick."

"Will you contact her Council and find out for me?"

Keary looked back at the man pinned to the wall behind him. "I'm a little busy right now. Would you mind if I check in a few hours? I think that's about all he'll last. I'm sure she can wait."

Sinow looked at him, then at the servant. "Put the man out of his misery, Keary. Let me know what you find."

"In due time, Sinow. And yes, I will report in as soon as I hear something."

He turned back to the servant as Sinow shifted. Sinow didn't have the stomach for it today. He'd been fighting with his regular demons since the meeting with his Council, and they had not fully emerged since. Darkness stirred deep within him, and he worried that if he stayed in the dungeon any longer, it would find a way out.

Shifting to his study, he buried himself in work to take his mind from Violissa. He hated the administrative pieces of his role but knew they had to be done. Those were the things he preferred to dole out to the Council, but today they were a welcome distraction.

Nose buried in figures that had his eyes blurring, he was thankful for the rap at the door.

"Enter," he said, rubbing his eyes. The sun had fallen, and both moons had risen. Under normal circumstances, by this time, he would have been relaxing and reliving the events of his earlier meeting with Violissa. He had expected this evening to be different, with memories of her skin against his or even still being tangled in bedsheets with her by this time. Worrying and waiting had not been what he had anticipated.

Keary entered the room, and he didn't have to say anything for Sinow to know something was seriously wrong. His frown said it all.

"What is it? What's wrong?" Sinow asked, rising from his chair.

"You were right. Something did keep her away today. She chose not to come."

"What? But why would she do that? Did I do something to offend her?" As the words fell from his mouth, he frowned at how weak they sounded. Until the memory of their last meeting returned and his frown deepened, his chest taking on an unfamiliar strain. They had both said so much, things that neither could take back. Things he had hoped she'd overlooked, just as he had. He ran his hand through his hair as doubt crept in. "Fates, I did, didn't I? We both did." He looked back up at Keary. "Tell me what it is, Keary."

"I'm not sure how to tell you this." He shifted his stance, breathing in deeply. "Violissa is taking vows with another."

The sudden rush of heat gave Sinow no warning. Rage overwhelmed his control, sending a fiery streak of red through his vision. His power broke free and hit Keary, sending him through the wall of the study and to the outer edge of the castle wall. Keary shifted back to Sinow in moments, dusting himself off and stretching his neck.

"By the Fates, Sinow, warn me next time," he grumbled. "I hate bringing you bad news."

A growl rose from Sinow. "Who is she taking vows with, and why?"

"I couldn't get all the details as she's apparently forbidden her Council from communicating with us. You're lucky I'm persuasive and Brom agreed to meet me. From what I could find out, she's seriously pissed about something you've done. Brom kept saying I should know and seemed alarmed when I told him I didn't know why she'd be upset with you. What have you done, Sinow?"

"Upset? I have done nothing to cross her. Sure, the last time we met, there were words exchanged, but nothing that should have caused this to happen. If she was that concerned about what I said that day, she should have said something about it. Why wouldn't she have called for me or one of you if that was the case?" The rumble of ire still stirred within his blood, but he had contained it, instead focusing on the mystery of the situation.

"I asked that same question and was told that she did. You weren't available, so she spoke with representation."

"I don't remember anyone meeting her, do you?"

"No, I'm just as puzzled as you are, Sinow."

None of this made sense. Violissa had never requested a meeting with him. No Council had met with her or her Council. He raked a hand down his face, seething that she had done exactly what she had threatened to do. Exactly what he had threatened to do when lost to his power, boasting of taking another to see her reaction.

"What else did he tell you?" Sinow asked.

"Only that the union will be to one of their own."

His fingers dug into his desk. "A Council? That can't be possible." The heat in his eyes told him they had darkened. "Who?"

"The Keeper, Daneele."

Sinow's rage had him in its grasp, his power fueling it so there was no stopping it. Magic flared from him, but this time he directed it to the wall behind them, blowing it from its foundation and sending the bricks flying out into the night.

"I need explanations, and Violissa is going to give them to me," he said.

"Sinow, don't do anything stupid," he heard Keary say as he shifted. He focused all his power on sensing Violissa, and when he did, he set his path to her. She'd made a mistake crossing him like this, and now she would truly see the power she'd quelled in him all this time.

***

Sinow landed with a resounding thunder. Ebony engulfed him, but he could make out shapes of furniture, sensing Violissa on the bed across from him. So, she was in her bedroom. That knowledge created tantalizing thoughts that antagonized the Darkness in him. Magic pushed against his skin—alarms triggered by his unexpected presence. The sensation would have disarmed any other Darkbearer, but for Sinow, it was merely an annoyance.

A bolt of blue magic struck the air, aimed at him. He caught it and sent it back out to light the room. Violissa sat in the bed, her eyes wide but their green lush. Her blankets had bunched at her waist, and his eyes followed the strap of her nightgown as it fell to reveal the soft crest of her breast. The sight disarmed him, lust shoving aside the anger. It almost tempted him to leave the emotion aside and rip the rest of the gown from her body. Almost until the thought of her sharing her bed with another flashed in his mind.

"Sinow?" she said, half-questioning, half-demanding. She pulled the strap back up her shoulder, never taking her eyes off him. The flutter of her heart paused for the three beats it did each time she saw him, the vibrations pulsing the air.

"Violissa," he snarled, not bothering to rein in the Darkness. There was no need. This wasn't a friendly interaction.

She waved her hand through the air above her, and the alarms stopped. Her sight shifted slightly, and he could see she was sending a message in enaigne to her Council. Pounding at the door came at the same time, and she huffed. "I'm fine. It was a false alarm. Everything's under control." Her voice was firm, the voice of a queen and not that of the girl he'd talked with so often in the glade.

"What are you doing here, Sinow?"

She rose from the bed, fire flickering in her eyes. His chest tightened as he watched the way her gown clung to her body, her silhouette stealing his breath and making it difficult to avert his eyes. Even with all this madness, he still wanted her desperately. He shook the thoughts from his head and focused on what she had done.

"Tell me you're not taking vows with Daneele," he demanded through gritted teeth.

Her eyes dropped, revealing the truth. When they flicked back to meet his, they had grown a shade closer to the forests at night. Danger danced in them, and her features sharpened.

"I can't."

"Why, Violissa? Why would you even think of doing something like this?"

"How dare you ask me that?" she spat. The vitriol in her voice caused him to step back. "You couldn't bother to give me answers when I asked the same of you. To face me when I needed you to give me some explanation." Her magic hit him, nearly knocking him off his feet as she stepped into his space. Her reaction was unexpected, and he wondered how he was suddenly on the defensive. "I don't owe you answers, you bastard," she continued, her face contorted in beautiful shades of venom. "You had your chance, and you gave me up. You made it perfectly clear you were moving on that day in the glade. I didn't believe you'd really do it, but you did." His mind spiraled as he grasped to understand what she was saying. "You are the reason I'm taking those vows, Sinow. You drove me to this."

Her fists pounded on his chest to emphasize each word, her anger throwing him off guard until he grabbed her wrists. Holding them, he glowered at her, towering over her but keeping his power contained, too worried about her behavior to let it loose. Too concerned to even notice how close they were standing.

"What are you talking about, Vi?" He searched her eyes, seeing the moisture in them, and his heart wrenched. She was hurting, and he didn't understand what he had done to cause her pain or to cause this reaction.

She looked up at him with those large, tear-filled eyes, and he had to catch his breath. He watched as she took a gulp of air and blinked back the tears.

"I'm talking about your own impending union."

He nearly laughed, except she had spoken the statement with such certainty. "Union? What union, Vi? There is no union for me. You kept turning me down, remember?" He smiled, relaxing once he realized she was still upset from their last meeting. The wayward curl that hung on her face was soft when he reached over and brushed it back. "Those were just words, Violissa. I would never think of taking vows with anyone but you."

Her reaction wasn't what he expected, the tension not fleeing her body. He still held one of her hands in his and he rubbed his thumb over her soft skin, wishing he could remove the confusion from her expression.

"But you told me," she said, her eyes growing larger. "The last time we met, you said you were ready to move on, to stop waiting for me. You said you wanted to take another woman." Her voice broke, and he brought both hands to her face to reassure her.

He shook his head, not wanting to believe that she'd thought he would go through with what he'd threatened. "They were just words spoken in anger, Vi. It wasn't really me speaking those words. I thought you knew that."

She twisted out of his hold, and the Darkness reared until he squashed it back. Something was still wrong, and his concern was growing.

"You of all people should know the power of words, Sinow," she replied, her voice terse.

"I do, but you must have known it was the Darkness talking, that I didn't truly mean what I said."

Eyes lowering, teeth biting her lip, she whispered, "At first, I did but...but then the wind..." Her vision snapped back to him. "The wind told me there was talk, and your people...they were discussing it." She scratched at her arm nervously.

He chuckled, dragging her back to him and loving how easy it was to have her in his arms. "That was a rumor started by a servant. That's all it was, Vi. Nothing more than a rumor."

Her head shook, her body still stiff in his hold as she pushed her hand against his chest and backed away from him. Brows furrowed, he tried to understand her actions. "I have punished the servant, and the Council has corrected the lies. You could have just asked me, Vi. I would have swallowed my pride and admitted the error of my words."

Violissa sat at the end of her bed, holding tight to the tall bedpost to steady herself. Her hand shook as her skin paled. "Fates, what have I done?"

"Vi?" He didn't like the nerves that slithered through him, the twisting in his gut that this was a turning point for them. One they could not turn from.

"I reached out to you. Every day, over and over, but you blocked me." She wiped her face with her arm, looking so distraught that he wanted to pull her back to him. But he refrained, knowing she was about to tell him something he didn't want to hear. "We tried to reach your Council, but no one would come." A shadow crossed her eyes. "Your brother. Your brother came. He confirmed it all. He said there had been discussion, that preparations were being made."

Embers that had simmered in his core, silenced by the mood in the room, roared to life. Flames that scalded at the mere mention of his brother, and he balled his hands into tight fists to keep them at bay. "Tynan? When did you speak to him?"

The crease between her eyes deepened, the guilt marring her beauty and twisting his insides.

"When Cyric requested someone meet me, Tynan came. I questioned him, but he said no one else could come. That he was your ambassador and that I would need to speak to him. He told me you were too busy and that your Council was making preparations. He led me to believe that those preparations were for a union with someone else." The anguish that accompanied that last admission reached into his heart and lanced it. He'd never had such an intense need to avenge someone, to leave a bloody trail of bodies in his wake to avenge her pain. But he did now. "Why would he lead me to believe that? Why would he want to hurt me?"

The burrowing of something in his chest was akin to someone carving it out and shattering it into a million pieces. "I don't know," he answered honestly as the Darkness in him surged with a need for retribution. "But I will find out, and then I will kill him myself."

He ran a hand through his hair, not believing what he'd heard. Tynan had met with Violissa, had neglected to tell him about it, had intercepted a request for that meeting, and then lied to her. Why? There was no answer he could come up with that made any sense. Betrayal was something Sinow had never experienced, and the sting of it he likened to having a dagger severing his chest in two. He wanted to leave and torture his brother as he'd mentally tortured Violissa, but he couldn't leave her yet. She wasn't in the right state, and he needed to reassure her there was no other so she could call off this farce and finally be his.

He moved to her, ignoring the Darkness that rippled in him. Learning of Tynan's actions had heightened it, but he needed to be near Violissa. Kneeling before her, he took her hands in his, marveling at how easy it was to touch her now.

"I'll deal with my brother when I return." He gave her a reassuring smile, wishing she would return it. "Now, tell me you didn't set up a union to get even with me?" There was no reaction, and he knew then that something was still wrong.

Guilt crossed her expression, and she sucked her bottom lip under her teeth again. Her eyes fell to their hands, and a longing passed over them. "I wanted you to know the agony that was debilitating me. It was agonizing, and I wanted you to experience that pain." He couldn't stop his smile from growing. There was a part of her that the Light didn't dictate, and he was looking forward to exploring that piece of her and freeing it. "I'm such a fool. I'm so sorry, Sinow."

He tipped her chin, forcing her to look at him. "No harm done," he said, his thumb brushing her cheek. "Call it off, and we'll take our vows. I think it's time to fulfill the prophecy they keep forcing on us. We'll figure out how to get past the problems with our powers."

She inhaled, tears pooling in her eyes as her lips parted. Anguish invaded her delicate features, and he tried to determine why she wasn't happy. Here they were as close as they'd ever been, their powers at bay, the obstacles no longer blocking their path forward, yet she seemed so fractured.

Lip quivering, a tear sliding down her cheek, she breathed, "I cannot, Sinow."

His grip tightened on her hand. "What do you mean, you cannot? It's not difficult, Vi. Call your Council and tell them it was all a misunderstanding. End this farce."

Lifting her hand from his, she let her fingers drift over his cheek, the sadness in her eyes stifling the tingling her touch caused. He wanted to take her face in his hands and pull her lips to his. To kiss and touch her, to remove the tears and lift the melancholy from her spirit. They should have been celebrating his control and the revelation that they had finally made it to this point and they could do what the Fates had intended for them.

"You don't understand."

"Then make me understand, Violissa." His frustration was

showing, her full name coming from his tongue as easily as his curt tone.

She tried to look away, but he gripped her chin tight, forcing her eyes to his. Eyes that leaked tears he wished to stop, but feared he would only cause more of if she didn't provide the right answer.

"If I could do that...if I could take it all back, I would in a heartbeat."

His mood was dipping, and he fought the Darkness that sought escape.

"I would explain quickly, Violissa," he growled, his hold on her chin tightening.

She flinched but didn't pull away. "The laws of my land forbid the renunciation. Once a couple announces their union, they cannot stop it, even if they have not taken their vows. Announcing is the first step in accepting it and is as sacred as the union itself."

Every muscle in his body went rigid, his grip on her chin so strong that she cried out.

"Sinow, you're hurting me."

Dropping his hand, he rose abruptly, staring at her and seeing the bruising where he'd hurt her before it healed. His eyes fell to his hands, his mind trying to make any sense of what she was saying.

"There are no exceptions," she continued. "Especially not for royalty." He drew his vision back to hers, understanding slicing through him like lightning on a stormy night. More tears fell from her eyes. "Your brother would have known this as your advisor."

Stunned, he continued to stare at her, his mouth trying to form the words. Tynan's actions had been deliberate. Sinow didn't know what hurt worse: his brother's part in this or the fact that Violissa had gone to this extreme. She would take vows with another man, an immortal at that. There would never be a chance to have her if she didn't stop this.

"That's absurd," he said, his steps heavy as he paced the room to settle his temper. "You would exchange vows with another man? You decided that was the best course of action because your feelings were hurt?" He hadn't meant to sound so nasty, but his chest ached in a way he didn't like, and his power was rising to shield him from it.

"Yes." She dropped her head in her hands, and he stopped his pacing. "I reacted hastily and foolishly. They warned me, but I didn't listen. I thought for sure you wanted another woman, that you had replaced me so easily, and it ached."

Her body shook with her tears, and she seemed so fragile in that moment that it softened his fury, the Darkness pushed aside as the man in him sought to comfort her.

With a sigh he asked, "Tell me you don't love him, Vi." He hated how weak he sounded, hated that a plea laced the words, a desperate need for her to say no.

Raising her head, her sparkling orbs searched his face before she rose from the bed. Her hands trembled as she neared him. "No, I don't love him. Not like that. I never wanted to take vows with anyone else." Relief rushed through him. "I was so hurt, so angry that I got caught up in my emotions and whatever game your brother is playing. That last conversation we had was so fresh I really believed you'd given up on all of it." Her head lowered, and he closed the distance between them, ignoring the surge of power that fought him. "I don't love anyone else," she whispered, and his heart leaped through his chest at the acknowledgement within that statement. He lifted her chin again, smoothing his fingers over the place where he had hurt her, hating himself for having done so. He never wanted to see her in pain again, especially by his hand. Her lips quivered, another tear falling. "What have I done, Sinow?"

Taking her hands in his, he said, "There's no way to get out of it? You are queen. Can you not simply change the law?"

The shake of her head devastated him as much as it frustrated him. "It's not my law to change. It's one created by our people long before even my father's reign. Our people take the sanctity of a union commitment very seriously. I cannot go against it without insulting them and turning them against me."

Tension made his jaw go rigid. The idea of putting a silly law in front of her own needs was ridiculous to him. "You care too much for your people and what they think, Vi. Do you ever put yourself before them? Ever think of putting yourself first in times like this? Because this is one of those times when you need to come before your people. You know the consequences if you do not."

His tone was callous, but he couldn't refrain. The Darkness swirled within him, ready to pounce on his loosening control. If she didn't stop this, her people would suffer. He would have no choice but to call her out for violating the treaty. Not just because she had missed the meeting, but because she was turning her back on the prophecy and him. Before, it had merely been a delay of their union, but now, with the prospect of her wedding another immortal, any chance he could have her was gone and with it, the prophecy's fulfillment. His people would demand retaliation, even if they didn't care for the Light, as would his Council.

"I do, but what I have done, I cannot undo."

Fates, she was so stubborn that it made him want to pull his hair out. All she needed to do was change a law. Why did she care what her people thought? He couldn't understand why this was such a problem for her. It seemed so simple.

"There must be a way around this, Vi," he replied, hearing the plea return to his voice and not liking it. Her presence made him seem so weak at times.

She pulled her hands free, and biting her lip, walked the length of the room. He observed her, hope building that she would talk herself into ending this and beginning anew with him. He was half tempted to grab her and steal her away. If he kidnapped her and forced her to take vows, her people could place no blame on her. Having Cirillians hate him would not differ from how they already thought of him. He momentarily considered it, then pushed the thought aside, knowing she was too strong for it to even be a feasible possibility.

"Vi," he said, needing to know the truth and not having the

patience to wait. "If none of this had happened, and I had asked you to marry me today, would you have agreed?"

Her steps faltered, and she swiveled toward him. Eyes of brilliant emerald shimmered with her smile, leaving him breathless. She rushed back to him, sending lilac and sunshine invading his senses. "Yes," she answered, and his heart thudded against its bounds. "I would have with no hesitation this time."

Lips of lush pink tempted him before he remembered this dream lay entangled in the web of a nightmare out of which he could not find his way. He ran the outside of his finger along her cheek, aching to kiss her.

"Look how close we're standing," she murmured. "You've been in control almost the entire time."

He smiled, wrapping his finger through a golden curl that skimmed her cheek. "I've been practicing for today." As soon as the words were out, he felt foolish but didn't care. He wanted her to know he had been fighting for her, that he would continue to fight for her in whatever way he could.

The emerald in her eyes danced invitingly, and he pulled her closer, unable to hold back his need for her any longer. He leaned down, his lips so close to hers they almost touched.

"I need you, Vi," he said. Her breath was warm and sweet, her heart pounding against his chest in rhythm with his. The moment was perfection, and as she tipped her head back, he no longer cared about the situation or her morals, nor did he care what her people thought about her breaking a tradition that needed to be broken. That he needed to break because she belonged to him. But just as he resolved to give in to his craving and take what the Fates had promised him, she lowered her head, her forehead scraping over his lips.

He breathed in her scent and savored the lush skin against his mouth as he fought the mounting disappointment.

"I cannot, Sinow. If I give in now, I won't be able to go through with this," she breathed.

"Isn't that a good thing?" he asked, moving his face so that his cheek rested on her hair. She buried her face in his chest, and he tugged her tighter against him, never wanting to let her go. The sensation of having her there was indescribable. Like she solidified a space that had been barren forever, waiting for her to make it whole. Even with the massive pressure from his Dark powers as they fought against it, he embraced it.

"Leave with me, Vi. Things will go on without us. In time, they'll even forget us." It was a ridiculous suggestion made in a moment of wretchedness. Impulsive and wild—things he never would have been if the situation weren't dire.

"You know we can't." She peered up at him, and the nudging that this was exactly how it should be, with Violissa in his arms, returned like a snowstorm in the early days of the warm season. She tilted her head and chewed her bottom lip. "But...I wonder..." She stepped from his hold, leaving him with a shallow emptiness.

"But what?" he asked, his mind reeling from the loss of her touch.

"Well, the true law states that the bond must be between two people and spoken with vows. It assumes love, but there is no specific mention of it." As she spoke, he could hear her excitement, her words becoming more rushed, her voice lifting. "Theoretically, the bond could be one of friendship." She turned back to him, the excitement reflected in her shining orbs, the emerald so bright it nearly knocked him over. "Daneele and I could go through with it, but take the vows as friends, which is what we are, and not as... well...as you and I would have been." She paused, awaiting his reaction.

"And I'm supposed to be happy with this...why?" he asked, scratching his head.

"Don't you see? I would still be without a true union as husband and wife. I would still be open to taking true vows with you, well," she gnawed at her lip, "once I figure out how."

"Dissolve the union after a short time," he blurted, wondering why he hadn't thought of it earlier.

"What?" she asked with wide eyes.

"Dissolve it, end it."

"I know what dissolve means," she retorted, "but I don't understand how it relates to a union."

He couldn't help but gape at her. "Don't tell me your people are so strait-laced they never break their unions. They don't all keep their vows for a lifetime, do they?"

She looked at him as though he'd lost his mind, and he squinted his eyes, not believing that was the case.

"Of course they do."

Rubbing his hand over his face, he tried not to laugh. "Don't be foolish, Vi. That's too incredible to believe."

"Why?" She seemed insulted by his suggestion. "I find it incredible that anyone would take a pledge of commitment and love, then turn around and break it. Is that what you would do to me?"

The urge to take her arms and shake her for even insinuating such a thing streaked through him. "Vi, be serious. First, the king never dissolves his union. The union always lasts for his mate's lifetime. Although it's not a law as it is in your land, we take it seriously. Second, do you really think I could take vows with anyone but you?" His jaw twitched when he remembered she had thought exactly that and believed it. "Given the circumstances, don't answer that." The truth still stung, but he didn't want to dredge it up again.

She looked unsure until she said, "So, you suggest I dissolve it after an appropriate period?"

"Yes," he replied, hope rising again. "Give an excuse like it just wouldn't work because of a conflict with his Council position. I don't know. Just give them something. They'll forgive you and get over it in time."

Lips pursed, she twisted the material of her dress in her hands. "I don't know, Sinow. It all seems wrong to me."

He dragged his hands over his face, grumbling, "You're right, Vi. Every piece of this is wrong, including the fact that you're taking vows with another man." He hadn't meant to raise his voice, but his irritation was growing. She looked away, and he could tell his statement had stung her.

"You don't understand."

"No, Violissa, I don't understand," he complained, grabbing her arms. A need to convince her to stop this madness overtook him, countered by the frustration that was driving his power over the edge. "I don't see how you can feel the way we both do and still want to go through with this."

"I don't want to do this, Sinow, but I have no choice now."

"You have a choice, Violissa." His anguish came through in his voice, and he dropped her arms, his power struggling with the show of weakness.

"I don't," she murmured. "But I'll find a way out of it before I must take vows. I promise you."

"You'd better find one, Violissa, and fast." He held his hand to his forehead, fighting to stay in control. A calming spell tingled against his skin, and he peered at her, seeing the question in her eyes and nodding to give her the okay to finish with it. The Darkness continued to berate him, but her spell muted it some, giving him the strength to ask her one more question before he would have to walk away.

"Why Daneele? Why one of your Council? An immortal? Why not some random villager with a shorter lifespan?"

Her hand came around the back of her neck, rubbing it as she avoided his eyes. "I could only convince myself to take the vows. I didn't want anyone else's touch on me." She peeked up at him, and there was a pressure in his chest he wanted to remove because he knew it couldn't last. Not with the truth of their situation and what she was forcing on them both. "I knew Daneele would want to keep his vow of chastity and would never ask anything of me. I trust him. He's like my big brother, so I chose him."

Unable to help himself, he went to her, his finger wrapping through the curl that had loosened again. It took every ounce of effort not to kiss her. He threaded his fingers further into her hair and pulled her into his chest, the calming spell enough to keep his power assuaged. Burying his head in her hair, he mumbled, "Don't take vows with him, Vi. If you can't break the commitment, then at least put off the ceremony. There must be a way out of this and to stop this. If you go through with it, I won't be able to control my powers any longer. You know what it will do to me." There was no hiding the strain this was causing him, especially having her this close, his mouth against her ear, her body pressed into his.

Her hands dug into his shirt, and her heart pounded with his. "I'll find a way. Just give me time and I'll think of something."

A ragged sigh escaped him as he rubbed his cheek along hers, resisting turning his head to capture her lips. "So, I guess this means I'm resigned to sit back and wait once again? I can't believe I'm even having this conversation."

The movement of her smile weighed against his chest. The wish to never let her go, to hold on to her for eternity, mounted again.

"I do remember you mentioning something about waiting for eternity to have me," she said.

Gently pushing her back, he rested his forehead on her head. "So, I did," he replied, breathing in her scent once more. "I didn't realize at the time that it would prove so difficult."

She chuckled, her hand releasing his shirt before smoothing down the material. He leaned into the sensation. Eyes peeking up at him, she slid her hand up his chest and brought it to his cheek. Power played in her eyes, and the Darkness in him clawed to be recognized.

"I may not be able to give you what you want tonight, Sinow, but I can give you something. A promise."

"The prophecy was a promise, yet still you remain out of reach." His lips grazed her forehead, following a path down her cheek. Heart pounding, he debated turning his face, claiming her lips like he craved, but she stopped him once again, bringing her finger to his mouth. It lingered there before hesitantly slipping away.

"Don't," she breathed, and he relented, disappointment seeping into the far reaches of his body. "This is all I can give you."

Her magic touched the air, her voice with it. Soft and haunting, the song wove a spell around him. He may have laughed if he weren't so captivated. The sound laced through his skin, embedding in his core, then spreading until every part of him was bound to her as they never had been. There was power in her voice. He'd known that, but this seemed different. Personal. Reserved just for him. The spell grazed his hair, his skin, his entire being, and he recognized it for what it was. A binding spell, powerful and unbreakable. Sung in Elvin, he could not understand the words, only the magic in it and a sense of longing that filled it. He didn't have to ask what it was she sang, the woe in her voice was enough to know it was their story.

As her last note hung in the air, he tipped her chin, brushing his finger over her lips and wishing he had forced her hand all those years before.

"That song is my promise to you, Sinow, and the binding of that promise. That's all I can give you." And he knew how much she had given with it, the risk she'd taken in sharing her voice with him again, the magic that lingered on his skin and nestled around his heart. "I'm sorry I can't give you more right now."

He breathed in her lilac essence one last time, sweeping her curl back and letting his finger drift through it. "It's enough," he said. "But..." She tensed, her lip tucking below her teeth as his finger followed the curve of her neck and pulled away just before meeting her neckline. "...you know what this means."

He watched her swallow, the gentle movement of her throat,

the rise of her chest before he dragged his eyes back to meet hers. Her nod was subtle, unlike the sensation of loss that struck him when she stepped from his arms. They both understood the consequences of her misstep. Regardless of how it had happened, her actions had broken a treaty that promised their union. Even if she didn't want to go through with her union with Daneele, her commitment to it dissolved the treaty. A treaty that had ensured Cirillia remained protected until they could fulfill the prophecy because they both knew, just as their Councils had predicted, that he had the power to bring down the boundary.

He had put this off long enough, relishing their closeness and their touches, praying there was some way to avoid this step. He moved further from her, inviting the Darkness to surface. His power barreled through him like an unleashed torrent, and he clenched his hands to restrain it. Calling on his power was the only way he would have the strength to follow through with what needed to be done.

"You know what must happen now, Violissa? You understand I cannot avoid it?"

She created a robe and pulled it over her exposed skin before holding her head higher.

"Yes."

"Then the time is at hand to discuss the inevitable."

CHAPTER 47

Fear gnawed at Violissa, threatening to erase the lingering of Sinow's touch that still sat on her skin. The urge to cry, to curl up in a ball and close the world off raced through her. She'd been such a fool, and Tynan had played her for one. She had trusted him because she trusted Sinow, and that trust had been misplaced. Now she was suffering for it, Sinow was suffering for it, her people would suffer for it.

Biting back the agony, she watched as Dark power morphed Sinow, overtaking the gentle side whose finger had wrapped through her curl, whose mouth had sat so near to hers that one tiny move would have changed their course, whose firm hold on her arms left her breathless. It took the man away and buried him under the power. His eyes became a shade closer to black, and she pushed her emotions aside. She had no choice, no matter how much she loved him. And she knew now that love was what hounded her, what drove her temptation to turn her back on the expectations of her people and pull his lips to hers. She knew the moment they kissed, the struggle would be over, their hearts would link, and they would never turn back.

But there she stood, awaiting the inevitable. Yet another

misstep on her path that she could not undo. She had only herself to blame. The Fate had warned her the path would be treacherous, and she suspected this was only the beginning.

Sinow stood taller, and she couldn't help but be aware of how massive he was. Muscles strained below his clothes, and he towered over her even with as tall as she was. But no matter how intimidating, he was beautiful, and he was hers, even if her foolishness was keeping them apart again. He rolled his neck, his hands flexing, and she steadied herself for what was to come.

"It's time to face the consequences of your decision, Violissa." A forlorn look crossed his face before the coldness returned. No matter how he didn't want to do this, he had no choice, just as she'd had none. These were the rules they lived by. She had a sickening suspicion Tynan had planned it all, knowing this would be the outcome.

Drawing her robe tighter, she waited, understanding what was coming and dreading it. She wanted to scream in frustration. She craved his touch, wanted to be back in his arms, but she was too proud to act on it, to let go of her stubborn need to abide by the rules. He was right. She put her people first, and now they would pay for it. The irony was not lost on her. Here they were, both at a point where they could accept their destiny, and once again, she had made the wrong choice. Once again, they were being pulled apart by her poor emotional decisions.

"Go on, Sinow, let it be done." She sensed the change in her eyes as she hardened herself to what was coming and locked her emotions away.

"Your decision to follow through with this farce," she shuddered at the vile sting of his words, "leaves me no choice but to consider the treaty broken and declare war on you and your realm, Violissa." She had expected it, but still a shiver raced down her spine. "I have no choice. The Fates and your Council promised you to me. You are mine, not another man's, and I cannot let your decision to disregard that fact go without repercussions.

Regardless of what agreement we've come to today, regardless of what we discussed, my Council will expect it, my people will expect it. I have laws of my land that I must follow, Violissa, just as you have yours."

He stopped, averting his eyes before they flicked back to her. She knew he hated doing this, and that was why he had summoned his magic. She made no attempt to weave another calming spell, knowing he would need to release his hold on the Darkness completely to silence his instinct to protect her. Another internal conflict for which she was to blame.

"I understand, Sinow."

"I'll give you time to place protection spells around your towns and ready your people and Council. When I tear down the realm boundary, you will have no more time. That is the most I can offer." The hues of brown in his eyes battled the ebony that drowned them.

"Thank you," she said, worrying over not only her people's safety but Sinow's. If he lost himself completely to the Darkness, there would be no bringing him back. The thought gouged her heart, but she had little time to consider it.

"I will deal with my brother swiftly and justly before that time. His punishment will be severe." His expression softened, an earthy hue overcoming his pitch orbs. "The only chance you have of stopping this is by calling off your planned union. Find a way quickly. I'll hold back as long as I can, but after that..." He trailed off, and she knew then that he, too, worried his power would grow unhinged and they would never return to what could have been. "Goodbye, Vi."

Sadness layered his voice, and it further fractured her heart. "Goodbye, Sinow," she replied as he shifted.

Emptiness encompassed her, and she brought her arms around her stomach, clutching her body to make it go away. She stood there for a long time, breathing in what remained of his scent and replaying everything in her head. Running after him was what she wanted to do, to tell him to forget it all, that the laws could go the way of the Fates for all she cared. But she didn't. Instead, she crumpled over and fell to the floor as the emotions of the evening and what she'd sacrificed came crashing down upon her.

THE COUNCIL HAD GATHERED, their voices spilling from the doorway as Violissa approached. She stood to the side, listening to them and hearing the dread in their voices. They had carried it since the day she announced the union with Daneele. A moment of weakness driven by emotions and one she now regretted.

Taking a deep breath, she ran her hands down her skirts before walking into the room. They fell silent, reading the seriousness of her stance and expression. If it was anything their queen was not, it was serious. A lifetime spent dallying in gardens and frolicking with her people had left Violissa ill-equipped for matters such as this. She hated that they would judge her, that this would validate their early concerns that a woman's temperament would make ruling a challenge. Not that they meant it as anything unkind. Never had a woman ruled or even held magic in Cirillia. Only the Elvin had female rulers. They were the only race where the line included more than a male. At least before Violissa.

And here she had gone and made yet another mistake that they would blame on her emotions and lack of preparedness. She was tired of her emotions ruling her, tired of pain and sadness, tired of being the only woman in a man's world. But mostly, she was tired of letting them down and reinforcing their notions. And she would no longer be that woman. She would own her mistakes and face this situation as a queen, not a quivering, crying ball of emotion.

Head held high, she took her seat, seeing the questioning eyes and confused faces as they sat. Light blood and Elvin blood ran through her veins. She was the heir to two thrones, the last of the

Elvin. This would not be her defeat, and what she did now would define her for eternity.

"Tenebron has declared war on Cirillia."

Large eyes and gaping mouths preceded the rise of voices.

"Silence!" She slammed her hand on the table as she stood. "You will listen and hold your questions and judgment until I have finished."

They sat back down, some giving her surprised looks, others like Cyric ones of pride.

Staying on her feet, she continued. "The king's brother has manipulated me, playing a game for unknown reasons yet with far-reaching repercussions."

Murmurs began, but she ignored them. "I will say this only once and do not wish to hear any more about it. I made a mistake. I rushed to judgment given the facts presented to me and made an unwise decision, letting my emotions guide me." She paused, waiting for the backlash but receiving none. "The king has not taken another, nor does he plan to." There were a few groans, and several of her Council slumped back in their seats, including Daneele. "Sinow has declared the treaty void, broken on the grounds that I have denied him what the treaty promised."

"Violissa," Cyric started, and she glanced at him, praying he wouldn't condemn her. "What do you intend to do?"

She released a sigh of relief, seeing the other Council lean forward in their chairs to listen.

"I need protection around the towns. The people need to be warned. Raise any army we can to protect the borders."

"He plans to bring the boundary down, doesn't he?" Anwell asked.

"Yes. He is giving us time to prepare and to research."

"Research what?" Daneele asked, his brow raising.

"How to take back our impending union." She saw the mouths open then close and knew they wanted to tell her they were right, that they had warned her. "I need a way out that will not jeopardize my standing with the people. But first, we must prepare. Cirillia has not felt the sting of Dark power since the days of my father. Our people know nothing of fighting, nothing of destruction. They know only peace. It is imperative that they be ready."

"And what will you do?" Cyric asked. He was the only one who knew the toll of war, who understood the severity of what was coming.

"I will be by your side until the boundary falls. After that, I will hold the protection spell over the realm to keep as much of our realm and our people protected."

"Fates, Violissa. The entire realm? You cannot hold a spell that long, nor do you have the power—"

"I do and I can," she retorted, severing Anwell's argument. "Now, much work is to be done. Sinow is already under the influence of his power, and I don't know how long we'll have until he slips completely."

"And what of his brother? You said Tynan manipulated this?" Cyric asked.

Sitting, Violissa gave a synopsis of what she had discovered, thankful they kept their opinions to themselves and didn't remind her of her misguided decisions. As they left her, off to fortify the realm and warn the people, Cyric approached her. Daneele remained in his seat, watching Cyric.

She wanted to avoid Cyric's knowing look, the crossed arms that told her he wanted to lecture her but was refraining.

"I know," she mumbled, forcing herself to hold his stare. "I messed up."

Daneele put his elbows on the table and leaned his head in his hands. If she could take it all back, she would, but it was impossible.

"You're a lot like your mother," said Cyric, and she turned her attention back to him. "Aradisa was impulsive and emotional. It drove your father mad, but he loved her for it. Elvin runs through your blood, and it has always driven your moods. That will never change, Violissa. Learn to listen to your Light side, to hear the reasoning it offers when the Elvin wants nothing more than to burn the world down."

He gave her a sad smile before he walked away, leaving her alone with Daneele. Flopping into her seat, she blew a strand of hair from her eyes.

"Go ahead," she said. "Tell me how you told me so. You're the only one I'll allow to say that."

He shook his head. "I won't because I know you've told yourself that enough times." He sat back, rubbing his beard. "I'll work with Cyric to find a way out of this. You could just break it off, you know. The people love you too much to condemn you for not following tradition."

"It's a sacred tradition, Daneele. Who would I be if I stomped on that and said I wasn't going through with something they deem so important?"

"The vows are the important part."

"Just as important as the announcement. I can't just tell them I changed my mind. It would lower the sanctity of every couple's decision to join. Lessen the meaning in it."

"You care too much for them," he said, to her surprise.

She looked away, saying, "So I've been told."

Talking was something she wanted to be done with. There were too many things that needed her attention, including figuring out how she was going to shield the realm from the full brunt of a Darkbearer attack.

Daneele left without another word, and she stayed there, contemplating all she had done and the horrors that awaited, wishing she had made different choices and cursing the Fates for letting her make the ones she had.

CHAPTER 48

Tynan looked around. Nothing. That's all he saw for miles and miles. Nothing. Banished for eternity in this blasted realm. The Banished Realm was a pocket of land sealed off from the rest of Tenebron by an early Dark King. A punishment worse than death for a criminal. Only the most vile of criminals received this sentence. It was death, but slow and torturous. No food, no water, nothing for a mortal to survive on. For an immortal, banishment was another type of sentence. A life of loneliness and madness. It was rare for an immortal to be banished but not unheard of. Dark Kings had unstable temperaments, and their Council were often the victims. Piss a Dark King off enough, and he wouldn't care if you were Council or not.

Tynan groaned in frustration and rubbed his neck. Shifting, he crashed back to the ground as he hit the magical barrier that held him prisoner. Picking himself back up, he took a deep breath. This was temporary, only temporary. He'd known Sinow would punish him, but he hadn't seen this coming. Although looking back, he should have.

What he had done to Sinow and Violissa had been perfection.

He couldn't have planned it better, and her jealousy was her downfall. The wind had done his bidding, and Violissa had done the rest. With a little persuasion from Tynan, of course. Laughter escaped him, fading into the vast nothingness that was now his home. Even with all that power, she was just as weak as any mortal woman and just as gullible.

The outcome had been worth this minor setback. He would wait for Sinow to come calling for him, granting him pardon. His brother's hold on his power was wavering, the Darkness driving him now that the truth of what Violissa had done was out. And when he lost himself to the Darkness, Sinow would turn to Tynan for help. Tynan would wait. He had waited this long. Rubbing his hands together, he thought about what awaited him.

He was so close. The book was secure, hidden where no one would find it before Sinow had banished him. A war was brewing, a war that wouldn't take long to begin. Sinow would have no grounds to hold the Council from calling for war. Violissa had violated the treaty, and they would jump at the chance to call for revenge. Once a battle began, Sinow's control of his Dark nature would fail. Sure, he talked big, telling himself and anyone who would listen that he had it under control. Tynan knew the truth, knew the call of their Dark powers all too well. Too much aggression would tinge the air for Sinow to fight it. When he finally tasted the true depth of power he held, nothing would stop him. Nothing except Tynan. Yes, Sinow would come crawling back to him seeking his advice again, and he would be back in Sinow's favor, all the while scheming for his downfall.

Tynan aimed his shift out a few miles within the Banished Realm's borders, finding no sign of anything or anyone. Not that he had thought he would. Those sent here were few, and there was no way for them to survive long in the dreaded barrenness. All he would find were the bones of mortals and the dust of long-dead immortals who had given up and returned their souls to the Fates.

Waving his hand, he created a small building for shelter. His magic would sustain him until Sinow called him back. It wouldn't be long, and when he returned, he'd break the secret to that damned book once and for all and bring Tenebron to its knees.

CHAPTER 49

As the days ran by, Violissa knew she was in trouble. No matter which way she worked it, she couldn't find a solution to ending the impending union. She argued constantly with her Council about the situation, and thankfully they refrained from reminding her of her fault in it.

The people were bracing themselves, her Council reinforcing supplies and teaching those closest to the Tenebron border to defend themselves. While they weren't certain, they suspected the Darkbearers had an army. Sinow's grandfather had built an army early in his reign and over the multiple millennia he ruled, it had become a nightmare for Cirillia. If that army was still in force, a ground war would complicate the magical war between the Councils.

She rubbed her head as the exhaustion from the lack of sleep and the stress of what was coming burrowed in her bones. Between Cyric and Daneele, they'd gone through options of calling off the union, but none offered what she needed. At this point, she wasn't sure what she was looking for anymore, and time was running out. Daneele wanted her to stop her stubborn need to keep the people happy, and she was considering it. Perhaps she was being foolish, and no one would judge her. Her fear was that by breaking off the union, she would disregard a sacred part of a couple's journey and set a precedent. Taking the vow to wed and announcing it to family and friends was a commitment that was honored. It ensured couples did not venture into that commitment without intending to see it through and have the union.

No other option was viable, and the threat was coming. It was in the air, in the ground, heavy in every breath she took. The wind, ever so apologetic about giving her erroneous information, had tried to make it up by feeding her news on Sinow. It told her of his swift punishment for Tynan and the ever-present sadness in his eyes. He had sentenced his brother to a fate most thought worse than death: banishment.

This didn't surprise Violissa. Tynan had betrayed Sinow and created a situation that was not easily fixed. Banishment was really the only form of punishment one could give to an immortal. Violissa feared, however, that as much as Sinow might hate what Tynan had done, he was still blood, and instinct told her Sinow had a soft spot for Tynan. Unfortunately, Tynan had taken advantage of that, and she prayed this weakness wouldn't become Sinow's downfall. Although she suspected it already was.

The air grew thicker, a prickling running over her skin, and Violissa lifted her head. She was sitting outside, taking a moment of peace in her garden. A rumble went through the ground, and she sensed Sinow's mind brushing against hers. Darkness invaded her mind, and she shivered before she shifted. Something was coming, and when she landed on the edge of the boundary where the ravine ran deep, she looked across through the boundary into Tenebron. The ravine split the two realms in half, only ending at the northern end of the boundary close to where the Sacred Groves were. It narrowed in some places and was minimal enough in certain places to be no more than a divot in the land, but no one saw it. The boundary hid it from view, all view but hers, and she suspected Sinow's.

From this viewpoint, she could use her powers to see far into Sinow's land. It was dawn in Tenebron, and the sunrise cast a brightness to the land that seemed ironic for what sat in the air. The land was dense with trees and lush green fields that welcomed the coming sunshine. Mountain peaks in the distance cast a shadow over part of the land, including Sinow's castle. A vast amount of cleared land backed the castle, while thick woods guarded the front. Even with the morning sun, a haze sat over it, thicker than usual. Sinow's power had spread like an infection across the land, and she knew he was losing his battle.

The invasive touch of his mind met hers, and she brought her sight to the left, seeing him on the other side of the ravine. Today was the day. War was coming, and she had not found a solution. She would have no chance to change her mind and simply tell her people she had been wrong. To let them down. But now that the full scale of her mistake was upon them, she wished she'd done that.

Eyes of pitch glared at her from beyond, the sensation in her mind softening when their eyes met. It had been so long since she'd seen him. An entire moon cycle had passed, and she knew he'd held this at bay as long as he could. He was waiting for her to announce the union had ended, but now he had no choice but to move forward. She understood the pressure his Council was placing on him to act. What else could he do?

Violissa. His voice caressed her mind, and she opened herself to it, bracing against the Dark tinge that sank into her veins and warred with her power. *Vi, I cannot deter them any longer. Are you prepared?*

She wanted to scream that she wasn't. To call her Council and tell them to announce her withdraw from the union. To make some excuse because anything would be better than what was coming. But it was too late for that. Once again, another decision had been wrong, and her emotions had led her astray. So instead, she said a simple, *Yes.*

I'm sorry it's come to this, but you give me no choice.

His voice was so smooth, she could tell he was holding his power back. The longing in it made her want to shift to him and give herself over to him. Her hands shook. A warning screamed in her mind, telling her to stop this, but she did nothing.

I understand the laws of your lands, as you have understood mine, she replied, wishing she could tell him what was really in her heart.

Goodbye, Vi. I will have them go easy on your people as long as I can, if that's possible.

She was thankful for that but doubted it would happen. Once the war began, the Darkness would take him, and he would unleash his Darkbearers on Cirillia with full force.

Sinow?

Yes, Vi. Again, the longing sat in his voice, and she questioned why she was being so stubborn. Why she couldn't let herself fail and admit to her people that she had messed up.

Take care of yourself. Don't let the Darkness cause you to lose control.

Take care, Vi.

He was gone, the thick, heavy sensation retreating from her mind. The absence left an emptiness deep in her core. The ground shook, stones crumbling down the ravine as an angry ebony filled the sky. With bated breath, she waited, her hand held to her chest as her heartbeat quickened below. Magic flashed in the sky, streaks of it along where the boundary sat. He was doing it. He was destroying the magical border that had separated their lands for thousands of years. The ascension had granted him the power to do so, just as her ascension had, just as her Council had suspected.

She did nothing to stop him, knowing it was no use. This war was inevitable; all she could do was watch and wait. The ground bucked, and the air quivered before the boundary shattered with a deafening thunder that split the air. Quickly, she wove a spell to dissolve the shards that splattered her realm. They changed into a fine powder, layering the ground like a light snow. Fear and panic hummed through the kingdom and vibrated on her skin. Overwhelmed by the invasive sensations, she backed away, trying to steady herself. Sinow shifted, and she stared at the empty space, foreboding crawling through her and warning her that this was a defining moment in her life and her reign, one that would test her tie to Sinow and the space he held in her heart.

THE BATTLE WAGED FOR YEARS, draining Violissa and pushing her Council to its limits. At first, it was just a battering of Sinow's army against her protection spells. Daily attacks on it with few infiltrations. Sinow kept his word to her, letting his army lead the fight until he had no choice but to involve his Council. Even then, he sent one or two, never more, to fight her Lightbearers. But she suspected they had grown frustrated and questioned him because soon the full wrath of the Darkbearers bombarded her shields and took aim at her Council who, lured out by their violent attacks, joined the fray.

The full force of magical warfare began. Violissa maintained her shields, but at times the fighting diverted her attention. It was then her shields would weaken, and soldiers would sneak through, never many but enough to do damage. Those Cirillians the Lightbearers had rounded up to fight lacked the skill of Sinow's army. His soldiers had years, if not more, of training, while hers had only weeks. Casualties rose, her Council too distracted to heal, and she too focused on maintaining her shields against Sinow to help. She remained as Sinow did: a witness to her mistakes.

And with their attention diverted, she and the others spent their time defending rather than finding a way out of the union. She had concluded that she needed to concede, no matter the opinions of her people, but then Sinow had shattered the shield, and her decision was lost in the hustle of war.

With each passing moon cycle, Sinow sank further into the Darkness. Violissa could feel it, sense him turning as he lost his struggle against the power. The fighting, the carnage, the violence fed the emotions of the people, and his Darkness fed upon them. Their pain, their anger, their violent battle cries fueled his Dark side, and it killed her knowing she had been the cause.

The wind, still apologetic for leading her astray, kept her abreast of Sinow's condition, and as it told her how he had forgiven his brother and welcomed him back to Tenebron, she knew she had lost him completely. Her hope of turning things slipped from her. Her worst fear was being realized, or so she thought.

As Sinow twisted further out of control, the actions of his troops and Council became worse. It went on so long that she almost forgot why the war had begun in the first place, and she was certain he had. Unable to take anymore, she reached out to her Council in desperation through enaigne.

This must end. I don't care that the people will hate me for breaking the vow. They'll hate me more for letting them suffer and die. I must do it. It's the only way to stop this.

As she awaited their answer, a blast of Dark power slammed into her so hard it threw her through the side wall of her castle and out into the air. Shock strangled her, and it took a moment to realize what had happened. Shifting mid-flight, she reappeared on the ground below. Eyes darting, she searched for any sign of Sinow. The magic that had struck her smelled of him but carried a foul tinge, almost as if it had spoiled. Over several moons, she had tried reaching out to him in enaigne, but that same foul aura had assaulted her, and she had eventually closed her mind from him to keep it from seeping in.

Now, it surrounded her again as she scanned the area. He was nowhere in sight, but another blast of magic raced toward her, and she threw her hand up, deflecting it. The forest beyond exploded, the trees screaming as magic tore them asunder. She folded over, clutching her head and fighting the onslaught of pain that reverberated from the forest. Summoning her power, she sent a wave of nature magic flooding into it, repairing the damage. As she straightened, she realized her mistake. The distraction had cost her. Sinow hit her with a strike that knocked her from her feet and threw her across the front lawn of her castle, the stone structure stopping her movement. The impact left her dazed until her body healed, but Dark magic scorched her skin, leaving her clawing at it until she quelled the fire in it and healed her burns.

He was too far into his realm to see, but his power still reached her, and so hers could do the same. Without risking another moment, she hammered him with a bolt of arcane magic, homing in on the source of the magic that had struck her. As it took hold, his roar enveloped the land, his rage palpable. The sensation of his magic pressing outside her mind and seeking entrance hounded her. It tempted her to open her mind and talk to him, but she thought better of it considering his state. Letting him in could cripple her, and she couldn't take the chance. She didn't dare shift and fight him on his ground. And if she was being honest, she didn't want to see him like this. The guilt she carried had yet to cease, and seeing him so far gone would crush her.

Spell after spell hit her, but she shielded herself to stop the damage, volleying his attacks. They continued battering each other, their powers so strong now that neither needed to leave their realm to do so. For every hit Violissa sent at him, he returned one with just enough force to irritate her. She was growing tired of the game when an ugly mass of black tendrils dropped from the sky above her and encased her before she could shift away. It suffocated her with tainted Dark power, temporarily blocking her senses so she couldn't respond.

Memories of being dragged under the surface with the Torathar entered her mind, and panic struck her. She scratched at the magic, trying to break free. Calling to her Light power, she let it pour from her. Blue arcane surrounded her, pushing back the ebony mass, and she drew a deep inhale as her sight returned. Annoyance claimed her, and she pulled the power back to her, letting it build until she released it in a rage of energy that shot through what remained of the Dark magic around her and stormed toward Tenebron with one goal in mind—Sinow.

She waited, expecting another attack, but there was nothing. All was quiet. Too quiet. And it was then that she noticed her protection of the realm had faltered. He had distracted her, purposely drawing her focus to him and from the shield she'd kept in place over the kingdom. Casting her senses out, she discovered the devastation. Sinow's troops had broken through and had pillaged the outer villages.

Pain, death, misery. The emotions pummeled her, and she teetered. Ire burned through her, cascading like a rogue wave through her body, and she shifted to the border, reaching out to any of Sinow's troops that remained. Most were gone, likely shifted back out by the Darkbearers not currently fighting her Council. A few stragglers remained hidden in the outer forests, however. She could perceive their intent, the excitement that streamed from their auras, the adrenaline that had fueled their violence. Finding them, she gave herself over to her Elvin side. Rage and anguish burst forth, and in a fury of emotion, she hunted them down, one by one, killing each with the vengeance of a predator. Roots burst forth from the land, some strangling, others impaling, and a few dragging their enemies into the ground, leaving only their muted screams. There was no mercy, but they had given her people none.

When she had killed the last one, she staggered forward, clutching a tree. The emotion calmed, and she turned her head and vomited, the realization of what she had done unsettling her Light side. Vengeance was a Dark emotion, and murder went against the code of the Lightbearers. But she was not only of the Light; her Elvin side ruled her as well. The toll of taking another life, however, left her in agony, and she buckled over, expelling the remains of what little was in her stomach. She had never harmed another, but Sinow had pushed her too far. And in doing so, he had unleashed a side of her she didn't like, one she would have to reconcile when this ended. If it ever ended.

Releasing her hold on the tree, she wiped her mouth with her sleeve.

"Do you still have the urge to run to him, Violissa? Still love the man who let his people slaughter ours?"

She whipped around to find Brom behind her, his blue eyes grave, the distress in them palpable. Weariness showed in his frame, the rounding of his once proud shoulders, and the grim tightness of his lips.

"Yes, I still love the man under the Darkness, Brom. You have your damned prophecy and the Fates to thank for that. His Dark power has control of him. For how long now, I don't know." She glanced back. Disturbed dirt was the only sign the enemy soldiers had ever been there. "Sinow has turned the tide of the battle, and it is now my fight and mine alone." Turning her sight back to Brom, she said, "And I promise I will bring the Darkness down around him if it's the last thing I do."

"The fight has always been yours, Violissa. It's time to act and join the battle. Only you can bring him back, and if you cannot, then only you have the power to defeat him. We will continue to fight the Darkbearers, but you need to take your stand and unleash what you've been holding back all this time. I've no doubt you'll bring him to his knees. It's what you do with him once you have him there that will define the queen you truly are."

That night was quiet. Nothing pounded at her shields, no one fought her Council, and no one screamed in pain or fear. Daneele and Brom took watch over the realm as Violissa tried to get a full night's sleep. The first in a very long time. But after spending the day comforting the grieving villagers, healing those who had been injured, and burying the dead, what little sleep she got was fitful.

She launched her assault on Sinow the next morning. Nerves

bounded through her, but it accompanied determination and anger that roared through her like a feral beast. Brom had been correct in his assessment of her. It was time to push back and end this war. She had hesitated, and even though it was mostly her people's blood that had spilled, she had not been willing to attack Tenebron and spill more innocent blood. Sinow, however, had given her no choice. She could no longer stand back and watch the destruction.

The cliffs of the ravine held firm below her feet as she looked out at the place Sinow had once stood and warned her of the impending attack. Closing her eyes, she relished the gentle touch of the wind on her face and prayed to the Fates to give her strength. When she finished her prayer, she envisioned the fiercest tempest, summoning her nature gifts and thinking of the storm coming down over Tenebron. She called forth the lightning and the thunder, commanded the wind to blow at its fullest strength, then she brought the rain down in thick sheets over the land.

With the storm slashing down over Tenebron, Violissa sought Sinow. Reaching far through the storm and the land, she found him. A vile essence permeated the aura that surrounded him, and she almost pulled her senses back to flee from it before she pushed through. Sending the full force of her Light magic at him, she ordered it to tear him from his bed and into the rain. His angry growl rumbled across the land, and she smiled. Not yet satisfied that he had suffered enough, a burst of her nature magic fled her, digging into the land and seeking its target. She commanded it to entangle him and drag him into the forest, battering him against the trees.

His power pushed against hers as he freed himself, and a rush of Dark power surged toward her. She blocked it, but not before his voice echoed across the expanse.

"Violissa!"

He counter-attacked again, but not in the way she expected. He directed his rage toward her people, a black band snaking through her shields and into the towns before she could protect them from the Darkness infecting them. The screams shattered her elation, and she moved quickly to shield them, sending a wave of healing energy out to those villages that had been impacted. She turned her attention back to Tenebron, holding her breath for the next attack. None came. He wouldn't let her off that easily, and she knew whatever came next would be worse because she had thrown the war in a new direction.

CHAPTER 50

A black fog billowed around Sinow as he cursed Violissa. Power sparked from his hands in streaks of red and gray, but he restrained it. She expected him to retaliate, but he wouldn't give her the satisfaction. Rolling his neck, he looked up at the gaping hole in the castle where his room sat. The bitch had struck while he was sleeping, her magic throwing him from his bed, through the wall, and out into the open. Rain pounded on his head, sending his hair into his face, and he shoved it back. The storm was her doing. She had finally made a move against him. The wait had been worth it, and he looked forward to showing her his full strength. He'd been waiting for her to do more than remain on the defensive. All these years and nothing but a relentless back and forth between the Councils, and all the while the Darkness in him grew stronger until there was nothing left of who he'd been before the war.

Shifting to his room, he stalked to the gap and stared out at the deluge. Her power was impressive, and he was looking forward to facing a formidable adversary. He had never even considered fighting her Council. They weren't worth his time, nor did he care to bother with the mortals. He wanted to fight Violissa, to see her suffer, to punish her.

Somewhere deep within him, an urge to end this battle slinked, but he quickly eviscerated it before it could claw its way to the surface. His damned conscious. He couldn't think of another name for it other than that. The remnants of his former self. The man with emotions for Violissa and controlled by the blasted prophecy. He had squashed that side of him early in the war, and he despised it even more than he loathed her. It had made him weak, keeping his powers at bay, living like a slave to his hunger for her.

The thought sent fire coursing through him, angering him even more. He had severed that part of himself and locked it deep within him where it would stay buried. Attempts to destroy it had failed. That would have been preferable, but no matter how he tried, that voice remained, lingering in the distance, and so he kept it submerged, vowing to never let it dominate him again.

Water evaporated on his skin, his power drying it before he grabbed a shirt and yanked it over his chest. Knowing he would sleep no more this night, he slammed through his doors, blowing them from their hinges and shattering them into tiny fragments. Violissa had already destroyed his room, and taking his frustrations out on the door relieved his need to go after her. His Council could deal with the mess in the morning.

Stalking through the halls, he could hear the storm battering against the keep. He knew her intention, but she underestimated his concern for his people. His code had warped, the call to protect his people lost in the madness that gathered in his mind. Soon the towns would flood, and many of his people would drown. He didn't care. She assumed he would, that his old self would overtake him and he would end the war to stop his people's suffering, but she was dead wrong.

Let them die. Since when did a Dark King care about his people? the Darkness taunted.

It hounded him now, the voice leading him, controlling his decisions and his power. His fingers flexed as he embraced the thought, thinking how different he was from his father, the weak link in the family line. Sinow refused to follow that path. He planned to be a legend of terror just as his grandfather had been, and he would start by finishing what his grandfather had started. He would annihilate the Lightbearers and their queen and bring Cirillia to its knees.

"Did you have a nice bath?" Tynan stood at the end of the hall, his arms crossed as he leaned on the wall.

"Shut up, Tynan," he groused, still questioning why he had brought his brother back.

It had seemed like a good idea at the time. Tynan was the reason they were at war with Cirillia, the reason Violissa had shown her true colors. How quickly she had turned her back on him again, choosing another man this time. The Darkness slithered through him, reveling in the hatred and envy that stirred. It fed from them, sinking deeper into his veins. It was better this way. He didn't need her.

"So she finally made her move?" Tynan said, falling into step beside Sinow.

"Yes." They rounded the corner into another hallway, and Sinow questioned why he hadn't shifted. "What are you doing here, Tynan?"

"I came to see what the commotion was."

Sinow stopped and turned on him, grasping his collar and slamming him into the wall. "Your quarters are nowhere near mine, so I will ask again, what are you doing in my wing of the keep?"

Tynan pushed his hands away, his eyes beady. "Let me take care of her, brother," he said.

Sinow tilted his head, evaluating his brother. Tynan had returned from the Banished Realm changed, but Sinow had yet to pinpoint what that change was or what it meant. There was something sniveling about him now, like a stalking predator who had yet to reveal himself. Even the Dark power didn't trust him; it was on edge each time Tynan was near. There was no tangible reason to doubt him. Tynan had been advising him throughout the war, his suggestions surprisingly good. The distraction that had allowed their soldiers to break into Cirillia had been Tynan's doing. But still, there was something that nudged at Sinow.

"No."

He walked away, hearing Tynan grumble behind him.

"It's beneath you."

Turning on Tynan, Sinow barred his teeth and growled, "You will not engage with the queen."

"Still touchy about Violissa?" Again, the way Tynan said her name itched at Sinow's tolerance. "I thought you were over that."

"I'm not touchy about anything. Leave Violissa to me. Your part in this is and always has been to advise. Nothing more, nothing less."

The clench of Tynan's jaw had Sinow's eyes narrowing, and he waited for Tynan's rebuttal.

"If that's what you wish," Tynan said, a hint of annoyance in his tone.

"It is. Now leave me. I've had enough aggravation for one night. Since you have nothing better to do than hang around in my wing, put yourself to use and fix my quarters. There's a hole in my wall, and my door needs repairing."

Thunder shook the keep, his molars grinding in reaction. "And I have an obnoxious bitch who needs reminding that I'm the wrong king to mess with." He stomped off, cursing the damned rain, his mind sifting through all the ways he was about to make Violissa's life miserable.

CHAPTER 51

Quiet crept over the kingdom, and within it sat an eerie sense of anticipation. Violissa expected Sinow to retaliate, but he didn't...not immediately. And so she waited, watching for any sign of his magic, barely sleeping, barely eating. Her nerves were a constant companion, and the day he struck again, they battered her so that she faltered, her shields slipping, her reflexes slow. Recovering, she engaged his attack, reaching out to her Council to warn them. His power rained down over the kingdom, and with the Darkbearers joining, the war began again.

Day after day, she and Sinow fought. There were days when he would send the Darkbearers to fight her Council, times when her concentration wavered and his troops would attack. But mostly, it was Violissa against Sinow, wreaking enough damage on the realms and each other to keep both their Councils busy cleaning up. The fighting was grueling, the land and the people constantly cowering in fear of the magical torrents that engulfed them. No matter what Violissa did, Sinow didn't stop. Nothing bothered him, and she eventually stopped the deluge over his kingdom, leaving the rain over his castle just to spite him for letting his people suffer.

As the war raged for its fifth year, exhaustion sank its fangs into Violissa. Between the fighting and the casualties, she could take no more. Sinow had volleyed a round of intense Dark magic at her, draining the last of her energy. Collapsing, she looked up at the sky.

"Is this what you wanted?" she asked the Fates. "Is this my punishment? If it is, you are too cruel. My mistake did not warrant this agony."

She crawled over to the side of the pond where she had fallen and splashed her face. As the water stilled, she stared at her reflection. Circles curved like dark crescents below her eyes. Hair lay matted and disheveled, its curls straight with the weight of her burdens. And skin that once held a delicate glow seemed pale except for the places where dirt marred it. Her emerald orbs had lost their shine and now held a sadness she didn't think would ever leave.

They had lost so much. And for what? For a misunderstanding and a stubborn need to protect her people. One that only hurt them. Well, she was done. Done being punished for her mistakes, done letting Sinow and his Darkbearers brutalize her people, done letting the Darkness own the man she knew was still in there. The man she loved. And yes, she still loved him because the man who had brought her to ecstasy in the Dream Realm, who had told her he would wait for her, who had held her the night her foolishness had set off this debacle was not the man who was inflicting so much harm on her and her realm.

She brushed her hair aside, sure she was leaving dirt on her face and not caring. A butterfly flitted near her, and she put her finger out to give it perch.

This had to end. The war had gone on for so long, they had lost the reason for it. The Council had stopped their research, and she had forgotten her decision to give up her reasoning and break off the union. Now she wondered if it even mattered anymore.

The people just wanted the war to end. And Sinow... He was another matter completely. The Darkness had its claws in him, and she was positive that side of him couldn't care less if she broke off the union with Daneele and announced it was time to move forward with the prophecy.

Chewing her lip, she stood, releasing the butterfly and brushing her hands over her dress. The Sinow she loved was in there, locked away somewhere and lost to his power, but she would find him. She had to, or this war would never end, and there would be only the two of them fighting an endless battle over nothing.

With reckless abandon, she shifted to Tenebron, sending her senses out to find him. Appearing before him, she swallowed back her gasp. She had not seen him since the night the war had started. They had fought at a distance, neither willing to face the other, their power substantial enough that the miles between them made no difference. They could sense each other as if they were only feet away.

Her eyes perused him, seeing the shell of the man who had once held her so tight it seemed he feared losing her. And of course, he had. He looked as broken and disheveled as she did. His ebony locks were long, running past his shoulders in an unkempt mess of thick strands. The stubble that had once framed his powerful jaw had grown in, a full beard in its place that would have looked sexy if not for the lack of grooming. Madness sat in his eyes of pitch, and a haze of black surrounded him. She no longer recognized the man who stood before her.

Rain poured down over them, the spell she had set over his castle ensuring it was never dry. His eyes met hers, and a slight flicker of brown disturbed their color. It was a tiny glimmer of hope, but it was hope, nonetheless. Sinow, her Sinow, was in there somewhere. He scowled at her, drawing his hand up as magic pooled around it.

"Enough, Sinow!" she screamed.

His magic pulsed through the air, hurtling toward her, and she threw up a shield. Still, it moved her back a pace, sending her feet sliding in the muddy ground. But she'd been prepared and sent the strike recoiling back at him. He blocked it with his hand, his lip snarling as a rabid dog might.

"No more, Sinow. I will no longer fight you. I renounce my union to end this blasted war and will take my vows with you no matter what the consequence."

His snarl faded, his face softening for a split second before it hardened again, but not before she noted the flecks of brown in his eyes again.

"I don't need your union or you, Violissa." He stalked closer. A shiver of fear tingled up her spine, but she stood her ground, knowing to move would only embolden him. "I want your land. You mean nothing to me. You are only an obstacle keeping me from my goal of ruling this world."

Thinning her lips, her power swimming through her veins and snapping for freedom, she said, "You lie. I mean everything to you, Sinow, and the man you have locked away knows that. He would never hurt me or my people." Dark power hissed at her like serpents.

"Come back to me, Sinow. Don't let the Darkness—"

His magic burrowed into her skin before she could stop it, her power bursting forth to protect her. Lines of black darted from him, tearing at her shield. She sent her magic out in streams that wrapped around his, the two exploding in a waterfall of violet hues. She stumbled back, stunned at the sight, and Sinow pounced. His magic encased her, burying her in a haze of black, daggers of magic driving into her skin as he dragged her to where he stood. It dropped her to her knees, and she glared up at him, debating whether to strangle him with her power or feign weakness. She chose the latter as he grabbed her face and held it. The move reminded her of how he had tipped her chin when he'd been in her room, but everything about this felt wrong. The flitter of brown returned before the black swallowed it once more.

"You are a thorn in my side, Violissa. A nasty Light woman I do not need in my life."

"That's not true," she argued. "Prophecy—"

"Damn the prophecy!"

Lightning slashed the sky, and he peered up, giving Violissa an opening.

She grasped his hand. "Listen to me, Sinow."

When he looked back at her, his eyes were as dark as the night.

"I will kill you, Violissa," he said, his hand encircling her throat as he leaned further down, "and I will enjoy every second."

Rain poured down her face, mud soaking into her skin through her dress, but still she brought her hand to his chest, intending to call forth the binding song she had woven that fateful night. Hoping it would awaken his heart. But he shoved her away, his power picking her up and tossing her across the lawn.

Her fingers sank into the mud as she lifted herself. "You can't kill me, Sinow, and you know it. Your threats are empty. I am the thorn in your ass you cannot rid yourself of. I am yours for eternity."

He drew his hand to attack again, and she knew this wouldn't stop. It would be a continuous battle of wills, the fight wearing her down and the Darkness wearing him down. Neither side would win, but both would lose. Their people would continue to suffer, their Councils would continue to do their bidding, and they would continue this madness. She thought of how she hadn't fought earlier and she had broken through for just an instant.

Quelling her power, she put her hands up, saying, "I won't fight you anymore, Sinow. I'm surrendering. Every part of me is yours, and I will bend to you if that's what's needed to end this war. Please stop this. Let it end."

He shook his head, and hope climbed its way through her like a vine. She clung to it, dropping her shields, knowing he would notice the move. Focus returning to her, he rubbed his temple before squeezing it, and she tried getting through to him again. One step, then another, she moved closer.

"Please, Sinow. I know you're in there. I know how you feel about me because it's the same way I feel about you."

His hand dropped, his sight snapping to her, and she held her breath as he released a blast of Dark magic, growling, "I feel nothing for you, Violissa."

The blow hit its mark, careening into her chest and sending her through the open field and into the forest behind them. Trees hammered her body, limbs tore at her skin until she slammed into a thick trunk. She slid down it, leaving a trail of blood. She had thrown a quick shield around the back of her head to protect it from sustaining too much damage, but her injuries were grave.

When her shield dropped, she had stilled her healing, something immortals rarely did. Only during their early years of training did they learn how and only to experience what the mortals did. To understand how injuries affected other functions, like thinking. Her wounds would have healed otherwise, but she needed Sinow to see her this way. It was her only chance to free him from the Darkness. She was getting to him, but she prayed the shock of seeing her hurt would awaken his protective side.

Blood ran down her forehead, hastened by the rain, and she blinked to keep it from her eyes. A gash throbbed on her cheek, and she had broken one of her arms, but it was the tree limb running through her chest that ached the worst. Every breath she drew was a wheeze. She'd forgotten how much pain a body could endure and how excruciating it could be. The threat of blacking out edged closer, and she debated whether this had been reckless after all. She was vulnerable in this state, and Sinow could kill her before she released her healing powers.

Closing her eyes against the harsh sting of rain and the agony of her injuries, she fought to stay conscious. Time seemed to freeze while she waited for his footsteps or even his voice, and with every passing second, her body shook more. Whether from nerves or from pain, she didn't have the wherewithal to think about. Gathering the small amount of energy she had, she wove a calming spell, hoping he wouldn't notice and that it would find its mark. If this didn't work, there was nothing more she could do. War would be all her people would know for eternity.

CHAPTER 52

Violissa was playing games. Thinking she could drag the weak part of him out from under the grave in which he had buried it. He knew what she was doing when she reached her hand out to touch him. As if he hadn't purged that damned song from his body the moment the Darkness woke completely in him.

He stomped toward the forest, that part of him he detested so much clawing at him again, trying hard to resurface and take control. He clenched his fists, hating how a rush of joy had seared him when she had appeared. The emotion had morphed to another emotion he refused to recognize. Seeing her that way—so tired and disheveled, the golden curls he remembered looping his finger through matted and flat, her eyes hauntingly beautiful—had given life to a place inside of him he wanted to remain dead.

He scratched at his scalp before he grabbed a handful of hair and tugged. The ache sent the thoughts tumbling into the recesses of his mind. Replacing weakness with strength.

That will be enough of you, the Darkness roared.

Two beings ruled his one body, and Violissa suspected that was the case. She had risked coming to Tenebron, and he imagined she was desperate, thinking she could reach the side that was no longer in control. And she had been right. That part of him continued to hound him as he walked, climbing further from the depths where the Darkness had stranded him. A struggle for survival had begun. His head pounded as he fought against it, taking his first steps into the forest.

A chaotic path of destruction lay before him, and he couldn't help but chuckle at the amount of damage such a small woman's body had caused. A path of downed trees formed a trail he followed. Why hadn't she stopped herself? Her shields had been down, her magic silenced, but healing was natural. He had blasted her hard, but she still should have been standing before him by now.

"Violissa, come out and play," he called, malice coating his words. "I can smell you, so I know you're still here."

It was the truth. He could smell that damned lilac scent that clung to her, but it was different now, mixed with another smell. He stopped and sniffed the air. The copper tinge of blood accompanied it, but that couldn't be. Immortals didn't bleed enough for the smell to be that pungent; they healed far too quickly. What game was she playing?

"Violissa?" he called, drawing closer. His voice wavered, and he shook his head against the invading worry.

He would not let that weak part of him surface. He needed to push it back down, but it was fighting to be recognized. That weak side was screaming to escape, screaming for freedom, so he could find out why Violissa was so silent. Anger raged through him, but it no longer held as much power. He froze, seeing her mangled body against a rock. The sight elated the Darkness but from within, the sharp talons of the man who loved her sliced their way through their prison and burst free. He wrestled for control, the white-hot streaks of fury caging the beast who had done this to her. A ragged inhale scraped the air, and he blinked away the acidic touch of his power to focus on Violissa. Blood pooled around her as the rain washed it from her skin. Cuts marred her delicate skin, and a thick, gnarled tree limb protruded from her chest.

Forgetting all else, he ran to her, dropping to his knees and using his magic to disintegrate the limb. Gathering her in his arms, he spoke her name, praying that the Fates would heal her and questioning what he had done.

"Vi?" he murmured, holding her tight and hating how limp her body was. She had sacrificed herself, refusing to heal so she could bring him back. He wasn't worth it. Nothing was worth doing this. "No, I won't let you give yourself to the Fates for me." She was so weak and pale. He was terrified that he'd been too late. "Vi? Please come back to me."

It didn't matter that the plea had sounded weak. It didn't matter that emotions were wreaking havoc on his mind, that they had softened him. Nothing mattered but her, and if he lost her, he didn't know if he could go on. The realization of that thought hit him squarely, the final chains around his heart breaking free. And he knew without a doubt that if he ever lost her, he wouldn't survive because he loved her.

CHAPTER 53

Strong hands held her, a familiar voice called her name, and Violissa fought to surface from the blackness that engulfed her mind and the numbness that sat in her limbs. She blinked her eyes open, pain slashing through her as consciousness returned. Sinow held her tight in his arms, his breathing strained, his muscles shaking. It had worked. He had returned, but the cost had been great for them both. She was close to dying, the pull of the Fates strong, the loosening of her tie to the physical world quickening.

Sinow's chestnut eyes met hers, and he pulled her closer, brushing her hair from her face. She wheezed, trying to speak.

"Vi? Thank the Fates. Heal yourself, please."

She should have, but her joy at seeing his face without the menacing look and the soulless black orbs overtook her rational thinking.

"Sinow." Her voice was a hoarse whisper, and blood trickled from her lips, only to be swept away by the rain. "You're back."

"Fates, Vi. Please tell me you didn't do this for me."

Pain accompanied her smile, and she coughed, more blood spilling from her mouth.

Sinow's eyes creased with worry. "Why did you let yourself become so damaged? Can you not heal yourself?"

"I was waiting for you to return to me."

"Well, I'm here. Now, by the Fates, please heal yourself."

Her body was so wounded she wasn't certain if she had the energy to draw her power. She could hear Anwell scolding her for being so reckless.

"Now, Violissa."

She narrowed her eyes. "I thought you knew I don't like being told what to do."

His lip twitched, but he turned it to a scowl. "I'll let the Darkness back out to play if you don't heal yourself before you bleed to death."

She wanted to reach up and drag his lips to hers, but given how painful it was just to breathe, she didn't think she could muster the strength to do that. His arms still enveloped her body, and she relaxed into his hold, reaching deep into her core to release the cage she'd placed on her healing abilities. A rush of power surged from it, forcing the air from her lungs, and she clung to Sinow as the magic went to work. Small wounds healed quickly, but the damage in her chest was extensive. Sinow held her through it, the concern fading the more whole her body became. He shielded her from the rain by leaning over her, streams of water falling from his hair. And all the while, he never took his eyes from hers.

"Do you think you can stop this blasted rain?" he asked her as mud squished below them.

She put her hand out so he could help her stand and fell into his arms, her feet sliding in the mud. Face turned toward the sky, she sent her magic out and the rain stopped. Sinow lifted his head and looked around before he dropped his sight back to her. The clouds dissipated, the sun returning, but she couldn't take her focus from him.

"You did that purposely?" he asked, and she nodded. "Why?

Why would you risk your life, knowing I could have easily killed you in that state if you didn't die before I found you?" His voice rose with each word, and she could hear the frustration in it.

"It was the only way to get to you, Sinow. I knew I couldn't reason with you, not in the state you were in."

"I'm not worth that risk, Vi."

"But you are to me. You were in there, locked away, and I wanted you to return to me." His hand came up and rubbed her cheek, and only then did she think of what a mess she must look. Drenched and mud-soaked. "I missed you," she admitted.

He dragged her closer, his forehead touching hers. The frantic thudding of his heart beat below his soaked shirt, and she could hear the ragged drags of his breath.

His hands rubbed her arms but stopped when he said, "Tell me you found a way to end the charade with Daneele."

"I did. You were right that night. No one will care, especially not after all the suffering they've endured."

"Suffering I caused."

She shook her head, bringing both hands to his face. "Suffering we both caused. It is my fault the Darkness took you, my fault you had to call for war. I cannot deny the blame. I accept it."

"But I lost control, Vi." Agony laced his words, and her chest ached again as if the limb still impaled it. "I tried to contain it, but with the fighting and the emotions, the Darkness took over. I warned you of the damage I would cause if you didn't move swiftly."

She could see the defeat in his appearance and hear it in his voice. The weariness of his internal battles reflected on his face, and she smoothed her fingers over the lines on his brow. He took her hands and held them.

"End the war, Sinow. Make it stop, and we'll move forward."

Moving forward would be difficult. The war had left the kingdoms devastated, with Cirillia taking the brunt of the damage. A faraway look crossed Sinow's eyes, and she knew he was calling his Council home and ordering them to stop the war, to bring his troops back. A calm settled over the realms. It was finally over, and now they could begin their life together.

CHAPTER 54

Confusion tangled in Tynan's mind as he rubbed his temples. No, this couldn't be good. There was only one reason his idiotic brother would call off the war. Something had happened with Violissa. Sinow was entirely more likeable when he acted like a true Dark King instead of the whipped puppy of the Light Queen. And calling off the war meant he was under her influence again.

A wad of spit left his mouth and splattered on the stone floor as he thought of her. She was ruining everything. He had a plan, one that was almost at fruition, and he didn't need this interference. Pacing his quarters, he tried to think of what had caused such a sudden change. The hatred Sinow had for Violissa in his current state was delectable. Just this morning, he had been spouting about his plans to punish her today for the damage she had done in yesterday's battle. The two of them had been going at each other like two wild beasts, and Tynan was enjoying every minute. He'd almost thought they were close to destroying each other and he wouldn't even need to get involved.

He needed time to think, but he knew he didn't have it. The Darkness had taken Sinow, leaving him on the brink of madness and following in their grandfather's footsteps. Sinow had welcomed Tyan back with open arms, and he'd been bending Sinow's ear ever since, stirring the Darkness to his advantage. After all this time, he still had no idea what Tynan was truly capable of, and Tynan had been planning to leave it that way.

Scraping his arm across his desk, he threw the books to the ground. He was so close to breaking the secret of the book, and he needed Sinow distracted. Needed him to weaken Violissa and keep his attention focused on her. The spell to perfect his plan was in his grasp. He had discovered it moons ago, but the fighting between Sinow and Violissa was too fun to stop. Watching Sinow fall apart as his only weakness, Violissa, destroyed him, was too enjoyable.

The spell was truly unique. A spell to kill an immortal. Never had there been such a spell. No one had even thought such a thing existed, and now Tynan had it in his hands. But with Sinow's message that Violissa had turned Sinow so easily back to a doting idiot again, he could no longer wait.

Picking the book up from the floor, he sifted through the pages, landing on the death spell. It was too simple. Tapping his fingers on the page, he thought about his options. He could use it to take Sinow out, but maybe there was another way to bring his brother to his knees. One that gave Tynan the chance to watch him fall, piece by piece until he was the shell of a king. Violissa was his brother's weakness, and today, she would be his utter downfall.

Tucking the book in his robe and adding a concealing spell to it, he stepped through his mess with a smile. It was time for the ultimate act to begin, and Tynan would be the only one standing in the end.

CHAPTER 55

Questions berated Sinow, but he shut them down, telling his Council to retreat with haste and he would meet them in time to explain. First, he needed to talk to Violissa further. She was still in his grasp, her soft skin below his hands. Even rain-soaked, she looked beautiful.

The fear that had seized his heart was long gone. The anguish at seeing her in such a fragile state and the helplessness of not being able to heal her himself were distant memories. Now, all that mattered was the woman before him. The woman he now knew without a doubt he loved.

"It is done," he told her, hearing her relieved sigh.

"Thank you," she said, her emerald eyes warming his heart. "I will make the announcement to end the union when I return. Please give me some time to take care of my people. There are still many wounded, and we need to repair their towns and their land."

Sinow winced. He had caused that damage, and nothing he could do would ever make it better. But he would spend eternity trying as long as she was by his side. "How long?" he asked, thinking of how easily he tipped to the Darkness. He tightened his grip on her arms. "I need you, Vi. You're the only one who calms the beast within me. Without you here, I fear I'll lose control again."

Understanding crossed her eyes, and she pushed his wet hair back, her fingers sinking through it. "Not long. But I can't leave them. They need me, too." He ached for more of her touch, but his state was precarious, the Darkness always one step away from freeing itself.

"I know that, but I don't know how long I can control my power."

Head tilting, she studied him, her brows scrunching. "Do you trust me, Sinow?"

His power bumped against his hold, disturbed by the question. "Yes," he said, ignoring it. "I trust you with my life."

The smile she gave him lit every shadowed crevice in his soul. "You need to embrace your powers. You struggle against them, always trying to subdue them. Don't. They are a part of you. Accept them and be as one with them rather than divided as you are."

Shaking his head, he dropped his hands and stepped back. "You don't know what you're asking. If I do that, there may be no coming back this time."

"Trust me, please."

He had every urge to tell her no. To walk away and maintain what little control he had. To admit that he would have this fight for eternity and face a life where her calming spells offered the only possible peace.

"Please, Sinow."

Her eyes pleaded for him to take the chance. And maybe that's what he needed to do. Take a chance and admit that everything with Violissa would go against his nature. Loving the enemy and letting her into his life.

"What is it you're asking of me, Vi?"

She closed the gap between them and took his hand. "I need you to do something that will go against your instincts." He tensed, uncertain he wanted to hear more. "Let your powers run through you, let the Darkness within you loose, but this time willingly."

Snatching his hand away, he said, "Are you mad? I barely controlled it this time. Every time the Darkness takes me, it becomes harder to come back." He grabbed her shoulders. "It took your broken body to make that happen, and I won't risk you suffering again."

"Sinow, you need to trust me. You won't lose control because you'll willingly hand over that control. There's a difference." Her eyes lit, excitement widening them. "Don't you see? You never fully handed yourself over to the powers you gained when you ascended. You fought against them, buried them, and feared what they would do to you. Feared they would turn you into your grandfather." He gritted his teeth, hating that comparison. Detesting how he had strived to be like his grandfather when the Darkness had owned him. That was a man he never wanted to be, and he would do everything in his power to never come that close again. "If you set that side of you free instead of fighting it, I promise you will finally be whole."

With a sigh, he moved his hands down her arms, contemplating her words. Was there truth to what she said? Had he never completely ascended because he had feared the Darkness owning him, feared the legacy his grandfather had left him?

Violissa's hand came to his chest, and he sucked in a gulp of air. "I'm going to let my power surface, and when I do, you release the hold on your magic."

Hands dropping, he stepped back again, but she bunched his shirt in her hands, stopping his movement. Scraping his hand through his hair, he said, "Violissa, that's a big mistake. You know what will happen."

"I know what will happen, but do you?" She moved back into his space, tipping her head up at him. "Trust me, Sinow." Her power simmered, and it prickled against his skin. The need to step away tore through him, but he refrained. "Don't stop looking into my eyes. Please trust me. This is the only way we'll ever be together. There can be no union if our powers aren't in harmony, and that will only happen if you are one with the Darkness." She released more of her magic, and his power strained for release. His muscles pulsed as he tried to control it. "Relax, Sinow, don't fight it. Let the power wash through you."

This was madness. Maybe she had hit her head when he struck her, and it hadn't fully healed. If he did what she asked, he would lose himself, and war would be their future. Violissa's eyes stayed locked with his, never wavering, and it gave him strength. She seemed so determined, so fearless, that he could only do what she asked. Trusting her.

Shallow breaths, sharp and uncomfortable, entered his lungs.

"Relax," she said, as if it were that easy. The Darkness within was rearing its ugly head, trying to free itself again, and he instinctively stopped it before remembering that he needed to deny that instinct. He closed his eyes, hearing her say, "Keep your eyes on me, Sinow."

Opening them, he met her lush green orbs, fierce and obstinate. "By the Fates, Violissa. If you're so keen on seeing me spiral back to my former self, then by all means, I'll cooperate."

"I have no intention of ever meeting that man again, Sinow. It's you I want. Only you."

She gave him a crooked smile, and he would have laughed but for the force of power swirling in his core. More Light power shimmered on the air, and he tightened his jaw, his muscles straining. No matter how he wanted to do what she was saying, he couldn't stop his desire for control over the insanity that boiled within him.

"Relax, Sinow. Remember, invite the power in. Let it run free through you. It should fill your veins, your limbs, and your mind. Let it course through your body and merge with your spirit." Her voice was sensual, and he thought of what doing this would bring. Violissa. Her kisses, her body, her cries. A lifetime of discovering everything that made her shatter and everything she could do to shatter him.

His pulse raced, and he relaxed, giving himself over to her words. He stopped fighting and welcomed the rush of power, embraced the burning fire that ran through him just as she had said it would. He sensed it deep within him, flooding his veins, coursing along the blood within them. It ran through his organs, through his limbs, down to his fingertips, surged through his heart, causing it to race even more, and finally wove its way through his head. The sensation was ecstasy, like a hand painfully caressing every inch of him from the inside out. A dark haze built around him, and he knew his eyes were an endless void of ebony.

All the while, Violissa continued to hold his gaze, her power shining around her like a beacon that summoned his. No fear touched her eyes, no worry darkened them. She held steady, calm and unwavering, like he imagined she would be through their lives. A force to stand beside him.

A sense of completeness washed over him, and he let the air flow from his lungs. Violissa's hand rested on his chest still, and he picked it up, her power flowing along his skin. His power danced with it, and he let it, noting how freeing it seemed. For the first time since his ascension, he was at one with the Darkness that coursed through him. He no longer feared it but welcomed it like it had returned home. There was no longer a need to control it, for it was part of him now. He shook his head and rolled his neck, letting the power flow through him. Blinking his eyes, he sensed the ebony fade, knowing his eyes were now a darker shade of brown, closer to his father's. And it was a shade that would remain now because the Dark power was a part of him he'd accepted. They would only turn to pitch when he needed the Darkness to punish, to follow his code. The code of his forefathers and every Darkbearer—to protect and punish only those who threatened his people.

The arch of Violissa's brow was gorgeous, and he lifted his finger to trace it as she asked, "Better?"

"Better," he said and noticed that for once there was no other voice inside his head fighting for dominance. He smiled at her and gently twisted his finger around her curl.

Being near her felt right, like it was where he had always needed to be. He lifted her chin, lowering his face and said, "Marry me, Violissa."

He heard the catch of her breath, the speeding of her pulse as his lips hovered over hers, awaiting her answer. Lilac filled his senses, and he never wanted to be without that smell again.

"Yes," she breathed.

A lingering moment separated them while he waited for the interruption that always happened before he kissed her. But none came, and only the pounding of his heart in rhythm with hers remained. Fingers threading through her hair, his mouth crashed into hers. Blood rushed through him, time came to a halt, and the land trembled before the world fell away and all that existed was them. She tasted of morning dew and ripe berries. Lips, supple and moist, parted and allowed him entry. His tongue danced with hers, his body melded with hers, and a sensation of rightness swam through him.

This was what the Fates had wanted, what they had created, and what he and Violissa had fought against for so long. But they had been wrong to fight it because this was their destiny. His soul reached to hers, embracing its other half, and he understood then that he loved her with every piece. That it had never been entirely his, that half had always belonged to her and always would. There could be no turning back from this now. He would die before he ever gave her up and kill anyone who threatened to take her from him. That certainty roared through him like a hunter settling over its prey with a possessive stance.

But as suddenly as his life had changed, it turned. Violissa pushed him away, breaking their connection. Her eyes were tight with confusion and hurt that nearly broke the heart that only moments before had been complete. Her eyes darted around as she backed further away from him.

"Vi, what's wrong?" he asked, fearing her answer.

"What have you done?" Her voice cracked as she brought her hand to her chest, holding it as if she were in agony. "How could you? I thought..." She stepped back again, her hand moving over her mouth to stifle the anguish that held her face captive.

"Violissa, what are you talking about? I have done nothing."

She never answered the question, shifting from him and leaving him confounded. He ran a hand over his face, trying to figure out what had gone wrong. Head snapping up, he looked to the east, sensing a disturbance in the balance of power. It wasn't massive, but it was noticeable enough to be concerning. The balance of power in the world had tilted to him. Darkness rose around him, his own powers rising with it. Something was very wrong, and he suspected that something explained Violissa's sudden exit. With a sense of foreboding, he followed the trace of her shift to see what had turned her mood so drastically, even though, deep down, he didn't know if he wanted the answer.

CHAPTER 56

That kiss. Never had Violissa imagined their first kiss would be so intense. Nothing they'd done in the Dream Realm came close, and they had done plenty there. Still, the kiss was one that wrapped its embrace around her heart and embedded itself in her soul. It was everything she'd longed for, topped with a sense of completeness where she'd never felt incomplete before. This had been a turning point, a defining moment that solidified the emotion she had carried for Sinow. No doubt remained. She loved him with all of her essence and would willingly tear the world apart to keep him.

But the slash of betrayal that gutted her demolished those emotions. Pain tore through her like a rogue wind, collapsing all the kiss had just built and sending it toppling into an abyss. Something had severed her tie to her Council, and no matter that she didn't want to believe it, only one person could be behind it.

She stumbled from her shift, deceived and hurt. That kiss had been so real, yet so had the loss of her Council's magic. An empty sensation sat in her chest, an awareness that their magic was no longer in the world, which could only mean they had been bound.

Sinow's denial had cut almost as bad as knowing his kiss had been nothing but a diversion. That he hadn't turned from the Darkness at all. But to bind her Council? It made no sense. Only a king could bind powers, and only those of his own Council.

The agony of that hollow sensation left her dazed, and she wasn't certain she'd found them. There was no trail to them, no magical tie that led her to them, but she had followed with blind instinct. She turned, faltering when something slithered into her. Slinking in her blood, like a snake moving stealthily toward its prey. Seeking her power. She dropped to her knees. Someone was binding her power. She scratched at her arms, hating the feel of the spell as it sought her core, sought to destroy the space that housed her power.

She needed to stop it, but the binding spell was hunting her magic down, trapping it and draining her. Pushing herself off the ground, she stumbled forward, only then seeing the truth. Before her kneeled her Council, magic holding them in place. She tried to draw on her power to free them, but it was too late; the spell had left her bound, her magic locked away too far to reach.

Only a king could bind one of his own Council, but no one could bind royal blood. No one had that kind of power.

"Well, well, Violissa. How nice of you to join us."

She whipped around, finding Tynan behind her. He wore a smug look, his eyes devious, his mouth forming a grin that only enhanced his disturbing aura. Reaching inward, she found a small pocket of magic the binding spell had yet to silence and sent it at him. His lips twisted in annoyance, and he jerked his hand out, blocking her poor excuse for a spell. When she tried again, there was nothing left to summon. The spell had imprisoned all of it.

"What have you done?" she asked, her legs threatening to send her toppling.

"I'm cleaning up a mess," he said just as Sinow shifted in.

The ground rippled when he landed across from her, and it left her even more unsteady. She was barely holding on. The hollowness of losing the connection to her power and her Council caused her to be unbalanced. Sinow looked around at the scene, taking a step back from her. He was distancing himself from her, and a small cry escaped when she realized she had been right. He had played her, just as she had tricked him into thinking he had mortally wounded her. A flood of emotions swept through her. She felt stupid and used, humiliated and hurt.

But that kiss. It had been perfect. There had to be an explanation, something she wasn't piecing together. She glanced back at her Council. The spell that held them kept their heads bowed to the ground, but she could see their discomfort in the distorted positions of their bodies. She had no way to help them, not without her magic. Sinow was her only hope, but the thought that only a royal could bind, and Tynan didn't have that kind of power, kept returning. He had to be behind this. There was no other explanation.

Defeated and weak, she realized no royal had ever had their powers bound until now. But Sinow was unlike any Dark king before him, more powerful and less predictable. And she had misjudged him. She turned back to Sinow, watching and waiting for his actions to prove she was wrong, to prove he had nothing to do with what was happening. The beautiful earthy tone of his eyes had shifted, returning to the color of a moonless night, and her heart cracked into a thousand pieces she knew could never put back together again.

CHAPTER 57

There was too much in the scene before Sinow to comprehend, and he was trying to wrap his head around it. The Lightbearers were on their knees, powerless, and just before he'd arrived, the shift of power had almost overwhelmed him. He understood the reason now. Not only had someone bound their power, but Violissa's as well. There was no Light magic left in the world, and so the balance had shifted to Darkness. The power swelled in him, almost overflowing, and he knew his eyes were changing to black with the sudden influx.

Tynan stood on the other side of Violissa, a smirk on his face and a devious glint in his eyes. What had his brother done? Sinow had released him from banishment, and all the while, he had been scheming. But to what end? To rob the world of Light magic? It made no sense.

Violissa turned back to him, her eyes meeting his, and he read her expression. She blamed him. Of course she would. Only a royal could bind power, but he had done nothing, and even he didn't have the power to bind Light magic. Only Dark. He didn't have time to defend himself; he needed to make this right, and that would show her the truth.

He looked over at Tynan. "What in the Fates are you doing, Tynan?" Magic shadowed his aura, turning the air around him gray, and he welcomed it.

"Do you like it, brother? It was perfect timing. What a great trick, to send out that message that the war was over. It made them easy prey, and I even found them all in one place, gathered here, kindly waiting for me."

"You really did this?" Violissa asked Sinow. The doubt stabbed him, especially after what they'd just shared. She stood taller, anger etched on her features.

"Violissa, I—"

But she turned to Tynan and demanded, "Let them go. Now, Tynan."

Sinow knew if she'd had her powers that even the Lightbearer in her would not have stopped her from bringing great pain to Tynan, but she had only her voice. He would have to do the job for her. He reached his hand up to strike.

"Uh uh, don't make me harm them yet," Tynan said, stopping him. "That wouldn't be any fun."

Sinow tempered his strike, not wanting any further harm to come to them. He didn't know what to do and was stuck between making things right and not doing anything.

So he did the only thing he could think of given the circumstance and he asked, "Why are you doing this, Tynan?"

If he'd known the answer Tynan would give him would be his undoing and further turn Violissa against him, he would have made another choice, gone down another path, but he didn't, and he would ponder that choice for the centuries to come.

"I'm doing what you commanded, brother."

Violissa took a step back from Sinow, her gasp mingled with a hoarse cry. The betrayal in her eyes was one he doubted he would ever forget. Even as he shook his head in denial, he knew deep down this situation would not get better, that he would never hold her in his arms again, that whatever Tynan was up to had cost Sinow. His chest grieved the loss before it even happened.

"What are you talking about, Tynan?" he asked, needing Violissa to believe this was not his doing. "I never told you to do this."

"Of course you did. You said the only way we could walk free in this world was by destroying the Lightbearers and their queen. I found the key to bringing that wish to fruition. And now you can watch as I purify our world and rid it of the Light, just like we discussed."

Sinow gaped at Tynan. "You take my words out of context. Those were words spoken while the Dark power had me in its clutches. You can't have seriously thought this was what I need? What our world needs?" His mind reeled. Had he really said those words? He'd said so many vile things that he very well may have. It briefly occurred to him that Tynan should never have the power to do such a thing, but that was not a battle that needed to be fought right now. Violissa was his priority, and he needed to turn things around before he lost her completely.

"Did you really say that?" she asked. "I thought...I thought you loved me. Fates, I'm such a fool."

"But Violissa, I—"

"This is beginning to bore me," Tynan interrupted, and Sinow clenched his fists, ready to turn his power on Tynan and be done with this fiasco. He would regret not doing that for far too long.

"Then let them go, and return my power," she pleaded.

"No." With that single word, Tynan threw a spell out toward Violissa's Council. Sinow vaguely registered her scream as the spell soared through the air toward them. He didn't know the spell, but he somehow knew it meant their death. Everything ran in slow motion as he instinctively yelled out a counterspell to undo the intent of the spell. He had only one chance, pushing his full power out and encasing the spell, morphing its purpose to send her

Lightbearers to the Fates and instead send them somewhere else, somewhere safe until he could fix all of this.

Charged with magic, the air sparkled with hues of black, gray, and red. His spell collided with Tynan's right before it hit her Council. A black ball of power slammed into them, and they disappeared, leaving the space where they had been empty.

"No!" Violissa screamed, turning toward Sinow accusingly. "You bring them back. Whatever you two did, you bring them back to me now!" The hatred in her eyes gutted him, and he wanted so desperately to make this better.

"Violissa, we'll get them back. I promise you."

"No, you won't," Tynan blurted, and Sinow swung his eyes to him.

Tynan raised his hand again, aiming it toward Violissa, and the spell left his lips. Sinow's power crashed through Tynan, sending him soaring backward, but it was too late. The spell was loose and heading toward her. There was no stopping it, and in those remaining moments, his instinct once again kicked in. The counterspell sped from him, accompanied by words in ancient Tenebron, and crashed into the death spell, but this time the power of his emotions warped his counterspell. He realized once it had left his control, but didn't know what the outcome would be until it melded into Tynan's, warping it and twisting the magic so that it was unrecognizable.

His eyes flicked to Violissa, whose face fear engulfed.

"Sinow?" she whispered just before the spell slammed into her. A spray of light shot out from where she stood, and she was gone.

Sinow stood in shock, too stunned to react. The pain of losing Violissa stormed through him. It almost seemed like half of him had disappeared, leaving his heart tattered and his soul severed. He turned to Tynan, Darkness coursing through him stronger than it ever had. A violent haze of black and red blinded him, and he threw a bolt of magic at Tynan. It smashed into his brother. A trail of mangled dirt and trees lay in his wake.

Sinow reached out with his power and grabbed him, pounding Tynan into the ground over and over, leaving a massive crater. Dirt whirled through the air, but Sinow disregarded it. Jumping down to where Tynan looked up at him, he grabbed him by the hair and flung him against the inside wall of the crater. Beaten and bloody, his wounds slowly healing, Tynan continued to smile at Sinow before a laugh that made even Sinow's skin crawl emerged from him.

His brother had lost his mind. Worried for so long that the Darkness was infecting him, Sinow had never considered that Tynan would be the one to follow in their grandfather's footsteps. Tynan lifted his hand, and Sinow sensed him beginning to build the same spell he had thrown at Violissa and her Council. It was one he'd never witnessed, but one whose intent he had known on a primal level. It caused every alarm in his mind to scream that it was wrong that Tynan knew that spell, that the spell was unnatural and the Fates had not meant for him to have it. And that was all the more reason to be rid of it.

Raising his hand, full power flowing through him, he yelled, "I denounce your spell and strip it of all power from here on. I bind the spirit of it and render it useless."

Tynan paused. "You can't do that. No one can do that." Just to prove his point, he picked the spell back up and tried to cast it, but the magic of it sputtered even before it began to form. Fear penetrated Tynan's eyes, and this time it was Sinow who smiled.

"I just did. I don't know how you got the strength to do the things you just did, but you are going to undo them. You will bring Violissa back now," Sinow growled, the power shaking the ground.

Tynan's laugh was maniacal. "Don't you see? I can't, and even you can't. Ha, it would take the Fates to bring her back now. My spell would have killed her, but yours, yours turned it into something so much more fun." Sinow stalked over and picked him up from where he still sat, shoving him into the dirt.

"Then you are useless to me. I bind your powers, Tynan, and curse you to live your immortal existence without them."

He threw Tyan across the crater. Tynan moved to block Sinow's spell, but Sinow was too powerful. The force of it caged Tynan. Black and gray mist swirled around him, forming a chain like a viper poised to sink its fangs into him.

"No!" Tynan yelled. The chain seeped into his chest as he fought back his screams. It threaded in and out of him before burrowing into his core and latching onto his power. Tynan thrashed as the chains continued to wind in and out of his body in a circular motion until they sank into his skin and disappeared from sight.

Sinow was certain that whatever binding spell Tynan had used was nothing compared to that of a true king. Otherwise, Violissa still would have been on the ground in agony when Sinow arrived. At the thought of her, his anger doubled, the air turning so black he could barely see.

"For treason to your king and realm, I banish you for the remainder of your existence or until I figure out how to kill you myself." He whipped his hand through the air, and Tynan disappeared just as quickly as Violissa had.

Silence encompassed him, and the weight of all that had happened came down upon him. He bent forward and rested his hands on his knees. Maybe he had acted too rashly, and he shouldn't have rendered useless the spell Tynan had cast on Violissa and her Council. He could have used it to kill Tynan, but he wasn't even sure how to use the spell and certainly didn't know how his Dark powers would influence it. Such a spell should not have existed. He would add it to the mystery of how his brother had known a binding spell to incapacitate the Lightbearers and their queen.

This was a mess. He needed to find Violissa. Straightening, he looked up to see his Council standing on the edge of the crater. He turned away and climbed out of the crater, keeping his back to them, not wanting them to see the anguish reflected on his face. How much they had seen, he didn't know, but it was likely enough.

"Find Violissa and bring her back to me. Find her Council and find her. Now," he bellowed, his voice both powerful and terrifying. The force shook the ground.

He sensed them all shift, all but Keary, and so he turned to face his friend.

"We'll find her, Sinow," he said, and Sinow didn't have to ask if he had seen it happen.

Sinow had no words. The despair was too overwhelming, and he refused to look weak in front of his Council, even Keary. He gave Keary a nod and turned from him, sensing him shift seconds later.

There was a hollow place inside of Sinow that he didn't like. If it had been there before, he had never noticed, but now it screamed like a void he didn't think he could ever fill. He walked to where Violissa had been standing, breathing in the lilac that lingered. A melancholy grew, and he knew in his heart they would not find her. If he'd thought there was any chance, he would have gone himself. The power of his counterspell had warped whatever magic Tynan had used. It had sent her somewhere, but wherever that was, it was nowhere they would find.

The balance had tilted. Darkness now completely overshadowed the Light, but he sensed a trace of it out there, so he knew they would find her Council. He could easily undo the binding spell on them and restore their powers, but the one he truly needed to save was now beyond his reach.

TIME DRAGGED TOO SLOWLY as Sinow waited for his Council to return. The events replayed in his mind countless times, and with each he cursed himself for not reacting quicker, for not realizing what was happening. He should have taken Tynan out and reversed the damage, but he had been too shocked to think that swiftly. And Violissa had been too quick to place blame, too eager to cut him off and not let him explain. Hands raking through his hair, he cursed again, hating that she had doubted him, hating that wherever she was now she still hated him, thinking he had betrayed her.

The air stirred, and Keary and Odhran appeared. Since they were the only two with the courage to face him, he suspected the outcome of the search would reinforce what he had known all along.

"We have found her Council. The spell sent them to the Banished Realm. The others are working to free them."

"Tell them to stop. I can free them," he said, rubbing his forehead and dreading the answer to his next question. "What of Violissa?"

Keary looked at Odhran, who nodded, then bowed to Sinow and shifted away. If Keary was the only one to give him the news, then it wasn't good. An indent formed between Keary's brows. "There is nothing. We followed every trace of her we could find, but she was nowhere. It's as if she no longer exists."

Sinow ran his hand through his hair. Hearing the words made him sick. Panic struck him, and he grabbed Keary's cloak. "I need her back, Keary."

Releasing him, Sinow backed away, hating the moment of vulnerability and thankful only Keary had been witness to it.

"Are you sure Tynan's spell didn't work? Are you positive yours changed the course of the spell?" Keary asked with hesitation.

If it had been anyone else, Sinow would have punished him for even asking.

"Yes, it turned the spell, redirected the magic. She's alive. I just don't know where." He paused, the emotion rising in him. "I can't sense her presence anymore, Keary. I could always feel her, even when we were young it was there. But now, there's nothing, just this emptiness." He hit his chest for emphasis before he turned away.

"We'll keep searching," said Keary, and Sinow knew it was only to appease him.

With a sigh, he told Keary, "Leave me. Tell the others I need to be alone."

Keary didn't question him, saying, "Yes, my liege." But he didn't leave and instead added, "We'll find her, Sinow. I promise you we'll do all we can to bring her back to you."

He was gone before Sinow could respond, leaving Sinow alone, more alone than he had ever been before. Emotion held him prisoner, and he dropped to his knees, no longer able to keep his legs steady.

He looked up at the sky, at the Fates he knew were watching, then lowered his head as moisture formed on his cheeks. He had never cried. Tears were a weakness not fit for a Dark king, but now they ran freely as the awareness that Violissa was truly gone eviscerated him. He raised his head in anguish, her name tearing from his throat in a wretched cry that resounded through both realms. The ground trembled around him, and the trees bowed their heads in pity as rain began to fall.

CHAPTER 58

Somewhere, many worlds away, in a small human town off the coast of what would someday be Ireland, Lidia grunted as she pulled the final potato from the hardened ground. The weather was turning cold too fast this year, ruining what crop they had left to harvest for the oncoming winter. The bitter wind whipped at her hair and stung her fingers as they rubbed the dirt from the potato. Slowly, she rose from her knees.

I'm getting too old for this, she thought at the cracking that emitted from her left knee.

Bending to pick up her basket, she heard a voice calling her name. She raised her hand to shade her eyes, spotting Kayla, the McDonough's daughter, running toward her.

"Miss Lidia, Miss Lidia," she panted as she stopped in front of Lidia, placing her hands on her knees to catch her breath.

"What is it, child?"

"It's Miss Emma, the baby...it's coming."

Lidia looked off into the distance toward where Emma's cottage sat. It would take her a few minutes to gather her supplies, and the trek to Emma's home would be tough on her old bones, but not a baby in the town had been birthed without Lidia's presence. She'd been a midwife since before anyone could remember.

She sighed. Of all the times. The warmth of her home called to her, but she knew Emma needed her. They'd thought she was barren. She and Lore had tried for so long. But here it was, her fortieth year and with child. Some said it was a miracle. So, Lidia trudged to her cottage, dropped the basket on the floor and gathered her things.

"Don't just stand there, child, run back down and tell them I'm on my way. Get some water from the well and some blankets ready. Go, go!"

The girl ran off, sending dirt through the air behind her.

It took Lidia almost an hour to get to Emma's home. By the time she entered, Emma was screaming in pain. She looked over at the woman and spotted the round shape of the baby's head crowning between her legs. Lidia cursed. This was unbelievable. Labor should have taken hours, as this was a first child.

"Sit her up more," she ordered to Lore, who'd been pacing next to the bed, not knowing what else to do. Most men would have bolted with the first cry of pain, but Lore was one of a kind, always attentive and dedicated to his wife. A man who still loved her after all this time.

Lidia pulled a stool to the end of the bed. "You must relax, Emma, or you'll harm the babe." She grabbed Emma's knees and spread them wider to get a better look. Yes, there was no doubt the babe would be born in the next few minutes. Kayla brought a blanket over which she placed under Lidia's hands.

"Now push, child, push hard." Emma strained and pushed. The head came out. "Push again, bigger this time," Lidia said, as she grasped the baby's head. "Push, child!"

Emma grunted, her face turning red from the strain. The baby fell into Lidia's hands as Emma fell back against Lore's large arms. This was possibly the fastest birth Lidia had ever attended. As Emma relaxed, Lidia cleaned the baby and cut the cord. She wrapped the child in the blanked and cleared the airway. Then she listened. No sound came from the child. She brought her hand back to smack its bottom to force the first breath, but stopped when she noticed the chest moving in a breathing motion.

"Is it a boy or a girl?" Emma asked, the concern pouring over in her voice at the silence. "Lidia, what's wrong?"

Lidia stared in amazement at the child. Never had she seen such a quiet and still babe. The child was beautiful. Blonde curls were drying on her small head, almost like a halo blessing her. Tears filled Lidia's eyes at the sight. When the baby opened her eyes, Lidia almost dropped her.

"Lidia, please!" Lore shouted at Lidia's silence.

Snapped from the spell of those brilliant emerald eyes, the midwife looked up and replied, "It's a girl, a beautiful baby girl."

---

*Thank you for reading Ascension. Be sure to look for book two, **Descent**, to find out the next step on the prophecy's path.*

If you enjoyed Ascension, please consider leaving a review. Reviews are like priceless gems to authors like me.

About the Author

J. L. Jackola is a writer of love stories with fantasy, darkness, feisty women, and morally gray men. She's an admitted sugar addict with a penchant for anything with salted caramel. When she's not weaving tales, snacking on sweets, or downing her morning cup of tea, you can find her logging miles in her running shoes, watching movies with her family, or curled up with a book.

She resides in Delaware with her husband and three children.

Visit her at www.jljackola.com and be sure to sign up for J L's newsletter to keep up with all the latest release news.

www.ingramcontent.com/pod-product-compliance
Lightning Source LLC
Chambersburg PA
CBHW061043310726
48969CB00004B/1059